# A Nymph Returns to the
## A Noir Urban Fantasy No

This is a work of fiction. Names, characters, organizations, places, events, and incidents are either products of the author's imagination or are used fictitiously. Any resemblance to actual persons, living or dead, or actual events is purely coincidental.

Copyright © 2022 by Douglas Lumsden
All rights reserved.
**ISBN:** 9798361836710

No part of this book may be reproduced, or stored in a retrieval system, or transmitted in any form or by any means, electronic, mechanical, photocopying, recording, or otherwise, without express written permission of the publisher.

Cover design and art by Arash Jahani (www.arashjahani.com)

# A Nymph Returns to the Sea:
## A Noir Urban Fantasy Novel

By

Douglas Lumsden

To Rita. Always.

## Books in this Series

Alexander Southerland, P.I.

Book One: *A Troll Walks into a Bar*

Book Two: *A Witch Steps into My Office*

Book Three: *A Hag Rises from the Abyss*

Book Four: *A Night Owl Slips into a Diner*

*(Standalone Novella): The Demon's Dagger*

Book Five: *A Nymph Returns to the Sea*

## Contents

Chapter One .................................................................................................... 1
Chapter Two .................................................................................................. 11
Chapter Three ............................................................................................... 21
Chapter Four ................................................................................................. 29
Chapter Five .................................................................................................. 39
Chapter Six .................................................................................................... 47
Chapter Seven ............................................................................................... 55
Chapter Eight ................................................................................................ 65
Chapter Nine ................................................................................................. 75
Chapter Ten ................................................................................................... 83
Chapter Eleven .............................................................................................. 93
Chapter Twelve ........................................................................................... 103
Chapter Thirteen ........................................................................................ 111
Chapter Fourteen ....................................................................................... 119
Chapter Fifteen ........................................................................................... 127
Chapter Sixteen .......................................................................................... 137
Chapter Seventeen ..................................................................................... 149
Chapter Eighteen ....................................................................................... 159
Chapter Nineteen ....................................................................................... 169
Chapter Twenty .......................................................................................... 179
Chapter Twenty-One ................................................................................. 189
Chapter Twenty-Two ................................................................................. 201
Chapter Twenty-Three .............................................................................. 211
Chapter Twenty-Four ................................................................................ 223
Chapter Twenty-Five ................................................................................. 233

| | |
|---|---|
| Chapter Twenty-Six | 245 |
| Chapter Twenty-Seven | 253 |
| Chapter Twenty-Eight | 265 |
| Chapter Twenty-Nine | 275 |
| Chapter Thirty | 285 |
| Chapter Thirty-One | 295 |
| Chapter Thirty-Two | 305 |
| Chapter Thirty-Three | 317 |
| Epilogue | 325 |
| Acknowledgements | 333 |
| About the Author | 335 |

# Chapter One

"It's not you. It's me," she said. We both knew it wasn't true, but it was sweet of her to accept the heat.

The first time I'd seen her, I'd been holed up in a corner booth at Lefty's, an upscale Midtown nightclub, celebrating the completion of a successful case in the company of some excellent avalonian whiskey. I was nursing my fourth glass when she appeared at my table, a cigarette tray at her waist above a pair of gams that wouldn't quit.

"Cigar? Cigarette? Reefer?" Her voice slid across my face like satin sheets.

I almost never smoke, but she'd come all the way to that dark corner of the room to offer her wares, and only a heel would have sent a doll like her away disappointed. Or maybe it was something about the way her dark eyes gleamed in the joint's dim light. Maybe I was just drunk and alone. Whatever the reason, I found myself asking, "Which cigar would you recommend?"

She arched her eyebrows and sized me up for a second or two. She smiled a smile that illuminated the dark corner of the room like a searchlight, pulled a cigar out of her tray, and held it up for my examination. "These come from Qubao. The leaves are soaked in rum, dried in the tropical sun for a month, and hand-rolled by barefoot peasant girls selected for their purity and beauty."

I couldn't help but smile. "Sure they are. I'll take one of those if you light it for me."

Her own smile broadened, deepening the dimples in her cheeks. "Of course, sir." Lifting the cigar to her lips, she gave it a quick twirl to moisten the tip before deftly snipping it off with a double-bladed cigar cutter. Returning the cigar to her mouth, she lifted a silver lighter from her tray, flipped open the top with a practiced hand, and, with a flick of her thumb, conjured up a flame on the first try. After firing up the cigar, she transferred it from her lips to mine. I felt warm blood rush into my cheeks. It was the closest thing to a kiss I'd had in months.

"How do you like it?" she asked.

I let the cool smoke swirl over my tongue and let a cloud form in front of my face. "I'm impressed. With the cigar and with the way you handle it."

Her eyes found mine, and I felt something tingle in my lower abdomen.

"How long have you been working here?" I asked her.

"Six or seven months now. I had this crazy notion that I was a singer and came in for an audition. They suffered through my act for an entire minute and offered me a job as a cigarette girl."

"You like it?"

"I meet some interesting people."

"More interesting than me, I'm sure."

She let her eyes drift from my face to my chest and back again. "I don't know about that. You might be surprised about what I find interesting."

If she was angling for a big tip, she was succeeding. "What'd you do before you landed here?"

"A little of this, a little of that. Nothing I'd talk about on a first date. What about you? What's your racket? Wait. Let me guess." She frowned as she stared into my eyes. "You don't look too respectable. Are you a bank robber?"

I chuckled at that. "Not quite. Not yet, at least. I might take it up if times get tough. No, I'm a private investigator."

She nodded. "Like I said, not too respectable."

"It could be worse," I said, taking a puff on the cigar. "I could be a lawyer."

She giggled. "Lawyers never drink here alone. They meet with clients, pick up the tab, and then bill the poor saps for the drinks. With interest."

Four glasses of good avalonian had rendered me bulletproof, so I blew cigar smoke into the air and asked her for her name.

A wayward strand of raven-black hair had strayed over the side of her face, and she pushed it back into place. "My parents named me Holiday. My friends call me Holly."

"My parents named me Alexander. My friends call me Alex."

"Are we friends, Alexander?"

I shrugged. "Not yet, but I'm working on it. Tell you what, Holly. If you let me buy you a drink, I promise not to bill you for it later." I raised the cigar to my lips and fell into her dark eyes.

*Holly bit at her lower lip and scrutinized me for a long moment. Then she smiled, a dazzling smile that revealed a stunning set of teeth. "I'm due for a break." She gestured toward my glass. "Order me one of those." She lowered her head toward me, as if taking me into her confidence, and her wayward strand of hair fell back down over her cheek. "But just one, Alexander. I have a feeling I'm going to need to keep my wits about me around you." She stood and let the strand fall against her lips. "Give me a minute to stash this tray and I'll join you."*

*The next three months had been swell. The month after that had not been so swell. Two weeks after that, we'd been washing down some deep-fried calamari with a good bottle of rye when she told me it was over, and that it wasn't me, it was her. But I knew better. Holly was a sweet gal, a picnic in the park. I gave her everything I thought she should want. She left me out of self-preservation. It was the only sensible play she had.*

*\*\*\**

Three months later, I was sitting in my whitish terrycloth bathrobe staring at a page in the morning paper, my mind diverted by the memory of Holly's hair splayed over her pillow like ravens' feathers as she slept. I was jolted from my bittersweet memories by something from the page of the newspaper poking at my subconscious with a stick, trying to grab my attention. The image of black feathery softness slipped away as my eyes focused on a familiar cognomen: Ten-Inch.

It was a slow news day. The top stories focused on the effects of the heavier-than-usual April showers that had been pelting Yerba City for the past three days. Waterlogged streets had caused a major traffic jam in the downtown area, and a few homes in working-class neighborhoods had suffered some damage. A photo on the front page showed a kid pushing a small wooden sailboat into a flooded intersection in the Porter District, the working-class neighborhood where I lived. As it happened, I'd been walking past that intersection when the picture had been taken. I'd stopped to watch them stage the event. Reporters in raincoats had stopped up the drains with old newspapers until the intersection was sufficiently underwater. Then they'd handed some local kid the toy boat, directed him into the puddle, and had him crouch down on his knees to make the water appear chest deep. Afterwards, they unstopped the drains. It took about two minutes for the pool of water to disappear.

I was more interested in the story at the bottom of page five. The article was only two paragraphs long and didn't rate a byline. The body of a young woman had been found in an alley behind an office building in the South Market District in the early hours of Tuesday morning. The woman was an adaro, a humanlike species of amphibious people from the southern waters of the Nihhonese Ocean. Full-grown adaro men could pull a medium-sized ship to the ocean depths, and they had a reputation for ferocity and aggression. Female adaros, impolitely referred to by some as "nymphs," emitted a strong pheromone that men and women alike found sexually stimulating. As a result, adaros were regarded with suspicion or misgiving by most respectable folk. According to the article, police suspected foul play in the death of this particular adaro, who had suffered grievous bodily injuries, and they were searching for a person of interest: a man known as Ten-Inch. The article stated that Ten-Inch was said to be a member of the Northsiders, described as a prominent street gang in Placid Point. The article further noted that the Northsiders and their principal rivals, the Claymore Cartel, had engaged in a number of turf battles over the past several years, and, although the article didn't say so directly, the implication was that the unnamed adaro was a victim of this unchecked gang violence.

Ten-Inch. That was a name that haunted my dreams. A stone-cold killer. How long had it been since we had nearly beat each other to death with our fists and our feet in one of the most brutal fights of my life, and then toasted each other's health with bottles of beer in his crib afterward? Two years? No, almost three now. The paper said that he was a member of the Northsiders. He'd been the boss of the gang—he'd referred to it as a 'tribe'—when I knew him. Was that still the case? The nature of his position was such that he was always subject to challenges from tough, violent young thugs, and he'd be, what, thirty-five now? Thirty-six? Maybe older. Was he still in charge? If he wasn't, if he'd been toppled from his throne, I doubted that he would still be associated with the gang. It wasn't in his nature to willingly subject himself to someone else's authority. On the other hand, he was apparently still alive, and gang leaders didn't tend to retire. Knowing Ten-Inch, if he was still kicking, he was most likely still calling the shots. Still, three years was a long time for an older street hood. And he was being hunted by the cops? Three years ago he would have been easy to find. I wondered what he'd gotten himself into.

I folded the newspaper and tossed it into my wastepaper basket. I had no reason to get myself entangled in anything Ten-Inch was involved with. My life was already full. The whiskey I'd splashed into my cup of joe was doing a piss-poor job of numbing my morning hangover, the result of the party I'd held for myself the previous evening in front of my television with a fifth of convenience-store hooch. They say you shouldn't drink alone, but I'd been thirsty and hadn't felt like sharing. Three vintage late-night movies later, I'd nearly polished off the bottle, and if it weren't for my magically enhanced ability to heal I would probably still be sleeping it off. Hell, I might not have survived the night. As it was, the drill bit boring through my brain when I woke up made me swear to give up drinking forever. A quick shot from the remainder of the bottle put an end to that nonsense, but I still wasn't ready to face the day.

After spreading a blob of peanut butter over my toasted waffle, I picked the newspaper out of the wastepaper basket, smoothed it on my tabletop, and turned back to the article about the dead adaro woman. Something about the article bothered me. I read through it again. The woman's body had been found in the South Market District. That was maybe two miles north from my place. The police were looking for Ten-Inch, "a member" of the Northsiders gang, which was active in Placid Point, another four miles or so to the northwest.

Four miles isn't far as the crow flies. But to a gang boss like Ten-Inch, South Market may have been on the other side of the moon. His turf was a section of Placid Point, one of Yerba City's larger districts. The district, perched on the tip of the peninsula, consisted of a sprawling patchwork of working-class housing, industrial parks, strip malls, and shipyards. It had its own business district, separate from the rest of Yerba City, consisting of deteriorating office buildings, cheap diners, and a disproportionate amount of pawn shops, tattoo parlors, and bars. The adaro settlement, where female adaros were housed as a "protected species" after they were relocated from the Nihhonese Ocean and registered by the Bureau of Adaro Affairs, was located off the water on the east side of the district, just past the busy ferry port. Ten-Inch was a notable figure in Placid Point, a person of importance. A prince of the streets. In South Market, a major business hub and center of tourism, Ten-Inch would have been just one more piece of working-class trash. Like me. And now he was the subject of a citywide search in conjunction with a murder committed in fashionable South Market? Something didn't fit.

Ten-Inch. The Northsiders. Placid Point. Images drifted through my alcohol-soaked brain. The old fisherman, who was more than he seemed, at the end of the abandoned pier, his line in the water, an old empty bucket at his feet. A smuggling boat in the dead of night. Bullets flying and people in gang colors dropping on the broken asphalt. Kraken, the young adaro lord, leaping out of the water. The image of an adaro woman, Leena Waterfowl, in a raging storm with a tiny gun in her hand popped into my head and sat there, like a worn-out black-and-white photo. My thoughts drifted to her sister, Mila, poor doomed Mila, stepping into my bathroom to take a shower, smiling at me over her shoulder, challenging me to feel something. That memory was torn away and replaced with the stark image of Stonehammer, his troll eyes glowing red, holding the tip of an icepick a hair's-breadth away from my eyeball.

I was overcome by a fit of shuddering as sobriety ripped through my brain like ball bearings from an IED. I wadded up the newspaper. After devouring half my waffle and draining the dregs of my coffee, I left the remains of my breakfast on the table for later and grabbed my hat and coat. I was in the mood for a crosstown drive.

***

A steady rain was falling, and I smelled salt in the wind whipping off the Nihhonese Ocean as I walked up the block to pick up my car at Giovanni's Auto Repair, where I kept it parked. Gio saw me coming from inside his office and waved at me to join him. I sensed he wasn't alone, and when I got to his office I found his youngest daughter, Gemma, sitting behind his desk shuffling through an unusual deck of playing cards. I gave the cards a quick glance. They were larger and more colorful than the ones we used on our poker nights. The backs of the cards were bright yellow and lined on all four sides with realistic images of wooden staves sprouting dark green leaves. The hum of magic emanating from the deck brushed lightly at my inner ears, like a half-heard musical note.

Gio indicated his daughter with his chin. "Look who got sent home from school early today. The plumbing got all backed up because of the rain."

Gemma smiled up at me. "There's shit all over the bathroom floor!"

Gio glared at the girl. "Gemma! Watch your mouth! Who teaches you to talk like that?"

Still facing me, Gemma rolled her eyes dramatically toward her father and pointed at him with her thumb. "Who do you think?"

"Yeah? Well watch it or I'll fuckin' belt ya one!" He lifted the back of his hand, threatening a slap that no one in the room believed for a second would ever be delivered, at least not as long as Gio was sober and hoping to stay married to Gemma's mother.

Gemma took an exaggerated breath and huffed it out through her nose. "Yes, Daddy." She glanced at me sidelong and flashed me a sly grin.

Gio shrugged in resignation. "Kids. What are you gonna do." He nodded toward his daughter. "Hey, Alex. I want you to see something. Gemma, show Mr. Southerland what you can do with your cards."

Gemma smiled up at me, revealing a set of white teeth constrained by chrome braces. What was she now—eleven? No, I remembered Gio telling me a couple of months before that she'd celebrated her twelfth birthday. The kid was growing up fast. I smiled back at Gemma, who loved cars as much as her old man and her older brother, Antonio. How old was *he* now? Sixteen? He'd be doing his mandatory time in government service soon, probably in the military. The thought made me wince. The kid would probably wind up in a combat zone in the Borderland. Despite the best efforts of the Tolanican government, rumors that Dragon Lord Ketz-Alkwat was attempting to produce an offspring were flying all over the internet. The other Dragon Lords were said to be in a full-blown panic at the idea of *two* powerful Dragon Lords in a single realm. Lord Manqu of Qusco had doubled his forces in the Borderland, and Lord Ketz had doubled his own forces in retaliation. And now Antonio, who had only just started shaving the peach fuzz off his baby face, was going to be in the middle of it all? In another year or two, he was going to have to trade in his skateboard for an automatic rifle. It didn't seem possible.

Lord's balls! Where does the time go? You didn't notice it so much with adults, but with kids you could see the years race by right before your eyes. I didn't envy parents, who I imagined must feel themselves one step closer to the grave every time their child outgrew a pair of pants or replaced a baby tooth with a permanent one. You turned around, and they were putting on makeup, getting their driver's license, and sneaking booze out of the pantry. Turn around again, and they were giving you their own kids to hold and calling you grandpa! No, I thought, the best way to keep from growing old was to avoid the company of children, since they refused to stay children for more than a few days, or hours, or minutes.

"I'm going to be a witch," Gemma told me. "I've got a talent with cards. I can tell fortunes. Want me to tell yours?"

I turned to Gio, whose smile couldn't quite hide the look of panic in his eyes. "What's this?" I asked him.

"They tested her at school. One of her teachers, Mrs. Keli'i, says that Gemma has a talent. A big one, she says. She's going to train Gemma. I guess I should have seen it coming. She's always had a knack of finding things the rest of us have misplaced. And she's always been able to predict things before they happen. Hey, it could come in pretty handy!"

"I could be a private eye, like you, Mr. Southerland!" Gemma was beaming at me.

"I'm sure you can find a better way to use your talent than that," I said. "Something that brings in some real dough."

Gio nudged me. "I keep telling her that she can use her witchcraft to find a rich husband."

Gemma rolled her eyes. "Oh, Daddy. That's so boring." She looked back at me, casually mixing her deck. "Come on, Mr. Southerland. Let me tell your fortune."

I smiled at her. "Sounds like fun. But I've got someplace I've got to be at the moment. Another time, okay?"

In response, she fanned the cards face down across the desktop. "Just a quick one. Pick a card. Any card. Pull it out from the other cards, but don't look at it. Leave it face down on the desk."

I looked at Gio, who shrugged. Turning back to Gemma, I said. "All right. Just one, though."

I slid a card from the middle of the deck. Gemma pushed the remainder of the cards together and set them off to one side in a pile. She focused a serious gaze on the back of the card I'd drawn. After a few seconds, she closed her eyes and placed her hand on the card. After waiting another second, she opened her eyes and flipped the card over with a snap. Withdrawing her hand with a flourish she stared down at the card.

The hand-drawn illustration on the card was innocuous enough: sheets of rain pouring down onto turbulent ocean waves from an impressive set of gray storm clouds. In terms of quality, it was a drawing you'd be more likely to find in a comic book than an art gallery. My reaction to the drawing, however, was intense. The moment I set eyes on it I felt the hairs on the back of my neck stand on end, as if I'd walked through a field of static electricity. From somewhere far off, I sensed Cougar, my spirit animal, stirring and sniffing the air, curious and alert.

"It's the Storm," Gemma proclaimed.

Gio shot me a surreptitious wink. "So you're saying Mr. Southerland is going to get stuck out in the rain? That wouldn't be hard on a day like today."

"It means more than that, Daddy!"

"What do *you* think it means?" I asked Gemma.

The girl thought about it and shrugged. "It could mean a lot of things, actually. I don't think it's a good card, though. But I'm still new at this. I should probably ask Mrs. Keli'i."

I held out my hand. "Can I see it?"

Gemma hesitated for a moment, and then handed me the card. I examined one side, and then the other, listening to the hum in my ears. "I don't know much about witchcraft, but I can definitely feel something at work here." I handed her back the card. "I'd be interested in hearing what your teacher has to say."

Gemma's eyes widened. "Maybe I can call her."

Gio gave her shoulder a squeeze. "Mr. Southerland has to go, Gemma. You can talk to Mrs. Keli'i later."

"But Daddy," Gemma complained. "It could be important."

Gio smiled at her. "Turning over a picture of a rainstorm on a rainy day doesn't seem all that big a deal to me." To me, he said, "Pretty accurate, though. I hope you have an umbrella."

"I've got a nice one. Too bad I left it at home." For some reason, walking in the rain had seemed like a good idea when I'd left the house. It had been such a light rain, and I'd been hoping it would let up after three days. Now I was beginning to wonder.

Gemma studied the card. "I don't know, Mr. Southerland. These cards aren't toys. You felt something when I turned it over, and I felt something, too. I think this card is telling you something more than it's raining." She looked up at me, a solemn expression on her twelve-year-old face.

I nodded at her in a way that I hoped was reassuring. "I think you're right. You've got a real talent, and there's real magic in those cards."

Gio frowned. "Do you think they're dangerous?"

I shrugged. "Magic is always risky, even when you know what you're doing. I can sense some things that most people can't."

"Because you're an elementalist?" Gio asked.

"Yes, and for other reasons. But I'm not a witch. I don't have that talent. Gemma does, though, I'm sure of that." I turned to the girl.

"Gemma, you need to be careful with magic. Don't try to do too much with your talent until you get some training. Okay?"

Gemma nodded, her face still serious. "That's what Mrs. Keli'i says."

"You listen to your teacher, sport."

"I will."

"Good."

Gemma's lips spread into a grin. "As soon as I find out more about this card, I'll tell you, okay?"

I gave her a hard look. "You'll let your teacher help you, right? Don't do anything until you talk to her, okay?"

Gemma's eyes widened until I was staring into two deep pools of umber-colored innocence. "I won't, Mr. Southerland. I swear."

## Chapter Two

Despite the rain, city traffic was no worse than usual when I pulled the beastmobile out of Gio's lot, and I was able to make Placid Point in only a little more time and with considerably less sweat than I could have reached it with a good unobstructed run. Maybe. It had been a while since I'd laced up my sneakers and pounded the pavement, and, although I'd been avoiding the scales, I suspected I'd been putting on some pounds over the past couple of months. Since Holly had moved on to greener pastures, in fact. Probably just a coincidence. My stomach began to churn, and I gritted my teeth, fighting back a sudden attack of nausea. The air inside the beastmobile was stifling all of a sudden, and I reached up to wipe beads of sweat off my neck. My hand scraped over the stubble on my unshaven face. More than stubble, I realized. How long had it been since I'd shaved? Three days? Four? It might have been at least that long since I'd showered, too. I took a quick sniff in the vicinity of my armpit and shrugged. It's not like I'd had any pressing reasons to clean up lately. I hadn't been within spitting distance of another live sentient being in at least a week. What was happening to me, I wondered. I was really letting myself go. I sighed, feeling old. Thirty-one going on fifty.

I opened the window a crack and sat up a little straighter in my seat. "Alkwat's flaming balls," I muttered to myself. This had gone on long enough. It was time to stop moping around like a pathetic middle-aged stumblebum and start getting myself back into fighting shape.

First thing tomorrow, I thought, as I unscrewed the cap off my whiskey flask and knocked back a slug of rye.

I inched my way through the streets of Placid Point's business district, unsure what I was doing there. Not that I had any other place to be. I was, as they say, "between cases" at the moment. In fact, I hadn't worked a case since..., well..., since Holly. Undoubtedly another coincidence. Private investigation isn't exactly steady work, especially when you run a one-man operation. Sometimes I'm swamped with more offers than I can handle, and I have to farm good potential clients off to my competitors. Other times, weeks can go by with zippo, like an imposed and unwanted vacation. To be fair, I'd turned down a couple of opportunities because I didn't think they were worth the bother. I'd scored a few high-paying jobs toward the end of the previous year, and lately I hadn't felt like peeking through keyholes to find out whether some sad sack's better half was making a monkey out of him, or tailing some crabby dame's son to find out who was selling him unlicensed blow. Those were jobs I would have taken ten years ago when I was just starting out. I was more established now, and I didn't need the dough that badly anymore. At least, I didn't think so. I couldn't remember the last time I'd checked my bank account. But none of my checks had bounced, so I figured I was okay.

I guess I shouldn't have been surprised when I looked out my window and found that I was cruising by the shuttered storefront of what used to be the Nautilus Jewelry and Novelty Shop, a place that had been owned by a decent joe called Crawford. He'd been a good pal, my best friend, I guess, until he'd been forced by the Lord's Investigation Agency to take a powder. Almost a year ago, I'd received a cryptic text message from him telling me that he was leaving the Realm of Tolanica for a while, but he couldn't tell me where he was going, and he'd asked me not to look into it. I'd texted him back asking if he was okay, and he'd said he was, and that was that. I hadn't heard from him since. I *had*, of course, been trying to find out what was going on, but so far I'd drawn a blank. I told myself that he was capable of taking care of himself, but I had a bad feeling about it. None of the Seven Realms were safe from the LIA, Dragon Lord Ketz-Alkwat's own security force, and if those bastards caught up to him they could erase him as if he'd never existed. I wasn't going to stop making inquiries, but I also didn't want to risk exposing him if he was still alive and running. I was doing my best to look on the sunny side, but it wasn't easy.

I left the business district and made for the north shore. The rain had diminished to a light drizzle, but traffic was stop-and-go for no discernable reason, and it took more than a half hour to cover the twelve blocks to Fremont Street, which ran along the northern tip of the Bay. Most of the traffic headed west on Fremont toward the Placid Point Pier, the new modern one. I turned right and drove past the abandoned original Placid Point Pier, keeping my eye out for a joint called Medusa's Tavern, which had served as the home base of the Northsiders last time I'd been there. It was a little early for the tribe to be gathering, but I thought I'd at least drive by and see if the place was still in business.

It wasn't. Even when I'd last seen the joint, Medusa's had appeared to be abandoned. It had been a ramshackle wooden structure set off the road across a dirt parking lot. The building had long fought a losing battle against the salt-filled winds blasting sand in off the coast. The shuttered windows had prevented light from leaking out from the interior, and the only exterior display had been a small carved wooden figure barely recognizable as the possibly mythical snake-haired Medusa. But now, as I pulled the beastmobile into the empty lot, I was greeted with only the blackened ruins of the Northsiders' former headquarters. The sorry old joint had burned to the ground.

 I parked near the remains of the building and stepped into the muddy ash and rubble, being careful to avoid broken glass and rusty nails. I didn't know what I was looking for. The structure had been in a state of near decay even before the fire had finished it off. Anything remaining of the roof and walls were scattered at my feet. The tables and chairs had been reduced to cinders. The bar counter had caved in, partially burying the scorched metal fixtures of the drink dispensers, sinks, refrigeration units, stainless steel kegs, and beer cans. I kicked a path through the debris to where the pool table had been and found nothing except chunks of blackened ceiling beams.

 I smiled then, remembering the time when a bunch of the kids in the neighborhood had tossed some stolen billiard balls into a dumpster fire to see if they would melt. The resulting explosions had been spectacular, although one of the kids had lost an eye when his mug had been seared by the burning resin and plastic. We all called him "Patch" after that, of course. He later got gunned down by a cashier while trying to rob a liquor store. I think he'd been thirteen. Kids. It's a wonder anyone ever survives childhood.

 I made my way to the space that had been Ten-Inch's office. Amidst the charred remains, I spotted a cast-iron safe. Unfortunately, the door was hanging open, and anything that had been inside had either been looted or burned. I dug through the rubble, but found nothing of interest. If I'd been hoping for clues to the fate of the Medusa or Ten-Inch's current whereabouts, I was out of luck.

 As I was about to leave the ruins, however, something began to nag at me. Had I overlooked something? I stood in the middle of the debris and did a slow three-sixty, trying to figure out what had caught the attention of my subconscious. All I could see were the wet ruins of an old decrepit building that had been thoroughly ravaged by fire and doused by rain. Not even the fiberglass insulation had survived, which meant that the flames had been pretty intense. Had the fire been the result of an explosion, perhaps from a drug lab? I didn't think so. If the Northsiders had been cooking meth, they wouldn't have been foolish enough to do it at their headquarters. And, anyway, the walls had all collapsed inwards, an indication that the fire had burned inside the poorly ventilated structure for a long period of time. The high heat and heavy smoke had sucked up the oxygen in the building, reducing the air pressure and creating backdraft conditions when outside air found fissures in the burning walls and rushed in to fill the vacuum. Had the Northsiders come under attack? Maybe they'd been raided by the Claymore Cartel. Or the cops. Either was a likely possibility. Or, just as likely, a short in the electrical wiring could have caused this fire. Or a discarded cigarette. The wonder of it all was how the old building had lasted as long as it did.

Something about the collapsed walls. I wandered to the back of the building and stepped outside the burned-out rubble. Scrub brush grew just outside the walls. Within inches of the walls, in fact. Even in the moist morning air, the brush was gray and brittle, typical of the vegetation that grew in the sandy soil this close to the shore. I bent down to snap off a branch, and it broke away easily. I tried to pull a bush out of the ground by its roots, but they held firm, even in the wet ground. In soil like this, these roots had to be deep, which meant that the brush had been there for a long while. Years, probably.

So why wasn't any of this brush scorched? I examined the growth carefully. I'm no expert, but it all looked perfectly healthy to me, untouched by excessive heat. I didn't know how long ago the Medusa had burned, but I'd stood inside the joint two and a half years earlier, so it had to have been sometime since then. If the brush had been charred, would it have already recovered? I wasn't sure. To my admittedly untrained eyes, however, it appeared to me that an inferno hot enough to collapse the Medusa had somehow left the dry brush next to the building unaffected.

Maybe it was nothing, but it bothered me. I'd have to find out when the fire had occurred and ask an expert about the likelihood of scrub brush outside the burning building surviving the conflagration unscathed.

By the time I reached the beastmobile, the light drizzle had turned once again into a steady rain. I drove out of the empty lot with my wipers running and headed for the apartment that had been Ten-Inch's last known address. I still didn't know why I was looking for Ten-Inch, but I thought maybe I'd figure it out on the way. Maybe I just wanted something else to think about besides the girl with the raven hair and shining eyes who wouldn't be waiting for me to come by her place later with some deep-fried calamari and a bottle of rye.

*\*\**

The four-year-old dark green soccer-mom van with the shaded windows parked across the street from the apartment where I'd visited Ten-Inch three years earlier told me the gang boss was still living there. Since the police were looking for Ten-Inch, I knew they'd have his place under surveillance, and the nondescript utility van—neither flashy enough nor shabby enough to attract attention—was typical of the vehicles the police liked to use on stakeouts. Not only did the two lethargic-looking gentlemen in the front seat of the van have a good view of Ten-Inch's apartment building, but the cigarette butts littering the street outside the front windows on both sides of the vehicle indicated they'd been watching the place for several hours.

I drove past the van and considered my next move. The cops would have picked Ten-Inch up if he'd been home, so he was probably on the lam. They had to leave a team there on the off chance he tried to sneak back home for some reason, or that he would send someone back to pick something up for him. The cops on the stakeout would be bored and careless, fully aware of how unlikely it was that Ten-Inch would make an appearance, knowing they were wasting their time. I parked around the block from the apartment building, out of the surveillance team's sight, and turned off the engine.

I hadn't known whether Ten-Inch still lived at the same address, or expected to find him at home waiting for the coppers to come calling if he did, but it had seemed like a good idea to check in on the place. Anyway, it wasn't as if I had another place to be, or any better ideas on where to find the old gangster. Although the cops were an indication that I'd come to the right place, their presence there was a problem. I wanted to get inside the building without attracting their attention. After considering the situation for a minute, I called up a sigil in my mind, opened my window a crack, and waited.

Twenty minutes later, a streak of wind zipped through my window and hovered in the air in front of me, spinning like a two-inch tornado and slinging droplets of rainwater in every direction. I wiped the mist out of my eyes and said, "Hello, Smokey."

A hissing whisper responded with, "Hello, Aleksss. Howzzz trickssss?"

"Aces. Are you ready to go to work?"

My favorite tiny air elemental hopped to my shoulder. "Smokey is ready to ssserve."

"Good. I was hoping that this rain would let up, but it doesn't look like it's going to. But I don't guess the rain bothers you much."

"See what Smokey can do." Before I could stop it, the elemental darted through the opening in the window into the rain. In another second, it shot back through the window and launched a thin jet of water into my face. The freezing water rolled down my cheek and into the inside of my coat.

It was going to be one of those days. Never mind that the "experts" all claimed that elementals were not supposed to possess independent thought, emotions, or wit. After working with elementals all my life, I knew better. Smokey definitely had a sense of humor. Not a sophisticated one, unfortunately, but who was I to tell an air spirit what it should regard as funny? I sighed and dried my face with a handkerchief. "That's very clever, Smokey. Don't do that again unless I ask you to."

"Smokey likesss water in windsss."

"That's swell. Alex isn't as pleased by it as you are. I wish I had thought to bring an umbrella."

I could have simply gone home, of course. That would have been the reasonable thing to do. But I'd already made the drive to Placid Point, and Ten-Inch's apartment building was right around the corner. My mother always told me I didn't have the sense to come in out of the rain, and at that moment I couldn't argue with her. I pulled the brim of my hat low over my forehead and instructed Smokey to stay on my shoulder as I stepped out of the car.

I stuffed my hands into my pockets and walked around the corner until I was in sight of the unmarked surveillance van. I pointed it out to Smokey and told the elemental to keep watch on the men sitting inside. "If either of them leave the vehicle, come tell me immediately."

Smokey zipped into the mist and disappeared from view. Nearly invisible even up close, I knew that the two cops would be unable to spot the air spirit as it watched them from overhead.

With the stakeout team now under my own surveillance, I circled the block and studied the apartment building on all sides. It was a narrow three-story structure with four apartments on each floor. The individual units could only be reached from the building's interior after entering through the front door, which was not only under observation, but was locked and barred. I remembered that Ten-Inch's unit was on the second floor in the front of the building with a window facing the street. It also had a window on the side of the building, out of the view of the observing cops, but entering the apartment through that window would be impractical, if not impossible. Getting inside Ten-Inch's apartment unseen in broad daylight was going to be tricky.

Crawford could have done it. He was a were-rat, a shapeshifter who could transform into more than a hundred rats. Rats have no trouble finding ways into old buildings like this one, as I'm sure the current residents were already aware. Then there was the Huay Chivo, an ancient scraggly goat-like creature who had once been a powerful sorcerer, and who now resided in my laundry room. Chivo possessed some sort of magical skill that allowed him to ignore locks and open doors with impunity, as if they were eager to usher him through. He was also insane, more beast than human, and nearly impossible to control, not to mention wanted by the government for study and disposal. Driving back to my place and bringing him back to help me was out of the question. Me? All I could do was summon and command small air elementals, like Smokey. I could get Smokey inside, but he wouldn't be capable of unlocking the front door and letting me in. I studied the building, searching for a way to get to the roof, and backed into the street a few steps to get a better view of the building.

As I stood in the street, my face growing numb in the wind and rain, I wondered whether getting into Ten-Inch's apartment would be worth the effort, even if I *could* find a way inside, which was doubtful. Ten-Inch was almost certainly somewhere else, and the chances of finding any hint of his whereabouts in his apartment were slim. The police would certainly have already searched the place. I shook my head, and water spilled over the brim of my fedora. The rain was coming down much harder now. Mother had been right about me.

I was about to forget the whole thing and return to the shelter of the beastmobile when I stopped in my tracks and stared at the apartment building. Something had scratched at my awareness, like the tiny prickling of a kitten's claw on my neck. I "saw" it then in a way that my vision didn't actually register: a distortion in the air above the building's roof, a hint of brightness, like pale sunshine fighting its way through the dark rainclouds. Only the distortion wasn't coming from above; it seemed rather to be glowing from a point just above the side window of Ten-Inch's apartment.

Nine months earlier, during the previous summer, I'd been sent on a spirit quest by a computer wizard named Walks in Cloud, who afterward became a good friend of mine. During the quest, I'd encountered Cougar, who had become my spirit animal. Even after nine months, I still didn't really understand how it all worked, but Cougar occasionally provided me with insights, as well as sudden bursts of animal strength. Since my initial encounter, I'd begun to perceive the world around me a bit differently than I had before. Colors were brighter, objects were more clearly delineated. And I could sense things I couldn't before, evidence of magic, for example, and places where our earthly realm intersected in varying degrees with... other places. These places were hard to describe, but everyone knew they existed and that things sometimes came through them, or disappeared into them. The most well-known of these places was Hell. Six thousand years ago, the Dragon Lords had emerged from Hell, bringing trolls, gnomes, and dwarfs along for the ride. The immortal Dragon Lords had overcome the elves, the former masters of the world, and established the Seven Realms, which they ruled ever afterward. The elves had been wiped out. Completely, according to the official accounts, but that, like much of what the government tells us, was only what you might call "political messaging." Or "bullshit," to use a more colorful and useful term.

What I saw, or sensed in some way, above Ten-Inch's window probably wasn't a portal into Hell, but it was something unearthly. Something supernatural. It might have been nothing, maybe just the lingering vestiges of a magical spell. But finding it in such close proximity to the last place I'd seen Ten-Inch struck me as more than coincidental. I wanted to get closer.

A shrill hissing whisper sounded in my ear: "Men in vehicle walk here now!"

Alkwat's balls! How long had I been standing in the rain, gawking at that apartment? I must have caught the attention of the surveillance team somehow. I turned to hustle my way back to the beastmobile and saw a black-and-white cop car headed up the street in my direction, the red light on the roof flashing. Just to make sure I got the message, the siren screamed for a couple of seconds before it was switched off.

I stopped in my tracks and sent out a mental command. "Smokey! Don't let yourself be seen by those men, but follow me wherever I go until I command otherwise. Got it?"

"Smokey gotsss it!" The elemental vanished in the rain.

A booming shout ripped through the wind. "Police! Freeze, asshole!"

Three years earlier, an elf had demonstrated to me that he was not, in fact, a member of an extinct species, and he'd jammed a magic crystal into my forehead to augment my awareness. My five senses played a role, but it was more than that. I could now "see" without using my eyes, even in pitch darkness, which proved to be handy for a guy in my profession. As a result of the elf's magic, I didn't have to turn around to know that the two plainclothes cops who had been staking out Ten-Inch's place were now advancing on me at a trot with guns drawn. I held my arms out to my side and turned slowly to face them.

"Hello, gentlemen," I said. "What's with all the hardware?"

## Chapter Three

"Get down on your knees and put your hands behind your head!" The cop doing the shouting had a barrel chest and a smooth baby face that appeared to have never been scraped by a razor, although the old scars that lined both his cheeks suggested he was no stranger to violence. If he'd been in a boy band, he would have been a real heartthrob among his teenaged fans. At the moment, however, his pretty face was distorted into a grotesque caricature of a street tough by his twisted lips and bulging eyes. It didn't work for me. He was trying too hard. I took an instant dislike to him.

By now, the police cruiser had skidded to a stop behind me, and two uniformed patrolmen had emerged, weapons at the ready. I now had four heaters pointed in my direction.

"On my knees?" I asked, keeping my voice steady. "In this weather? Is that really necessary?"

I should have seen it coming, but I was having a bad morning. As I shot a quick glance over my shoulder at the uniformed officers, the plainclothes bull with the scarred baby face advanced on me as quick as a cat and buried his fist into my solar plexus. It was a short jackhammer jab with no wasted motion and a couple of hundred pounds of hard-packed muscle fiber behind it. My breath left my lungs with a whoosh, and I was on my hands and knees before I felt the impact. I spent an uncomfortable few seconds attempting to inhale and having little success.

"Hands behind your head, asshole!" My head was stuffed with cotton, and Scarface's shout sounded like it was coming from the bottom of a well.

I was almost ready to breathe again when Scarface launched a kick at my midsection that threatened to empty half-digested waffle and booze from my gullet.

"I told you to put your hands behind your head!"

Under the circumstances, that struck me as an unreasonable request.

The pudgy older copper at his side was more reasonable. Keeping his heater trained on me, he put a restraining arm on his agitated partner. "Now, now, Modoc. It's okay. It's not him." Raising his voice to the cops behind me, he shouted, "Relax, boys. Stay cool. This isn't him."

None of the cops lowered their gats, but the reasonable one, apparently in charge of the team, crouched down until his face was level with mine. "Do you think you can stand, sir?"

"Give me a second," I managed.

I took a much needed breath, stood, and brushed mud off my coat.

"We're going to pat you down," said the reasonable copper. "You don't mind, do you?"

I shrugged. "Sure, go ahead. I'm not packing a weapon."

The older cop sent his excitable friend to do the honors, and he wasn't gentle. Something about the bull with the scars on his smooth cheeks rankled me. I couldn't put my finger on it, but it was something apart from the fact that he had decked me with one punch, kicked me when I was down, and was groping and pawing at me like a vice cop frisking a streetwalker. I'd had worse, and I took it without complaining. It was quick and efficient, and he didn't find anything on me except my wallet, which he pulled out of my back pocket and opened.

"This says he's Alexander Southerland. He's got a buzzer here that says he's a private dick." He said it like he'd caught me kicking a baby, and his face didn't get any less red as he glared at me with narrowed eyes. I figured he had anger issues. I was feeling a little angry myself, but I kept it in.

The pudgy copper digested this information, stroking his short gray beard with one hand and looking thoughtful. "Mr. Southerland, I'm arresting you for jaywalking." He indicated the cops from the black-and-white. "These men will take you back to the station."

"Jaywalking!" I barked, fuming a little. "You can't be serious."

The cop adjusted his glasses and addressed me in the kindly, but firm manner of a wise father in a TV sitcom gently chastising his wayward son. "We caught you walking in the middle of the street, Mr. Southerland. You were a danger to any passing motorists and to yourself. Especially with the rain interfering with a driver's visibility."

"Lord's flaming balls, officer. What would you have done if I'd've had a gun? Shoot me?"

He smiled, but I could tell he didn't mean it. "My partner and I aren't officers. We're detectives, and you will address us as such. And, yes, shooting you would have been a consideration." The smile turned to a frown as he took in a deep breath through his nose. "Is that booze I smell? Shame on you, sir. Looks like I'm going to have to slap you with a public drunkenness, too. Go on along with these men, Mr. Southerland. None of us like standing around in this rain."

\*\*\*

The uniformed cops took me to the Placid Point Precinct stationhouse, where I was fingerprinted, relieved of my wallet, phone, and keys, and led to a holding tank. Two drunks were sleeping it off on the only bench in the cell, their rhythmic snorts and snuffles providing backup harmony for snores loud enough to peel paint emerging from the ragged dwarf curled up in the corner. Five other occupants, all human, slumped or sat against the walls. They glanced briefly at me as I entered the cell before returning their attention to the tops of their shoes.

I leaned against a section of unoccupied wall and tried not to gag on the odor of stale booze, fresh farts, unwashed flesh, and a hint of bleach. I'm not a sociable guy by nature, but after a few minutes of nothing but snores, sniffs, and coughs, I began to miss the sound of voices. I turned to my neighbor, a defeated-looking mug barely out of his teens with unwashed strands of dank black hair plastered to the sides of his face and hanging down his back, and asked, "Rough night, buddy?"

The young man shuffled his feet but didn't look up. "Could say that," he muttered.

It was an opening, so I decided to see where it would lead. Maybe I could make a friend. "They nabbed me for jaywalking," I told my new pal, leaving out the other charge. "That a serious crime in these parts?"

He smiled a little at that and gave me a sidelong glance. "You're not from around here, are you."

"I live in the Porter District."

He grunted. "Lucky."

"How so? The Porter isn't exactly the Galindo. We're no less working class than Placid Point."

My pal shook his head and straightened a little. "You have no fuckin' idea."

"That so? Maybe you can enlighten me."

The disheveled young man looked me up and down, like he was trying to decide whether he could trust me. "Jaywalking. Huh. Whereabouts?"

"I was on Spruce Street just off Miller."

He nodded. "Residential area, right?"

"Yeah. Near an apartment building."

"You cross the street without using a crosswalk?"

"Actually, I was standing in the street a few feet off the sidewalk. I was trying to get a view of something."

My new pal smiled. "Then you're fucked."

"Really? They're that serious about walking violations?"

My pal's face hardened. "Look, man. The laws here are fuckin' insane. The cops grab you for all kinds of petty shit. Vagrancy, loitering, trespassing.... Jaywalking is one of their favorites. A lot of the neighborhoods around here don't even have sidewalks, so the only way you can get anywhere on foot is to walk across someone's yard, which is trespassing, or on the street, which is fuckin' jaywalking."

I considered what he was telling me for a few moments before asking, "What are *you* in for?"

He scowled. "Rolling through a motherfuckin' stop sign. So they say. Or maybe it was failing to signal for a right turn. Last time it was for driving with a broken taillight. Funny thing about that. The fuckin' taillight was fine before the son-of-a-bitch cop pulled me over. The asshole broke it with his flashlight. I watched him do it. Then he wrote me up for it."

"No shit?"

"No fuckin' shit. Alkwat's balls, man! You can't fuckin' drive through this town without getting nailed for something."

"I've driven through here lots of times. No one has ever pulled me over."

He looked me up and down again, examining my leather trench coat. "What kind of car do you drive?"

I hesitated. "Nothing special." The beastmobile required a lot of explanation if I was going to go there at all.

"Expensive?"

"It's... big. Yeah, I guess it's on the high end."

My pal nodded. "They don't usually mess with anyone who looks like they can afford a fuckin' attorney."

Which reminded me that the police owed me a phone call.

A gentleman tucked into a corner of the cell had been listening to the two of us talk and decided to jump in. "They got me for disturbing the peace. I was about to cross the street when a car ran the light and almost plowed into me. I yelled at him and flipped him the bird as he went by. Next thing I knew some eager-beaver cop was putting me in cuffs and pushing me into the back of a squad car. They wanted to pin a

D and D on me, only I hadn't been drinking yet. I was on my way *to* the bar when they put the arm on me. So they settled for disturbing the peace."

By now, the other mugs in the room, the ones who were awake, at least, were showing signs of interest, grunting, shuffling, and nodding.

"They got me for loitering," said a voice.

"Jaywalking," said another. He looked at me with half a smile and nodded, as if acknowledging that we belonged to the same club.

My longhaired pal turned toward me. "Here's what they do. They get you for piddly shit and hit you with a fuckin' fine. A big one. More than most of us can afford to pay." He looked around the room. "Am I right?"

Nods all around. Mutterings of "Fuckin' A," and "That's right."

My pal continued. "Then they give you a notice to appear. The date is set a couple of months down the road. And the law says you gotta appear in person, on that date, at the specified time. Then they fuckin' charge you interest on your fine. And you can't pay early to avoid the fuckin' interest, either. There's no way to pay except in person, in cash, and when scheduled."

"And if you fail to appear, or if you don't have the dough on you, then that's another fine," chimed in one of the other men in the cell. "And it's bigger than the original fine."

"And with another notice to appear." This from the dwarf, who had been awakened by the growing hubbub.

"And if you can't pay, they put you in the slammer for a month," a new voice piped in. "Good luck keeping your job after that!"

"And all the while, the interest on your fine keeps growing," another one added.

The dwarf stood. "I was in the joint for failure to pay the fine on one citation when my court date to pay the fine on another came up. Naturally, I couldn't make that date, because I was in the fuckin' joint. So I got nailed with another fine for failure to appear! How is that fair?"

More grunts and grumbling.

"It's a motherfuckin' racket!" My new pal wasn't exactly shouting, but he was working up to it. "It's a major source of revenue for the city. They cite you for fuckin' anything, and then they make it as hard as possible to pay the fine. Then they charge interest, and the penalties keep racking up. I've got five fuckin' tickets pending, and I can't pay none of them! And every month I don't pay, the debt gets bigger. I fuckin' got fired from my job because I had to take the fuckin' day off to appear in court. They're going to impound my fuckin' car, but that won't even pay the fuckin' interest on what I owe. I'm fuckin' screwed man. I'm fuckin' screwed." He shook his head and sat on the floor, his energy depleted.

"How long has this been going on?" I asked.

My pal groaned. "Long as I can remember. But it only got real bad this past year. Toward the end of last summer."

"That's right," said one of my cellmates. "That's when the cops started citing people for all kinds of petty shit. And that's when they made it so you had to pay your fines in person. Used to be you got a ticket, you could mail a check or go online and charge it to your credit card. Not anymore. And good luck trying to find anyone to take your money. Most of the time there's just one window open at the counter and a fuckin' line to get there. And only during certain times of the day. Thing is, they don't want you to pay on time. They want to charge late fees and interest. Get a few citations, add some fees, and next thing you know it's more than you can fuckin' afford!"

Confirming grunts sounded from around the cell.

"They foreclosed on my house when I couldn't pay my fines," one man grumbled.

"I lost my house last week," complained the dwarf. "Paid off my debt in full, but they nabbed me last night for sleeping in an alley. *Big* fine for that one, I'm guessing. More than I'll ever be able to pay. Guess it's prison for me. At least I'll have a roof over my head."

Everyone was awake now, and the grumbling was growing into a steady buzz, like the droning of angry hornets. A loud pounding on the door announced the arrival of one of the precinct goons. "Keep it down in there!"

We all glared through the barred window at the cop on the other side. I recognized him as Modoc, the baby-faced asshole who had humbled me earlier in the day.

Seeing his face caused my hackles to rise, along with my blood pressure. "Hey, Modoc!" I shouted at him. "How long are you planning on holding me here?"

"Shut your fuckin' hole, juicehead!" Coming in from the rain hadn't made the detective any friendlier.

"When do I get my phone call?" I asked.

"Fuck off!"

I would have pressed the issue, but the prick didn't wait around to hear it.

"This is bullshit," I muttered.

My longhaired pal sneered up at me from the floor. "Welcome to Placid Point. Make sure you close the gate on the way out. Be sure to visit our website and fuckin' rate your stay."

## Chapter Four

They transferred me to a sweatbox fifteen minutes later and left me there to contemplate my predicament. I noted that the room was similar enough to the interrogation rooms I'd grown familiar with in the Yerba City Police Department headquarters downtown. No doubt they were the same everywhere: bare walls, metal table attached to the center of the cement floor, uncomfortable folding chairs, one-way glass, a camera you're not supposed to notice in the corner of the ceiling. A single bare bulb hanging from the ceiling lit the center of the room with a harsh yellow-tinged beam and left the corners of the room in shadows. Faded gray stains on the floor and walls were a reminder that interrogations could get rough if the cops wanted it that way, which they often did. By design, the room was too warm and too claustrophobic for comfort. I glanced up at the one and only air vent in the ceiling and noted the slightest of distortions that told me Smokey was still keeping watch over me. I tested the chain running through the metal loops under the tabletop to the cuffs around my wrists and waited to see what the Placid Point coppers wanted from me.

After letting me sweat for a good half hour, the door to the room opened and the two detectives from the surveillance van stepped inside. Modoc leaned his bulky frame against the wall and glared at me, murder in his eyes. I didn't take it personally. In fact, I was flattered. He was doing his best to appear tough for my benefit, but he couldn't quite pull it off, even after the way he had roughed me up earlier. Not with that freckled baby face of his. It didn't help that the scars on his cheeks were less obvious in the shadowy edge of the interrogation room than they'd been outside. Once again, I felt a visceral reaction at the sight of him, as if driven by some sort of animal instinct. Judging by the expression on his face and the swelling of the veins in his neck, he was feeling something similar toward me. Something was happening that I couldn't quite understand, something beyond a reaction to my earlier humiliation. Something primal. My heart began to pound in my chest, and I seized control of my breathing to slow it down.

The other detective took a seat opposite me and removed his hat, revealing an ash gray hairline that had retreated three-quarters of the way up his dome, reminding me of a deserted beach at low tide. He pushed a paper cup to my side of the table.

"You're probably thirsty," he told me, smiling. "I thought you might want some water."

I tore my attention away from Modoc and sniffed at the cup. "What, no coffee?"

"Trust me, the water is better."

I held up my cuffed hands, and the chain scraped the underside of the table as it pulled tight. "Think you can do something about these?"

"I might. Depends on how cooperative you are." He scratched at the soft gray whiskers on his chin.

I found that the chain had just enough slack to allow me to pick up the cup and bring it to my lips if I slumped over the table a bit. The water was warm and tasted like metal, but it felt good going down.

"I'm Detective Sims," my benefactor told me. He was going to be "good cop."

I nodded toward his partner, whose eyes had never left me. "What's your baby bull's name?" I asked.

The baby-faced detective didn't move, but his eyes narrowed into slits. He was going to be "bad cop."

Sims smiled. "That pleasant fellow is Detective Modoc."

"He's a little young to be a detective, isn't he? What is he, sixteen?"

Modoc's eyes widened, but the older detective chuckled. "He's a cutie, isn't he? The other cops have to hide their daughters from him. But he's older than he looks. Can you believe he spent six months in a Special Forces search-and-destroy unit?" He turned toward his partner. "Tell the gentleman how many Qusco insurgents you killed in the Borderland."

Modoc pushed his fedora to the back of his head, and a shock of thick honey-colored hair fell over his forehead. "Twenty-seven with blades. Fourteen with my hands. At least another three or four dozen with various types of firearms. Maybe more. I stopped counting after a while." He let his eyes bore into mine.

Sims turned back to me. "And he returned to the provinces without a scratch on that pretty face of his. Can you believe it?"

"How many has he killed since he came back?"

Sims ran a hand over his bearded chin. "You don't want to know. We have a few questions for you. Answer them honestly, and you can be on your way. Sound fair?"

"Sure," I said. "Who did you think I was when you came down on me with all that iron?"

Modoc was on me almost before I knew he had moved. His backhanded slap rattled my teeth and snapped my head to the side. "We'll ask the fuckin' questions, asshole!"

My jaw tingled, and I launched a wad of blood-streaked spittle to the cement floor. Deep inside me somewhere, I felt an inaudible vibration, a sound below the register of human hearing. A sour feline odor reached my nostrils, and I sensed the presence of Cougar, my spirit animal, riding the crest of my growing rage. I met Modoc's eyes, and I thought he sensed something, too. His nose twitched and I heard him draw in a sharp breath.

Sims made a half turn in his partner's direction. "Now, now, Modoc. The gentleman's question is legitimate." Modoc hesitated a moment before resuming his spot against the wall. His glare never wavered, and his lips widened a fraction into a tight, cold smile.

Sims turned back to me. "As you've probably surmised, we were on the watch for a dangerous criminal we believed might be in the area. You and he are approximately the same size and build, and it was difficult to distinguish your features clearly in the rain, so we elected not to take any chances. We apologize if we gave you a scare. I trust there was no harm done?"

I swallowed my anger. "It was a harrowing experience, but I'm managing to get past the fright."

"Good. My partner is right, though. We'll get through all of this unpleasantness a lot faster if you leave the questioning to us."

"Fine. Maybe I can save you some time. I was jaywalking. I admit it. You caught me fair and square. If you let me know where and when I can pay my fine, I promise to take care of it."

Sims removed his glasses and began working at them one lens at a time with a pocket handkerchief. "That's a good start, Mr. Southerland. You *are* Alexander Southerland, correct?"

"That's me."

"And you're a licensed private investigator?"

"I am."

Sims slid his glasses back over his nose. "Thing is, Alex—may I call you Alex?"

"All my friends do."

"You got a lot of friends?"

"A few. Not many."

Sims nodded, as if I'd given him a valuable piece of information. "Hmmm. That's interesting. Thing is, Alex, there's also the matter of public drunkenness. We caught you wandering about in traffic—"

"Excuse me, Detective Sims," I interrupted. "There wasn't any traffic in the street when you arrested me. And I wasn't wandering. I was standing there admiring that apartment building."

Modoc started forward, but Sims held up a restraining hand, and his junior partner settled back into the wall with an actual snort, as if he were a caged lion. Sims folded his hands on the table and met my eyes with his own. "Still, Alex, you were in the middle of the street near an intersection. At any moment a car could have come around the corner, and we would have had an incident. Especially with the rain limiting visibility. In the position you were in, you were a danger to yourself and to others." He held up a hand as if I were going to interrupt. "And, Alex, you were clearly intoxicated."

"Was I? I was never tested."

"I could smell liquor on your breath. That's all the testing we need."

"Really? I don't think that will hold up in court."

Sims's lips parted as his smile broadened. "You clearly have no experience with the Placid Point court system. Trust me. My testimony will hold up. We'll convict you for public drunkenness, or, given the situation, a drunk and disorderly. That's serious business in Placid Point. For a long time, this district had a reputation as a rough part of Yerba City. Especially after they closed down the old pier. We lost a lot of tourist trade when they did that. A lot of businesses closed down. And, of course, the adaro settlement is on the edge of our district. That's a high crime area, and a lot of bad shit was spilling out of that sewer into our better neighborhoods. Into the business section, too. Illegal drugs, gang activity, unlicensed prostitution.... Well, you get the picture. But then a year and a half ago, the citizens of the district elected a new council, a bunch of law and order types with a mandate to clean up the streets. Make Placid Point a pleasant place to live and visit again. The department was instructed to come down hard on crime. Not just the big stuff, but the little stuff, too. The idea is that we leave no infraction unpunished. We can't clean up the district if we turn a blind eye to the small shit and let it smolder and fester into a bigger mess. So when we see an obviously intoxicated man creating a disturbance in the middle of a public street, we can't allow ourselves to be sloppy about it. We have to take immediate action."

Sims leaned back in his seat and rested a hand over his paunch. "You're not from this district, Alex, but you seem like a basically decent man. You might want to cut down on your drinking, though. Let today's little episode be a lesson to you. Do what we've been doing. Stop the sloppiness in your own life before it gets out of hand and grows into a bigger problem. It's jaywalking and public drunkenness today. Who knows what it will be tomorrow if you give yourself a pass."

I had to give it to Sims. Sure, he was a patronizing little shithead, and I wanted to slap the smile off his chubby face, but I had to admire the way he exuded calm and confident authority. I wondered what his real position was in the department. With his gray beard, his balding head, his glasses, and his soft, broad midsection, he looked more like an insurance salesman than a street cop. Or a bank manager. Despite his relaxed, deceptive charm, I pegged him as a man in charge, secure in his role as a key working piece in the Placid Point District's mechanism for funneling loose change out of the pockets of its residents and any visitors who happened to fall unsuspecting into its snares. I didn't doubt that a nice chunk of that change found its way into Detective Sims's own pockets.

What Sims didn't know was that I had an ace up my sleeve, a close working association with a skilled mouthpiece whose ability to bend and twist the legal system in his favor was matched only by his extensive files on the personal habits and history of every important government official in the county. I doubted there was a judge in Yerba City's thirty governing districts that Robinson Lubank, attorney at law, didn't have the goods on, or who didn't owe him a favor. Sims might think he had me thoroughly leveraged, and I was certain that he wanted more from me than a contribution to his district's coffers, but I was just as confident Lubank could free me from the clutches of Placid Point's legal extortion racket and any other trouble I'd stumbled into. I also knew that any help from Lubank would be expensive. The corrupt chiseler wasn't a guy who let something like friendship and a steady business relationship stand between him and as much dough as he could squeeze out of a situation. I planned to keep him in reserve as a last resort.

I slumped forward and made a show of sighing in resignation. "All right, detective. You said you had some questions for me. Ask away. I'm ready to answer."

Before Sims could launch into his interrogation, the door to the sweatbox opened, and the fattest troll I'd ever seen waddled into the room with the aid of a cane, turning slightly sideways in order to squeeze through the doorway. Modoc's glare turned into an eye roll, and Sims regarded the newcomer with a patient smile.

"Who's this here?" The troll's thin tenor was unexpected in a creature with his bulk.

"He's nobody, captain. Just a vagrant we picked up outside Ten-Inch's apartment."

"Does he know where Ten-Inch is?"

"I don't think so, sir. But he was jaywalking, not to mention drunk and disorderly, so we thought we'd better bring him in before he caused any mischief and disrupted our surveillance."

The troll frowned. "Well, if he doesn't know where Ten-Inch is, get him processed as quickly as possible and get back out on the street. We don't want to miss Ten-Inch if he goes back to his apartment."

Sims's smile remained locked in place. "Don't worry, captain. We've got two cars out there now keeping the place covered."

The troll nodded. "Well, okay. But you two get back out there yourselves as soon as you can. Ten-Inch is our first priority."

"Of course, captain. We just have a few questions for this gentleman."

After the troll squeezed his way out of the interrogation room, Sims glanced briefly at Modoc, who was shaking his head in what appeared to be disgust, before turning his attention back to me. "That was Captain Flinthook. He's in charge of our investigation."

I heard a short contemptuous chuckle burst its way through Modoc's smirk.

Sims gave me a paternal smile, not unlike the one he'd used with Captain Flinthook. "We'd best get on with this, Mr. Southerland." The detective leaned forward and rested his forearms on the tabletop. "What were you doing on Miller Street today?"

I could have stalled them, but I didn't see the point. "I was looking for Ten-Inch, same as you."

Sims didn't miss a beat. "What is your association with Ten-Inch?"

"We met a couple of years back. I saw his name in the paper this morning and got curious."

Sims frowned. "You got curious? Care to elaborate?"

Actually, I didn't, partly because I didn't know myself exactly why I'd decided to go looking for him. That wasn't something I wanted to admit to the cops, though, so I blurted out the first thing that came into my mind. "It sounded like he was in trouble, and I'm not working any cases at the moment. I thought maybe he might want to hire me."

Sims raised his eyebrows. "Really? What did you think he might want to hire you to do?"

"I'm a private investigator. I thought he might want me to investigate."

"Investigate? You mean the dead nymph?"

I nodded. "Sure. According to the papers, you guys were looking for him. It doesn't say so, but I'm assuming you think he was involved in the girl's death. Maybe you think he did it. Hell, maybe he *did* do it. But if he didn't, then maybe he might want to know who did so he can clear himself."

"Ah." Sims reached up and straightened his glasses. "And that's where you come in. You think he'll hire you to find out who topped the adaro dame. So you went to check out his place, in the rain, to see if he was home."

I shrugged. "It was worth a shot." The more I elaborated, the better the idea seemed to me.

Sims stroked at his beard and looked thoughtful for a moment. "Well, Alex, I'll have to say I find that a little odd. You knew we were looking for him, and that we hadn't found him yet. Did you think maybe we'd neglected to come knocking at his door?"

"I assumed you'd already checked his place out."

"So what made you think he'd be home when you came looking for him?"

"I figured it was a longshot. But I thought some of his friends might be around, and that maybe one of them might tell me where he was." Some of his friends? I was winging it, but it sounded reasonable enough to me.

"Hmm. I see." Sims gave his beard another stroke. "And did you see any of his friends?"

"I didn't get a chance. I got arrested."

Sims smiled, showing his teeth. "You should thank us. We not only got you out of the rain, but we saved you a lot of trouble. We questioned everyone in that building. None of them know where Ten-Inch is hiding out. And before you ask, yes, we're sure. Our questioning was thorough."

"I'll bet. Did your baby bulldog kill any of them with his hands?" I gazed back at Modoc, who was still leaning against the wall. He met my gaze with his tight smile.

"It wasn't necessary," Sims said. "Not this time. We know the identity of every member of Ten-Inch's gang. The Northsiders, but I guess you already knew that. In fact, two of them *do* live in Ten-Inch's apartment building. They are very dangerous young men, by the way. But, like Ten-Inch, they're not currently at home. You're lucky they weren't there to catch you snooping around. They might not have liked that very much."

"I'm sure I was safe. Detective Modoc was around to keep things from getting ugly."

Sims removed his glasses and breathed on the lenses to steam them up. He rubbed each lens vigorously with his handkerchief. When he was finished, he held them up to the light to catch any remaining smudges. Satisfied, he put them back on and leaned over the tabletop.

"When was the last time you saw Ten-Inch?" he asked me.

"Like I told you, a couple of years ago. Maybe three."

"Actually, you said that you *met* a couple of years ago."

"Did I?"

"Yes. You did. I have a good memory for detail. Have you been in contact with him since?"

"Nope."

"You're sure about that?"

"Yep."

"He didn't contact you and send you back to his apartment to retrieve something for him?"

"Nope."

"Or to check it out to see if the police were still watching his place?"

"Nope."

"You just decided to take a walk in the rain to see if any of his friends were hanging about?"

"Well, maybe I was thinking I might break into his apartment to see if I could find any hint of where he might have gone."

A smile came and went on Sims's face. "Breaking and entering is against the law, Alex."

"Good thing you stopped me. Business has been slow lately. I can't afford too many of your citations."

Sims sighed. "I think you're telling me the truth. I appreciate your cooperation, Alex, although my partner might be a little disappointed that we didn't need him to drag it out of you."

Modoc stepped forward and rubbed a hand over his fist. "Are you sure about this? How do we know Ten-Inch didn't send this fuckin' mugwump to his place to get something for him? Maybe some hidden dough, or some heaters he's got stashed under the floorboards. Give me five minutes with this motherfucker, just to make sure."

Sims heaved himself out of his seat with a groan and rubbed at the side of his knee. "That won't be necessary. Even if Ten-Inch sent him to his apartment, he didn't get inside."

Modoc wasn't satisfied. "He still might know where Ten-Inch is."

Sims turned to me. "Do you? No, I don't think you do. Anyway, you're not going to be seeing Ten-Inch anytime soon."

That got my attention. "What are you talking about?"

"We're going to keep you here a while longer, Alex."

"Why? For jaywalking?"

"You keep forgetting the D and D. But, no, there's something else. When we brought you in, we ran a computer check on you to see if you were in our system. Turns out you are, but when we opened your file it was flagged."

I was legitimately puzzled. "Flagged? What do you mean?"

"It means we can't access the information in your file. But there was a notification on it. We were required to call a number and let the person who answered the phone know that we had you in custody. That person told us to hold you until further notice."

"What person?"

Sims raised his arms from his sides and lifted his shoulders in a shrug. "I don't know. I'm assuming a representative of some government agency. The mayor's office, perhaps. Or the governor's. Maybe it goes all the way to the top. Who knows, Alex. It's possible that you've come to the attention of the Lord's Investigation Agency. I'd sure hate to be in your shoes if that's true. But you know what they say, don't you? It never rains but it pours. And last I checked, it was coming down in buckets."

The LIA? Well, wasn't that swell. Lord Alkwat's flaming balls!

## Chapter Five

They stashed me in an empty cell with a double-decker bunk and gave me a lunchmeat sandwich (I didn't inquire about details) with a cup of tepid coffee. Smokey followed me in unnoticed. I'd heard about high-level security equipment capable of detecting elementals or even preventing them from entering buildings or rooms uninvited, but that kind of system was too expensive for a cophouse in a precinct like Placid Point. Those systems required a fair amount of magical enchantment, and that kind of powerful magic costs serious dough. Not even the main police headquarters in downtown Yerba City could afford anything as sophisticated as that.

I sent Smokey off to keep a watch on Sims. I told the elemental to listen especially for any mention of Ten-Inch. Most elementals are capable of remembering and repeating back overheard conversations, and Smokey was better at it than most. I didn't know how long they were going to keep me on ice, but I hoped to use that time to get a lead on where I might find the Northsiders' boss when I finally got out.

When I was alone, I lay down on the bottom bunk, closed my eyes, and conjured up a mental image of a waterfall in a jungle clearing I'd wandered into when I'd been stationed in the Borderland. It was a place of peace that an army therapist had taught me to call up from my memory at will during times of stress. It was also a place where I could sometimes contact Cougar, provided the spirit was willing to show up. He might have been my spirit animal, but that didn't mean I could command and control him the way I could small to moderately sized air elementals. The best I could do was make myself receptive to his presence and hope for the best.

I'd sensed something about Modoc, and I thought he'd sensed something about me, too. Each time I'd seen him I'd felt a profound and irrational sense of hatred toward the man. It wasn't just that he'd put his hands on me. Everything about the guy pissed me off, and I didn't know why. Clearly, the feeling was mutual. It was as if we had an instinctual animosity toward each other. I found myself relishing the opportunity to face off with him. Sure, he was unnaturally quick, and his punches packed a real wallop. But he'd caught me off guard when he'd punched me in the street, and I'd been restrained in the sweatbox. Lying on that jailhouse bunk, I was craving a rematch with the obnoxious punk. I had just enough presence of mind to wonder why. I'd sensed Cougar's presence in the sweatbox, and I was hoping he would come to me and offer some enlightenment. Unfortunately, the unpredictable spirit refused to show up. Spirit animals. I'd once been told that they were mostly good for filling our heads with riddles and laughing at our efforts to figure them out. I fell asleep waiting in vain for mine to make an appearance. If I had any dreams I didn't remember them.

As it happens, I didn't stay locked up for long. After what couldn't have been more than an hour, Sims opened my cell and stood in the entrance.

"You've got a visitor," he told me.

I sat up in my bunk. "Who?"

"He didn't say."

"Did he tell you who sent him?"

"He appears to be a man of few words."

"What if I don't want to go with him?"

Sims smiled. "I suppose you could knock him out and run away."

I stood. "Thanks. I'll consider it."

A short, solidly built middle-aged man in a black suit and wraparound shades awaited me in the lobby. I'd never seen him before, and he acknowledged me with only the briefest of nods. The desk clerk returned my belongings to me, and I made sure that nothing was missing. I considered what to do with Smokey. I hadn't had a chance to hear a report from the elemental, and I decided to leave it with Sims for a while longer.

Turning to the man in the suit, I motioned toward the door. "Shall we?" Without speaking, the man opened the door and waved me through ahead of him into the rain.

Once outside, the man led me to an expensive luxury sedan and opened the door to the back seat. I slid in, and the man took his seat behind the wheel. He pulled out of the precinct's parking lot and into traffic.

"Where we going?" I asked. The man glanced at me in the rearview mirror, but didn't answer.

Fine, I thought. I wasn't feeling especially sociable anyway. I wrinkled my nose and sniffed. What I needed after half a day in the cop shop was a hot shower. I settled back into my seat and watched the skies rain down on the city outside my window.

Wherever we were going, the man in the black suit seemed in no hurry to get there. He drove erratically through the driving rain, changing lanes frequently and making several sudden turns, many of them with no warning and with little regard for our own wellbeing. Even before he sped up suddenly to run a red light, causing the other vehicles in the intersection to swerve out of danger, I realized my silent driver was trying to ensure we weren't being followed. Useless, I thought to myself. Any decent elementalist could use an air spirit, like Smokey, to tail us. And my driver could never have evaded someone using an enchantment to track our movements, no matter how many stoplights he ran or drivers he terrified. I kept these thoughts to myself. If he was going to get us to wherever we were headed in one piece, my driver needed to keep his attention on the road.

I was more than a little relieved when the driver pulled the car into a three-story parking garage only a few blocks from the precinct house and drove it to the top floor. After pulling to a stop behind a small economy car, he turned to me and said, "Get out here," the first words I'd heard him speak. I slid out of the sedan, and the driver continued on toward the exit, leaving me to study the economy car in front of me.

I recognized the car. I recognized the figure climbing out of the car, too: a gnome, four-feet tall, in a ridiculous green checked suit with the world's most obvious hairpiece perched precariously between his large round gnome ears. The gnome pulled a cigar from his lips and blew a cloud of smoke in my direction. "Alkwat's balls, Southerland. I'm getting pretty fuckin' tired of pulling you out of jail cells."

I raised my fedora and wiped sweat out of my hair before putting the hat back on. "Leave me in next time, Lubank. The lunch was free and the coffee wasn't half bad."

\*\*\*

"Let me get this straight." We were sitting in Lubank's office and I was freshening my coffee with a dash or two of rye from the bottle he'd pulled out of his desk drawer. "You have flags on my files in the police database?"

"Clever, right?" Lubank was obviously pleased with himself. "Anytime they pull your file, it gets blocked and they get a notice to call a number for further instructions. The number goes to my answering service, and the operators have instructions to answer without giving out my name, or any name, and forward the call to Gracie's private cellphone. She takes it from there. Those cops probably thought we were the fuckin' LIA!" He toasted me with his cup before taking a sip.

The pleasantly curvy woman with the pretty girlish face and coiffed blond hair blew a puff of smoke from her cigarette into the air above my head. She sat on the corner of Lubank's desk, her plump legs crossed and dangling over the side. "We set it all up a few months ago on the account of you always getting in trouble with the cops. It was all my idea. I'm sure glad it worked, sugar. I hate the thought of you getting your pretty face slapped around in those sweatboxes."

"Thanks, Gracie," I said. "It's all part of a day's work. But how were you able to get into the police computer system without them knowing about it?"

Gracie's red lips spread into a glowing smile. "Walks helped me. She's a real magician when it comes to data systems."

"She was in on this?" I shook my head.

"Of course, sweetie! You know how much she cares for you. You need to call her, by the way. When's the last time you saw her?"

"I brought some lunch to her shop a couple of weeks ago."

"More like a month ago, baby. She asked me about you yesterday. You should stop by and see her more often. I swear! The two of you are such hermits! You never have any fun. You both need to get out more."

"Look who's talking, Gracie. When's the last time you and your grumpy little hubby went out on the town?"

Gracie turned her smile to Lubank, sitting across his desk from her. "This sweet little guy and I have all the fun we can handle right here in the office. Don't we, honey?" She blew some smoke in his direction.

Lubank smiled back at Gracie and then scowled. "Th'fuck, Gracie! Lunkhead over there doesn't want to hear the gory details of our gnome-on-human private life. You know how insanely jealous he gets."

I forced down a mouthful of coffee, trying hard not to choke on it. "Maybe another time. Right now I want to hear how much your husband is charging me for monkeying around with the police department's database. I never asked for that, you know."

Lubank pointed at me with his coffee cup. "It's in our contract."

"The hell it is!"

"It's covered under 'client protection.' Tell him, Gracie."

Gracie looked back at me over her shoulder and batted her eyes. "As your attorney, Robbie has the power to protect you from undue police harassment. He thinks you need extra careful looking after."

"I'll bet. It's just another way for him to bleed me dry."

Gracie's lips curled into a pout. "Oh, sugar. You *do* need looking after. Look at how many times Robbie has had to pull you out of the clutches of the police."

"And how many times he's added a few thousand to the bill he says I owe him."

Lubank laughed. "It's only money, you ungrateful cheapskate. Besides, I'd do it out of the goodness of my heart, but Gracie wants a new pearl necklace."

Gracie turned back to her husband. "My old ones are starting to yellow."

"See what I mean?" Lubank shouted. "Lord's balls! Never get married, Southerland. You'll fuckin' live longer!"

Gracie shook her head. "Oh, Robbie. Don't tell him that. Can't you see how lonely he's been the past few months?" Turning back to me, Gracie crushed her cigarette butt out in an ashtray. "I was so sorry it didn't work out between you and Holly. But it's time for you to pick yourself up and get yourself back into the dating scene. I hate to say it, Alex, but you're not getting any younger. You need a woman in your life. I'd volunteer, but..." She nodded in Lubank's direction, "Robbie can't spare me. His practice would fall apart if I split my time between the two of you. And, sorry to say it, baby, but, while you and I would have a ball together...." She paused and leaned toward me, exposing a generous amount of cleavage for my viewing pleasure, before continuing. "He pulls in a lot more dough than you do. Pearl necklaces don't fall out of trees, you know." She giggled.

I tore my eyes away from my attorney's wife's luscious bazooms and swallowed another sip of coffee. Turning to Lubank, I asked, "Where did you find that driver? With that black suit and those shades I thought sure he was LIA."

"You mean Luano? He's a client of mine. I got him off on a grand larceny charge. He was the getaway driver in a bank job. I convinced the jury that he'd been hired to drive a group of jaspers downtown and back, but that he had no idea they were there to pull off a heist. I had to spread a little of his take from the robbery among a few of the jurors in order to help them see the case my way, but it all worked out. I send him out on jobs from time to time so he can work off his debt."

"He drives like a maniac. Did you tell him to make sure he wasn't tailed?"

"Fuck no. What would be the point? Those cops thought you were being taken away by the LIA. No fuckin' way would they want to screw around with *those* bastards! I doubt they ever expect to see you again."

"Well, your man drove like the cops were hanging on his bumper and he was trying to shake them off."

Lubank laughed. "Lord's balls! Luano's a little excitable. Good man, though. Did he keep his cool in the police station? I told him to keep his face blank, act bored, and say as little as possible."

"I'd say he followed your instructions to the letter. I only heard him say three words the whole time I was with him."

"Good! I knew I could count on him. You owe him. Gracie, take whatever you chipped off Luano's account and put it, plus ten percent, on loverboy's tab. That way we all come out even."

I shook my head. "How come whenever we all come out even, I end up broke and you wind up making money?"

Lubank's face lit up with a pleased grin. "Because I'm a genius and you're a fuckin' idiot."

I snorted. "I should get another lawyer."

Lubank leaned back in his office chair and raised a cigar to his lips. "If you had another lawyer...," He paused long enough to take a puff from his cigar and release a cloud of smoke toward the ceiling, "you'd still be cooling your heels in a cell at the Placid Point cophouse."

I couldn't argue with that. Not that I didn't want to. Lubank and I had a tidy little business arrangement. I did investigative work for him, and he acted as my attorney. We billed each other for our services, but, no matter how many cases I worked on his behalf, I was forever on the red side of the balance sheet. Sure, part of it was because my business all too often found me in a precarious position with various legal authorities and in need of a capable, if expensive, mouthpiece to preserve my freedom. But Lubank had a way of ensuring that a mug like me was always going to wind up in his debt. I didn't fight it. I needed a smart operator like Lubank on my side, but the duplicitous son of a bitch was about as reliable as a rattlesnake. As long as he considered me a steady source of revenue, however, he wasn't going to turn on me. He might cheat me a bit, but he wasn't going to risk losing me as a client. Besides, Gracie liked me, and Gracie was the only person in this world that Lubank loved more than money.

Lubank had other business to take care of, other clients, fat cats, and politicians to fleece, flatter, and threaten, and he chased me out of his office. Gracie walked me to the front door, linking her arm in mine and holding me closer than necessary. She was a vicious tease, but I didn't mind. I knew she was devoted to her husband, and she knew that I knew. That didn't stop me from getting a few small thrills out of my visits to Lubank's office, though.

Rather than disengaging herself from me when we reached the door, Gracie drew me in and held me in a full-body hug. She stretched herself up until her lips were an inch from my ear and whispered, "Call Walks in Cloud, you big lug. She misses you."

I put my hands on Gracie's shoulders. She loosened her hold on me, and I stepped back a few inches so I could meet her eyes. "I'll stop by when I can. But we're not an item, and she's too wrapped up in her work to miss anybody."

Gracie's face was serious. "She works too hard. It's not easy for her to get around in that chair, and she doesn't try hard enough to have a social life. I know that she has... limitations... when it comes to having an intimate relationship, but that doesn't mean she doesn't get a kick out of having a ruggedly handsome man come around for a cup of coffee every once in a while."

I put a mock-insulted look on my face. "*Ruggedly* handsome? Well, I guess a man with a mug like mine better take any kind of compliment he can get."

Gracie patted my cheek. "You might not be no matinee idol, sweetie, but you ain't all *that* bad, either."

I rolled my eyes. "Gee, thanks, gorgeous."

Gracie opened the door. "I'm serious, Alex. Call her. Bring her some lunch. Or, better yet, take her to dinner."

"I took her to the Gold Coast Club."

"That was months ago. She told me she had a great time. You should do it again."

I grunted. "That place is a palace. I couldn't have afforded it if I hadn't been given a free pass. Business has been slow lately, and your husband likes me to pay him something every month. And besides...." I looked down at my shoes. "I met Holly after that."

Gracie put a hand on my elbow. "In case you haven't noticed, sweetie, Holly's not in the picture anymore. Anyway, Walks isn't looking for that kind of relationship with you or anyone else. But she's your friend, and you've been avoiding her."

I was going to protest, but I just sighed, instead. "Okay, Gracie. I'll go see her. You're right. Holly's gone. Crawford's gone. They took Troy away. I suppose I haven't felt much like seeing people lately. I've been skipping out on my poker nights, too." I raised my eyes to meet Gracie's.

She stroked my cheek and smiled. "You need to climb out of that hole you've fallen into. A lot more people care about you than you think. Don't turn into one of those eccentric recluses. Not while you're still young. It's not a good look for you." She gave my face a playful slap. "And try to stay out of jail, you bastard! It scared me to death when I heard they had you locked up. And in Placid Point, of all places! Robbie was upset, too."

"Rob was upset?"

Gracie smiled, a ray of light shining through the smoke-filled room. "Of course he was, you big goon! The little guy doesn't want you to know it, but he cares about you, too." She glanced back over her shoulder toward Lubank's inner office. "But don't tell him I said so. He has an image to maintain, you know."

"Yeah? Well tell him to quit gouging me until I can drum up a little more business. I'm barely paying my rent these days."

Gracie giggled. "Don't forget who keeps the books around here, bub. Robbie never checks. He thinks I'm bleeding you dry. But, remember, I have access to your financial records. I never bill you for more than you can afford." She winked. "And if you ever need a little extra dough to take someone special to a place like the Gold Coast Club, just give me a buzz on my private cel."

I didn't know what to say. "Thanks, Gracie," I managed.

She leaned in toward my ear again. "You'll owe me, honey. I think I'd like having a big strong man like you in my debt."

I took a cab to the beastmobile, still parked near Ten-Inch's apartment. First thing I noticed when I saw my car was that someone had boosted all four of my hubcaps. I checked for cop cars, but didn't see any. "Figures," I muttered to myself. At least the thieves had made a good clean job of it. After a close inspection, I concluded that the beastmobile had suffered no additional damage, and it gave me no problems as I drove it home.

Once I was showered, properly fed with a microwaved frozen pizza, and comfortably seated at my desk with a cup of molten black coffee seasoned with a generous splash of rye, I touched on that part of my mind that only elementalists possess and sent out a call for Smokey. It was time to find out what Detective Sims had been up to all afternoon in Placid Point.

## Chapter Six

My coffee cup was empty by the time Smokey streaked through the seam of my imperfectly sealed front door, trailing rainwater into my office and scattering a fine mist of cold droplets into my face. It was kind of refreshing, actually. I'd been close to dozing off.

Well-trained elementals like Smokey are like tape recorders. I'd used Smokey to listen in on conversations a number of times, and the tiny elemental's skill as a mimic had improved with practice. Smokey could not only reproduce the sounds it heard in detail, but it could do a passable job of imitating the unique nuances of an individual's voice. In Smokey's hissing rendition of Sims's conversations, I could clearly distinguish the detective's part in them from whomever he was speaking with.

What an elemental, even a talented one like Smokey, could *not* do was analyze a conversation and highlight the important points. Smokey had spent several hours with Sims, and I would have to listen to all of it in full in order to learn anything useful. I poured myself another cup of jacked-up joe and sat back to take it all in.

Most of it was as boring as I imagined it would be. Lots of routine office procedure: locating files, typing letters and reports, going over duty rosters with Captain Flinthook, and so forth. Scattered conversations about cases unrelated to the death of the adaro and the department's interest in Ten-Inch: detectives were sent to break up a domestic dispute involving an out-of-work husband and his stay-at-home wife; patrolmen brought in a street kid suspected of vandalizing a tattoo parlor on Carlotta Drive just after midnight on Monday morning; the two hooded thugs who had robbed the convenience store on Fremont Street last Friday night were still unidentified. One side of a phone conversation between Sims and his wife: leftover chicken stew for dinner was fine, and he'd get around to replacing the torn screen in the bedroom window the following Saturday afternoon.

But some of what Smokey reported caused me to sit up and take note. As Lubank had surmised, Sims and Modoc believed I was now securely in the hands of the LIA, and they weren't happy about it. I'd told Sims that I'd had no recent contact with Ten-Inch, and he'd said he believed me. He'd lied. In fact, he'd been convinced I had some sort of close connection with Ten-Inch, and he'd been hoping he could use me to lead him to the gang boss. When he'd discovered that my file had been flagged, he'd concluded that I was an LIA asset of some kind. An informant, maybe. Perhaps even an undercover agent. That gave me a good chuckle. He'd been pissed when he'd been forced to hand me over to the man he thought was from the Lord's Investigation Agency.

Smokey's report confirmed what I suspected: Modoc hated me as much and as irrationally as I hated him. The junior detective didn't explain the animosity he felt for me to Sims, and Sims hadn't asked him about it, but the venom in the younger cop's voice as he spoke with his partner about me was evident in Smokey's account.

"Next time you put me and that motherfucker in the same room," Smokey hissed in a distorted, but recognizable, version of Modoc's voice, "I'll rip him open and eat his heart!"

Not if I see you first, I thought to myself, and I felt my heart beat faster at the prospect.

Sims had been on the phone when I'd called on Smokey to end his surveillance and report to me. Smokey had only heard one side of the conversation, of course, but it piqued my curiosity. According to Smokey, Sims had spoken in a lower than normal voice, almost a whisper, as if he hadn't wanted to be overheard.

Sims: "Hello. ... It's okay, the office is practically deserted at the moment. ... Nope. Nothing. ... Hey, we're looking, but I'm not expecting much. Flinthook had me and Modoc staking out his apartment this morning with two squad cars. Was that your idea? ... I didn't think so. ... That's what I told him! Ten-Inch knows we're looking for him. He's not likely to come waltzing up to his own apartment. ... Yeah, we need to be sure, but one squad car would have been plenty. Me and Modoc should have been casing the settlement, questioning some of his known associates. We're detectives, for fuck's sake! It was a poor use of resources, but you know Flinthook. ... Sure, he does what he's told. But he's an idiot. You have to be careful what you tell him. ... I don't know. Modoc thinks he's left the city, and he might be right. ... I agree. That would be for the best. ... By the way, we picked up this character outside Ten-Inch's apartment. A private dick named Southerland. He says he was looking for Ten-Inch. You know him? ... Southerland. First name Alexander. ... No? Are you sure? His files are flagged, and he got picked up by some well-dressed mug who screamed Leea. ... No shit? Well, that's odd. I guess we'll have to find the dick and pick him back up again. ... I wouldn't worry about it. He said he was trying to drum up some business. He read in the paper that we were looking for Ten-Inch as a person of interest in that other business. ... Right, the dead nymph. Anyway, the dick told us he knew Ten-Inch from a couple of years ago and was hoping he would hire him to clear his name, or something like that. ... Well, I thought he was Leea, but maybe he was telling the truth. ... Yeah, okay. We'll run him down and pick him up again. No problem. ... Of course. But, like I said, I think that gangster's long gone. He's not dumb enough to hang around now that he knows every cop in Yerba City is looking for him, but if we run across him you'll be the first to know. ... Modoc? Don't worry about him. He does what I tell him. ... Sure, he'd like that. ... [Chuckle] Yeah, he's a bloodthirsty bastard. ... Sure, same as always. We'll feed the body to the sharks, and no one will be the wiser. ... Yeah. ... Right. ... Got it. ... Motherfucker." The last word had been mumbled, and I assumed it had come after the call had been disconnected.

After Smokey finished his report, I released him from his task and sent him on his way, no doubt to bask in the haze of the rafters at the Minotaur Lounge, the elemental's favorite haunt. Mine, too, for that matter. I checked the time. It was early enough in the evening for me to beat the late-night mid-week crowd. A glance out the window revealed that the rain had diminished to a drizzle, and I decided to take a walk to the joint and consider what I'd heard from Smokey over a bowl of fried calamari and a cup of hot coffee with a kick.

As I walked the eight blocks from the building that served as both my office and apartment toward the warmth of the Minotaur Lounge, fending off showers with an old umbrella the wind was trying to tear out of my grip, avoiding puddles that just might be water elementals waiting to seize and hold me under until the breath left my body, listening to the traffic splashing through the wet streets, and breathing in the cold, rain-soaked city air, I went over everything Smokey had overheard.

I wondered whom Sims had been speaking with at the end of Smokey's report. It sounded like a contact in the Lord's Investigation Agency. It didn't surprise me that the LIA had someone from the Placid Point Precinct at their beck and call. It was always a good idea to assume that Leea—the LIA—was everywhere. It sounded like they were issuing orders to Captain Flinthook and using Sims to inform on him behind his back. Typical double-dealing Leea, covering all the bases. It also sounded like Sims and Modoc were involved in a lot of unsavory activity, either at the direction of the LIA or on their own. Something that involved turning their targets into shark food. My stomach grew cold at the thought. I was suddenly very happy to be out of the Placid Point PD's holding cell.

I was thinking about the connection between the Placid Point cops and the LIA when another possibility occurred to me. What if Sims hadn't been talking to the LIA at all? Could Sims's unknown contact have been from the Hatfield Syndicate, instead? The Hatfields were the most powerful crime family in Yerba City, and I knew they had a lot of cops in their pocket. Yerba City was a thriving municipality, a place where you could find anything you might want to help you through your day—or night—provided you had the dough-re-mi. Since every trade in the city was regulated, licensed, and taxed by the city government, as well as the Province of Caychan and the Realm of Tolanica, those so-called "non-essential" goods and services that added spice to life and made it interesting tended to be expensive. One could make a case that booze, narcotics, games of chance, and exotic sensual pursuits were as necessary for a good life as food and shelter, but that's neither here nor there. The legal versions of these items set you back some serious dough. That's where the underworld came in, and the Hatfields were the kingpins of the city's underworld.

Your typical working-class lug can't afford a steady supply of high-end avalonian whiskey or imported sparkling wine from the world's most renowned vineyards, but people are going to drink. So the underworld provides enough unlicensed hooch to keep everyone pickled to the gills as often as they want to be. You want to get gloriously buzzed on premium government-regulated cocaine or heroin? No problem. Just pay your authorized certified retailer. But if you're short on serious coin, cheap blow and mass-produced skag is also readily available, provided you're willing to sacrifice quality and risk impurities that might leave you blind, deranged, or dead. Are upscale casinos, arenas, and tracks outside your price range? No problem. Off-site betting, underground bookies, and neighborhood lotteries satisfy your same desires for a shot at easy money. You feeling that itch that only a professional sex worker can scratch, but you don't have the scratch for a legit escort or companion? The underground sex trade accommodates any size budget and offers a wide variety of possibilities, most of which are desirable, some—like deception, disease, and sudden unexpected death—not so much.

In Yerba City, the Hatfield Syndicate provided for all your unlicensed and illicit needs and desires. Technically speaking, the Hatfields operated in the shadows of the city, but they were never more than a step from the light. The municipal government didn't bother them, especially once their chosen man—Montavious Harvey—was put into the mayoral seat. Some people claimed that Ketz-Alkwat, the Dragon Lord himself, controlled the underworlds of all of the major cities of Tolanica, including Yerba City's, but I didn't know what to make of that idea. Still, I wouldn't put it past old Lord Ketz to control both the legitimate *and* illegitimate business conducted in his realm. The totality of a realm's economic activity was a vast operation that an immortal unkillable hundred-foot fire-breathing flying master of magic would certainly be capable of maintaining. And everyone knew the Dragon Lords loved their gold. On the one hand, the Hatfields, who worked outside the law, and the Lord's Investigation Agency, which reported directly to Lord Ketz, seemed to work at cross purposes often enough to make me doubt whether they could be part of the same team. On the other hand, an apparatus as large as the Dragon Lord's Tolanican government was bound to contain some internecine rivalries. Politics. It all left my head spinning, and I tried to spend as little time as possible thinking about it.

My own relationship with the Hatfield family was complicated. They'd offered to make me a part of their operation. They'd tried to kill me more than once. Holly used to tell me that I saw the fingers of the Hatfields in everything, and that they were making me paranoid. I told her it wasn't paranoia if they were really out to get me. She'd called me crazy, and I'd responded, "That's me, sister: crazy, man, crazy!" We had a good time with that, and, for a while, 'crazy, man, crazy' became a kind of running joke with us. I'd say something about the Hatfields, and she'd shake her head and say, "Crazy, man, crazy."

When the Hatfields really *did* come for me, I didn't tell her about it. I thought I was protecting her. Turned out I was driving her away. Oh well, live and learn, right? Right.

If Sims was working for the Hatfields, then the Hatfields were not only looking for Ten-Inch, but they wanted him dead. And my search for Ten-Inch might once again bring me face-to-face with the lords of the Yerba City underworld. Part of me welcomed the idea. Maybe Holly was right. Maybe I really *was* crazy.

And that brought me to the question that troubled me the most, namely, did I really want to find Ten-Inch? Why? No one was asking me to. No one was paying me to find him. I'd told Sims I was looking for Ten-Inch in the hopes he might hire me to clear his name. I'd had to tell Sims something, and that was the first thing that had come to mind. Was there any truth in it? Maybe. Part of my brain sometimes worked separately from the rest of it, and I often went along for the ride to see where it was taking me. More than anything, though, I was just curious. Curiosity was serious business for me. It was part of what made me who I was. I knew that curiosity was one of the things that had driven me to become a P.I. It was a big part of my success, the thing that gave me the drive and determination to see a tough case through to the end. I was also convinced that curiosity would be the thing that killed me one day. That night, as I sat shaved and showered in a back corner booth at the Minotaur Lounge, slurping juiced-up coffee and wondering what had compelled me to get mixed up in an unidentified adaro's death, a police search for a gang boss, and a possible encounter with the underground mavens of my fair city, I wondered if that day might be drawing near.

Crazy, man, crazy.

\*\*\*

As I made my way home from the Minotaur, concentrating on walking a straight line and avoiding the puddles that had formed where the rainwaters had spilled out of the gutter onto the walkway, I was struck by a sudden attack of vertigo, as if the sidewalk beneath my feet had suddenly tilted to one side. I lurched and caught myself before I fell to the curb, but it was a near thing.

Swell, I thought to myself. I shouldn't have had that one for the road. I looked around to see if anyone was getting a kick out of watching me, another rummy staggering his way home through the night. I lifted my face to the sky, took a deep breath of rain-washed air, and set out in what I hoped was the right direction.

I was dangerously close to the street when a car zoomed over a pothole and swamped me with enough water to fill a small swimming pool.

"Alkwat's flaming balls!" I shouted. "Shit!"

The day had been fucked up from the start, and it didn't want to end. I shook water off my hat and coat, feeling more than a little sorry for myself.

"Fuck me," I muttered under my breath. I launched into a lecture, meant for my ears only. "This is no one's fault but yours, tough guy. When did you start drinking today—about, what, eight in the morning? You haul your ass off to Placid Point with no plan, looking for Ten-Inch for no reason.... You let yourself get beat up by a cop.... You dumb fuck!" I said that last part loud enough to make me aware that I was babbling into the night like an old drunk. I didn't get the obvious message. Instead, I continued to babble about corrupt cops and underworld crime families. Eventually, I started thinking about Holly. I didn't want to talk about her, so I shut up.

Another wave of vertigo struck me, and this time I couldn't keep my feet. Facedown on the wet sidewalk, I felt a strange flutter in my gut. My throat grew tight, and I felt a burning in my eyes. When I felt tears beginning to form, I bit back down on them and forced myself to my feet. Anger replaced the sense of futility that had been welling up inside me. I'm not a bum, I told myself. I had a rough day, and I had too much to drink tonight, that's all. I'll get over it. My father was a drunk, but I'm not. I've made something of myself. I've had rough days before. I can handle myself. I need to snap myself out of this mood and get home. I'll be fine.

As I was selling myself on this claptrap, I became aware that I wasn't alone. A man stood on the sidewalk in front of me, regarding me in silence. The night had become thick with fog all of a sudden, and even with my enhanced awareness I couldn't quite make out his features. Adrenaline poured into my bloodstream, and I squared to defend myself. The man didn't move to attack me, however. In fact, he didn't move at all.

Muscle by muscle, I allowed myself to relax. "Sorry, mister," I said. "I didn't see you coming. I've had a little too much to drink, and you kind of snuck up on me there."

The man still didn't move, but the fog between us began to clear, bit by bit, until the details of his face became more distinguishable. He looked vaguely familiar: dark eyes that burned with the intensity of a killer, a permanent frown, a shaved head, a black beard, streaked with gray.... The beard on the right side of the man's face was patchy. I studied it more closely and saw that it was having trouble taking root in a deep scar that stretched from cheek to chin.

It was the scar that triggered my memory. His hairline had been receding when I last saw him, but it hadn't been shaved. He hadn't had the beard back then, either. But there was no mistaking the way he held himself, like a fighter who never expected to lose a battle. "Ten-Inch?" I sputtered, my breath catching. "Is that you?"

The figure shifted his weight from one foot to the other, but didn't speak.

"Ten-Inch? I've been looking for you."

The figure's eyes moved from my face to my feet and back to my face again, a slow once-over. His mouth twisted into a scowl. His head shook slightly from side-to-side, a disapproving dismissal. He lowered his eyes and turned away from me, his head still shaking slowly from side to side.

"Ten-Inch?"

Although his legs never moved, the figure receded swiftly away from me, as if someone were pulling him with a rope, and within seconds he disappeared into the fog.

I stared into the spot where I'd last seen the figure. The fog faded into translucent wisps, and then the night was clear. Ten-Inch, if that's who I'd really seen, was gone.

My umbrella was lying on the sidewalk, and a steady rain was pouring down on me. Had the whole encounter with Ten-Inch been a drunken hallucination? It had felt real enough, but then I guessed that's what a drunken hallucination would feel like. Lord's flaming balls, I thought to myself. Next it would be swarms of insects, mice, and snakes crawling all over my body. Was this what happened after you reached your thirties? It didn't seem that I'd had as many drinks as all that. I sighed. Maybe it was time to quit and find a new vice. Like what, I asked myself—heroin? I smiled at the idea. Fat chance of that. Maybe I'd just start watering down my whiskey. My smile broadened. Even less chance of that.

I picked my umbrella off the sidewalk and walked the rest of my way home with a purposeful stride. I wasn't teetering now, and I had no more bouts of vertigo. Thankfully, no ghosts stepped into my path. When I reached my front door, I spotted something out of place on my porch. I bent to examine the smooth curved chrome object, wondering what it meant. I picked it up and took a closer look at the block letters scratched on the surface: KISIKISI. I studied the characters for a long time before unlocking my front door and bringing one of the beastmobile's four stolen hubcaps into my office.

## Chapter Seven

Holly's first meeting with Chivo had gone reasonably well, aside from the part where he'd tried to kill and eat her. I'd prepared Holly in advance, assuring her that I could protect her if things got out of hand.

"He and I have an arrangement," I told Holly. "As long as I keep him fed, he doesn't try to murder me in my sleep."

"What do you feed him?" she'd asked me.

"Yonak. I get it from the butcher counter at the corner market."

"Yonak? That's the stuff trolls eat, right? Isn't it just raw meat?"

"Pretty much. Soaked in blood with some kind of seasoning I don't want to know about."

"Yuck! What kind of meat is it?"

"I don't ask. Probably whatever happens to be handy."

"And this creature—the Huay Chivo? He likes this swill?"

"He thinks it's swell. Especially when it's been sitting in the open air for half a day."

"Again, yuck! Doesn't it smell?"

"You bet. And so does Chivo. But I've got an elemental in my laundry room who spends twenty-four hours a day siphoning the bad air out of the room through the window. Good thing, too. I've got a little home gym set up in the room. I bang a heavy bag and lug a few weights around whenever I get the urge. So it's kind of a competition between Chivo and me to see who smells the worst. Siphon—that's what I named the elemental—has a tough job. I'm lucky that it's willing to keep doing it."

"He doesn't mind?"

"It. Elementals don't have genders. It seems happy enough. I've tried to free it from its service, but it won't leave. Elementals tend to bond to places, and Siphon has bonded to my laundry room."

"Lucky for you."

We'd come back to my place in the late evening, about the time Chivo normally woke up and ate before disappearing into the night. My plan was to introduce Holly to the creature and let her scoop some yonak into his food dish. I entered the laundry room first and found Chivo still curled up in his bed. Siphon was all but invisible, but the soft whooshing sound told me that the elemental was on the job. Holly's nose crinkled. The room didn't smell all that bad to me, but maybe I was used to it.

"Chivo!" I called in a gentle voice.

The creature lifted his goat-like head and his eyes opened a slit.

"I've brought someone here to see you. She's a friend, so be nice to her. Okay?"

Chivo blinked a couple of times and yawned.

I called Holly into the room. "Holly, meet—"

With no warning, Chivo sprang from his bed and rose on his hind legs, the spikes along his spine standing at attention, his bare rat's tail rigid behind him. He fixed Holly with a stare, his red eyes glowing with their own inner light. Holly made a retching noise and fell to her knees. Chivo lowered his head and prepared to skewer her with his long, lethal horns.

I stepped between them. "No, Chivo!" I shouted.

Chivo's eyes met mine, and a wave of nausea swept through me. "Stop that right now, Chivo!"

The nausea subsided, and, after a long moment, Chivo lowered his eyes.

"Get down, Chivo."

The creature lowered himself to all fours.

"Sit!"

Chivo lifted his head and glowered at me, but didn't otherwise move.

"Okay, don't sit. But behave yourself! Holly is our guest."

I helped Holly to her feet. Her face was drained of color. I kept a hand on her arm to steady her. "Are you okay?"

"I... I think so. What happened? I thought I was going to barf!"

"That was Chivo. He stuns his prey by making them sick before he attacks. Try to avoid looking into his eyes."

"He's not going to do that again, is he?"

I gave Chivo a menacing look. "No, he isn't." I held the look until Chivo hung his head and looked away.

Holly turned from Chivo to me. "How come you don't get sick when he looks at you?"

"I'm immune. Mostly. Not that he doesn't try sometimes." I glared at the creature, but he stood with his head drooped and wouldn't meet my eyes.

Holly sniffed at the air and turned toward a shelf in the wall above the dryer. "Is that the yonak? Should I give him some?"

"Sure. Scoop it into that bowl over there."

Holly, scrunching her nose and breathing with short gasps, filled the dish with the rancid slop. Chivo watched her with interest.

"Try approaching him with the bowl," I told her. "Nice and slow. Don't look him in the eyes, but don't back off. If he tries anything, I'll rip off his horns and use them to cut out his heart. You listening to me, Chivo?"

Holly took a tentative step toward the creature and forced herself to smile. "Handsome boy, Chivo," she cooed, as if the creature were an infant. "What a handsome boy you are."

Chivo snorted and tried to catch her eyes in his death glare.

"I don't think he's buying the flattery," I said.

Holly spared me a quick glance. "It works on you, doesn't it?" Turning back to Chivo, she continued to coo at him. "Oh, but he's such a good handsome boy."

As Holly pushed the food dish in his direction, Chivo lowered his eyes, turning his attention to the yonak. His nose twitched and his mouth fell open. Holly placed the bowl in front of him, and he sniffed at it suspiciously. With one last quick glance at Holly, Chivo pushed his snout into the bowl and began gobbling up the contents, oblivious to the rest of the world.

We waited until Chivo had cleaned out the dish, lapping up the last blood-soaked remains with a thin tongue. Apparently deciding to let us live, the sated creature slunk out of the room, down the hall, and out the back door into the alleyway without so much as a glance in our direction.

"Rude," I said. "He could have thanked you."

Holly stared at the empty bowl. "He didn't eat me. That's all the gratitude I need."

I led her out of the laundry room, through my office, and up the stairs to my apartment.

\*\*\*

Chivo was sitting on the floor in front of my desk when I stepped out of the rain and into my office. When he saw me, he padded up to me on all fours and sniffed at the hubcap I had carried inside. Concluding it wasn't edible, he walked past me to the door, sat back on his haunches, and looked back over his shoulder at me.

"I keep telling you, buddy. Holly's not coming back."

Chivo gave the door one last look and climbed back to his feet. He crossed the room, snorted as he passed by me, and disappeared through the back door into the hallway. The door slammed shut behind him. Seconds later, I heard the door to the alleyway slam shut.

"Whatever," I muttered. He hadn't waited for me to feed him. I hoped all the neighborhood cats and dogs were being kept safely indoors. I figured the raccoons and possums were fair game.

Once I was seated at my desk, I gave the hubcap a good going over. I had no doubt the chromium moon hubcap had come off my car, and that someone was sending me a message. My beastmobile wasn't the only automobile on the road with caps like this one, but the coincidence was too strong. The surface had been polished clean, and the scratch marks stood out sharply in the light of my desk lamp. KISIKISI. The word was unfamiliar to me. Was someone trying to send me a message? I found no other marks anywhere on the hubcap. Pulling out my phone, I did a quick internet search. KISIKISI gave me nothing. Did the letters stand for something? I couldn't begin to guess what that might be. Whatever message someone was trying to send to me, it was awfully opaque.

I looked at the hubcap with senses other than my sight, drawing upon the awareness given to me by the elf, and the different kind of sight given to me by my spirit animal. I smelled the chrome. The reflected lamplight danced in front of me as I tilted the curved object this way and that. I felt for magic. I detected nothing unusual.

I thought about what I knew. Someone who had recognized my car had taken the hubcaps. One of the hubcaps had appeared on my doorstep with a string of letters on its surface where I could clearly see it. The other three hubcaps were still out there somewhere. Whoever had put this one outside my office had known I would find it, which meant that this someone knew where I was based. I'd found the hubcap after my strange meeting with Ten-Inch, assuming that hadn't been a hallucination. I drew my own conclusions. Whether my "meeting" with him had been real or some kind of vision, Ten-Inch wanted me to find him, and KISIKISI was some kind of clue that would lead me to him. I didn't know if I had drawn the correct conclusion. I had no reason to believe that I had. But it was the conclusion I wanted to draw, so I drew it. The letters had to mean something. I decided they meant I had a case. Ten-Inch had hired me to find him.

I'd worry about details like contracts and fees later.

It was time to go to work, and I knew where I wanted to start. The police were looking for Ten-Inch in connection with an adaro woman who had been found dead in South Market, not far from where I lived. I needed to find out everything I could about the woman and how and why she had been killed. Maybe I'd run into something or someone called Kisikisi, or an acronym consisting of those letters. I'd start by finding the crime scene. I knew the South Market area well. My morning runs often took me through the Porter District and on into the streets and alleys of South Market. At least they did back when I was running. Back before Holly had left me.

I checked the time and was surprised to discover that it was well after two in the morning. I'd been holed up in the Minotaur longer than I'd thought. How long had I been drinking? What had I been thinking about? It had been a long, event-filled day. Had it just been that morning that I'd read the article about the adaro woman and the search for Ten-Inch? Since then, I'd stood outside the gang boss's apartment in the rain, been picked up by the cops, questioned, and put on ice. Lubank had rescued me, and I'd spent the late afternoon listening to Smokey's report. Then I'd gone to the Minotaur to sort it all through like a good detective.

Right. Except I'd spent most of the evening moping about Holly over beers and shots. Had I eaten anything except fried calamari? Anything except bar squid? I shook my head. Was this my life now? Was I going down the same road as my father? Forgotten memories of him lying in bed, shivering and shaking, forced themselves into my consciousness. Had he suffered from hallucinations? I couldn't remember any episodes, but maybe he and my mother had hidden them from me. Since coming back from the Borderland I'd enjoyed drinking alone in crowded places, but I'd told myself it was a hobby, a way of watching the rest of the world from a distance, listening and learning, honing my observation skills and sharpening my mind. I didn't think of myself as a juicer. Had I been kidding myself all along? Maybe it was all nothing but an excuse to be solitary and uninvolved, to be numb and untouched.

But things felt different now. Sure, a nice girl had decided she didn't want to be part of my life. Who could blame her? She'd done the right thing. And, okay, I was a little down in the mouth about it all. That was a normal reaction to being dumped, wasn't it? Don't they write songs and poems about that kind of thing? They make whole movies about it, right? So why shouldn't I drown my sorrows in a neighborhood bar if I felt like it? That's what people do, don't they?

Lord's flaming balls. What did that make me, except just another poor sap trying to chase a woman out of his head with a flood of alcohol. Is that who I was now? A punchline to the world's oldest joke? You got dumped, Southerland. Boo-fucking-hoo. It was time to get off the barstool and get on with my life.

The night had been a numbing blur of background muttering, washed-out colors, sticky glasses and tabletops, sharp prickles in the soft tissues at the back of my throat and in my nasal passages, and the rancid odor of my own sweat, stale beer, and lingering whiskey, but my vision (if that's what it was) of Ten-Inch had cleared my head. The thought of bedsheets, pillows, and sleep made me sick to my stomach. Fuck that! I lifted myself out of my chair with an audible groan, grabbed my umbrella, and walked out the door. Maybe I wasn't up for a run, but a two-mile walk to South Market in a steady all-night rainstorm seemed like the most wonderful idea I'd had in months. Or the most ludicrous? Probably both. At that point, I simply didn't care.

\*\*\*

A few moments later, I stepped back inside and poured some rye into a traveling flask. To stave off the cold, I told myself as I walked back out the door.

\*\*\*

Back into the stormy night, it took me the better part of an hour to reach the South Market alleyway the newspaper had identified as the place where the adaro had been discovered on Tuesday morning. She'd probably been killed in the alley or dumped there late Monday night, which meant the crime scene was now more than forty-eight hours old. The alleyway was a block long, and the cops had taken down the tape marking the scene once they'd finished with it, so the precise location where the body had been found wasn't obvious. Not that it mattered. Even if the cops had overlooked a valuable clue or two the odds against finding anything useful were high, especially since it had been raining steadily for a couple of days. But, there I was. I stepped slowly through the alley, the driving rain beating down on my umbrella, the darkness near total, my senses, augmented by elf and spirit-animal magic, on high alert, my expectations set close to zero. Despite my pessimism, I felt more alive than I had in weeks. I was on a case, right? Authorized by some gibberish scratched onto the surface of a hubcap. The scene of the crime seemed like the logical place to start, even if I came up empty.

Office buildings lined both sides of the alley, and it didn't take me long to become aware of a figure tucked into a recessed back doorway. The old dame, who probably wasn't as old as she looked, was sitting just out of the rain, huddled in an old blanket that appeared to be too thin to give her more than the illusion of warmth. A large dog with matted fur and smelling like..., well..., wet dog was curled at her side and eyeing me with a look of deep suspicion as I drew near.

I stopped in the center of the alley about ten feet from the pair of them and let the rain pour over me. The stub of a homemade cigar hung from her lips, and I recognized the odor drifting from it into the rain. It was a unique scent. The smell reminded me of old burning socks, but I knew that it came from the leaves of a laurel tree native to the Baahpuuo Mountains in the Province of Lakota, and that it was seasoned with a kinnikinnick made from bearberry oil and other stuff I didn't know about. I'd only known one other person to smoke that awful shit.

"Excuse me," I called to the old dame. "Are you okay in there?"

She stared at me with dull eyes, took a puff off her cigar stub, and said nothing. The dog didn't move.

"I've got a flask," I said, and reached slowly into my pocket to bring it out. "Whiskey." I held it up for her to see.

Her eyes locked on the flask, and she pulled the cigar from her lips.

"You don't have to do nothing for it," I told her. "I just have a couple of questions. If you don't mind."

She licked her lips. A hand wearing a glove with no finger coverings emerged from underneath her blanket and motioned me forward. I approached her one careful step at a time, aware that the old dame's canine protector was becoming increasingly tense. But the dame laid a hand between the dog's shoulders, and it visibly relaxed.

When I was close enough, I extended the flask toward the woman, and she snatched it away from me as if she were afraid I might change my mind. She unscrewed the cap, and, never taking her eyes off me, she threw back a shot, gulping it down without blinking as if it were water instead of hundred-proof rye. She held my eyes for a moment or two and drained another couple of swallows, this time more slowly. With obvious reluctance, she reached to pass the flask back to me.

"Hold on to it for now," I told her, and she pulled it back without arguing. She put the cigar stub back into her lips and stared up at me with questioning eyes.

"Were you here a couple of days ago when the police found the body?"

The woman shook her head. "I don't know nothing about a body. Wish this rain would stop." She took one last puff from the cigar stub and crushed it out on the pavement. Looking up at me, she added. "You're wet."

"Yeah. Say, where'd you find that cigar?"

"I didn't steal it."

"I know. You found the stub somewhere in this alley, right?"

"That's right, mister. It was laying on the ground over there. No one was around. It was wet, but I got it lit." She smiled at her cleverness and indicated a spot farther up the alley with a nod. "Half a cigar! It's my lucky day. First a cigar and then some booze. Let the good times roll!" Her mouth opened and she choked out a single laugh that sounded like the caw of an angry crow. This was followed by a fit of wet coughing that wracked the old dame's body until I thought she would break into pieces. When she was done, she sniffed noisily and spit a greasy-looking blob into the rain. She eased back against the doorway, wiped her nose with the side of her half-gloved hand, and knocked back another snort of rye before casting a wary eye in my direction. "You sure you don't want nothing from me for the booze, mister? You try to take advantage of me and Hunter here will rip you to pieces."

"I'm good. So you don't know anything about the woman who was killed here the other day?"

"Killed you say? Here?"

"Somewhere in this alley."

"I don't know fuck all about that, mister. That's the Lord's truth. That water is washing up into this doorway."

"You gonna be okay?"

"Sure, mister." She held up my flask. "This helps." She guzzled down the rest of the whiskey, letting out a long, satisfied breath when she was done. Then she held the flask over her open mouth and tried to shake out any remaining drops.

"I'll take that back now," I said. She'd put away more than half a pint.

"Sure, mister. You're okay. Stop by anytime. I might even blow you next time." She pulled the blanket up to her neck, huddled herself back into the doorway, and closed her eyes. Her dog laid its head over her feet, still watching me.

"I'll keep that in mind," I mumbled. Within seconds, thick, sonorous snores were emerging from deep inside the woman's chest and echoing through the night like the rumbling of distant thunder.

## Chapter Eight

I spent the next hour poking through the alleyway, searching for clues I knew I'd be unlikely to find. Although I was fairly sure I'd located the spot where the body of the adaro had been discovered, I found nothing to indicate how she had died or who had killed her. But the cigar stub the old dame in the doorway had been smoking told me who I needed to go to for more information, provided he was willing to give it to me. I returned home satisfied that I'd done all I could for the night.

I woke with the sunrise after a good three and a half hours of untroubled sleep. A hot shower and a cold breakfast later, I called a number that, as far as I knew, only I had access to. When it went to voicemail, I left a message: "Call me, asshole."

Assuming it would take a while for the "asshole" to get back to me, I placed another call to a slightly more accessible private number. Expecting to have to leave another message, I was surprised when a familiar female voice answered after the second ring.

"Southerland?" Detective Laurel Kalama seemed surprised to hear from me.

I slouched in my chair and let my legs stretch under my desk. "You sound tired. You getting enough quality sleep?"

"I just came out of a meeting, and I haven't finished my third cup of coffee yet. What's up? Did you kill somebody?"

"Not me. I'm calling about the adaro woman you guys found the other morning."

Kalama paused for a beat before asking, "What about her?"

"I've got questions if you've got time."

"Oh, sure, gumshoe. This is a peaceful city. We homicide dicks got nothing to do but sit around hoping nosy private citizens like you call us up for a chat. Makes the day fly by."

"The paper said something about foul play. Are you working the case?"

"That one? Nahhh. It's too high-level for us city coppers. The adults swooped in and took it away from us."

I'd been afraid of that. "So the LIA's got it?"

Kalama snorted. "We heard about it from them."

"Are you saying it was Leea that found the body?" I knew how personal Kalama took it whenever the LIA assumed jurisdiction over a homicide case in Yerba City. "How is this their case and not yours?"

I heard Kalama sigh. "It's an adaro. That makes it a realm matter."

After the Dragon Lords had launched their war to seize control of the South Nihhonese from the amphibious adaros, who had dominated those waters before humans crawled out of the trees, the surviving female adaros were forced out of their bombed-out ocean homes and herded into settlements in several of the Seven Realms, including the one in Placid Point. They were designated as a "protected species" and held in "protective custody" as the first step in assimilating them into the larger community. Life in the settlement wasn't ideal, and some of the adaros found their way into the city, usually as part of the sex trade. The adaro men, or "bucks," who couldn't live long on land, were hunted down by naval forces and subjected to a process government reps called "pacification," and the adaros called "genocide." I don't know that they caught many, though. Male adaros can survive indefinitely in the deepest reaches of the ocean, places where not even female adaros can go, much less their hunters. Sightings of male adaros were extremely rare. In my life, I'd only met one male adaro, and he'd seemed like a decent enough lug. More brawn than brain, maybe, but honorable. And he'd saved my life, which made him a right gee in my book.

"I get that the adaro settlements are run by the realms," I said. "But isn't a dead adaro in downtown Yerba City a local police matter?"

"Usually." Kalama paused a beat before continuing. "Under normal circumstances, Leea hands cases involving adaros over to us. This one must be different somehow."

When the detective didn't elaborate, I prompted her. "Different? How?"

I could almost hear Kalama shrugging. "Beats me. It's not like I'm not busy with a half-dozen other cases anyway."

I stared out my front window into the grayness beyond. The rain had stopped, and a thick haze was rising from the pavement. When I didn't say anything, Kalama asked, "Why are you calling me about this adaro, gumshoe?"

"She's related to an investigation I'm working on," I said. It wasn't exactly a lie. I *was* working on an investigation, even if I hadn't been hired to do so in any conventional sense.

"That right? What do you know about this girl?"

"Nothing except what I read in the newspaper," I admitted.

"Your client didn't tell you anything about her?"

"Not yet." I regretted the words as soon as they came out of my mouth.

"Not yet? What does *that* mean?"

I hesitated. I didn't want to admit to Kalama that I had no legitimate business looking into the adaro's death, and that I was merely scratching at an itch because I had nothing better to do with my life at the moment. "It's a long story," I said, finally.

"Do you know her name? Or what she was doing downtown?"

"No. I was hoping *you* might be able to tell me."

"That's some client you've got. You're saying you don't know anything about this nymph? Anything at all?"

"Like what?"

"Hmm." Kalama sounded skeptical. "For now, let's assume you aren't lying to the only member of the Yerba City Police Department who wouldn't drag you into an interrogation room just for asking about this particular case. That means you're investigating the death of someone you know nothing about. Nothing at all. Not even her name. And since your client won't provide you with any essential information, you're hoping to get it from *me*, a homicide detective, even though you know full well that coppers don't share information about active cases with the general public."

"When you put it that way, it *does* sound a little crazy," I admitted.

"Let me guess, gumshoe. You don't have a client. No one has hired you to investigate this dead nymph. You read about it in the paper and got curious. You've got no one to turn to for information about the vic, so you're trying to sweet-talk it out of me, because we've worked together a couple of times, and because my husband and I have had you out to the house for a barbecue. That about sum it up?"

"I've got a client. I just haven't had a chance to talk to him about the case yet."

"Oh? And why is that?"

"Well...." I cleared my throat before continuing. "He's missing, and I haven't found him yet." As soon as I said it I wished I hadn't. It sounded lame, even to me, and I could feel my ears warming as blood rushed into my cheeks. I felt like I was twelve years old and trying to explain to my mother why I had skipped school that day.

"Are you okay, gumshoe? You're not making a lot of sense."

I tried to recover. "According to the article I read, the police are looking for Ten-Inch."

"Right. The gang banger who helped you kill Graham."

"I didn't kill Graham."

"Sure you didn't. When's the last time you've seen Ten-Inch?"

"Not since that night on the pier." Unless you count possible drunken hallucinations, but I didn't want to get into that just then. This conversation was proving to be uncomfortable enough as it was. I was definitely off my game. I should have caught another couple of hours of shuteye before calling the detective.

"But you're looking for him now?" Kalama asked.

"I am," I said. "Are you?"

I heard Kalama sigh. "In the spirit of cooperation, Leea has delegated that portion of their investigation into the adaro's death to the YCPD. We are to apprehend the subject alive if at all possible and hold him for the LIA. All departments are, in fact, requested to make the finding of said suspect a priority. We're all very excited about it." The detective's tone, dripping with sarcasm, ran counter to her words. "Fuckin' LIA thinks they run this department."

I made a sympathetic chuckling noise. "They think they run everything. They might be right."

Kalama snorted. "Hmph! Why are you looking for Ten-Inch? Are you telling me he's your missing client?"

"When I find him he's going to hire me to find out who killed the adaro."

"Oh really!" Kalama sounded more than skeptical. "And why would he do that? Are the two of you still tight?"

"We've never been tight. We shared a few beers a while back, that's all."

"In other words, you're running off half-cocked again. Knowing you, you read about the nymph's murder, your curiosity got the better of you, and now you're looking for someone to pay you to find someone who you're looking for anyway."

I hesitated for a moment or two before admitting, "Maybe."

"Right. Good luck, gumshoe. You got cops and maybe some LIA agents looking for Ten-Inch, too. Try to stay out of the crossfire."

Kalama disconnected the call, and I let out a breath. I regretted calling Kalama and wondered how much of her respect I'd lost with my feeble attempt to pry information from her. The homicide detective was one of the smartest people I knew, certainly one of the sharpest law enforcement professionals I'd ever run across. Despite my fumbling, however, I'd learned a couple of things I hadn't known. The LIA had discovered the body and kept it from the police. That was unusual. And they had the entire YCPD looking for Ten-Inch. What kind of mess had the gang leader gotten himself into? Why was the LIA so keen on finding him? And what possible reason could I have for thrusting myself into an affair that was clearly much bigger than I'd thought it was when I read the throwaway article about the dead nymph on the bottom of page five of my local newspaper?

I pulled a half-empty bottle of rye out of my desk drawer. I stared at it, longingly. It was early. Not even nine o'clock. I'd been hitting the sauce awfully hard lately. Maybe it was time to start cutting back and rounding myself back into shape. I pinched the roll of fat that seemed to have crawled out of nowhere in the past few weeks to surround my midsection. I didn't have anything specific planned for the rest of the morning, and I got the bright idea to spend an hour banging away at the homemade heavy bag in my laundry room. I was inordinately smug about my sudden decision to take better care of my health. I was so pleased that I limited myself to only two swallows from the bottle. I lasted a full ten minutes with the bag before hitting the showers. Okay, maybe it was five. Sue me.

When I came out of the shower, I noticed I had a text from a number I didn't recognize. The text consisted of a four-character message: "10pM." The "10" meant eight. The capital "M" was a code telling me where to meet. I checked the time and was surprised to see my "workout," such as it was, had ended well before lunchtime. Thinking of my conversation with Gracie, I decided to take care of an obligation I'd been neglecting for far too long.

Picking up the phone, I called a number I had on speed-dial. A weary-sounding woman's voice answered on the third ring. "That you, Jack?"

"Maybe. Aren't we all Jack to you?"

"There are Jacks, and there are Jacks. What'd you want, Jack? I thought you were dead."

"Funny. I've been busy."

"You've been moping."

"Yeah, well, maybe. A little. Thought I might bring you by some Huaxian takeout if you're up for it."

"Well aren't you the knight in shining armor. Sure, come on by. As long as you don't mind watching me work."

"I won't be in the way?"

I heard her draw in smoke from a cigarette, which I knew would be dangling from the corner of her mouth. "It's nothing exciting," she told me. "Just optimizing some code. I can do it while we're having lunch. Hey, can you do me a favor? I'm out of coffee. I've been straining water through the same sludge for three days, and it's weaker than a starved mouse. Can you pick some up on the way over? Some of that eastern Ghanaian bean I like. Oh, and get me a pint of cream, too. And a quart of hooch. Any brand will do."

"Bitter coffee, sweet cream, and cheap whiskey. Got it."

I grabbed my hat and headed out into the late morning.

\*\*\*

*I'd been working on a grocery list with Holly when a Tolanican god seized control of my hand and used it to write me a message. Holly had offered to cook me a special oyster stew if I would buy the ingredients she needed. I was halfway through "paprika" when my pen began scribbling letters in large shaky handwriting that wasn't mine. When I was done, I dropped the pen and read what my hand had written:*

paprFRONT DEKS HAWHTORNE PAKCAGE 9 TONIHGT TROY

*Holly had been looking over my shoulder while she dictated her list, and now she was staring at me wide-eyed.* "What does all that mean?"

"It means that Thunderbird's dyslexia is improving."

"What?"

"It's a long story. You'll probably want to sit for it."

*Once Holly was comfortably seated, I explained to her how I'd met Troy, a ten-year-old homeless troll who was the embodiment of Thunderbird, an extremely powerful Tolanican spirit. Another powerful spirit, known as Night Owl, had kidnapped Thunderbird from Lakota Province and brought him to Yerba City, where, thanks to the arrival of a diminutive nirumbee warrior named Ralph, Thunderbird had freed himself and created a new persona, a young troll with a serious case of expressive aphasia that made it difficult for him to speak. Cougar, my spirit animal, referred to him as "the boy who talks backwards," a legendary figure in ancient Native Tolanican folk tales, and directed me to keep him safe. With some help from Ralph,*

Crawford, and me, Thunderbird was able to overcome Night Owl. Along the way, Troy and I formed a bond, and I'd actually looked into adopting the boy. It didn't work out. Ralph convinced me that the boy needed to return to Lakota, where he could be trained to fully assume his role as Thunderbird. I didn't like it, but I knew Ralph was right.

Holly was not so sure. "Did Troy have a choice in the matter?" she asked.

"He's a child. Children don't get to make choices."

"I don't get it. Does he have family in Lakota?"

"In a manner of speaking. The boy we call Troy didn't exist until Thunderbird created him. Ralph told me that Thunderbird usually manifests himself in a baby as it is being born, but this was kind of an emergency situation. He was in a hurry, so he just kind of conjured up a ten-year-old Troy on the spot. But there are people in Lakota who are descended from a very old tribe. Some of these tribal people have the job of, I don't know exactly how to say it..., of 'maintaining' Thunderbird. Part of that involves training the 'new' Thunderbird whenever he renews himself. I don't know. Ralph explained it all to me, but a lot of it went over my head. Anyway, these people will take better care of Troy than I ever could."

"But what about that writing?"

I'd chuckled at that. "Yeah, it's weird. It's called automatic writing, and I've gotta admit it kind of creeps me out. When he wants to talk to me, he takes control of my hand and writes me a note. You'd think he'd just pick up a phone. But old habits die hard, I suppose, and he's a very old spirit."

Holly poured herself a drink at that point and gulped it down. "You lead a strange life, baby. What if you don't happen to be holding a pen when... this spirit—Thunderbird—when he wants to mail you a letter?"

"The first time it happened, I scratched the message into the side of a wall with my key."

Holly shivered. "Yikes! Remind me to steer clear of you when you're holding a knife. Does he talk to you often?"

"No. You know how kids are. They never call. They never write."

Holly pointed at my grocery list. "What's this about a package? Is that supposed to be Hawthorne? The hotel?"

"Yeah. Looks like I have to pick something up there at nine o'clock."

"Why?"

*She had to ask. I couldn't blame her. We had become very close in a short period of time. The dinner she wanted to cook for me was to mark our one-month anniversary, thirty days since the evening we'd met at her club. It had been quite an evening. We'd wound up at her place after she punched out for the night, and we'd wasted no time getting better acquainted. Much better acquainted. I took her out for breakfast after we'd come up for air the next morning. Thirty days later, and we were still acting like a couple of dopey teenagers and loving every minute of it.*

*But there were things I didn't want to tell her. Couldn't tell her. Things about an old elf and about a scheme he'd gotten me involved in over the past couple of years. Maybe we should have had a conversation about it all, but we never did. I told myself she was better off not knowing, that it would be safer for her if she were left in the dark. Like most people, Holly had heard fairy tales about vicious elves who feasted on wayward children, stories parents told their kids in order to frighten them into obedience. She'd also read the horror stories and seen the lurid movies about bloodsucking elf monsters who roamed the streets at night, preying on the weak and unwary. But these were just fantasies, and Holly, like most people, believed that elves were an ancient species eradicated by the Dragon Lords and their troll allies long ago.*

*I didn't want Holly to know that I'd met an elf, and that I owed the elf a large debt. Not only had the elf's gift of magical awareness saved my life on more than one occasion, but he had intervened in some way I didn't understand when a witch's poison had left me just outside the gates of death. After he'd helped the witch bring me back I was never entirely sure whether I'd been rescued from the brink of death, or if I'd literally died and somehow been revived. In any case, I was now involved, more or less against my will, in the elf's plan to overthrow the Dragon Lords, including our own Lord Ketz-Alkwat. Ralph was part of that plan. So was Troy, and I knew his message to me concerning a package I was supposed to pick up at the Hawthorne Hotel was part of it, too. It was a long-range plan, and I was privy to none of the important details. My role in this grand conspiracy was small, but it could often be inconvenient, not to mention hazardous. Let's face it: the Dragon Lords weren't going to go down easy. As for me, I didn't really care one way or the other. I had nothing in particular against the Dragon Lords. They'd never bothered me much, at least not directly. But if Old Lord Ketz ever found out I was a part of a plot against him, my life wouldn't be worth a plugged nickel. And to make things worse, the elf was in league with the Hatfield Syndicate, the lords of the underworld. Which meant I was, too, though I tried hard to keep them at arm's length whenever possible. Things were complicated, to be sure, and I didn't want Holly to be wise to any of it. The less she knew, I convinced myself, the better off she'd be.*

*I should have known that no good relationship can survive secrets like the ones I was keeping. Maybe I did know it. When she told me it was over, I can't say I was surprised. All things considered, it was probably for the best. Safer for Holly, more convenient for me. But that didn't make it hurt any less when she walked away from me for good.*

## Chapter Nine

I arrived at the unassuming, almost inconspicuous workshop of Yerba City's premier computer wizard at half past noon with a bag full of Huaxian and walked in without knocking. Walks in Cloud, wearing a shapeless flannel gown she'd probably slept in, appeared to have been poured into her wheelchair behind a computer. I knew she had a small apartment adjoining the shop. I also knew she didn't use it for much more than sleeping. That morning she looked as if she hadn't been in the apartment all night. Her unmoving eyes were glazed and dull. The cigarette hanging from her mouth had an inch of ash hanging precariously from its tip over a small pile of ash on the tabletop. Only her pudgy fingers, too quick to follow with the naked eye, moved as she tapped at her keyboard.

She spoke without looking up. "I'm on a roll, Jack. Be a lamb and make the coffee, wouldya? The food smells great. I'll be ready to eat by the time the coffee's ready."

"Pulling an all-nighter?"

Walks didn't bother to respond.

I set the cardboard containers of Huaxian food on her worktable next to her computer. "Gracie says hi. She says we're both a couple of hermits and that we need to get out more."

The computer wizard continued typing, her eyes still locked on her screen. "Get out more? Where am I supposed to go? Dancing? The bod's useless from the waist down. You held me up on the dance floor once. I don't need to put you through that again."

"It was fun."

"Uh-huh," she muttered absently. Her typing never slowed.

"Gracie also says I've been neglecting you. I'm sorry."

"Jack?" The computer wizard still didn't look up.

"Walks?"

"Shut the fuck up and make me some coffee. I drained my last cup hours ago and I'm about to chew on the grounds. And don't be stingy with the cream."

As she continued typing, I made my way past boxes of used electronic equipment to the table where Walks kept her grinder and coffee pot. After I finished grinding some beans, my attention was grabbed by... something odd. A sensation of some sort. A noise? No, it was more like the cessation of an almost inaudible background sound. Like when air that has been streaming quietly from an air-conditioning vent all day long suddenly stops flowing. Or maybe it was more like a silent implosion deep inside the back of my head. Whatever it was, the sensation felt familiar somehow, though I couldn't put my finger on what it was. Something in the room.... I stopped what I was doing and closed my eyes. In my mind, I conjured up mental images of sigils, stringing them together in a specific pattern. When I opened my eyes, I could see the world of air elementals superimposed over the dim light of Walks's shop. I could see the air drifting through the room, pulling motes of dust along in the wakes of languid currents. I scanned the room from one side to the other.

There! Near the ceiling above and behind Walks—a tiny air elemental, no longer moving on its own, drifting with the dust motes. The tiny spirit, a spherical bubble no bigger than a coffee bean, aware that I had spotted it, shot toward the front door of the shop. Instinctively, I formed a sigil in my mind and shouted a command: "Stop!" The elemental slowed, but I could feel it resisting my will. I refocused, but in the next second I felt my connection to the elemental snap. In an instant, the spirit was through an imperceptible seam in the doorframe and lost to the world outside.

Walks had stopped typing. "What happened? Why are you shouting?"

I sighed. "An air elemental. It was under someone's control, I think. Either that, or it was stronger than it looked. It got away."

The computer wizard's eyes narrowed. "An elemental? Here?"

"It's been watching you work. It had a good view of your screen."

Walks, frowning, crushed out her cigarette in an ashtray already filled with butts. She reached back and pulled the end of a long braid of black hair over her shoulder and down into her lap. "It couldn't have seen anything important. I've just been tightening up some programming for a customer. Routine shit. No big deal." She absently stroked her braid.

I shook my head. "No telling how long the elemental has been watching you. Have you worked on anything unusual or sensitive over the past few days? Or weeks?"

The frown on the computer wizard's forehead deepened. "Oh dear."

"What?"

Walks tapped a few keys and pushed at her computer mouse. She shook her head. "Could be a lot of stuff. I've been busy for a while, and some of this shit is *highly* sensitive."

"Anything in particular?"

She pondered the question for a few seconds, running her braid through her fingers. "Hard to say. It would depend on who was interested."

I considered the problem. "Have you worked on anything today that could be trouble?"

Walks shook her head. "I don't think so. Like I said, just some routine shit. An insurance company is updating its software, and the new code they developed is kind of clunky. They hired me to make it more efficient. But it's nothing that would interest anyone outside the company's IT department. I started on it first thing this morning and I was just wrapping it up. It's the only thing I've been working on so far today."

I let out a breath. "Whoever sent the elemental is probably monitoring you for something specific. They've probably been watching you for days. They must not have the answers they want yet, or you wouldn't still be under surveillance. I think I chased their bug away before it discovered anything useful."

The computer wizard pushed her braid back over her shoulder and tapped at the top of her worktable. "This isn't good. Important people come to me because they trust me to keep their shit confidential. I've got all kinds of gear in here protecting against unwanted intrusions, both electronic and magical. Against elementals, too. No elemental should have been able to penetrate my security."

"This one was tiny. And very quiet. Almost impossible to detect."

A tight smile appeared on Walks's round face. "*You* detected it."

"I'm good."

"I know."

"Real good."

"I know."

I met the computer wizard's dark eyes with my own. "Whoever sent that elemental is better."

Walks stopped smiling. "Do you have any idea who sent it?"

I shook my head. "No. Lots of elementalists are better than I am. But I'm guessing that they're all working for powerful people."

"Or government agencies?"

I nodded. "That's a possibility, too."

Walks stared at her computer screen, as if searching for the identity of her intruder in its depths. After a few moments, she lifted her eyes to meet mine. "Hey, Jack. You don't think..."

I stared back into the dark eyes of the computer wizard. "The thing you've got stored away?"

Walks lowered her eyes. "Lord's balls," she muttered under her breath.

Lord's balls indeed, I thought. The formula for Reifying Agent Alpha. The substance the Tolanican Dragon Lord needed to make himself a new little dragon ally. The formula that had been destroyed and, despite the best efforts of engineering minds around the globe, never replicated. The formula only Walks and I knew still existed somewhere in the deepest hidden recesses of the spirit realm of the Cloud.

"You haven't accessed it lately, have you?" I asked.

Walks opened a container of pan-fried spiced duck and rice. "I haven't touched it since I tucked it away. You think I should look in on it and make sure it's still there?"

"No. It's safe, right?"

"It couldn't be in a safer place." Using chopsticks, the computer wizard scooped out a small bite of the duck. "Mmm. This is good!"

"Then leave it. If anyone's watching, you don't want to show them the way in."

Walks frowned. "Until you chased that elemental away, I wouldn't have dreamed that anyone could look in on me like that." She reached into a file cabinet drawer and pulled out a device I recognized as a high-end portable bug detector. "Wanna help me check the place over?"

I nodded. "Sounds like a swell idea."

"I'll check for electronic surveillance. You check for spying spirits."

I mentally conjured up the appropriate sigils and began to focus on them. "I can spot any air elementals that might be in the room," I said, "but I don't do earth, water, or fire."

"That's fine, Jack. Do what you can." Walks began waving the bug detector slowly over her desk, concentrating on electrical fixtures, electronic equipment, and other likely spots for a listening device or miniature camera.

I moved around the workshop, examining every nook and cranny. I'd been able to spot the tiny air elemental from several yards away, and I was confident in my ability to detect any other similar spirits that might be hanging about. I also searched for physical evidence of other types of elementals: clumps of dirt, small puddles of water, unusual sources of heat. I searched for anomalies that might indicate the presence of magic or otherworldly portals, though I knew Walks would be more sensitive to the presence of the supernatural than I was. Still, I wanted to be thorough. It wasn't a large shop, and after twenty minutes of poking through it I was ready to pronounce the room clean.

Of bugs, that is. Kneeling in a far corner of the shop, I picked an ancient cracked coffee mug off the floor and sniffed at it. Judging from the size of the mold deposit inside the cup, I concluded it hadn't been used in several months. "Hey, Walks!" I called across the room. "How often does your shop get cleaned?"

"Who's got time to clean?" came the response.

"Don't you have a service?"

"I don't want anyone messing with my stuff."

I stood and tossed the mug into a nearby wastepaper basket. "I'm coming up empty. You find anything?"

Walks, who had wheeled herself from one end of the shop to the other, returned to her station behind the worktable. "Nah, Jack. I'm not picking up anything electronic or magical. The Cloud Spirit assures me that I'm in no danger. All of my security is in place and working. I think we're good. Let's eat before this food gets cold."

I pulled a chair up to the other side of the worktable from the computer tech and opened a container of egg rolls. "Did you ask the Cloud Spirit about the elemental I chased out of here?"

"She's puzzled by that. She says she's looking into it."

"She's puzzled? That doesn't sound good." I bit off half an egg roll that was a lot less warm now than it had been when I bought it.

"Air spirits shouldn't be able to sneak past her. She's an air spirit herself, about as powerful as they get. The good news is that she should be able to track it down pretty easily. Maybe we can find out who sent it."

I wondered about that. The Cloud Spirit was more to Walks in Cloud than a mere spirit guide. The bond between the two was older and stronger than the relationship between Cougar and me. Walks was something like a priestess to the Cloud Spirit, who had given her a number of supernatural gifts and protections in return for her service. And her legs. But if the elemental had been able to enter this protected space undetected and keep watch on the computer wizard for an indeterminate length of time, it might also be able to avoid the Cloud

Spirit's attempts to find it. Calling the capabilities of the powerful spirit into doubt with her devoted quasi priestess didn't strike me as an advisable course of action, so I kept my peace and bit into another egg roll.

We were washing down the last of the Huaxian with some strong Ghanaian coffee when a knock sounded at the front door. Walks and I looked at each other. The computer wizard's business was not listed in any directories, and she had no signs or markings of any kind outside her front door. Her operation catered to an exclusive clientele. Few people could afford her services, and she agreed to work with fewer still. New customers came to her only by referral.

"You expecting anyone?" I asked.

"Nope. It's probably nothing. An ambitious solicitor maybe. Just ignore it."

The knock was repeated, and when the door handle turned I stood to meet whoever might be walking in. Ice formed in the pit of my stomach when I saw who it was.

"Detective Modoc." I suppressed a growl.

The baby-faced detective's eyes bored into me as he smiled. "Fancy meeting you here, peeper. Long time no see."

"Not long enough. What are you doing here?"

Modoc's eyes scanned Walks in Cloud's shop as he slowly made his way inside. "Happened to be in the neighborhood and thought I'd see about getting a new computer."

Walks spoke over her coffee cup. "Then you're in the wrong place. I don't sell computers, mister."

"It's detective. Detective Modoc. From the Placid Point Precinct."

Walks put down her cup and pointed off to her left. "Placid Point's that way, detective. About two blocks down the street. This is Nihhonese Heights. You're out of your jurisdiction."

"Our two departments aren't fussy. We're all part of the greater Yerba City police force, after all." He nodded in my direction. "This man escaped our custody yesterday, and I've been instructed to bring him back. But there's no reason for you to be involved."

He turned to me. "Come along quietly, Southerland. We can do this the easy way, or we can do it the hard way. You'll wind up coming with me either way, but I'd hate for us to mess up this nice crippled lady's shop in the process."

Heat rose from my neck into my cheeks, and I felt blood surging through my temples. "Why don't we take this outside, Modoc."

Walks in Cloud had other ideas. "No one's taking anything anywhere," she said. Modoc's eyes shifted in her direction, and I turned to see the computer wizard pointing a sawed-off shotgun at the detective. "Get out of my shop, *mister*, or this 'cripple' will drop you where you stand."

If Modoc was alarmed at looking down the barrel of a scattergun, he didn't show it. "Are you planning on shooting a policeman, ma'am? I wouldn't advise it. Our law enforcement system doesn't take kindly to cop-killers, and that chair of yours won't buy you any sympathy."

Walks lowered the barrel of the shotgun a few inches. "Maybe I'll take out your knees and you can get yourself a chair of your own."

Modoc's eyes narrowed, and his lips pinched. "Ma'am, put that gun down before you get yourself in real trouble."

Walks raised the barrel until it was pointed at Modoc's face. "Nah, forget the knees. I think I'll just blow your fuckin' head off, instead."

Modoc's eyes found mind. "You gonna let a crippled dame fight your battles for you? You're a bigger pussy than I thought, Southerland."

"It's her shop," I said. "The way I see it, she's defending it from an intruder. It's none of my business one way or the other."

The detective glared at me for a second before letting out a breath. "Another time, Southerland." He turned his back on the scattergun pointed in his direction and, without hurrying, walked out the door.

Walks lowered the shotgun. "He was rude."

"Is that thing loaded?" I asked.

She frowned at me. "Of course it's loaded. I wouldn't be able to do much damage if it wasn't, would I?"

"Would you have really pulled that trigger?"

Her face relaxed. "I'm a disabled woman living alone in a seedy neighborhood, Jack. If he'd come one step closer, I'd've emptied both barrels into his handsome face. Then I would have asked you to pick up the body and dump it in my trash bin out back. And then I would have reloaded my gun for the next motherfucker who came into my shop uninvited and called me a cripple."

"You think he's handsome?"

She smiled. "If he wasn't such a prick, I'd've let him kiss me."

"Huh. And here I was all worried about you."

Walks frowned. "If I were you, I'd be more worried about saving your own skin. He came here for you, not me. And I don't think he likes you much. What'd you do to him, anyway?"

"Nothing. He and his partner, a senior detective named Sims, picked me up yesterday for jaywalking."

"You're shitting me."

"Nope." I told her about the dead adaro and Ten-Inch, and how I'd been bagged by the cops outside the gangster's apartment. I also told her about how Lubank had extricated me from custody.

When I was done, Walks shook her head. "So how'd he know you were here?"

"Good question. I wonder if it had anything to do with that elemental I scared off."

Walks frowned. "Maybe. But why would the Placid Point cops have me under surveillance?"

I shrugged. It didn't make any sense to me, either.

Walks looked down at her shotgun. "Anyway, I need to have a good long conversation with the Cloud Spirit. She's supposed to be keeping this place secure." She looked up at me. "In the meantime, you need to watch out for that asshole cop. The way he looked at you—that had nothing to do with police business. There's something personal going on there."

It was a good point. I tried to shrug it off, but the prospect of having to constantly be on guard against a Placid City cop with a hard-on for me was something I couldn't afford to take lightly. I opened my own container of spiced duck and rice, which I hadn't yet touched. I stared at it for a moment and reached for the bottle of rye I'd brought over instead. I splashed some of it into my lukewarm coffee and took a healthy sip. Bitter coffee and cheap whiskey. I'd had worse.

## Chapter Ten

*When Holly first laid eyes on Badass, she radiated lust. Whether it was toward me or toward the powerful air elemental hardly mattered. She had not only been instantly captivated by the primal intensity of the elemental, but by my ability to summon and command it. I'd explained to her that Badass had assumed the role as my personal guardian and protector, and that it was always near at hand when I called.*

She had stared, enthralled, at the twelve-foot dynamo of whirling fury. "She's beautiful," Holly had pronounced at last.

"It," I reminded her. "Elementals don't have genders, remember? And why do you think it's a she?"

"Look at that raw turbulence," she'd answered. "That's exactly what I feel inside myself all the time."

I'd pulled back and examined her with a critical eye. Even in her euphoric state she'd appeared to be calm enough. "It doesn't show," I'd said.

"That's what women do," she'd told me. "We've got all this energy. But when we're little girls, we're told to keep still and act like ladies. When we're growing up, we're told that aggressive behavior isn't ladylike. Let the man speak first. Be supportive. Don't show him up. Don't compete with him. Don't make him uncomfortable. So we keep all our aggressions in check and all our energy bottled up. And when we can't keep it inside anymore, when we explode, then they call us hysterical. They say we've had an ing-bing, a tantrum. Or that we've gone crazy."

"I think I'll stick to being a man. It's less complicated."

She'd turned to me with a derisive grin. "You think so? You do the same thing, you know. With your emotions. Especially your more tender emotions. You're so withdrawn. You hold everything inside. You act like you don't have no emotions at all."

"I've got emotions," I'd protested.

"I know you do, dear. You just don't like for them to show."

"You'd like me to cry?"

"Sure I would, if you felt like it."

"I never feel like it."

"Yes you do, dear. Often. You're like most men, though. Worse, even. You try to be so tough all the time. You don't trust emotions. You think they're only for women and sissies."

"It's not good for men to get emotional," I explained to her in my most reasonable voice. "It makes them dangerous. When my father got emotional, my mother and I would have to hide in the bathroom. Of course, he was usually drunk then. Afterwards, when he was sleeping it off, my mother would hurry out and clean up all the shattered glass and broken furniture so he wouldn't get mad all over again when he came out and saw it."

Holly had looked at me with interest, like a scientist studying a new kind of bug. "Who's the most emotional man you know?" She'd asked me.

I thought about the question. "Lubank, I guess. He's angry as a hornet most of the time."

"Hmmm.... You ever notice that when you think about emotion in men, the only thing you talk about is anger? Do you think that's because anger is the only emotion your father ever expressed toward you? Maybe that's why you're afraid to show your emotions. Anger is the only emotion you're familiar with."

I remember how I'd bristled at that. "I'm not afraid of showing my emotions."

She'd smiled at that. "Aren't you?"

I'd bit back hard on a response, took a breath, and turned my attention to Badass, a tightly contained tempest disturbing an otherwise calm afternoon like a rip in the fabric of the universe. "Do you know that Badass can generate enough wind power in close quarters to push over a small automobile? I once saw a picture on the internet of a plastic straw that a tornado had driven into the side of a tree like a nail."

After a moment, I'd felt a gentle hand on my shoulder. Holly lowered it until she was gripping my arm above the elbow. "Show me!"

When I turned my head and saw her face, it was lit up with a glow that looked to me like lust.

"All right," I'd said, smiling. "Let's go knock something over."

\*\*\*

Once Walks had eaten, she was eager to get back to work. I'd brought trouble to her doorstep, and I was feeling guilty about that, but knowing she could take care of herself made me feel a little better about leaving her to her own devices and getting on with my day. I had an eight o'clock appointment at the old Placid Point Pier with a dangerous little man, and I wanted to get a little work in while I had the chance.

Back at my place, I tried to find some information on Modoc. A simple internet search turned up nothing useful on Detective Lionel Modoc. He'd been assigned to the Placid Point Precinct for the past three years, but I found no information on where he'd been before that. He didn't seem to have any presence at all on social media, which might have been considered odd for a young, good-looking cop, but it wasn't unheard of, either. I didn't know Modoc well enough to know how he spent his spare time, but he didn't strike me as the kind of mug who spent a lot of time typing into a computer.

I searched for info on Sims, too, and discovered that Detective Samuel Sims had only come to Placid Point in the previous summer. He'd transferred from Yuma City in Yuma Province, where he'd been a detective in the special crimes unit. Further research indicated that Sims hadn't been in Yuma for long, just a few months, and that he had served in an unusually large number of departments in western Tolanica, often for only a few weeks, and never for more than three years. I looked for explanations for his frequent transfers: controversies, demotions in rank, anything that might indicate a pattern of contentious behavior toward his fellow cops or supervisors. I found nothing. In fact, he'd held the rank of detective or senior detective at every one of his stops. I wondered at that, but before I could dive deeper into my research, I was interrupted by my phone's ringtone.

It was Gio's daughter, Gemma, who told me she had more information on the storm card that was supposed to represent my fortune.

"I talked to my teacher," she told me. "She says not to worry. That card is coming up in a lot of readings these days."

"Makes sense," I said. "It's raining pretty hard out there, and it doesn't look like it's letting up anytime soon."

"True," she agreed. "But...."

"Something more?"

Her voice was hesitant. "Yeah. I mean, maybe. Remember how when you were here before, you took the card and held it for a while, looking at it? Well, when you did that, you left some of your skin oil on the card, and, well, I was able to use that to do a more detailed reading. I hope you don't mind." I heard the apology in her voice in that last hurried comment. "Mrs. Keli'i says it's not ethical to take material like hairs, nails, or skin oil from people without their knowing about it."

"It's okay," I said. "You should have asked me for my permission first, though."

"I know. I'm sorry. But I wanted to make sure the cards weren't trying to warn you about something."

"And?"

"And, well...," Gemma hesitated, as if she didn't know how to continue. "Well, I mean, I'm not sure, but, I mean, I'm getting a bad feeling."

"Gemma? Does your dad know you're talking to me?"

I heard her suck in a breath. "I haven't told him. You won't tell him, will you? I mean, I just finished doing the reading, and I thought I should call you right away."

I didn't like the sound of that. Gemma might just be a kid, but I had no doubt that she had the witch's gift. "All right. What did you find?"

Gemma's voice grew serious, and her hesitation vanished as her words flew at me in bursts almost too fast for me to follow. "The storm isn't normal. There's an otherworldly influence behind it. A powerful one. From the West. Or Southwest. Anyway, it's connected to the Nihhonese Ocean. But the storm is dangerous. And not just for everyone, but for you in particular. I see... I see death. For you. Not for certain. But maybe. It's... it depends on... on other things." She caught her breath. "I'm sorry, Mr. Southerland. A lot of it isn't clear to me. But you have to be careful. The cards say you are in danger from someone you think is on your side. At least, I think that's what they say. I could be getting that wrong. So... so be careful, Mr. Southerland. Watch out for unexpected betrayal. Betrayal during a bad storm. I'm not real good at this yet, but that's what I see. Okay?"

I put a smile in my voice. "Don't worry, Gemma. I'm always careful. But I'll be even more careful now. Thank you."

"You won't tell Daddy, will you? He told me I wasn't supposed to use these cards without a teacher watching me."

"I won't tell your dad, but he's right. No more using the cards without your teacher's supervision. You said it yourself, those cards aren't toys. Bad things happen to people who use them without proper training. You hear me?"

"Yes, Mr. Southerland. I hear you. And I promise."

"You promised before. You need to really mean it this time."

"I know. And I do. I won't do any more readings without my teacher."

We chatted a bit more and I disconnected. Gemma's warnings were too vague to act on, and I couldn't go around suspecting everyone I knew of having it in for me, but I'd try to be extra careful about trusting people for the duration of this storm. It wouldn't be hard. I wasn't inclined to trust too many people in the best of times.

I decided to pack it in for the afternoon and clear my head by punching at the heavy bag in my laundry room. I lasted a good fifteen minutes this time and I was feeling smug when I hit the shower. I knew I was far from being in tip-top shape, but fifteen minutes was better than five, or even ten. When I was dried off and dressed, I celebrated with a couple of swallows from my flask—but just a couple! After that, it was time to get myself ready for a trip to Placid Point, which mostly meant frying up a cheeseburger for dinner and making sure my flask was topped off.

\*\*\*

I arrived at the parking lot of the abandoned pier at eight-fifteen. Somewhere behind the thick layer of clouds, the sun was low in the western sky. A light rain was falling, and the breeze sweeping in from the ocean was heavy with frigid seawater. I didn't know whether to use my umbrella to shield myself from the rain falling from overhead or from the ocean spray blowing into my face, so I said "fuck it" and left it in the beastmobile. I pulled my hat low on my forehead, pushed my hands deep into the pockets of my raincoat, and headed across the lot to the pier.

Even with my magically augmented awareness, the shadowy stump-like figure at the far end of the pier was practically undetectable in the mist until I was almost on top of it. Even then, all I could see was the glowing tip of a stogie poking from the hood of a thick gray overcoat. A voice sounding like it was coming from a chain-smoking twelve-year-old emerged from deep within the hood: "You're late."

"I'm wet, too. You could have picked a better place to meet. And a better night."

"This place is secure. We'll be aware of anyone approaching long before they can come close, and I've already checked the pier for surveillance devices. And Yerba City doesn't have better nights. How do you live in this shithole? I haven't had the pleasure of a warm evening since I left Lakota."

"I thought it was always cold in Lakota."

"Sure, but it's a comfortable cold. Lots of pristine dry snow and clean mountain air. And it's only cold in the winter." The shoulders of the overcoat rose an inch and fell again. "Okay, fall and winter. And early spring." The tip of the stogie glowed red for a moment, and smoke emerged from the hood as the voice resumed speaking. "The cold here is like drowning in salty ice water. It freezes the insides of my bones. And it's all year round."

I stared down at the nirumbee warrior, less than half my height. "What do you want, Ralph? You didn't bring me out here to bellyache about the weather."

"I'm not bellyaching about the fuckin' weather. I'm bellyaching about the fuckin' climate. That's two different things, dimwit. I brought you out here because you left me a message. What do *you* want?"

"You could have called me back."

"Phone calls aren't secure."

My nose twitched at the odor of bearberry kinnikinnick wafting up from Ralph's cigar. "It's about the adaro stiff you guys found in an alley in South Market a couple of days ago."

"What makes you think I have anything to do with that?"

"I took a walk in that alley last night. I found a homeless old dame smoking the stub of a homemade cheroot that smelled like week-old carrion. She said she found it on the ground a few yards from where the adaro's body was found. You shouldn't be so careless, Ralph. No one outside the Baahpuuo Mountains smokes that skunkweed by choice."

Once again, the shoulders of the overcoat lifted and fell slightly. "It's an acquired taste."

"What were you doing there?"

"Smoking." Another foul-smelling cloud rose from the nirumbee's hood.

"More important, *when* were you there?"

"When do you think? Alkwat's balls, you think I wander through alleys in my spare time for kicks? I was there at oh-dark-thirty on Tuesday morning getting that nymph's body off the street before Joe Q. Public started filing in for work. Can't have them starting their day by tripping over some fuckin' roadkill. That kind of thing upsets people."

"How'd you know the body was there?"

"Someone ran across it. I don't know who. Maybe a drug dealer with a sense of civic duty. Maybe the killer. Who knows? Anyway, he—at least I think it was a he—tried to report the body to the Bureau of Adaro

Affairs, but naturally they were closed for the night. He got a recording that provided him with a number to call in case of an emergency. The number happens to be the LIA tip line. He called our operator—the LIA never sleeps—and I was notified of the call. I went out to investigate."

I frowned. "Why did they call you? It was just a dead adaro. Why not notify the local cops and let them take care of it?"

"It was an adaro. Adaros are realm business."

"Since when is the simple murder of an adaro realm business?"

"Who said she was murdered?"

"The paper said foul play, and you just speculated that the killer may have been the one who called your tip line."

"I said that? Huh! I'm getting careless in my old age."

"You aren't old. And you're dodging my question. Why is the LIA interested in this adaro?"

Ralph tried to draw in a puff of his foul-smelling weed, but his cigar had gone out. He produced a match from somewhere inside his coat, struck it on a wooden railing—a real trick in the wet weather—and took the time to fire the stogie up again before answering me. Clouds of smoke were blowing out of his hood by the time he did. "This nymph is special. According to our anonymous caller, she didn't have a registration number tattooed on her wrist. Naturally, that got our attention. First thing I did when I got to the body was check her wrist. The caller was right. No tattoo. So I called in a team to secure the crime scene and take possession of the body."

I stared down at the nirumbee. His voice had betrayed no trace of concern, and now he was puffing on his cigar as if he didn't have a care in the world.

"You waited until you had seen the body before calling in a team?"

"That's right."

"So you were notified by your people that some unidentified person had found a dead unregistered adaro, and you went out by yourself to investigate?"

"Yep."

I watched the smoke from the nirumbee warrior's stogie drift away from him to be caught up in the breeze and carried down the length of the pier toward the wharf. The rain had let up, but occasional beads of water still dripped from the brim of my soaked fedora. I brushed ice-cold moisture out of my eyes and off my face.

I crouched so that I could meet Ralph's eyes inside the hood of his coat. After another cloud from his cigar had vanished into the night, I asked, "Did you kill her?"

Ralph barked out a wheezing laugh. "Don't be an idiot, Southerland."

I stared into his hood, trying to read his feral eyes. "It wouldn't be the first person you'd executed for the LIA."

Ralph sniffed noisily and shot a kinnikinnick-infused blob to the wooden platform between my feet. "Let me tell you something. That nymph was roughed up something fierce. You know that's not my style. So quit insulting me, or I'll break your fuckin' nose. Again."

"You say you received an anonymous call. You say you were notified about it and you went out to investigate on your own before calling in an investigating team. How do I know you didn't kill her yourself and *then* call in a team?"

Ralph removed his cigar from his teeth and pointed it at me. "You know because I'm telling you."

"That's supposed to mean something?"

Ralph grinned and returned the cigar to his mouth. "I guess you're just going to have to trust me."

"And why would I do that?"

"Think about it, dimwit. You learned about the nymph from an article in the newspaper, right? You think the paper would know anything about her if I had punched her ticket?"

I thought about it. It was a good point. Not conclusive, maybe, but enough to make me doubt an idea I hadn't put a lot of stock in to begin with. I nodded and resumed standing. "I had to ask."

Ralph sighed. "I suppose you did at that. But I didn't chill that nymph."

"Do you know who did?"

The hood shook side to side. "Not yet."

"It wasn't the LIA?"

Ralph didn't say anything at first. He took a final puff on his cigar and tossed the stub over the railing into the water. "I don't know. You know how it is. Too many big chiefs. We underlings are split into so many factions.... The agency is supposed to know everything, right? But we can't even keep track of ourselves."

"You're the section chief, aren't you?"

"I'm not *the* section chief, I'm *a* section chief. We've got five section chiefs in Yerba City that I know of. And who knows who they actually report to. I've got no doubt at all that some of the people under my charge report every fuckin' move I make to someone else in the agency. You wanna know how I know this? Because I've got agents in the other sections reporting on *their* superiors to *me*! It's a big fuckin' can of worms." He let out a breath. "So in answer to your question, who knows? Leea might have eliminated her. But I have to ask the same question I asked you: why would someone from the LIA leave a stiff behind for anyone to stumble over? It seems more likely that someone left the body there for us to find. Anyway, I've got the body now, and my own people are looking at it. But anything they discover will find its way upstairs. You can fuckin' count on it."

I felt the tide, as high as I'd ever seen it, rolling through the pilings of the rickety old pier, a long, inexorable assault on the structure that would someday bring it crashing into the waters. "How did the papers find out about the body?"

"How do you think? I leaked it to them, of course. A controlled leak."

"Why'd you do that?"

"Ten-Inch. The agency has the police looking for him. I wanted him to know about it."

I frowned down at the nirumbee. "Why?"

"Because I don't want him to get caught. Not by the police, and not by the LIA. The only one I want to find Ten-Inch is me. Or you."

"Why?"

"Because somebody very high up in the LIA wants to question him about something. And I don't want them to."

"Question him? About what?"

Ralph peered up at me from inside his hood. "They want to ask him about the Eye of Taufa'tahi."

The rain was no longer falling, and the evening air, although cold and wet, had become remarkably calm. Ralph was still staring up at me, trying to read my face. Some people claimed they could detect lies by watching a person's eyes. According to the theory, the eyes of a right-handed person trying to access a memory would look off to their left. But if the eyes instead darted to the right, that person was about to lie. For a left-handed person, it was the opposite, so that a left-handed person who was about to lie would look to the left. I was right-handed. I let my eyes drift off to my left.

"The Eye of Taufa'tahi? Never heard of it," I lied.

## Chapter Eleven

The package I'd picked up at the Hawthorne those many months ago had been a rectangular cardboard box wrapped in plain brown paper with my name printed across the top in bold capital letters. I'd opened the package in my car. Inside the box I'd found a red gemstone the size and shape of an egg, with one end larger than the other, and a message for me written on a sheet of Hawthorne Hotel stationary. The message, written with a fountain pen in elegant calligraphy, was direct enough: "Mr. Southerland. The enclosed object is known as the Eye of Taufa'tahi. Without delay, place it in your mouth. Speak of it to no one." The short note was followed by an odd abstract symbol consisting of interlocking loops. It might have been a signature written in a script unfamiliar to me. Or it might have been some casual doodling.

After noting that the reverse side of the notepaper was blank, I read the message twice. I didn't have a chance to read it a third time, because the paper burst into a bright orange flame that vanished in an instant, leaving behind a pungent odor I couldn't identify: slightly bitter, but not unpleasant.

I didn't know what to make of it all. The Eye of Taufa'tahi? The name meant nothing to me. I made a mental note to do an online search once I got back to my office. I picked up the gem and examined it: red... precisely cut.... It looked valuable. I thought it might be a ruby, but any red gemstone would look like a ruby to me. Crawford would have been able to tell me what it was, but I had no idea if I'd ever see him again. As for putting it in my mouth, I dismissed the idea out of hand, and not just because the stone was large enough to gag me. I was about to return the gem to the box when I became aware of a faint vibration, along with the sensation of warmth, emanating from the stone. It felt somehow alive, and I knew that it was infused with an unearthly energy. At the same time, I caught the whiff of a feline odor and sensed the presence of Cougar in my mind. He didn't speak, but I felt a desire, almost like hunger, to taste the gemstone.

I resisted for a moment, but gave in. After all, if I couldn't trust my spirit animal... well, I wasn't actually sure I could trust Cougar. I certainly didn't understand who he was and exactly what kind of relationship we shared. But Cougar hadn't brought any harm to me yet, and he'd been useful on several occasions. I pulled the gemstone to my mouth and touched it with my tongue. Nothing happened. What the hell, I thought. Closing my eyes and bracing myself, I forced the gem into my mouth.

I felt... nothing. I probed the inside of my mouth with my tongue. It neither touched nor tasted anything. The gem simply wasn't there anymore.

"Hmph," I grunted, opening my eyes. The world didn't seem any different to me. I felt no trace of the magical forces I'd detected in the gemstone. Cougar was gone, too. It was as if I had passed the gem to my spirit animal, and he had run off with it. Maybe he was going to pawn it.

Back at the office, I'd searched online for the "Eye of Taufa'tahi" and discovered very little. I ran across references to underground cults among the Nihhonese Islanders centered on various unearthly spirits. The name "Taufa'tahi" or "Taufa" popped up several times in these references, but with few details. No mention was made of an eye, or an egg-shaped gem or artifact. When I'd finished my research, I was only sure of a few things. Taufa or Taufa'tahi was a powerful spirit of the sea who had been worshiped by the inhabitants of the South Nihhonese Islands before the advent of the Dragon Lords. Stories about him were contradictory, but they all agreed that he was a proud and paternalistic spirit who was protective of his people. Maybe even a bit over-protective on occasion. As with many pre-Dragon Lord ruling spirits, a conscious effort had been made to obliterate any knowledge of Taufa from historical records. This effort hadn't been completely successful: the memory of Taufa'tahi had been kept alive by Islanders in an unacknowledged subculture that the Dragon Lords could never quite suppress.

The Lords had been successful enough, though, I concluded. After two hours of uninterrupted and mostly fruitless research, I decided I'd had enough.

That night, I dreamed of a land of dark forests and sandy beaches touched by gentle ocean waves. A quarter moon surrounded by bright stars shone down from above, and swarms of fruit bats flitted through the night sky. Human figures appeared in the corners of my vision, only to disappear when I turned to get a better look at them. It occurred to me that I should have felt frustrated by these fleeting visions, but a numbness had spread through my brain, and I was overcome by a sense of peace and quiet.

*Later, when Holly asked me about the package, I told her there must have been a mix-up. The Hawthorne hadn't been holding anything for me to pick up.*

\*\*\*

"You're lying, Southerland," Ralph accused.

"Sure I am," I admitted. "But how did you know?"

"Because you're doing that eye thing in reverse to try to make me think you're telling the truth. But I know that you know how it's supposed to work, so I'm concluding the opposite of what your eyes are telling me." His mouth spread into a grin that exposed his pointed choppers. "Thing is, dimwit, that theory about eye movement isn't actually reliable enough to be useful. It's strictly amateur hour, and you really should know better."

"Really?" I said, surprised. "It doesn't work?"

Ralph pulled a hand out of his pocket and waved his palm in a "maybe yes, maybe no" motion. "Not much more than half the time. Sixty-forty at best."

"Huh. You don't say."

"Anyway, I'd already heard from the elf that he'd sent the Eye to you for safekeeping."

I gave the bastard some side eye, and he chuckled.

"I assume you've got it hidden away somewhere secure?" he asked me.

"Yeah. I swallowed it."

Ralph shook his head. "Very funny."

"Anyway," I said, getting us back on track. "What does any of this have to do with Ten-Inch?"

The smile left Ralph's face, and he pulled on his hood as if trying to bury his face farther within. "There are people in the agency, higher-ups, who suspect Ten-Inch got his hands on the Eye. That unregistered nymph we found.... We'd heard she infiltrated the settlement a few weeks ago. Maybe a few months ago. Anyway, word came down that she was searching for a special enchanted object: the Eye of Taufa'tahi, a sacred doohickey from the Southern Nihhonese Islands. The Eye predates the Dragon Lords, and it supposedly has some real heavy duty clout."

I frowned at the nirumbee. "What do you mean?"

"Hell if I know. Some people think the Eye was destroyed a long time ago. Or that it's just a legend and never existed at all. But others say it's an actual artifact, a gem of some kind, that's been loaded with lethal magical properties."

"What's it supposed to do, turn you into a toad?"

"From what I hear, it summons sea monsters and causes deadly floods."

I grunted. "Hunh. A flood doesn't sound like something we need at the moment."

Ralph shrugged. "Yeah, something like that would be handier during a drought. But they say the Eye can cause floods big enough to wash away the South Sea Islands."

I considered Ralph's story. "So if this adaro was looking for the Eye, what makes the LIA think Ten-Inch has it?"

Ralph removed a hand from his pocket and reached up to scratch his chin. "Word is Ten-Inch was working with her. They'd made some sort of deal. The old gang boss was on the outs, and I guess he thought a legendary enchanted artifact would help him get back in."

I looked at Ralph, searching for his eyes within the depths of his hood. "What do you mean he was on the outs?"

"You hadn't heard? The Hatfields are trying to take control of the gangs in the adaro settlement."

"The Hatfields? What for?"

"For the dough, of course. That's why the Hatfields do anything. The settlement is a huge source for drugs and whores. Weapons, too."

"Lord's flaming balls." I let out a slow breath, which condensed into a cloud of fog and drifted away from me. "The elf is working with the Hatfields, isn't he?"

The nirumbee was turned a little away from me, and I couldn't see his face inside his hood, but I could hear a scowl in his voice. "The Hatfields have given some of their drug labs over to the elf, and they're providing the elf with workers and security for his project. But this business in the settlement has nothing to do with that."

"Let me guess. Ten-Inch doesn't like the idea of taking on a corporate sponsor."

Ralph stared out over the ocean to the west, where the setting sun was visible only as a pale glow in the low-lying layer of storm clouds. "The way I hear it, Ten-Inch is dead set against selling out to the Syndicate, and they've been threatening to get rid of him if he doesn't. Maybe even if he does. Did you hear the gang's old headquarters got burned down?"

"The Medusa. I saw what's left of the place yesterday morning."

"It looks like the Hatfields were trying to intimidate the Northsiders. Trying to turn them against their leader. They're set up in a new place now, some dive in the settlement." Ralph let out a snort. "Not much of an improvement from what I hear."

I tried to process what I'd heard so far. "So this adaro comes out of the Nihhonese looking for the Eye of Taufa'tahi. She meets Ten-Inch, who's getting strong-armed by the Hatfields, and the two of them come to an arrangement. And now the adaro is dead—murdered—and Ten-Inch is in the wind. Could Ten-Inch have killed her?"

Ralph hesitated, then nodded. "It's possible. I saw the body. Someone gave her a good working over before she died." The nirumbee looked up at me. "Also, our medical examiner found semen in her."

"Shit," I breathed. "She was raped?"

"The bruises and defensive wounds suggest that's the case. Either that, or she'd had some very rough consensual sex. But she was an adaro. Men lose their minds around those nymphs. My money's on rape."

I shook my head. "But that means you know who did it, right? Or you will as soon as the DNA reports on the semen come back?"

Ralph crossed his arms. "The medical examiner sent samples to the lab by courier. The samples never got there."

I frowned. "What do you mean?"

Ralph sighed. "They were intercepted by someone from... upstairs. By people who don't want me in the loop."

My shoulders slumped as I let out a breath through my nose. "Lord's flaming balls."

"Exactly."

I took a little time to mull this information over in my mind. "But you think Ten-Inch did this?"

The nirumbee's head shook. "I didn't say that. I just said it was possible. Maybe he and the nymph had a falling out. But you know Ten-Inch better than I do. Would he put his fists on a woman? Would he rape her?"

I considered the possibilities. What did I really know about Ten-Inch? "He might rough up a woman if he thought the circumstances called for it. But rape?" I shrugged. "I don't know. I don't see it. We weren't exactly buddies, and I didn't spend a lot of time with him. Still, I think I understood him a little. Who he was, and all that. Beating up a woman isn't something he would have done for no good reason. The Ten-Inch I remember was a legitimate tough guy, a warrior. He didn't have to rough up a woman to prove to himself or anyone else what a big man he was. He was also a man with a high degree of self-control. I can't see him as a rapist. A killer, yes. A rapist? That would surprise me. But that was three years ago. He wasn't exactly a model citizen. He might not be entirely sane. The war.... We all leave a piece of our sanity behind when we come home. Some more than others." I shook my head. "I don't know what he's been going through since I last saw him. He wasn't stable then. I don't know what kind of man he might be today."

Ralph didn't respond, and I looked down at him. "What do *you* know about him? Have you ever run into him?"

Ralph shook his head. "We've never met face to face. I've read the reports on him that the agency has compiled. He's a decorated veteran of the war in the Borderland. He was an outlaw gang boss with a reputation for violence and extreme cruelty. I know a lot *about* him. But I don't *know* him at all."

I chuckled. "Funny. If the two of you ever met, I have a feeling you'd understand each other just fine." I remembered something Ralph had said earlier. "Why don't you want the LIA to question Ten-Inch about the Eye?"

Ralph's hood slid back a few inches as he looked up at me, and I got a good look at the determined expression on his face. "The elf sent the Eye to you because he doesn't want anyone, least of all the LIA, knowing about it. He's got his reasons. If Ten-Inch has any information about the dingus, I want to find him before the agency has a chance to question him."

I peered inside the nirumbee's hood to search for his eyes, two dark dots completely surrounded by white. "And if you find him?"

"Then I'll find out if he knows anything about the Eye."

"And if he does?"

Ralph's expression never changed. "If he knows anything about the Eye that the LIA would find useful, I'll probably have to kill him."

"And you want me to help you find him?"

"Yep."

"So you can kill him?"

"If necessary."

"Seems a little extreme to me," I said.

"If the agency gets their hands on the Eye, you'll find out what extreme really means. Can you imagine the LIA with the power to cause major floods? Or summon sea monsters? Can you imagine Lord Ketz with that kind of power?"

"He can't do that already?" I asked. "They say he can do just about anything."

"Don't believe the propaganda. He's not all-powerful."

"Sure. He's been ruling for six thousand years because he's a pussycat. Everyone thinks he's adorable."

That got a chuckle out of Ralph. "Let's see about finding Ten-Inch."

I held up a hand, palm out. "Not so fast. If you want me to find Ten-Inch for you, you're going to have to hire me."

Ralph's head whipped around so fast I thought he'd get whiplash. "What?!"

"Standard rates plus expenses. I'll email you a contract for your signature."

"Have you lost your fucking mind?"

"I'm a professional. If you want my services, you'll have to pay for them, same as everyone else."

Ralph took a step in my direction. "You're already looking for him! Alkwat's balls! Why should I pay you to do something you're gonna do anyway?"

"Sure, I'm gonna look for him. But if you want me to tell you where he is when I find him, you'll have to hire me."

"Bullshit!"

I shrugged. "You can always get the information from your buddies in the LIA. Oh, wait a minute. They've decided to leave you out of the loop."

"Don't get cute, Southerland. I'm an agent for the elf, and you owe the elf."

"Fuck the elf. And fuck you, too, Ralph for playing that card. So maybe I owe the elf a debt. Maybe he's saved my life a time or two. But I'm tired of being his errand boy. If he wants something from me, let him come talk to me man-to-man and tell me what he wants and why he wants it. Then we can deal. And if I don't like the job, I'll tell him where he can shove it."

"It doesn't work that way, Southerland. He's the elf!" Ralph hissed at me. "He's a seven-thousand-year-old force of nature. He can crush you with a thought and drink your blood when he's done."

"Yeah? Well if he's so fuckin' tough, he can do his own dirty work. Next time you talk to him, tell him to find Ten-Inch himself."

Ralph took a long breath. When he spoke again, his voice was calm and reasonable. "Southerland. You've got to look at the big picture. The elves are trying to free the world from the rule of the Dragon Lords."

"That so? Why should I care? I've got nothing against the Dragon Lords. Who are the elves going to put in their place? Themselves? What makes anyone think we'd be better off under elvish rule? A boss is a fuckin' boss. Seen one, seen them all. Better the ones we know than the ones bent on replacing them."

"Now you're just being stubborn. Whether you like it or not, we're in the middle of a power struggle between the Dragon Lords and the elves. In a confrontation like that, no one gets to be neutral. At some point, you're going to have to pick a side."

"I've got a side. It's called 'my side,' and I like it just fine. I'm apolitical, which means I work for the dough, not out of belief in a cause."

"Be reasonable, Southerland. What's the problem here? Is it because I said I might have to kill your buddy? It probably won't even come to that. Only if it's what's best for all of us. But maybe we can make a deal. If you think the best course of action is to let Ten-Inch live, I'm willing to listen."

"Are you willing to pay my rates?"

"Alkwat's flaming pecker!" Ralph started to say something more, but stopped. Finally, his shoulders slumped. "Fuck me. Fuck me sideways." He sighed. "Okay. But no paper trail. Strictly a handshake agreement. And don't try to tell me I'm not fuckin' good for it, either! I'm a man of my word. Deal?"

I met his eyes in the depths of his hood and held them for a few seconds. "You don't kill him unless I say it's okay."

Ralph stared back at me for another moment before nodding. "I can live with that," he said, and held out an oversized callused hand.

I extended my own hand. "Deal."

The diminutive nirumbee warrior gripped my hand just tight enough to show me he could crush it like a grape if he felt like it. "You're a stubborn fuck, Southerland. But I'll figure out a way to get the agency to reimburse me. It will take some creative paperwork, but I think I'll be able to manage it. And to show my good faith, I'm going to give you a retainer." He released his grip and stepped toward the end of the pier. "Not cash. Instead, I'm going to give you some help finding Ten-Inch."

"What kind of help?" I asked.

In response, Ralph bounded cat-like to the top of the rain-soaked rail with one leap so that he was peering out at the Nihhonese Ocean. Putting two fingers to his mouth, he let out a piercing whistle.

In the next instant, a towering funnel of water shot out of the ocean and splashed over the railing. I took several steps back to keep from getting washed over the edge of the pier, but still managed to get drenched by the deluge. I wiped the salt water off my face with the soaked sleeve of my raincoat until my eyes were clear. When I could see again, I stared up at the figure towering over me. Nearly as tall as a troll, but broader in the shoulders and chest, his dank head of golden hair hanging past his shoulders, dark blue eyes, gills in the sides of his neck, massively muscled from head to toe, wearing nothing but the ocean water dripping from his bronze skin and the silvery scales that covered his legs and lower abdomen, was a young male adaro.

The adaro's lips stretched into a wide smile as he stared down at me. "Hello, Dickhead. You're *gruuub-grurr* soaked!"

## Chapter Twelve

"Kraken?" I looked up at the hulking sea creature.

"That's my name. Don't wear it out."

I shook my head. The young adaro was still more brawn than brain. I looked him over. He'd grown since I'd last seen him. Not so much taller, but more defined physically. He'd been a developing adolescent. He seemed more like a completed adult now. "Long time no see, kid," I told him.

The smile on Kraken's face widened. "You and me are going to go find Ten-Inch."

Ralph was back on the platform standing opposite Kraken and me. We were an interesting trio. The top of the nirumbee's head barely cleared my knees. Without tilting my head, my eyes were level with the center of the adaro's chest. The adaro could have stepped on the nirumbee's head without breaking stride.

I shot a glance at Ralph before looking up at the adaro. "Do you know where he is?"

Kraken shook his head. The mane of wet blond hair surrounding his broad face made me think of a lion on a rainy day. "We're going to make the Northsiders tell us where he is."

"Sure we are." I turned back to Ralph. I was going to wrench my neck trying to talk to both of them at once, so I settled on the nirumbee. "Lord's flaming balls. Is this your plan? I take this heavy piece of ordinance into gang headquarters and rough up some hoods until they talk? I'm adding hazard pay to our deal."

Ralph was as drenched as I was, and he'd let his wet hood fall back to reveal his oversized bulb of a head, with its arched eyebrows and pug nose. "I figured you could good-cop-bad-cop 'em. You can be the good cop. The kid can be your out-of-control enforcer."

I looked up at Kraken. "You want to take on an entire street gang?"

The adaro's smile vanished. "We're going to find the *borrgloop-borrbl* who killed Kanoa. She was a *kwuurlplup*."

"A what?" I turned to Ralph. "Kanoa? Is that...."

Ralph nodded. "The nymph from the alley. That's right. Look, Southerland. I'm not free to do everything I need to do. If someone from the LIA whacked her, then I have to watch my ass. I need an independent out there doing the legwork. You're already looking for the gangster anyway, right?" He indicated Kraken with his chin. "We just want to help you."

"We?"

"Me, Kraken, and the elf."

I frowned. "Because the elf doesn't want the Eye falling into the hands of the LIA?"

Ralph's face grew hard. "That's right. And he doesn't want information that could lead to the whereabouts of the Eye dropping into the Dragon Lord's scaly lap, either. You may not care for the elf's 'cause,' as you put it. But do you really think your life will improve if Lord Ketz gets his claws on a device that can sink islands?"

I turned back to Kraken, my eyes lingering on his right hand, which was missing a finger. I remembered the troll who had bitten it off. I lifted my gaze and looked the adaro buck in the eyes. "What's in this for you, kid? Why do you want to find Ten-Inch?"

The big adaro's face tightened. "I want to know what happened to Kanoa. She was a *kwuurlplup*. Ten-Inch will tell me."

"A what?"

Kraken opened his mouth, hesitated, and shook his head. "I don't know your word."

I let out a breath. "All right, forget that for now."

Kraken's face brightened. "Ten-Inch can tell you when we find him."

I frowned. "I don't know, kid. You may be a big deal in the ocean, but you're literally out of your element here on land. Maybe I should do this on my own."

Kraken's lips stretched into an unsteady smile. "You and me are going to find Ten-Inch. He's going to tell me what happened to Kanoa."

I turned to Ralph and found him glaring at me, teeth still bared. "Take Kraken, Southerland. Don't be a sap. He can get you into the Northsiders' new hangout. That's your best bet for finding their missing boss. You'll never get in there on your own."

Kraken began to pace. "Let's go find Ten-Inch. We'll make the Northsiders tell us where he is."

I kept my eyes on Ralph. He'd planned this from the beginning, and I knew he wasn't going to let me work on my own. "All right, swell. You want to be useful? Do something to keep the cops out of my way. Some hard numbers from the Placid Point clubhouse are on my ass. It won't do either of us any good if they find Ten-Inch first and set him up for the LIA."

Ralph opened his mouth to respond, but Kraken cut him off. "The cops are looking for Ten-Inch? Why?"

I looked up at the earnest face of Kraken. "They think he might have killed Kanoa."

Kraken glared down at me. "Ten-Inch didn't kill Kanoa. The cops are *gruuub-grurr* stupid!"

"Why do you say that?"

Kraken snorted, producing an odd noise that sounded like a sneezing trumpet, and water sprayed from his nose and gills. "Ten-Inch was helping Kanoa. He was protecting her. He was her friend!"

I shook my head. "If he was protecting her on the night she died, he might be harder to find than I'd hoped."

Kraken started to say something, but he stopped short as a look of confusion swept over his face.

It was Ralph who spoke. "He was *supposed* to be protecting her. Whoever killed Kanoa might have killed Ten-Inch, too."

Kraken's eyes widened. "Ten-Inch is dead?"

"He's missing," I said. "But I don't think he's dead."

Ralph looked up at me. "Why not?"

"Because I think the son of a bitch stole my hubcaps."

I told Ralph about the hubcaps, and about how one of them had turned up on my doorstep. Kraken nodded along, but the look of confusion never left his face. He shrugged when I told him about KISIKISI. Finally, the adaro asked, "What did you say Ten-Inch stole?"

I suppressed an eye-roll. "My hubcaps." When Kraken's questioning gaze remained unchanged, I added, "Those are the metal coverings on the tires of a car. You remember my car, don't you?"

Illumination came to Kraken, and his face was lit up by his smile. "The big shiny one? It's cool, man, cool! You let me sit inside it when we went to Medusa's."

That reminded me of my most recent visit to the old dive. "Right, Medusa's. Do you know what happened to it?"

Kraken nodded. "It burned down. The Northsiders don't meet there no more. That's why we have to go into the settlement."

"Kraken, you used to hang out with the Northsiders. Have you ever been to their new place?" I asked him.

Kraken's gaze fell to his feet. "No. I don't hang out with them anymore. Not since Mila died. Anyway, I don't like them now. They make adaro women do bad things."

I cast a glance at Ralph before turning back to Kraken. "I heard that the Northsiders run an adaro prostitution racket."

Kraken nodded. His eyes met mine, and they hardened. "I'm going to make them stop. It's not right."

I turned back to Ralph. "Was this Kanoa a prostitute?"

Ralph scratched at his chin with his taloned fingers. "I don't know for sure, but I don't think so."

Kraken was done with talking. "Come on, Dickhead! Let's go make the Northsiders tell us where Ten-Inch is. And then Ten-Inch can tell us who killed Kanoa."

I looked at Ralph and let out a breath. I looked back up at Kraken. I didn't think I could spend the rest of the night jerking my head back and forth between them. "Okay, big guy. You and me. Let's go pay us a little social call on the Northsiders. I'm sure they'll be thrilled to see us."

*\*\**

"Cool!" Kraken exclaimed.

Spotting the beastmobile in the otherwise deserted parking lot, he'd run up to it and embraced its hood like he was greeting a long-lost lover. Looking back at me, he shouted, "Come on! Let's go!"

I looked him up and down, watching seawater drain from his nude body. "Don't you have any clothes?" I asked him.

His only response was to run to the passenger door and try the handle, which was locked. Looking back at me again, he waved me toward the car. "Come on!"

I sighed, resigning myself to a soaked car seat and carpeting.

Inside the car, Kraken gawked at the lights on the dash with wide eyes and an open mouth. He reached out to poke a finger at each display, as if touching them would fill him with some sort of secret revelation. He turned to the seat itself, running his hands over the upholstery with reverence, as if he had never touched leather. He turned again to watch the world speed by out the windows.

"Make it go faster!" he pleaded.

"Sorry, pal. We've got speed limits."

Kraken began pounding the dash with his heavy hands. "Faster!" he demanded.

I shot him a glance, intending to tell him to relax, when I was struck by a wave of mild nausea as the darkness outside my windshield suddenly began to swirl and shimmer. "What th'fuck!" I exclaimed, slamming my foot on the brake.

The car behind me screeched to a stop, and the driver leaned on his horn.

Kraken turned to me, his eyes wide. "Why—"

Whatever question Kraken was about to ask me was cut off by the crash of an object falling onto the hood of the beastmobile. Kraken and I both raised our arms reflexively, and I might have shouted something incoherent. I blinked once and noted that the distortion I'd seen in the night air had ceased. I also saw what had fallen onto my car.

Kraken was still staring at me. "What happened?" He turned to peer through the windshield. "Are we under attack?"

Instead of answering, I switched off the beastmobile's ignition and, after taking a second to regain my composure, stepped outside the car. When I climbed back in, I was holding the metal disk I'd retrieved from the hood. I held it out for Kraken to see.

The adaro's eyes narrowed as he studied it. "Is that a... a.... What did you call it again?"

"It's a hubcap," I told him. "It's one of the hubcaps that Ten-Inch took off my car."

"Is Ten-Inch out there?" Kraken reached for his door handle, but I stopped him.

"I don't think so," I told him. I was fairly sure the hubcap had dropped or been thrown through a portal from somewhere far away. The question was, "Why?" I ran my fingertips over the smooth curve of the hub.

"There's a message written on the surface," I said.

Kraken's eyes narrowed. "Are you sure? I don't see anything, and I can see a lot better in the dark than a human can, even when I'm out of the water."

"I can feel it etched into the surface." In truth, the scratches were faint, and the message would have been invisible in the darkness for most people, but my heightened awareness working through my senses of touch and sight allowed me to decipher the short message that had been lightly imprinted onto the metal surface.

"What does it say?"

I frowned. "I'm not sure. LEITI LA'AKA?" I pronounced all of the letters. "I don't know what that means."

Kraken smiled. "It's a name."

I turned to look at him. "Anyone you know?"

The adaro shook his head. "I don't know her."

"She's a woman?"

Kraken's smile widened. "She is now. But she was a boy when she was born. That's what the Leiti part of her name means. But I don't know Leiti La'aka."

"So she's a transgender?"

"I don't know that word. Does it mean a girl who was born a boy?"

"Close enough."

"Then she's a transgender. The Leitis live on the islands. They are..." He faltered. "What's your word? People who control spirits?"

"Elementalists?"

Kraken shook his head. "No. All adaros control *gruurbluurbls*, what you call elementals of the water. Leitis control... different spirits. Spirits that come from... from here. This world. But deep inside it." He waved an arm to encompass the whole of his surroundings. "They live in things. Plants, trees, animals, people, rocks, buildings, storms.... Everything," he finished.

"Hmm. Is she an adaro?"

Kraken let loose with one of his trumpeting snorts, spraying fishy-smelling water throughout the front seat of the car. "Humans can change their.... How do you say it? Whether they want to be a man or a woman?"

"Never mind," I said.

Kraken shrugged. "Such a change is not possible amongst the adaros. Adaro men and women are very different, more different than human men and women. Male adaros are a lot larger and stronger than female adaros. But female adaros can breathe outside the water as well as they can in the water. We men get weak when we're out of the water for too long. Adaro men can swim deeper than women." He shot me a sly smile. "That's how we get away from them. We hold our meetings in the deeps where women can't interfere." He turned to stare into the night outside the car. "We are different in other ways, too. An adaro man could never become a woman, even if he wanted to. It's impossible."

I studied the hubcap, feeling every part of it to see if I could discover any other messages. "I don't think it was an accident that this was sent to me here. We were headed for the adaro settlement. Maybe that's where we'll find this Leiti La'aka."

Kraken's mouth opened, and his eyes narrowed. It was the expression that fell on his face whenever he was attempting deep thought, something that never came naturally to the big fellow. After a few moments, he blinked and asked, "Do you think she knows where Ten-Inch is?"

"I don't know. Maybe. Let's find her and ask."

Kraken's eyes narrowed again. "How will we find her?"

"I'm an investigator. Leave it to me. First things first, though. I need you to show me where the Northsiders meet."

The adaro's face lit up. "I can do that. They meet in a bar, like Medusa's, only not as cool."

"You've been there?"

Kraken's eyes fell. "Not inside. I've seen it from the outside. I don't like it. It's not a cool place. Not like Medusa's."

Medusa's was cool? The Medusa's I remembered would have needed a drastic upgrade to qualify as a dump. "What's the new place called?"

Kraken sounded the words out with care: "The Dripping Bucket."

"Sounds awful," I said.

Kraken scowled. "I don't like it. It's a bad place."

## Chapter Thirteen

Kraken could have been describing the whole adaro settlement, especially everything south of Fremont Street, away from the ocean. A branch of the Tolanican Navy, working under the authority of the Bureau of Adaro Affairs, registered the female adaros and processed them into the community. Initially, the settlement had provided modest, but adequate housing, along with food, water, power, and waste management services, all established by the Tolanican Navy and policed by the Navy Master-at-Arms, or MAs. Over time, however, the number of adaro women herded into the settlement had overwhelmed the existing infrastructure, and the Tolanican government had found better things for the Navy to do than expand and improve it. As the settlement inevitably degenerated into an overcrowded inner city, the Navy's response had been to contain the problem, rather than fix it.

The settlement might have been a blight on the city's landscape, but it was a vital center of local trade, especially the kinds of transactions most often executed under the cover of darkness. As we rolled down Fremont Street into the settlement on this Friday night, traffic was stop-and-go in all four lanes, and Kraken was growing increasingly impatient with our slow progress.

"Go around these assholes!" he demanded.

"I can't go around them. The road's jammed."

"Then get off the road!"

"I can't get off the road without driving through those houses." The south side of the settlement had been rapidly developing into a slum over the past several years. I pointed at the constructions lining Fremont Street to my right, in truth little more than hastily thrown-together slabs of plywood, strips of sheet metal, and hanging cloth, which served as dwelling spaces for the settlement's inhabitants. In some places they were crowded so close to the street that Kraken couldn't have opened the passenger door of the beastmobile without bumping it into the side of one of the makeshift structures.

Kraken's nose wrinkled in disgust. "Knock them down. They're ugly. Our women shouldn't be forced to live in those places. They belong in the ocean with us men."

"Maybe so, pal. But you know how it works." He did, and he didn't like it. Adaro women were allowed to enter the water in a secure patrolled cove just outside the settlement, but they were prevented from traveling into the open sea by an elaborate underwater series of walls and nets. BAA and naval officials made it clear that any tattooed female adaros caught in the waters outside the cove were subject to execution on the spot. "Besides," I pointed out, "not all of the people living here are adaros."

Kraken nodded, aware that the adaro women in the settlement shared the space with humans and others who either didn't have the means or were too socially maladjusted to live in other parts of the city. Many of these inhabitants were hopheads who found it convenient to live in close proximity to the unrestrained trade of cheap drugs in the settlement. Many were crooks, deadbeats, street scum, or just plain misfits seeking refuge in the chaos of the slums. Way too many veterans of the Dragon Lord's wars, their brains scrambled or haunted by the memories of what they had endured, were searching for peace of mind in those ramshackle shelters. Many of their neighbors were otherwise respectable working citizens who chose to save a bunch of dough by living in squalor rather than paying the high rents charged by legitimate landlords and property management firms. Officially, the settlement was a subdivision within the District of Placid Point, clearly outlined on the maps issued by the Yerba City Planning Commission. In reality, the adaro settlement was its own little universe, separated from the rest of the city, as well as from the Realm of Tolanica itself, by unseen boundaries stronger than concrete walls and barbed wire. When outsiders crossed into the settlement, they left the laws and social conventions of the mainstream world behind, sometimes just long enough for an illicit transaction, or for a night or two of decadent thrill-seeking, other times in search of a new beginning to a life that had taken a wrong turn.

Kraken turned to me, eyes blazing. He let loose a string of burbling noises from his native language before transitioning into what he referred to as "human." "Fuck this! Let's walk."

"I can't just abandon the car. Hold your horses, big man. How far do we need to go to get to The Dripping Bucket?"

"We'll be there soon if we run."

That was only marginally helpful. "You're a naked adaro buck," I pointed out. "The MAs will shoot you on sight if they catch you in the open."

"Let them try."

"Just sit back and tell me how to get there."

"It's that way." Kraken pointed past the front of the car and slightly off to the right.

Great, I thought. The Dripping Bucket was in the slum. "Fine. I'll turn at the next light. Traffic should be lighter when we're off the main road."

Kraken crossed his arms and slumped back into his seat, a giant prince of the ocean depths in full pout mode. I bit back on a patronizing smile and kept my eye on the road.

Five minutes later, I turned right off Fremont onto an unlined road that continued veering to the right into the ramshackle dwellings until I found myself traveling deeper into the slum in a direction exactly opposite to where I wanted to go.

"You're going the wrong way!" Kraken informed me, unnecessarily.

"Not a problem. I'll take the next left."

"You need to go that way," Kraken told me a few minutes later, pointing to the north. At least I thought he was pointing north. Which meant I was now heading east. Or eastward. Truth was, I was starting to lose my sense of direction.

I took the next left, but it wasn't left enough. "That way! That way!" Kraken was pointing in a direction no road seemed to want to go.

"I'm working on it," I told him.

I saw a left turn up ahead, but when I got to where I thought I'd seen it, I found that it was actually a little farther ahead.

Kraken shifted in his seat and looked back over his shoulder. "Not this way," he shouted, exasperated. "Wait. I thought I saw a turn back there." Then, "No, I guess not."

"I'll take the next left," I told him. "That will get us back in the direction we want to go."

But we didn't pass any left turns, and the road I was on was veering to the right. "Up there," I told Kraken.

Kraken stared out the window. "Where?"

"Just ahead. I'll turn there."

But when I reached the intersection I'd seen coming up, I saw that the road only continued straight or to the right. Or did it? When I blinked and looked back again, a left turn seemed to appear out of nowhere. Squealing the tires, I cut across the oncoming traffic and turned into the road I'd spotted.

Kraken made a noise that sounded like something between a gasp and a choke. "Dude!" he sputtered. I glanced at the adaro, his confused expression back on his face. He shrugged. "I don't know how you did that."

I looked ahead at the road and swore. It was veering off to the right, taking me further in the wrong direction toward the southern part of the settlement away from the ocean. I became aware of a faint high-pitched buzz in the back of my head, and I was having trouble concentrating. Something otherworldly had descended in the night like a mist, and the road kept twisting in ways I wasn't expecting. "This place is insane," I muttered. "It's a fucking maze."

Ten minutes later I was regretting having ever turned off Fremont. I was hopelessly lost, and Kraken, glowering out the side window, was pointedly refusing to speak to me, or to even acknowledge my existence. The street I was on was so narrow I found myself snaking through unlit shacks lining the avenue no more than two yards from either side of the beastmobile. I knew I was somewhere in the slums that dominated the southern fringes of the settlement, and I strongly suspected I'd been guided there by unnatural forces. I stopped the car and stared at Kraken, waiting for him to turn around.

He finally did, glaring at me with hooded eyes.

"Which way to the bar?" I asked him.

He continued to glare. I pointed to my left, more or less at random. "That way?"

"I. Don't. Know." Kraken sighed. "I don't know. The ocean is that way." He pointed to the back of the car. "I don't know where The Dripping Bucket is from here."

I didn't either, but I knew that Fremont was between our current position and the shore. Once I got back on Fremont, I was sure that we would be able to find The Dripping Bucket, even if I'd have to endure bumper-to-bumper traffic in the company of an impatient adaro buck in order to get there. "We need to go back the other way. But I need to find a place to turn around." I eased the beastmobile ahead.

I'd advanced no more than fifty yards when I reached a point too narrow for the oversized vehicle to continue going forward. I shifted into reverse and turned to look out the back window. Dark figures in darker jackets and headbands were dragging a length of barbed wire into the street behind my car. I turned to look ahead of me. A dozen hoods in headbands emerged from the shacks on either side of the road and stood in the glare of my headlights. Kraken and I were surrounded.

Kraken let loose with a string of adaro burble and started to open the door.

I put a restraining hand on his arm. "Stay put. Let me handle this."

The massive beastmobile was a weapon in itself, and under the circumstances I felt that staying inside was the best option for both of us. Kraken had other ideas, however. The adaro shrugged my hand off his arm and slid out of the car. I sighed in resignation. Best to present a united front, I thought. I switched off the engine, opened my own door, and stepped out to face the music.

Without turning to look, I knew I stood in the midst of eighteen members of a street gang. The color of the headbands and the emblems on the jackets told me I'd been waylaid by the Claymore Cartel, a well-known citywide gang with branches throughout the Province of Caychan. I wondered what I'd wandered into. Eighteen of them seemed to be too many for a simple robbery.

"Nice automobile, bitch." The voice came from the center of the group in front of the beastmobile. "I've seen it before, I think."

I peered at the source of the voice and found myself looking at a dark-haired hood with purple wings tattooed on his face below the eyes. I recognized those tats.

"Jaguar? Is that you?" When I'd last run into the Placid Point division of the Claymore Cartel, Jaguar had been leading them.

The hood smiled. "You remember me, bitch. I'm fuckin' flattered."

"You put a bullet in my leg. I'm not likely to forget that."

"Do you remember everyone who's taken a shot at you, Southerland?"

"Only the ones who didn't miss."

Jaguar's smile looked to me like genuine amusement. He turned to regard the adaro buck on the other side of the car. "And you must be Kraken. We've never met, but I've heard a lot about you, brudda."

Kraken's only response was to roll his head from side to side to loosen his neck and shoulder muscles. The popping as bones slid into place was ominous, and the atmosphere in the street grew thick with tension.

The last thing I wanted was a fight. Even with a legendary sea devil on my side, I wasn't happy with the odds while we were on land. Talking seemed like a better option to me under the circumstances, so I decided to give it a try. "What's this about, Jaguar? A robbery? You can't have the car."

"How are you going to stop us, bitch? We've got enough firepower to take down the big man, and you don't look like you'll be much of a problem."

I held my arms out from my side. "We don't need to fight. I'm unarmed. So is Kraken, but I guess you can see that for yourself."

Jaguar stared across at Kraken's midsection and chuckled. "Unarmed? I don't fuckin' know about that. That fuckin' rod of his looks like a deadly weapon to me!" Some of the others let out chortling laughs of their own, and someone whistled, as if astonished.

A gust of wind blew cold rain up the street from behind me. "It's freezing out here, Jaguar. Tell me what you want so we can do whatever it is we're going to do."

Jaguar's smile disappeared, and the others looked in his direction to see how he was going to play things. "You're intruding on Claymore territory, brudda. Now, what that normally means is that we take a payment from you as a toll. Maybe we even take this fuckin' military assault vehicle, if that's what we decide we want from you. And we fuck you up good if you decide to give us a fuckin' hassle." He turned to Kraken. "We could get big money by turning the adaro over to the Navy. I hear they want to cut you up and find out what you're made of." He turned back to me and waved a hand in dismissal. "But we're not about that. And anyway, you're here by invitation."

I frowned. "By invitation? What does that mean?"

Jaguar's smile returned. He liked to smile. It was an easy smile, the smile of a man in charge. He held out his arms to indicate the other members of the Cartel. "We're the welcoming committee, brudda. We're here to make sure you find the right house."

I glanced at Kraken and watched his face twist into its default confused expression. I was as discombobulated as he was. I turned back to Jaguar. "We weren't looking for a house. We were trying to get to a bar. This settlement is a damned maze. I must have made a wrong turn." I pointed back behind me. "Fremont is that way, right? That's where I'm going as soon as I get my car turned around."

Jaguar shook his head. "No bars for you tonight, brudda, but you might have a drink waiting for you inside. We've been expecting you. The Leiti told us you were coming. She's waiting for you, too. Both of you."

"The Leiti?"

"Leiti La'aka. My boys will escort you to her place. Follow me."

The back of my neck tingled at the mention of Leiti La'aka. "What about the car?" I asked.

"Don't worry about the car, brudda. Come on." He started off toward his left.

"It will be safe?"

"Safe? Sure, sure. Safer than fuck. Don't worry. We'll treat it real good. Won't we, boys?" He shared amused glances with the other members of his gang as he passed by them. Some of the hoods chuckled, and I heard a "Fuck yeah!" from somewhere behind me.

I didn't move. "I'll bet you will. Especially since I've got my own security system."

Jaguar stopped walking. "Th'fuck you sayin'!"

I called up a sigil in my mind, and within seconds the wind on the street began to gust. A roar sounded in the distance, and it increased in volume as a funnel of distortion, about a dozen feet in length and darker than the night, descended rapidly from above until it halted a few feet above the roof of the beastmobile, whirling like a miniature tornado. Dirt and debris shot through the street in all directions, and the hoods all stepped back in amazement. Even Kraken drew back a pace, his eyes wide as saucers. A few of the dimmer hoods produced gats. Right. Like a little flying lead would set things right.

I leaned against my car, holding on to my hat. "Hello, Badass."

A howling moan deeper than midnight emerged from the fiercely spinning twister. "Hello, Alex. How may I serve you?"

I patted the roof of the beastmobile. "If anyone but me gets close enough to this car to touch it, hurt them. Understand?"

"This one understands."

Turning to Jaguar, I said, "All right, let's go."

The hoods all gave the beastmobile a wide berth as we followed Jaguar off the street.

## Chapter Fourteen

Our escort led Kraken and me away from the street into a labyrinth of hastily erected structures ranging in size and quality from a sturdy three-story multi-unit building that wouldn't have been out of place in some of the working-class districts of the city, to patched-up shacks and lean-tos that didn't look like they would survive another strong rainstorm. A few appeared to have collapsed during the most recent one. The pungent fragrance of pepper and other spices competed with the putrid stench of rotting fish and the fetid odor of old garbage, raw sewage, and too many unwashed bodies. As we snaked our way through the muddy unpaved alleyways of the slum city, feral eyes peered at us through windows, some covered with glass, plastic, or cloth, some nothing more than holes in the walls. Most of the eyes were human, I noted. Many were adaro, and the remaining few belonged to dwarfs, gnomes, and even an occasional troll. No one came out of their dwellings to confront the Cartel hoods or the giant adaro buck, though I suspected the situation would have been far different had I been alone.

It didn't take long for Kraken to show signs of frustration. "How much longer?" he muttered to no one in particular. I caught him scowling at a pair of furtive eyes before they blinked away behind a crack in the wall of a wooden shed.

"What's the matter, Kraken?" Jaguar aimed a mocking smile at the big adaro. "This part of town a little rough for you?"

In response, Kraken aimed a barefooted kick at a corrugated metal wall that threatened to bring the makeshift shelter tumbling into the mud. A stifled feminine scream came from within the hut, but was immediately cut off.

"Hey, asshole!" Jaguar stepped up to Kraken until he was standing inches in front of the adaro, head to chest. "People live in these shacks! You might not like it, but these shacks are people's homes." The gang boss put his finger in the big adaro's chest. "You're a guest in this neighborhood tonight. Act like one!"

I had to admit that I felt something like admiration for Jaguar at that moment. Kraken wasn't the most even-tempered creature around, and he had the strength to crush the gangster like a bug, but that didn't stop Jaguar from standing up to the bigger man on behalf of people who were undoubtedly unable to defend themselves.

"This is a bad place," Kraken muttered.

"That's not for you to say," Jaguar told him. The two glared daggers at each other, and I saw Jaguar's gangsters reaching into their pockets.

I put steel in my voice and lifted it over the sound of the pouring rain. "Hold up, boys. Stand down, Kraken. This isn't what we're here for."

With his eyes still on Jaguar, Kraken opened his mouth to say something, but Jaguar suddenly turned away from him, his attention caught by something behind the adaro. He pointed to a wooden hut with newspaper-covered windows across the alleyway. "What the fuck!" Jaguar shouted. Turning to one of his men, he said, "Take care of that."

I turned to look at whatever it was that had distracted Jaguar and spotted a silver oval that had been spray-painted on the wall of the hut under the window. As I watched, one of the gangsters took a spray can of his own out of his coat pocket and covered the oval over with a blob of gold spray paint.

I nodded at Jaguar. "Rival gang?"

Jaguar snorted. "Nah. Just some stupid adaro shit. It's nothing. Come on. We want to get you two to the Leiti before this fuckin' sea slug tears down the whole damn neighborhood."

Our fifteen-minute tour of what I hoped was the worst of the adaro settlement felt like it took half the night. Jaguar stopped outside a solidly built wooden shack with a sheet-metal roof. The door opened upon our arrival, and Jaguar motioned me forward. Kraken, who'd barely spoken since leaving the beastmobile behind, accompanied me. I wondered how long he would be comfortable out of the ocean. Noting that his breathing was unlabored, I concluded that he would be fine for the time being. Physically, at any rate. His eyes were cold, and his lips were twisted into a disapproving scowl.

"Keep your cool, buddy," I muttered at him. I watched his hands clench into fists.

"This is a bad place," he muttered back.

Jaguar waited outside the door to the shack. "Go inside," he said. "Both of you. Leiti La'aka is expecting you. I'm leaving three of my boys here. They'll show you back to your car when you're done."

"You're not coming in?" I asked.

"Fuck no. I got better things to do. I might be seeing you later."

"Really? Why?"

The gang leader smiled. "Talk to the Leiti. Then we'll see." He turned to Kraken and looked him up and down. Still smiling, he shook his head. "Damn, man." He chuckled once before gathering his crew and walking away.

Kraken looked down at me. "What's *his* problem?"

"I think he likes you," I said.

Kraken snorted. "*Gruuub-grurr* little human. I don't like him."

I nodded toward the open door. "Let's go meet the Leiti."

I stepped through the door into a space that was surprisingly homey. Light blue wallpaper covered the walls, and an area rug large enough to fill the room lay atop a polished hardwood floor. The interior of the shack was lit by two smoky oil lamps sitting on a wooden coffee table in the center of the room. On one side of the table, an enormous woman was sunk into an overstuffed cloth-covered chair with leather patches sewn onto the armrests. Getting her out of that chair was going to be a problem. Thick, wavy hair, black but liberally streaked with gray, poured down from a multi-colored headscarf and spilled over her broad shoulders. Deep grooves radiated from the corners of her brown eyes, and her eyelids were dyed the color of amethysts. Her tan cheeks were round and dimpled, and her lips were coated with a black lacquer that made them gleam in the dim light. The spaghetti straps on her loose-fitting low-necked dress exposed a complex network of bold black interlocking bars that had been tattooed on every visible part of her voluminous body from the neck down. An unearthly energy pulsed through those inked bars like neon through glass tubes, humming with a sound I couldn't quite hear, but which caused my back teeth to vibrate.

A slim female adaro, probably not yet out of her teens, stood next to the chair and stared at Kraken, her pale blue eyes opened wide. Her waist-length dark blue hair partially obscured the gills on either side of her neck, and silvery gloves covered the tattooed registration number on her wrist. She was wearing one of those loose islander floral dresses that left one shoulder bare, something that worked in the South Nihhonese, but not so well on a cold Yerba City night. I tried not to stare.

The large woman remained seated as we entered, and she indicated the couch on the other side of the table. "Please, come in and make yourselves comfortable," she said in a soothing and slightly accented contralto, just loud enough to be heard over the clatter of the rain falling on the sheet-metal roof. "I'm Leiti La'aka. This young lady is my apprentice, Tahiti. Welcome to my humble abode. I'm glad you managed to find me without undo complications. Would either of you like something to drink? I have rum, beer, and water, both salted and filtered."

I moved to the couch. "I could use a beer," I said, meaning it.

"Water," said Kraken.

The Leiti turned to the young adaro woman. "Tahiti, please bring beer and seawater for our guests. Thank you, dear." Without a word, the adaro disappeared through a hanging cloth door into an adjoining room.

Once we were all seated, the Leiti regarded me with an amused expression. "You must be quite confused, Mr. Southerland. I needed to speak with you, and I confess that I have expended no small amount of effort in bringing you here. I hope you will pardon the intrusion. I promise that it will prove worthwhile."

I glanced at Kraken, who was staring after the adaro girl with a surprised expression. Turning back to the Leiti, I said, "What do you mean when you say you directed me here?"

She nodded. "It's not something I can easily explain, nor would I wish to bore you with a lot of technical detail. Let me say first off that I did nothing to you directly. Your minds have not been touched, so you need not worry about that. My influence over the natural spirits in some parts of the settlement are strong. By manipulating certain aspects of these spirits, I made some passages along your route seem desirable and others difficult to detect." She looked directly at me and smiled. "I had a tougher time of it than I was expecting. You were not easy to deceive. You persisted in turning down streets that should have been hidden, and I was obliged to redirect you. I apologize for the frustration this must have caused. In the end, you wound up where you needed to be. I hope Jaguar and his people were well-behaved. They were forced to wait for you a little longer than we were expecting, and active young men become impatient so easily."

The young adaro—Tahiti—brought our drinks in and set them on the table in the center of the room. She placed a wooden bowl partway filled with a brown liquid I didn't recognize in front of the Leiti. The liquid emitted a pungent fragrance that, while familiar, I couldn't quite place.

When Tahiti drew near, I picked up a strong musky scent and found myself growing mildly aroused as I regarded the way the thin fabric of the slender young woman's dress hugged the contours of her hips and thighs. I reminded myself that adaro females naturally emitted a heavy dose of pheromones, an evolutionary consequence of coming from a species in which females outnumbered males by ten to one, and only the most alluring of the women received the opportunity to become mothers. I also reminded myself that the girl wasn't much more than half my age. I mentally slapped myself in the mouth and forced my libido back into the cave where I'd been hiding it since I'd last seen Holly. The girl's smile, however, was not directed toward me, but rather at Kraken, who sniffed the air once and glared at her with a disapproving frown. Tahiti's eyes narrowed as if she'd been rebuked, and she backed quickly away to stand by the Leiti.

I picked up the glass of beer, which, to my dismay, was warmed to room temperature. Looking across the table at my host, I said, "You could have just called me, you know."

Leiti La'aka's face tightened. "The LIA monitors the phone frequencies, Mr. Southerland. Surely you know that."

I sipped the warm beer, which was surprisingly refreshing. "So I keep hearing. I think people exaggerate the ability of the government to intrude into our lives. Cellphone calls are reasonably safe."

The Leiti's lips spread into a condescending smile. "If you say so," she said. She picked up her bowl with both hands and sipped at the liquid.

On the couch next to me Kraken was becoming restless. He shifted in his seat, downed most of his water, and sighed. "What are we doing here, Dickhead?" He set his glass on the table and shifted in his seat again.

I eased back into the couch, trying to demonstrate to Kraken how relaxed I felt about our current situation. "It's okay, buddy. We got a little sidetracked. These things happen."

Kraken wasn't having it. "What about Ten-Inch? We were going to make the Northsiders tell us where Ten-Inch is."

"We will," I assured him. "First we're going to see why the Leiti sent for us. We won't be here long." I turned back to the Leiti. "Isn't that right, Leiti La'aka?"

"That depends," the Leiti responded. "Personally, I have all night. But your adaro friend is young, and as I pointed out earlier, young men tend to become impatient." She sipped more of her drink. "Let's get right to it. The two of you are going to meet the Northsiders at The Dripping Bucket. I want you to take my apprentice with you."

I was going to ask the Leiti how she knew this. Before I could open my mouth, however, Kraken exploded. "No! That bar is a bad place for a *kwuurlplup*."

I turned quickly to Kraken. "For a what?" Was that the same word he had used when referring to Kanoa? I thought so, but it was difficult for me to make any sense of the adaro language, in which every word sounded like gases bubbling to the surface in a pool of hot oil.

Kraken's eyes never left the young adaro girl. "A *kwuurlplup*. She.... I don't know how to say it."

"She's a priestess," said the Leiti. "That's an oversimplification for a word that can't be properly translated, but it's close enough. Let's just say that she is a revered figure among the adaros."

Turning back to Kraken, I asked, "Do you know her?"

Kraken continued to regard the young woman with a disapproving expression that contained no hint of reverence. "I've never seen her before. But I know she's a *kwuurlplup*." His lips twisted into a scowl. "She can't go to the bar. She's just a *bluugblorl* girl."

If I was surprised that Kraken could recognize a seemingly innocuous adaro girl as a priestess, I was downright flummoxed when Leiti La'aka responded to the massively muscled and imposing adaro buck with a short sharp burble in his own language. Kraken fell back into the couch as if he'd been sucker-punched.

"Mind your place, fool! You know better than to speak that way to a *kwuurlplup*, regardless of her age. And, anyway, she isn't much younger than you are, you little snot. The *kwuurlplup* will do as she pleases, and you will do everything you can to assist her." The Leiti caught the giant adaro's fierce blue eyes with her dark unblinking ones, and she stared him down.

For several long moments, Kraken's face was twisted by a number of conflicting emotions before his expression settled on surrender. He slumped his shoulders and, with downcast eyes, nodded. "I apologize, Leiti," he mumbled. "I will do as you say."

The Leiti's eyes softened, and she turned to me with a benign smile. "Mr. Southerland, you, of course, have no obligation to take Tahiti to the Northsiders, but I hope you will do so anyway. I assure you that she will be perfectly safe with them."

I set my glass down on the table. "Let me get this straight, Leiti La'aka. You expended unearthly energy to flag me down like a taxi so that I would drive your... priestess... to a bar?"

The Leiti's black lips stretched into a wide smile. "I suppose when you simplify it like that it sounds rather excessive, doesn't it. And yet, that is essentially the gist of it. Although I'd say that vehicle of yours is more of a luxury town car than a taxicab."

"That may be, but I'm going to charge you for the damage that hubcap did to it."

Leiti La'aka tilted her head and frowned. "Excuse me? Did you say 'hubcap'?"

I regarded the Leiti's puzzled expression. "You didn't drop a hubcap with your name on it on the hood of my car through a portal in the sky?"

"I most certainly did not." Her gaze slid away from me to an imaginary point over my shoulder. "That's most curious. Quite curious." She focused her eyes on mine once more. "A hubcap? And my name was written on it?"

"Etched into the surface." I thought about that for a moment. "I might not have been so willing to let Jaguar and his gang bring me here if I hadn't received your calling card."

A chuckle forced its way through the Leiti's throat. "That was no calling card of mine. I'm not in the habit of dropping hubcaps from the sky. Or anything else, for that matter."

I scratched my chin and nodded. "Okay, let's say I believe you. Nevertheless, Leiti La'aka, I'm not a passenger service. I'm a private investigator."

"I'm aware of that, Mr. Southerland. You're searching for Ten-Inch, the leader of the Northsiders gang. Tahiti will not impede your search in any way."

"Did you know I was going to The Dripping Bucket before I walked through your door?"

"Of course. Just as I know you will come back to the settlement tomorrow, if you are able, in order to pursue your investigation."

"How?"

"I know many things, Mr. Southerland. I'm a Leiti. Do you know what that means?"

I shrugged. "I had never heard of Leitis until tonight. You were born male?"

Leiti La'aka's smile accented the dimples in her cheeks. "No. I may have been born with male parts, but I've always been female."

"I gather that's not the whole story, though." I nodded at her with my chin. "I can feel the magic in that ink."

Leiti La'aka's face grew more solemn. "Yes, I touch the *manu* and perceive the *tapu* of this place with these sacred tattoos, and through them I communicate with many of the *Otua*, the children of Taufulifonua and Havea Lolofonua. The Leiti are trained in these arts." Her smile returned to her face. "Tahiti assists me. She is a great vessel of *manu*."

Right. I could feel my brain shutting down from the sudden overload of unfamiliar sounding syllables. "You'll have to excuse me, Leiti, but I didn't catch much of that. I'll just accept that you have some heavy mojo. You say that Tahiti assists you. But she's not a Leiti, correct?"

Leiti La'aka chuckled. "Dear me, no. She's an adaro. There are no Leitis among the adaros. It's strictly a human thing."

"Kraken tells me that adaros can't be transgender."

Leiti La'aka shot a half-smile at Kraken, sitting glumly at my side, and the Leiti's eyes seemed to twinkle in the smoky light of the room. "Who can tell?" She turned back to me. "But, no. Adaro men don't have the brains to be women."

"Hey!" Kraken protested.

"Relax, dear," soothed the Leiti. "You adaro bucks are as strong as bulls, and that's what's important, right?" She shot me a quick wink.

"We're *stronger* than bulls!" Kraken corrected her.

"That's right, dear."

I wasn't as young as Kraken or most of the Cartel hoods, but I could feel my own patience beginning to ebb. "What can you tell me about Ten-Inch? Do you know where he is?"

The Leiti folded her hands on her ample lap. "Ten-Inch is a man of great fortitude, but limited vision. He rules a small tribe with an iron hand. He values the independence of his tribe, and he has been fighting to keep them that way." She shrugged. "Not everyone in his tribe shares his commitment to independence. The Hatfield Syndicate has dazzled them with promises of increased power and money. Ten-Inch has been struggling to keep them together in opposition to the attempts of the Syndicate to take them over. As to where he is now, I'm not sure. He went missing earlier this week and has been hidden from me."

"Hidden from you? Who could do that?"

"Ten-Inch was touched by a great spirit." Leiti La'aka closed her eyes for a second before reopening them to meet mine. "I have good reason to believe it was Maui-Kisikisi."

## Chapter Fifteen

I succeeded in maintaining my poker face, but it wasn't easy. "Who?"

"Kisikisi is either the youngest son or brother of Maui-Motu'a, or Old Maui, the most revered of the island spirits. Given the incestuous nature of the spirits, Kisikisi may be both his son *and* brother. Regardless, Kisikisi is a powerful spirit, but not a reliable one." She frowned. "He's something of a trickster, actually, and a real bastard. It's just like him to intervene in a fight and run off with the prize." She grinned at me. "It would also be just like him to drop a hubcap on your car from out of the sky."

Smoke from the oil lamps hung in the room like fog creeping in from the Nihhonese. I looked through the haze at the Leiti. "I see. In fact, the hubcap with your name on it was the second I received. I received the first late last night. That one had Kisikisi's name inscribed on it."

Leiti La'aka's grin widened, and the grooves in the corners of her eyes deepened. "You see? He was introducing himself. Cheeky little bastard."

"And it looks like he wanted me to meet you." I remembered the supernatural presence I'd detected outside Ten-Inch's apartment before the cops scooped me off the street. I wondered whether this Maui-Kisikisi was helping Ten-Inch or using him for his own purposes. My own experience with unearthly spirits had given me little reason to trust them. Being otherworldly, they had otherworldly ways of thinking. But that was Ten-Inch's problem. My job was to find him.

The Leiti reached up and extended a finger to her lips. "Hmm. Yes. I believe that Kisikisi wanted us to meet. I'm even more convinced now that you need to convey Tahiti to the Northsiders."

As the big woman sipped more of her drink, I remembered where I had experienced that unique fragrance. It was the bitter scent I'd detected when the sheet of stationary from the Hawthorne Hotel had flared into flame and vanished.

"What is that drink?" I asked the Leiti.

She lowered the bowl and favored me with an amused grin. "It's called kava," she told me. "Would you like some? It has pleasant qualities." She extended the bowl to me across the table.

I had to admit I was curious. "Pleasant? What do you mean?"

"It's a soporific. For most people, it has a mild calming effect. Drink enough of it, and it will expand your mind."

"It's a hallucinogen?"

"It can be."

"How's it taste?"

"Most people find it bitter. It's something of an acquired taste, like coffee, but once you get accustomed to it you can't get enough."

"Don't drink it," came a warning voice.

I turned to Kraken. "Why not?"

Kraken was scowling. "It's for witches."

Leiti La'aka made a scoffing sound. "Ohhh, poo. Don't listen to him, Mr. Southerland. It's true that kava is used in ceremonies and as the foundation for a variety of potions, but I assure you that the kava in this bowl is perfectly harmless in small quantities. Among my people it's polite for guests to share a bowl of kava with their hosts."

Kraken was still scowling. "I will not drink it. I don't want to turn into a mudfish."

The Leiti rolled her eyes at the adaro. "I'll have you know that mudfishes are considered sacred in many parts of the world." She turned to me. "How about you, Mr. Southerland. Are you brave enough to risk an offer of my hospitality? Kava has been known to bring clarity to a troubled mind."

I didn't want to be rude, and I could always use a little clarity, so I leaned forward and reached for the bowl. "I'll give it a try."

The Kava *was* bitter, but then so is black coffee. At least the coffee I like to drink. I decided I could get used to it, given the opportunity. "Not bad," I said.

The Leiti's black smile reached her purple-shaded eyes. "Come back to my humble home one day, Mr. Southerland, and I'll give you enough to make a proper Islander out of you."

"Sounds intriguing. So when do I turn into a sacred mudfish?"

The Leiti's only response was an enigmatic smile.

After she took the bowl from me, Leiti La'aka sought out Kraken through the smoky haze with refocused attention. "Kraken, adaro men rarely visit us here on the land, and they don't stay long when they do. I sense you have a question you'd like me to answer before you leave."

Kraken set his glass on the table. "Do you know who killed Kanoa?"

The Leiti's eyes fell. "Sadly, I do not, and I'd very much like to." She raised her eyes again. "Perhaps you and Mr. Southerland will find out. If you do, I'd like to hear about it."

"Maybe you can help," I said. "What can you tell me about her?"

"As it happens, I have some information you might be able to use." She refolded her hands, preparing to launch into a story. "Kanoa entered the settlement in secret from the ocean two months ago. She somehow managed to avoid the authorities and was never registered."

"Does that happen often?" I asked.

The Leiti's eyes twinkled. "Now why would a free adaro woman want to leave the sea for an unfree life on the land?"

I shrugged. "Sabotage? Espionage? People on the internet claim that adaro terrorists are organizing in the settlement."

"So I've heard." The Leiti's tone told me what she thought about such unsubstantiated allegations. "Kanoa was no terrorist, believe me. Those conspiracy theorists on the internet have no imagination. Kanoa's story is actually more interesting than that. She was a much revered person in the adaro community, a servant of the sea spirit Taufa'tahi. She claimed to have a message from him. Many of the adaros called her a prophet."

"Leiti!"

All eyes turned toward Leiti La'aka's apprentice, who was staring at the Leiti with alarm.

The Leiti placed a reassuring hand on her assistant's arm. "It's fine, Tahiti. Kanoa wasn't exactly discreet. Everyone in the settlement knew about her."

"The *adaros* knew," Tahiti clarified, glancing my way. "But the settlement authorities didn't."

"Please, dear. Kanoa may have been a prophet, or she may have been a disturbed young woman. If the latter, then it doesn't matter if Mr. Southerland knows what she was doing in the settlement. If the former, then he *needs* to know. Everyone does."

Tahiti was clearly unconvinced, but she nodded and kept her peace.

Leiti La'aka turned her attention back to me. "Kanoa wandered through the settlement telling everyone who would listen that a great disaster was going to strike Yerba City."

"What kind of disaster?"

"Storms. Floods. Tidal waves. That was before it started raining, so you can guess what people are saying about her now. According to

Kanoa, the entire peninsula is going to be buried under the sea by the wrath of Taufa'tahi, who, again according to Kanoa, has been angered by the aggression of the Tolanican realm and wishes to help the adaro reclaim possession of the Nihhonese Ocean. He will destroy Yerba City and free the adaro women. Kanoa was encouraging the adaros to resist their human oppressors in the settlement and escape into the sea."

I glanced up at Kraken, who snorted. "Sounds good to me," he said. "But our women spread stories like that all the time. Ever since the Dragon Lords destroyed our homes, these crazy women swim around claiming that our guardian spirits are going to destroy the humans. Smart people don't listen to them."

I caught Tahiti glaring at Kraken. She caught me catching her and made an effort to compose her features. Too late, though. I knew the truth: Leiti La'aka might be skeptical, but her apprentice was a believer.

Me? I had an open mind. I looked up at Kraken. "It's been raining for days. Some of the streets are flooded."

Kraken snorted again. "The land is still the land. I can't swim through your city, Dickhead."

"Most of the adaros in the settlement were as skeptical of Kanoa's prophecy as you are, Kraken," Leiti La'aka said. "For them, it is too much to believe. Kanoa tried to convince the adaros the time for a mass escape was at hand. She told them that they wouldn't survive the coming disaster unless they were safely in the depths of the Nihhonese when the storm was at its peak."

I studied the Leiti as she dabbed at the corners of her lacquered lips with a paper napkin in a most ladylike fashion. I couldn't help thinking about the circumstances of her birth. I looked to find something mannish about her, but couldn't detect anything in particular. It occurred to me that there was no reason why I should.

Leiti La'aka was waiting for me to ask her more about Kanoa, so I did. "Something puzzles me. You say Kanoa was encouraging the adaros to resist their human oppressors and escape into the sea. But the settlement isn't a prison. The adaros are free to come and go. If they don't like it here, why don't they leave? Not all adaros live in the settlement."

It was Tahiti who answered. "It's not that simple, Mr. Southerland. According to your government, we're in protective custody until we can be assimilated into your culture. But that's a lie. We're actually hostages in the war between the Dragon Lords and our men, who know that our lives would be at great risk if they decided to launch an invasion. Yes, any of us women can move out of the settlement, but where are we going to go? We can live on land, but our home is the ocean, and we don't like being too far away from it. You've seen adaros in the city, but they don't thrive there. The settlement may not be surrounded by walls, but we're treated like criminals everywhere we go." She pulled off her glove to show me the numbers tattooed on her wrist. "We're registered with the government. This number means our records can be accessed by any law enforcement agency in the realm. Not many employers will hire us. If you see an adaro in the city, the first thing you're going to think is that she's a sex worker. And you'll probably be right."

"Then why don't you swim away? I know that the Navy patrols the waters outside the settlement, and that they can legally execute any tattooed adaro they find, but what's stopping you from hiking up or down the coast and escaping from there?"

Tahiti lifted her eyebrows. "You don't know?"

I stared at her and didn't say anything.

Leiti La'aka filled me in. "The adaros aren't just tattooed when they're registered. The Navy also injects a tracking device under their skin."

This was news to me. "You sure about this? How come I've never heard about it?"

The Leiti shrugged. "The Dragon Lord's government is filled with secrets. They don't see any reason to broadcast this one."

"Okay." I didn't try to hide my skepticism.

Leiti La'aka went on. "The numbers tattooed on the wrists of the adaros are really just a convenient visual indication that the adaro is registered. The tracking device is on at all times, powered by the adaro's own electrical impulses. Whenever an adaro leaves the land, the government knows about it and sends a vessel to intercept. The tracking signal broadcasts the adaro's registration number, too, so they know the location of any particular adaro at any particular time. They also know where they've been."

Tahiti nodded. "The government doesn't need bars to make us prisoners."

The Leiti glanced at her apprentice before looking back at me. "But that's not the real reason why the adaros aren't making a run for it. Kanoa was having a very difficult time stirring the hearts of the settlement's residents. She was ridiculed. There were some unfortunate incidents. She was obliged to secure the services of Ten-Inch for protection. It might surprise you to know how reluctant most of the adaros are to leave the settlement, regardless of how unfree they might be."

"Really? I would think that the adaros would be happy to escape this shithole."

The Leiti's lacquered lips stretched into a smile that didn't reach her dimples. "Don't be so judgmental, Mr. Southerland. Home is what you make of it. You might not find the settlement to be an attractive place, but it has its own charm."

I shook my head at this, and the Leiti continued. "Many of the adaros have been here for years. They've settled in."

"Don't they miss the ocean?"

"Of course! But there are parts of their old lives they don't miss so much."

Tahiti glared at the Leiti, and my surprise must have shown on my face. I was going to have to work on that before I played poker again.

Leiti La'aka threw a glance at Kraken. "Ask your large male friend about the lives of the adaro women in their native communities."

I looked up at Kraken and found his default confused expression on his face. "What's she mean?" I asked.

"I don't know." He glared at the Leiti. "She's babbling."

The Leiti's eyes crinkled in amusement. "I don't want to get into the gender dynamics of adaro life. Maybe Tahiti will be willing to enlighten you on your way to see the Northsiders. For now, let's just say that many adaro women find themselves more liberated outside their native communities—even within the confines of this supervised settlement—than they ever did before. It's my belief that, in time, the adaro women will find their new lives on the coastal land more fulfilling than their old lives in the sea, where they were dominated, exploited, and routinely abused by the adaro men."

Kraken's eyes flashed. "That's not true!" he bellowed.

The Leiti's smile widened, and the dimples deepened. "So says the representative of the adaro patriarchy."

Kraken's look of puzzlement returned. "Huh?"

"Never mind, dear," said the Leiti. She turned back to me. "Kanoa was quite passionate, though wrongheaded, in my opinion. She was a product of thousands of years of cultural conditioning, and that's hard to shake off. As for her so-called prophecy, I talked to her many times. She was a remarkable woman. Quite passionate and self-assured. She was like a queen from the days before the Dragon Lords. I'm convinced she truly believed her message. But, Kraken's right. Those sorts of prophecies have been flying around for decades. Centuries, even. This rain, I believe, is just rain."

The Leiti seemed to lose herself in thought, and I let the silence linger for a few moments before breaking it. I shot a glance at Tahiti, aware that she had been watching me for some time. I was conscious of her scent, the softness of her lips, and the curves her loose-fitting dress couldn't obscure. A suspicion was growing in my mind, and I wanted to test it. "You say Ten-Inch was protecting her. That doesn't sound like the Ten-Inch I know. Did she seduce him?"

Leiti La'aka's eyes focused on mine. "To some extent, perhaps. But the two of them never entered into a sexual relationship."

I smiled with half my mouth. "How do you know that?"

The Leiti's expression remained serious. "Because Kanoa was a *kwuurlplup*—a priestess. And the *kwuurlplups* are all virgins."

I couldn't help shooting a glance at Tahiti, who was biting her lip and gazing at me like a girl weighing her duties against the desires of her heart.

Leiti La'aka continued. "If a *kwuurlplup* loses her virginity, she also loses her connections to the *manu* and the *Otua,* the ancient spirits of the Nihhonese Ocean. But even without entering into a sexual relationship with a man, a *kwuurlplup* possesses a great deal of persuasive power. Even the unfulfillable promise of sex can be a very potent weapon. Especially for an adaro." Her eyes dropped toward my lap. "But you already know that."

I glanced down and immediately felt a tingling in my cheeks as blood rushed into my head. Without my noticing, my body had been responding to the powerful scent of the hormones emanating from the young adaro woman. I was suddenly aware of the adrenaline coursing through my bloodstream, the pounding of my heart, and the thickening of my breathing. I looked up at Tahiti, whose lips were parted in a way that made me want to smash the wooden coffee table between us into kindling.

I forced myself to turn back to the Leiti and draw in a slow breath. "Are you enjoying this?" I asked her.

"My living space is small, and you've been in the presence of a young, desirable adaro female for quite a length of time. Many men would find themselves so uncomfortable in your situation that they would have to go outside for air. Or find themselves a cold shower. You have an admirable amount of willpower, Mr. Southerland," she said, an exasperating grin on her face, "but, like most men, parts of you seem to have a will all their own."

I couldn't help shooting a glance at the naked adaro on the couch next to me. Kraken seemed maddeningly relaxed under the circumstances and was smirking at me. "Humans. You have no control over your dicks."

I pondered pouring the water from Kraken's glass over my head—or into my lap—but settled for knocking back a king-sized swallow of beer and thinking about dead adaros in alleyways, instead.

"Do you know where Kanoa was going when she left the settlement Monday night?" I asked the Leiti.

She dropped her eyes. "I do not. Once she left the settlement, I lost all connection to her."

I drew in a slow breath. "Leiti La'aka, there's something I have to tell you. I've been told that there is a strong possibility that Kanoa was raped the night she was murdered."

Beside me, I felt Kraken stiffen. I glanced his way. His teeth were clenched, and I could feel the heat radiating from his body, but he stayed silent. It didn't take magically enhanced awareness to sense his stifled rage. I'd hate to be on the receiving end when he was ready to release it.

After a few moments, the Leiti raised her eyes. Her face was composed, and I could sense how hard she was struggling to keep it that way. But she couldn't keep her eyes from welling with tears, which spilled out the corners of both eyes and trickled down her cheeks. "I have little power outside my territory. My 'turf,' as Jaguar would say." She cleared the tightness out of her throat and reached up with a napkin to wipe the tears away. "I have attempted to discover the reason for her disappearance, but have met with no success. Perhaps you will have better luck."

"I'm just trying to find Ten-Inch. Maybe he'll be able to tell me something about why Kanoa was leaving the settlement when I find him."

The Leiti nodded. "I, too, would like to hear what Ten-Inch has to say for himself. If he was with her when she... when she died, he has a lot to account for. I've used all my resources to try to find him, but I don't think he's in the settlement, or in Placid Point, for that matter. I am certain I would know if he was." She turned toward Tahiti. "Help me up, dear." With the adaro's help, the Leiti pushed herself from the chair to her feet. "Mr. Southerland, I believe that I have taken up enough of your time. Tahiti can guide you straight to The Dripping Bucket, and with her help you should be able to reach it in no more than ten minutes, provided nothing falls on you from out of the sky." She allowed herself a small grin at that, but I didn't feel reassured.

Kraken and I rose from the couch, and I nodded toward Tahiti. "What am I supposed to do with her once I get her there?"

"Nothing at all, my dear. Nothing at all. All I ask is that you get her through the door." The Leiti turned her eyes toward Kraken. "You should be able to handle that without difficulty."

Kraken shot a glance at Tahiti before turning back to the Leiti and nodding. "I'll do it," he said without enthusiasm. "But she shouldn't go there. It's a bad place for her. A bad place for a *kwuurlplup*." He frowned. "It's a bad place for anybody."

## Chapter Sixteen

Before we left, Tahiti fastened a woven mat around her waist over her dress. "It's called a *ta'ovala*," Leiti La'aka explained. "Our people wear it on formal occasions."

"This is a formal occasion?" I asked. "Maybe we should find a tie for Kraken."

That got a brief smile from both Tahiti and Leiti La'aka, and a scowl from Kraken.

"The Claymore Cartel has entered into negotiations with the Northsiders over this Hatfield business," explained the Leiti. "Both sides have asked for my assistance. Tahiti will be bringing a gift from me to the Northsiders." She winked. "I'd like to know who's running the gang in Ten-Inch's absence, and what he thinks about the Hatfield Syndicate."

"And you're sure you're not putting Tahiti into any danger?"

"She'll be safe. She's a much more capable young woman than you are giving her credit for." The Leiti handed Tahiti a spiral conch shell with a brilliant pink interior that practically glowed. Tahiti carefully placed the shell inside a leather carrying case about the size and shape of a hatbox and slung the case over her shoulder. The two women gave each other a brief embrace, and Tahiti accompanied Kraken and me out the door.

We were escorted back to the beastmobile by the three gangsters Jaguar had left outside the Leiti's home, and Jaguar himself was waiting for us when we got there.

"About fuckin' time, bitch," he said when we reached him. He glanced up at Badass, who was still hovering above my car. "I've been getting to know your guard dog. He doesn't talk much, though."

"It. Elementals don't have genders. And it's not a dog." I turned to the elemental. "Badass. Did anyone touch the car?"

"Nooo." came the sonorous baritone.

"Did you have to hurt anyone?"

"Nooo."

"In that case, I release you from your service. Thank you."

Without another word, the elemental launched itself into the night.

Jaguar watched it until it disappeared. He shook his head. "Damn. I wish I had one of those. If it weren't for him, you wouldn't be here now, brudda. That motherfucker saved your sorry ass that night on the pier."

"It was just a leg wound. It wasn't that serious."

"I wasn't aiming for your leg, bitch, and I don't miss what I aim at. I wasn't figuring on a fuckin' tornado to alter the trajectory of my shot." He turned to me. "Did you drink any of the Leiti's kava?"

"I had a taste."

He grinned. "Try to stay awake, my brudda. Kava and driving don't mix."

"It was just a swallow," I said. "I think I can handle it."

"Famous last words, motherfucker." He indicated Tahiti with his eyes. "You think you can handle *her*, brudda?"

I shrugged. "Nuthin' to handle. I'm just transport."

Jaguar looked me up and down. "Hmm. Good luck with that. Don't fuck it up."

Tahiti and Kraken got into the car, but I stayed out to have a word with Jaguar. "What's this about?" I asked him. "The Leiti told me some kind of negotiation is going down. You're the leader of the Cartel. How come you're not a part of this tonight?"

The gangster smiled. "Nuthin' for you to worry about, brudda. Just get the girl inside and don't piss anyone off. The rest will take care of itself."

"Yeah? What's in it for you? Are you thinking of selling your gang out to the Hatfields?"

Jaguar's lips twisted into a scowl that pushed against the wing tattooed under his left eye. "The Hatfields are fuckin' bottom feeders, just like the Northsiders." He shook his head. "Fuckin' Northsiders. They better hope Ten-Inch comes out of whatever hole he's hiding in. They're shit without him. Less than shit."

"I thought you and Ten-Inch hated each other."

Jaguar's scowl turned into a tight smile. "Sure, brudda. I hate the motherfucker. But I give him his due. That fucker took a bunch of scum-sucking nobodies and carved out a territory with them. Not a big territory, just a few shitty blocks no one else wanted, but he made sure they held onto it. I did my best to take it from him, too, just to give my boys some action. Lord's fucking balls, we had some bloodbaths! Fuckin' Ten-Inch don't care how many of his people he loses, as long as they fight for him. That fucker is crazy, man! He's the most bloodthirsty son of a bitch I've ever seen."

"Any idea what happened to him?"

"The Hatfields happened to him, brudda. That's my guess."

"Have you heard from him lately?"

Jaguar clammed up then, and I didn't think he was going to answer. But just as I was about to give up and get into the car, he started talking. "Fuckin' Hatfields. They think they're big fish because they feed off this city, but the Cartel is bigger than the city. We're all the fuck over Caychan. We're bigger than the motherfuckin' Hatfields. We rule the streets in Aztlan and Angel City, and it's only a matter of time before we rule the streets of Yerba City, too." He turned to me and smiled. "Soon, my brudda. Soon. Shit's goin' *down!*" He winked and turned to our three escorts. "Come on, bruddas. We're done here."

*\*\*\**

It was Holly's night off, and we were enjoying rum cocktails in a midtown club that wasn't Lefty's. I was in my best (and only) suit, with my darkest tie. Holly was making a little black number she'd bought off the rack look like something she'd borrowed from one of the city's top runway models. On the stage, a well-known comic was firing up the crowd by humiliating drunken hecklers with his grab bag of devastating zingers. Three jaspers drinking gin and tonics in the back of the lounge near the table where Holly and I were sitting were finding their own rib-tickling banter far more entertaining than anything coming from the professional on stage, and their out-of-context snickering and chortling was eliciting harrumphs and scowls from neighboring patrons who had come to enjoy the marquee show. Holly and I sipped our drinks and tried to ignore everyone except each other.

We were not having a pleasant moment.

"You don't need to protect me, Alex." Holly peered at me over the top of her cocktail glass. "You can't do what I do without knowing how to take care of yourself."

I set my glass on a coaster and stared at it for a second before meeting Holly's dark eyes. "I'm just saying that fighting off the advances of rich drunken lechers three times your age is no way for a young lady to spend her evenings."

"I like my job. The pay is good and the tips are great. So what if I have to show a little thigh and flash a smile at a bunch of fresh geezers in order to earn my dough. It's perfectly harmless—and it's good dough! I'll bet I made more money last month than you did."

I looked away. My case load had been light the past few weeks, and we'd had to split the cover charge in order to get into the club that night. "The money isn't the point," I said. "It's not safe. What happened to Ella could happen to you."

"Ella's fine. Nothing worse than a split lip. She's a tough little broad, believe me. Anyhow, she should have known better than to try to break up a fight like that. Lord's sake--she's a cigarette girl, not a bouncer! You'll never catch me in the middle of a fracas like that."

I stared down at my drink, remembering that I didn't particularly care for rum cocktails and regretting that it wasn't a whiskey, neat. "I don't like the way those wolves put their hands on your ass. It's not right."

Holly rolled her eyes. "Honey, it doesn't mean a thing. It's all part of the attraction. Lefty's packs them in every night. How many of them would keep coming back if we girls weren't parading around in those skimpy costumes and encouraging them to misbehave a little. Anyhow, I only let the big tippers touch me like that. Anyone else gets a spiked stiletto in the top of their foot."

One of the jaspers laughed out loud in the middle of one of the comic's jokes, and faces with disapproving expressions turned in his direction.

I twisted my glass on the coaster without picking it up. "A touch for a tip. You know what that makes you, don't you?"

I didn't need to see Holly's glare to know I had gone too far. "Call me a whore and I'll throw this drink in your face."

"I'm sorry. I didn't mean that." I looked up from my drink. "I know how the game works, and I know you'd never let it get out of control. It's just... I mean... couldn't you make just as much dough sitting at a typewriter? Secretaries make a good living."

Holly leaned away from me and stared at me with widened eyes. "Oh, Alex. You can be such an asshole sometimes. You want me to be somebody's gal friday? Park my butt at a desk and type contracts for ten hours a day? Sit on the boss's lap and take dictation in between making him coffee?"

"Not all bosses are like that." I knew I shouldn't be flapping my yap, but I couldn't stop myself.

Holly smiled without humor and shook her head. "You liked what I was doing well enough the night we met."

"That was different." I mentally winced as I said it.

Holly's eyes never left me as she slowly lifted her glass to her lips and took a drink. I took a quick sip of my own and noticed the jaspers looking in my direction and whispering to each other.

Giving up and apologizing again would have been a swell idea. That's what I intended to do when I opened my mouth. What came out instead was, "Why don't you come work for me? I could use someone to answer my phone and research information on the computer, and I'd even get my own coffee. You could still sit in my lap while I did dictation, though." I smiled, believing for some reason that she would find that last bit amusing.

Holly's face tightened, and, too late, I realized that I needed to leave comedy to the professionals, like the one on the stage. He was getting big laughs. Me? I was about to get the hook.

Holly leaned toward me so that she wouldn't have to shout. "Now you listen to me, buster. I was working in a nightclub when we met, and it wasn't because I was looking for some strong man to scoop me up and take me away from all that. I told you that I like my job. I liked it before I met you, and I like it now. It's fun. It's exciting. I like the atmosphere. I like it when people around me are having a good time. I even like it when people get a little rowdy when they've been drinking. And you wanna know something else? I like it when they look at me. I'm an attractive dame, buster. And if you can't handle that...."

"Hey lady. Is this bum bothering you?"

I looked up to see one of the jaspers at our table talking to my girl. The two gentlemen he'd been drinking with suppressed snickers as they looked on from two tables away.

Holly raised her eyes to the jasper. "This ain't a floor show, honey. Scram."

I put my drink on the coaster and gave loverboy my steeliest glare. He ignored it.

"Don't be like that, baby. I bet my buddies over there that you'd let me buy you a drink. Come on. Let me buy you one drink, okay? Where's the harm in that?" He flashed a set of choppers that couldn't have been brighter if he'd coated them with white shoe polish.

Holly took a sip from her drink. "I've got a drink, honey. And you've had more than you should've." She put the drink down on the table. She also took her purse off the table and lowered it to her lap.

I decided it was time to step in. "Go back to your friends and tell them you lost the bet, champ. Go back while you still have your teeth."

The jasper ignored me, which I thought was rude. Still working on Holly, he said, "You're a beautiful lady. But you should smile more."

Holly turned to him, face expressionless. "You should stupid less."

The jasper frowned. "Huh? I don't get it."

Holly nodded. "I know, dear. Cut your losses and beat it."

That was language the jasper understood. "Hey. Don't be like that. Why do you want to make me look bad in front of my friends?"

Holly's voice remained even. "Oh, I doubt you'll ever need help looking bad. It just comes natural to you."

The jasper's face reddened beneath his impeccably cut head of hair, and he glowered at Holly, a threat in his eyes. "Don't be such a bitch, lady. I was being nice to you. But when my buddies take out the trash...." He gestured toward me. "We won't be so nice." He put a hand on Holly's shoulder and squeezed. "Now why don't you and—"

That was enough for both of us. I leapt from my seat, but Holly moved first. Her hand darted from beneath the table, and a thin spray of liquid streamed from the canister in her hand directly into the jasper's eyes. Like a hot knife through butter, the sharp scent of pepper cut through the cocktail fragrance that filled the room. None of the blast came my way, but tears began to pour from my eyes, giving me the faintest hint of the spray's effect on her would-be suiter.

The jasper released Holly's shoulder and clawed at his face, squealing like a pig in a slaughterhouse. The two members of his cheering squad decided this was their cue to charge into the fray. I kicked loverboy away from Holly, and the table he fell into collapsed under his weight, spilling drinks to the floor and scattering its screaming occupants. Loverboy's drinking companions were heading in my direction, and I turned to face them. Taking a step to my right to flank them and lead them away from Holly, I ducked under a flailing bunkhouse left and countered with a sharp left jab just south of the gentleman's appendix. He bumped into his partner on his way down to his knees. I pivoted to face off with the second member of loverboy's cheering squad, but before I could close with him he turned away from me screaming, the stiletto heel of Holly's shoe buried in the soft tissue of his cheek.

I turned to Holly in surprise. She shrugged and gestured toward the man she had struck. "Well? Are you going to get my shoe back for me, or do I have to go home barefoot?"

*It cost me a good month's pay to keep the cops from hauling Holly and me to the station. Later that night I offered Holly an apology from deep in my heart. She let me dangle for a good hour before letting me off the hook.*

*Later, she raised her lips to my ear and whispered, "I told you I could protect myself."*

*"I'll never argue with you again," I whispered back. A groan escaped through my throat as she reached down and took me in her hand.*

*"Good. After we get out of bed, you're buying me breakfast and taking me shopping for a new pair of shoes."*

***

The beastmobile had room enough in the front seat to accommodate three trolls in comfort, but I'd opted to put Kraken in the back seat so that Tahiti could sit far enough away from me to keep our bodies from accidentally making contact during turns. I felt I was doing a bang-up job of keeping my baser impulses in check, but I was keenly aware of her scent, and I wanted to keep my head as clear as possible. It didn't help that the soothing effects of the kava were beginning to chip away at my carefully repressed inhibitions. I'd barely had a sip; I shuddered to think what a bowl of the stuff would do. I glanced at Tahiti, and it seemed to me the lovely adaro was gazing at me cow-eyed like a lovesick teenager. Damned kava was messing with my mind, I thought, and forced myself to concentrate on my driving.

The rain had returned in force, and traffic had slowed to a crawl to accommodate it. As Tahiti guided me along the twisting route to The Dripping Bucket, I tried to get an idea about what we'd be in for when we got there.

"Have you been to this joint before?" I asked.

"No. This will be my first time."

"It's a bad place," chimed in Kraken from behind me. His face sagged as he sat slumped in the roomy back seat, and I had the distinct impression that after our frustrating journey through the labyrinthine back streets of the settlement the beastmobile had lost much of its magical allure.

I glanced over my shoulder at Kraken. "What's so bad about it?"

"It makes my eyes hurt. And it smells like *pwrrrpluuhh*."

Tahiti raised a hand to her lips as she stifled a laugh. For the first time, I noticed that she had a faint spray of freckles on either side of her nose. I turned my eyes back to the road and drew in a long, slow breath.

"Turn left at the next intersection," Tahiti instructed me.

"Got it." I shot her a quick glance. "I know that the Leiti assured me you will be safe. But do you know what you're getting into? The Northsiders aren't exactly a sewing circle."

Without looking at her, I could sense the adaro smiling in my direction. "I'll be fine. Don't worry about the Northsiders. They know better than to upset the Leiti. And, anyway, I don't sew."

The left turn put me on a narrow muddy unpaved street. My beastmobile was the only car in sight. "Are you sure this is the way to The Dripping Bucket?"

"It's a shortcut."

I gave her a hard look. "All due respect to the Leiti, but the Northsiders aren't exactly known for their respect for authority."

I heard a loud snort from behind me and felt a spray of seawater on the back of my neck. "They'd have to be pretty stupid to piss off a Leiti," said Kraken.

I had no response for that, so I didn't say anything.

Tahiti pointed up ahead. "It's right up there. We're coming in from the back. You'll have to circle around to get to the front."

Through the driving rain, I saw a two-story corrugated metal building with no windows. Four small tired-looking trailers were lined up behind the building, forming a short alleyway. I turned past the trailers and drove slowly down the alley toward the street, taking the time to study both the trailers and the building itself.

Only one door led out the back of the building. As I drove past it, the door opened, and two figures emerged. The first was a dumpy broad with dirty bleached blond locks whose expansive bare belly spilled over the top of a pair of shiny gold-colored shorts meant for someone half her size. She had obviously picked up her t-shirt in the children's section of the local discount clothing store, and, just as obviously, she was wearing nothing beneath it, probably due to lack of room. A boy barely in his teens, decked out in Northsiders colors, followed the broad a bit unsteadily out the door and past a dumpster. As I passed them by, the broad led the kid across the alley and into one of the trailers.

I steered the beastmobile to the front of the bar, where I encountered a collection of motorcycles and muscle cars parked haphazardly in a half-filled dirt lot. I found a spot away from the cluster of vehicles near the street where, if necessary, I could make a quick exit.

After parking the car, I turned to my two passengers. "When we get to the door, let me do the talking." Tahiti and Kraken nodded their assent.

The front of the building looked much like the rear: no windows and one door. It was unmarked, save by a gallon-sized iron bucket the color of pewter hanging from a metal hook mounted on the wall. Rain was falling into the bucket, and streaming right out again through a rusted-out hole in the bucket's side near the bottom, the bucket not so much dripping as urinating into the parking lot.

The beer-bellied lug standing near the door, perhaps inspired by the bucket, was also pissing into the lot. His taller, lankier partner leaned against the door, his arms hugging his chest in a futile attempt to stave off the chill. Both wore hooded raincoats, although Beerbelly's was hanging open to facilitate urination. He straightened and zipped up when he saw Tahiti, Kraken, and me drawing near. His partner peered out at us with sleepy eyes from deep within his hood.

I was in the lead, the only one carrying an umbrella, but Beerbelly ignored me completely. I watched him give Tahiti the once-over, mouth stretched into a leering grin, and then his eyes widened in something like shock as he got a load of Kraken. He either knew Kraken, or he'd never seen an adaro buck in the flesh before.

I tipped my hat to the doormen. "Evening, sirs. Party of three. We have a reservation, I believe."

Beerbelly ripped his eyes off Kraken and locked eyes with me as if I'd popped out of a hole in the ground. "Th'fuck you sayin'!" His breath reeked of stale beer.

Before I could further regale the thugs with my wit and charm, Kraken changed the game. "We're looking for Ten-Inch," he announced. "Let us in."

So much for leaving the talking to me.

Beerbelly snapped his head toward Kraken and put a hand into his coat pocket, probably reaching for a sap. But the lanky thug slouched against the door never moved, except to lift his eyes. "Howdy, Kraken," he drawled. "I'd ask you how it's hangin', but I guess we can all see it plain enough for ourselves."

Kraken stopped in his tracks, his face twisted into an all-too-familiar look of confusion. The thug straightened and pushed his hood back, revealing a lean face marked by an impressive handlebar mustache. "We can't let you in tonight, big fella," he said. "Private party. Tribe members and guests only. You were never officially a member, and we haven't seen you since Mila died." He gave his head a small shake. "That was a real tragedy. There's still a lot of us here who remember her. She was a warrior."

Kraken blinked. "You knew Mila?"

"Of course," said the thug. "I remember you, too. Mila's squeeze. You should have kept coming around afterwards. You were always welcome, you know. Ten-Inch would've admitted you into the tribe if that's what you'd wanted."

I'd been studying the lug's distinctive mustache. "Wait. I remember you. Doctor something...."

A sad grin appeared on the thug's face, and I thought he looked a little embarrassed. "Doctor Death. I was a kid when I gave myself that handle. Back then it sounded cool. I just go by Doc or the Doctor now, though." He stared at me with penetrating eyes. "You're the guy who took Ten-Inch down, aren't you. The Sarge, right?"

"Alexander Southerland," I said. "My sergeant days were a long time ago."

Doc nodded. "Ten-Inch talked about you a lot after that night. You're still the only man I know of who ever beat him in a fair fight. I still don't know how you did it."

I remembered the bloody corpse of Quapo hanging from the rafters of the Medusa as Ten-Inch beat me to within an inch of my life. "Lucky punch," I said.

"Hey!" Beerbelly, who was getting more and more agitated as his eyes narrowed at the Doctor and me as we spoke, decided to interrupt our little nostalgia party. He pulled the sap from his pocket and held it up to Kraken and me, letting the lead weight swing back and forth from the handgrip like a pendulum. "You mugs heard the man. Place is closed to the general public tonight. Take the little woman with you and scram!"

"Put that toy away, Hangman," Doc drawled. "You couldn't hurt either one of them with it."

Beerbelly, or Hangman, scowled. "Says you. Let's find out if fuckin' fish boy's head is as soft as his—"

That's as far as he got. With the suddenness of a rattlesnake, Kraken's arm shot out from his side. The adaro ripped the sap from the thug's fist and, in the same motion, flipped the lead weight back over his shoulder into the far end of the parking lot, where it clanked off the side of a parked midnight blue testosteronemobile.

Doc and I stared at Kraken for a moment in silent respect, but Tahiti's patience was exhausted. She wedged herself between Kraken and me, dismissed the openmouthed Hangman with a quick shake of her head, and turned toward Doc. "My name is Tahiti Whiteshell. I represent Leiti La'aka. Are you familiar with her?"

Doc nodded. "Sure. The Fakaleiti."

Hangman, trying to regain some face, stepped over to join his partner in the doorway. "She's that fat witch in the slum, right?"

Tahiti ignored him and continued to speak to Doc. "The Leiti sent me to speak to Ten-Inch, assuming he's still the chief of the Northsiders. If that's no longer the case, then I wish to speak with whomever has succeeded him in that capacity."

Hangman squared his shoulders and tried in vain to pull the front of his pants over his belly. "Look, sweet cheeks. Like I've been telling you, we're closed. If the witch wants to talk to our boss, tell her to call for a fuckin' appointment. Take a hint, lady. Tell your goons here that it's time to go home." He turned his head and belched, covering his mouth with the back of his hand.

Doc let his eyes close for an extended beat and gave his head a slight shake. "Hangman, go tell Doman that he's about to have company. Tell him Kraken and the Sarge are here, and they've brought a representative of the Leiti to speak with him. He'll know who they are."

"But—"

"Just do it." Doc patted Hangman on his shoulder.

Hangman puffed his cheeks and favored the three of us with a steely-eyed glare. "Fuck that," he said. With a grunt, the thug buried a lightning-like body shot into Kraken's midsection, his fist crashing into the big adaro's belly with a smack that could be heard a block away.

He may as well have punched a brick wall. Kraken didn't even let out a breath. As the thug gazed up at him in shock, the massive adaro swept Hangman aside with one arm, launching him face-first into his own still-steaming puddle of piss. After a second, the fallen palooka pushed himself to his knees with a groan, wiped the sludge out of his eyes, and spat into the mud. He tried to stand, thought better of it, and crawled over to sit against the wall of the bar.

Doc turned to Tahiti and sighed. "I'm sorry about Hangman. He may seem like an asshole, but once you get to know him you'll find that he really is an asshole."

"Look, Doc," I said. "My two friends may be right at home in this weather, but I'd really like to come in out of the rain and have a drink." I turned to look directly at Kraken. "We're not looking for any trouble."

Doc pulled at the end of his mustache. "You won't find Ten-Inch in here, and you ain't gonna like the drinks much. Plus, I can't promise that Doman will want to take the time to talk to any of you. But I wouldn't mind having a sit-down with the Sarge here. I'll get someone else to stand out here in the rain with Hangman for a while. The three of you can come in as my guests. But I'm gonna hold you to that 'no trouble' promise."

He opened the door, and a din of babbling voices poured out into the rainy night. "After you."

I folded my umbrella and stood back to let Tahiti enter. As Kraken and I followed her inside, I heard the big adaro grunt.

"Something wrong?" I asked him, glancing his way.

Kraken's upper lip curled. "This is a bad place," he muttered.

"You won't get any argument from me, big fella," I said.

Together, we crossed the threshold into The Dripping Bucket.

## Chapter Seventeen

I've frequented my share of dives. I'd thought Medusa's Tavern would be the most unappealing bar I'd ever see in my lifetime. I was wrong.

Stepping into The Dripping Bucket was like walking into a mad artist's nightmare. The first thing that struck me was the stench. I'd once watched a marine rescue team haul a sea lion out of a cove where it had beached itself a few days earlier and died. The gases that had caused it to swell to twice its size had been recently released when vultures ripped open its underbelly, and the fetid stink of dead sea creature had, until that night, been the foulest odor I'd ever encountered. No longer. Combine the scent of untreated puke, piss from a hundred cats, a week-old pile of dead fish, the deepest bowels of the most unwashed sewers of the city, and tank after tank of spoiled beer, and you'd have something that smelled like perfume compared to the interior of The Dripping Bucket. With an effort, I closed my throat to the bile that was making its way up my pipes.

The floor of the joint was covered with a six-inch layer of muddy shrimp shells and peanut husks. I shuddered to think how much worse the place would have smelled if the husks hadn't absorbed at least some of the stink. Rain leaked or poured through the ceiling in a number of places, soaking the shells and husks. Randomly placed oil lamps cast the only light in the bar. Cast-iron tables and benches were scattered chaotically across the floor, and thirty or so gangsters and hangers-on sat, stood, leaned, or lay amongst them. A row of metal crates, about four feet tall, were pushed together at the back end of the room to form a makeshift bar counter. Stenciled labels on the crates identified them as "Property of Tolanican Naval Forces." A haggard human woman behind the crates handed unmarked aluminum cans of warm beer to the bar's patrons in exchange for wads of paper money and piles of coins, which she tossed into a plastic garbage bag. The beer smelled like it had been homebrewed in a rusty bathtub, and scores of discarded cans littered the floor. I saw evidence of no other beverages.

Food? Yes, The Dripping Bucket served food: piles of shrimp, deep-fried almost into mush in vats of black cooking oil, which I suspected hadn't been changed since the bar first opened its doors.

Besides shrimp, raw peanuts were piled across the crates and on each of the tables, not to mention among the empty shells on the floor. The shrimp and peanuts were apparently free of charge.

I caught up to Tahiti. "How are you not retching from this smell?"

She glanced at me out of the corner of her eye. "Adaros filter and process scents differently than humans. We're better equipped to tolerate unpleasant odors."

Kraken shot an amused sneer my way. "Humans. So delicate. So weak."

Doc turned to us. "Wait here. I gotta find someone to man the door."

Tahiti scanned the room. Thugs in gang colors sat in clusters at the tables. Most of the gangsters were men. Three were definitely women, and a fourth could have been either or both. A handful of the thugs looked to be in their thirties, the rest either in their twenties or early-to-mid teens. Mandatory service for the Realm of Tolanica robbed the gang of members between the ages of eighteen and twenty-one. A few of the thugs, including one of the gals, had women sitting on their laps, joy girls in too-tight t-shirts and shorts, tattoos of flowers and birds on their exposed skin, needle marks on their arms, faces caked with makeup to hide acne scars and other signs of wear and tear. Two gangsters were stretched out on the floor, one of them lying in a pool of fresh vomit. As I watched, one of the thugs, a tough number with a broken nose and legs the size of tree trunks, tossed a giggling joy girl over his shoulder and carried her around the makeshift bar and out the back door.

Tahiti and Kraken were the only non-humans in the place. I wasn't surprised. Even though the bar was located in the settlement, an adaro woman in this crowd would likely incite a riot. The one I'd come in with was already the subject of many dark looks, and the babble we'd walked into when we'd first stepped through the door waned to near silence as more and more eyes turned in our direction.

"Which one do you think is in charge?" Tahiti asked me under her breath.

I spotted an older thug seated with his back to the wall to the right of the entrance in an actual chair, rather than on a bench. His jacket was off and hanging on the back of the chair, exposing a shoulder holster complete with a military issue nine-millimeter heater. He was counting a stack of bills while a teenaged banger sitting on a bench on the opposite side of the table looked on. A beefy bruno in a tight tank top stood at his side flashing muscles and watching Kraken and me from under a hooded brow. I nodded toward the seated figure. "That could be him. Let's go ask."

The older thug looked up as the three of us approached, seeing us for the first time. He held up a finger to let us know he needed a minute, and we waited while he finished counting up the dough. Task completed, he nodded, handed the young banger a couple of bills from the top of the stack, and deposited the rest of the bundle into a metal cash box. "Good job, Meat," he told the banger. "Your first brew's on me.'"

With Meat out of the way, the older thug stood and sized the three of us up with a critical eye. He smiled at Tahiti, and I noticed that his two lower front teeth were capped with gold crowns. "I know you. You're Leiti La'aka's apprentice."

"Yes. I'm Tahiti Whiteshell. I'm here as her representative. I was hoping to find Ten-Inch here tonight."

"I'm Doman, Ten-Inch's chief of staff. Unfortunately, Ten-Inch is unavailable. I'd offer you a drink, but I don't think a classy frail like you would like what we've got to offer."

The barest of grins appeared on Tahiti's face. "Thanks anyway, Mr. Doman."

"Just Doman, please." He shrugged. "They call me that because I handle the dough."

I think Tahiti wanted to groan, but she suppressed it. "I see. Then Doman it is." She placed her carrying case on the table. "I wish to discuss some important matters, but, before we get started, I brought something for you. Leiti La'aka would like to present the Northsiders with a gift." She opened the case and pulled out the conch shell. "She hoped it might contribute to the ambience of your meeting hall."

In the dimly lit bar, the conch shell gleamed like an orange and pink jewel as it reflected the light from the oil lamps. Doman stared at the shell, lifted his eyes to Tahiti, and glanced back down at the shell again before breaking out into amazed laughter. "The ambience of our meeting hall?" he choked out between laughs. "Fuck yeah! This place could use a little sparkle, am I right?" He wiped the corner of his eye and gave Tahiti a warm smile. "Shit. That shell is way too beautiful for this dump, but we'll gratefully accept the Leiti's gift and all the good will that comes with it. Thank you very much."

He looked out over the room. "Keahi!" A twentyish woman with a joy girl wrapped around her like an overcoat turned to look back over her shoulder at Doman, who signaled her to join us. With some difficulty,

Keahi extricated herself from her clinging companion and made her way across the room, dragging her feet through the moldy shells and husks.

Doman lifted the conch from the table. "Put this in a safe spot. Someplace where everyone can see it, but where no one can touch it. Got it?"

Keahi took the shell from Doman as if it were made of soap bubbles. "It's beautiful," she said. "But it won't last long in here with these fuckin' animals."

Doman's eyes hardened. "Spread the word. Anyone who breaks this answers to me."

Keahi sighed. "Don't worry. I'll figure something out."

After Keahi had taken the shell, Doman turned back to Tahiti. "Let's get down to business. Please, have a seat." He indicated the bench recently occupied by Meat.

Before sitting, Tahiti turned toward me. "I want to thank you for bringing me here, Mr. Southerland. I know that you and Kraken have other business. I'll find you when Doman and I are finished speaking."

"You sure you're okay being alone with this mug?"

"I'm a representative of the Leiti. I'm sure Doman respects that. I assure you, I'm perfectly safe."

I looked up at Kraken, who seemed torn between fulfilling his duty to the priestess and his desire to knock a few heads together until someone told him how to find Ten-Inch. "It's okay, Kraken. You can keep one eye on her while we go talk to some of the Northsiders."

Kraken frowned in thought as he considered his choices. After a moment, he nodded. "Yeah. Let's you and me go find Ten-Inch."

Once Tahiti and Doman were seated, the chatter in the joint picked up again. I scanned the crowd, looking to find Doc. Several eyes were on Kraken, who stood out like, well, like a naked seven-foot tall tower of muscle and scales, but no one seemed inclined to confront him. The adaro might be an enemy of the realm, but that didn't mean much to the patrons of The Dripping Bucket.

I spotted Doc at an empty table holding a can of beer, and he waved us over. Kraken and I stepped over a body lying prone on the shell-covered floor as we made our way across the room. I could tell the body wasn't dead because it was emitting chainsaw snores loud enough to be heard over the general din.

"Welcome to The Dripping Bucket," Doc said as we joined him. "Either of you want a beer?"

Kraken snorted, sending a spray of water from his gills.

The hood wiped moisture out of his eyes and smiled. "I'll take that as a no." Looking at me, he said, "How 'bout you, Sarge? Care to risk going blind?"

"Thanks. I'll pass. So this is where you moved after the Medusa burned down."

Doc pursed his lips and shrugged. "Quite a dump, isn't it? Not that the Medusa was anything special, but I miss it."

"How long have you guys been here?"

Doc thought about it. "Let's see.... The Medusa went up in flames about six months ago. Ten-Inch bought this place right after that. We chased all of the old customers away and turned it into our HQ." His nose wrinkled, and he looked around the place as if seeing it for the first time. "It's gone a little downhill since then, but I'm sure we'll clean it one of these days."

I heard a buzzing noise in my ear and waved a swarm of gnats out of my face, wondering what sort of ecosystem was thriving in that layer of peanut husks, shrimp shells, used beer cans, puke, and urine beneath my feet. "What's the rush?"

"Right." Doc propped his forearms on the table and leaned in to speak without shouting. "What do you think is happening over there?" he asked, indicating the table where Doman and Tahiti were engrossed in discussion.

I threw the question back at him. "What do *you* think?"

"The nymph is Leiti La'aka's girl, right? Word is the Leiti is trying to unite the street gangs that operate in the settlement to try to keep the Hatfield Syndicate from muscling in."

"Any chance of that happening?"

"Not much." Doc took a sip of his beer without choking. I guess he was used to it. "The Northsiders and the Claymore Cartel got too much bad blood between 'em. Besides, everyone knows that the Cartel are cozy with the Leiti. They'll get all the advantages in any deal she offers, and we're not going to accept anything that makes us answerable to the fuckin' Cartel." His lips twisted into a leering grin. "Some people think Jaguar is fucking her. They're saying she gave him some kind of drink that turned him into her personal sex toy." He looked across the table at me. "Have you met the Leiti?"

"Yes."

"Did she give you a drink?"

I thought about the Leiti's kava. "Just a sip."

I ignored the gangster's leer. "What do you think Ten-Inch would say about an alliance with the Cartel?"

Doc let out a sharp laugh. "Ten-Inch? He would tell the Leiti to go fuck herself. He would say, 'Screw the Cartel!' Then he would throw wave after wave of Northsiders against the Hatfields until none of us, including himself, was left standing. And then we'd all be dead, and the Hatfields would be in control of our territory."

"Is that what *you* want?"

Doc sighed. "What I want is a big pile of dough, a couple of dishy dames who'll let me keep most of it, and a good scrap every once in a while without a big-time outfit like the Hatfield Syndicate elbowing their way in and messing up a good thing." He punctuated his thoughts with a loud extended belch. "But that doesn't matter, does it. Everyone knows the Hatfields are coming. The only question is whether to stand up to them or stand aside. If we stand up to them, we're fucked. And if we stand aside?" He shrugged. "We're a different kind of fucked."

"So why not unite with the Cartel? They're a big outfit. That might give you a chance."

"We'd still be fucked." Doc sipped from his beer can. "The Cartel has chapters in a lot of cities, but they're only connected by their name and their colors. Basically, the Cartel here in Yerba City is just another neighborhood street gang, like us. We're minor league. The Hatfield Syndicate is the big leagues." He sighed. "That doesn't mean some of the dumb shits in here aren't interested. But if you ask most of the people in this room, they'll tell you they'd rather fight and die like warriors than roll over and live like dogs. With or without the Cartel, we'll fight. We can at least make the Hatfields bleed before we die. That's what Ten-Inch will tell us, if he's still alive."

"Do you think he's alive?"

Doc's shoulders slumped. "I want to. I don't know. And maybe it's better if he isn't."

"What do you mean?"

The hood's eyes lit up. "I was there that night. The night you took Ten-Inch down."

"Were you? I don't remember."

"I'm not surprised. I was one of the faces in the crowd. Ten-Inch had you on the ropes, but just when we all thought you were fuckin' dead on your feet...." He shook his head. "Th'fuck, man, none of us saw it coming. Ten-Inch was out like a fuckin' light, and we thought you'd finish him off. But you didn't." He paused, staring at me. "I almost wish you would've. Things kind of went downhill after that night."

"How so?"

Doc tilted his head and stared into the ceiling, thinking about what he wanted to say. After a few moments, he lowered his eyes and met mine. "Ten-Inch thought of the Northsiders as his children, and he saw himself as the stern-but-fair daddy he probably never had for himself. He was older and tougher than any of the rest of us. Fuck, he was tougher than any three of us put together." He sipped at his beer and set the can down on the table, screwing up his face as if he were tasting the bitter slop for the first time. "And then he was out cold on the floor with a busted wing, and you were standing over him. It was something none of us ever thought we would see. Once we *did* see it, though...."

Doc shook his head. "It wasn't the same after that. He used to tell us we were going to do something, and we would do it, no questions asked. We had a neighborhood, and it was *our turf*. Period. We owned it, and he was the fuckin' boss of all of it. He didn't put up with nobody fuckin' with his turf. Everyone in the neighborhood paid us for protection, and they only bought our shit. Anyone who crossed us paid in full, and there weren't any fuckin' two ways about it."

Doc flicked a stray peanut shell off the table. "When we saw him broken on the floor, it was like our eyes opened and the sun broke through the fog." He smiled and pointed at his head. "We started thinking. 'Why are we going out and selling these cheap-ass drugs and guns and women, and running our dumbass lotteries, and getting' shit for our troubles?' 'Why are we puttin' the hit on this guy or that guy? What'd they do?' 'Why are we shootin' it out with the Coyotes or the Strobes, or the Cartel to defend this street? Why don't we grab that one?' Everything he told us to do, now we wanted to know why. It wasn't like that before, and he didn't like it one fucking bit. Things got tense, and it got worse and worse. We had trouble recruiting. Ten-Inch started to look old. Some of his people challenged him for his leadership." Doc smiled. "They all lost. Fuck, Ten-Inch was old, but he was still the toughest motherfucker in the tribe."

Doc had stopped talking. "When did the Hatfields first approach him?" I asked.

Doc leaned further across the table and lowered his voice. "It was late last year, maybe seven or eight months ago. They came to all of us. Members of the Hatfield family, high-ranking friends, some of their torpedoes.... They came at us on all levels, talking big and flashing dough.

Ten-Inch had us ruling over a neighborhood. It seemed like a big neighborhood to us, but the Hatfields made us see how small it was. We didn't get nuthin' for it except the right to lord it over our little bit of turf. The Hatfields said we could be part of something bigger. We'd still run our rackets, but we'd be running them for the Hatfield Syndicate and with their support. We'd roll in dough. We'd have all the pussy we wanted. You know how it is with the Hatfields. They have it *all*, man!"

"But Ten-Inch said no?"

"Ten-Inch said *fuck* no. The Hatfields didn't have nuthin' he wanted. He said, 'We are the motherfucking Northsiders, and we are free!' He was stubborn like that. There wasn't nuthin' no one could tell fuckin' Ten-Inch. Ever."

"What happened?"

Doc sighed. "Ten-Inch thought he was our daddy. But the tribe didn't want to be his children anymore. Then Medusa's burned down. We didn't know how it happened, not at first, but Ten-Inch started to look weak after that. Some of us started thinking we'd be better off under the Hatfields. A boss is a boss, right? And the Hatfields had more to give us. I thought the tribe would just break up."

"But it didn't."

"Nope. Most of us are still loyal to Ten-Inch, especially us older members of the tribe. But there's been a lot of grumbling among the newer members, and some of the senior members..." he looked meaningfully in the direction of Doman, "started to rethink the status quo, if you get what I'm sayin'. Then last week, the Hatfields got the word out to us. 'Emergency meeting of the Northsiders at The Dripping Bucket.' We showed up, but Ten-Inch wasn't there. That was on Monday. We haven't seen him since."

I waved gnats out of my face, "And Doman took over?"

Doc lowered his voice even further. With my enhanced awareness, I knew what he was saying, but I doubt that Kraken could hear him over the noise. "He says he's holding the fort until Ten-Inch comes back, but he's a lying bastard. Maybe I shouldn't be telling you this, but I know Ten-Inch respected you, and that goes a long way with me. I don't trust that son-of-a-bitch Doman. He's always thought the Northsiders should be less of a family and more of a business. I'd be surprised if he didn't already have some kind of deal in place with the Hatfields. Whatever happened to Ten-Inch, I think Doman knew it was going to happen. He might have even been in on it. If the Leiti is really trying to keep the Hatfields out of the settlement, you should make sure she knows that."

I nodded. "I'll tell her. I'd like to talk to Doman sometime when he's away from the gang."

Doc thought about that. "He has a place somewhere in the settlement. I've never been there myself, so I can't say exactly where it is, but it's close to the marketplace. He runs a racket there. He uses an adaro crew to hook the outsiders who come in to shop. The crew lures them to his place for what they think is going to be the time of their lives, and Doman shakes them down. He pays off the authorities to turn a blind eye. It's a chickenshit hustle, strictly chump change. I think he does it more for the fun of it than for the dough."

A mealworm that had appeared seemingly out of nowhere was making its way over the tabletop, and I brushed it away with a backhanded swipe. A shadow fell over the table. I looked up to see a muddy Hangman and two other thugs looming over Kraken and me. They had hard looks in their faces and gats in their fists. Two of the gats were pointed at Kraken. The other was pointed at me.

"Th'fuck you two doing in our HQ?" Judging from his breath, Hangman had bolstered his courage with a can or two of the house brew and sounded just drunk enough to be dangerous.

## Chapter Eighteen

"It's cool, Hangman." Doc flashed his erstwhile partner a benign smile. "These two men are old friends of Ten-Inch."

"Za'right?" Hangman's eyes never left mine. "You should never have let them in. They're fuggin' outsiders, so take them outside."

Kraken rose to his feet, which put an end to any chance this encounter was going to defuse peacefully. Two gats rose with him, each aimed at the adaro's massive chest. They were twenty-twos, which weren't likely to kill the big sea creature outright, but there was a chance they could cause some damage.

I put a hand on Kraken's arm. "It's okay, Kraken. These mugs are just fuckin' with us."

Kraken shook my hand off. "I don't like to be fucked with." His lips curled into a snarl.

Before anyone could make a move, a voice cut through the heavy air. "Stop that this instant!" I glanced over Hangman's shoulder and saw Tahiti on her feet, heading in our direction.

"Put those stupid guns down before someone gets hurt!" Tahiti shouted.

A smile stretched slowly across Hangman's face. The gangster took a step away from me and turned his heater on Tahiti. "Back off, you little bitch," he said, his voice filled with contempt. "I don't take orders from fuckin' skirts."

Kraken was tensed to spring, but Tahiti caught his eye and shook her head. Her blue eyes gleamed in the lamplight as she turned them back on Hangman. "I'm asking you nicely one more time to please put your gun down. I won't ask again."

Hangman sighted down his pistol. As I prepared to launch myself from my chair, Hangman let out a yelp of surprise, and his head spun to his left. I saw his eyes widen with fear before his head spun back to his right, and he aimed the gat in the general direction of his two companions, who reflexively turned their weapons away from Kraken and aimed them at Hangman. Kraken's arms shot out almost too fast for me to see as he grabbed each of the gunmen by the sides of their heads and rammed them together with a crack that shook the air. The two gunmen plopped to the floor as if their bones had fled from their bodies.

Hangman screamed. "No, don't!" He waved at something only he could see. He fell to his knees and whimpered, "Mama? No, please. I didn't mean it. I didn't...." Slowly, the gangster turned his gun until it was pointed at his temple. "No... please... don't." Tears streamed down the sides of his face. "Please...."

"It's okay, Tommy." Tahiti's voice was soothing. "I've decided you may live. Put your gun down on the floor and go sit in the corner."

Hangman cried out loud, huge racking sobs. "Thank you, Mama. Thank.... I promise, I'll be good. Thank you." He crawled across the room, pants sliding past his hips to reveal threadbare undershorts and the crack of his ass, gun left behind on the floor. He made little whimpering noises all the way to a corner of the bar, where he sat facing away from the rest of the room, and sobbed piteous sobs.

All eyes were on Tahiti as she scanned the room, meeting everyone's stare. With a satisfied smile, she turned back to the visibly shaken Doman. "Let's wrap this up. I think we've done all we can for our initial meeting."

***

None of us spoke as I pulled the beastmobile away from The Dripping Bucket. The streets were flooded in places, and even with the windshield wipers on high, they couldn't keep pace with the intensity of the driving rain. The wipers showed me the road in flashes, clearing the windshield for split-second intervals before the pelting raindrops covered it over again. No lights illuminated the back streets of Tahiti's shortcut, and even with my magically enhanced awareness I had to ease off the pedal and proceed with caution.

I kept throwing sidelong glances at Tahiti, who stared straight ahead without moving. After a time, I asked, "What did you do to that gangster?"

Tahiti closed her eyes for a moment and sighed before turning toward me. "I touched a *tapu*, opened doors to memories he was suppressing and fanned the flames of the fears and regrets associated with those memories. It's not something I enjoy doing, but I thought it necessary."

"Your aim wasn't that precise," I said. "For a second there, while that hood was losing his mind, I felt just like I did the first time I went on jungle patrol in the Borderland. I could even smell the bark of the kapok trees. I wanted to dig a hole and jump in."

Tahiti's face fell. "I'm very sorry. Every *tapu* is volatile, and my control needs work. The Leiti has been teaching me, but I still have much to learn."

I glanced into the rearview mirror at Kraken, who was sitting in the back seat with a sulky expression. "How about you, big guy? Did you feel anything?"

"I don't want to talk about it," Kraken grumbled. "We didn't find Ten-Inch."

"That's true," I said. "But I learned a few things from Doc. Doman is probably working with the Hatfields, and he might know what happened to Ten-Inch. Maybe he even had something to do with it. If I can get him alone, I'll find out."

Kraken sat up straight. "Let's go back and get him now!"

"Easy, champ. We need to get Tahiti home. Doman doesn't spend all of his time with his gang. Tomorrow I'll find out where he stays when he's not with them."

"We'll both go," Kraken insisted.

"Sorry, pal. This is going to be a daylight job."

Kraken wanted to protest, but he knew he had no case. Sneaking around the settlement after dark in a car with shaded windows was one thing, but he was an enemy of the realm, and the Navy MAs would gun him down in the street if they caught him strolling around in broad daylight. He sat back in his seat to brood. He looked like he needed a drink, which probably meant he wanted to get off the land and into the ocean. I definitely needed a drink. I thought about the flask in my coat pocket, but elected to wait until I'd returned Tahiti to Leiti La'aka. The road was narrowing, and I knew we didn't have far to go.

I parked in the same place I'd parked before, the spot where the road narrowed until I was pinched in. No members of the Claymore Cartel came out to greet us this time, and the three of us walked down the dark meandering alleyways of the slum to the Leiti's shack. My umbrella was almost useless against the force of the storm, and I was soaking wet within minutes of leaving the beastmobile. I hid my misery, knowing that the rain was having no effect on the adaros. No lights shone from the surrounding structures. I heard no voices, either. Other than the drone of the rain pounding on the wood and metal roofs, the settlement was as still as a ghost town. I could almost believe that the neighborhood had been evacuated after we'd left for The Dripping Bucket. I put it down to the lateness of the hour, well after midnight, but still a few hours short of dawn.

When we reached our destination, I discovered the real reason for the preternatural quiet: Leiti La'aka's home was crawling with cops.

\*\*\*

Tahiti strode up to the first uniformed cop she saw. "What's the meaning of this? Is the Leiti all right?"

The cop shined a flashlight on the adaro. "Who are you?" The thin fabric of Tahiti's dress was plastered against her skin by the rain, and the cop's eyes honed in on her breasts.

"I live here. I'm Leiti La'aka's assistant. Where is she?"

The cop responded without moving his eyes. "You can't go in. This is a crime scene. Wait! Is that...?" The cop's eyes widened as he aimed his light at Kraken. "Buck!" he shouted. He reached for his sidearm.

Instincts honed by years of combat training replaced conscious thought, and before I was aware I had acted I had a firm grip on the cop's wrist just as he was pulling his weapon from his holster. With my other hand, I forced the barrel of his pistol up and back until it popped loose from his fingers. I moved behind the cop, wrapped my arm around his neck, and squeezed.

Pointing the cop's gun into the air, I shouted into the rainy night. "Nobody get nervous. All right? Keep your hands away from your pieces and no one gets hurt. Maybe we all have a beer when this is over."

Four bulls in official cop raingear stared at me, stunned and unmoving. I knew that wouldn't last.

"Who's in charge here?" I asked.

Before I could get an answer, Kraken began striding to the front door of the shack like he owned the place. One of the bulls moved into his path, which I thought was a poor decision on his part even before Kraken grabbed the cop by the back of his collar and, with no visible effort, flung him through the air. He came down in a heap in the mud a couple of dozen yards up the street.

Two of the other officers froze in their tracks, but the third cop pulled out his firearm, pointed it at Kraken, and shouted, "That's far enough, fish man! Stop right there!"

Kraken turned to the cop and grinned. Keeping my own gat pointed at the sky, I said. "Put that thing away, officer. You can't hurt him with that peashooter. You'll just make him mad. Now, who's in charge here?"

The cop kept his heater pointed at Kraken, but was hesitant to do anything that might anger the adaro buck. "Who wants to know?"

I indicated Tahiti with my chin. "This is Tahiti. She lives here. Where's Leiti La'aka?"

Two men stepped out of the Leiti's shack. One of them aimed a flashlight at my face, and a familiar voice shouted, "What the fuck is going on out here?"

I shielded my eyes from the bright light. "Detective Sims? That you?"

The portly detective adjusted his glasses and squinted behind the frames. "Southerland? What are you doing here? What are you doing with that officer? And what's that buck doing with you?"

Next to him, Modoc began pulling at his fingers, causing the knuckles to pop one after the other. A smile formed on his face beneath his cold eyes. I think he was happy to see me.

Tahiti stepped in front of me. "I'm Tahiti Whiteshell, detective. I live here with Leiti La'aka. Where is she? What has happened here?"

I released the cop I was choking, and he staggered toward Sims, who put a hand on his shoulder. "It's okay, officer. I'll take it from here." He raised his voice in order to be heard by the other cops. "If that adaro buck moves, shoot him. Ditto for this mug here." He turned to glare at me. "I'm going to call in the MAs."

Sims took out his phone, but Tahiti put a hand on his arm. "Where's Leiti La'aka? Is she okay?"

Sims turned to her, and his face softened by a degree. "There's been an incident, ma'am."

Tahiti released the detective's arm and put a hand to her face. "Is she okay?"

"I'm afraid not, ma'am. She's dead."

A choked yelp forced its way out of Tahiti's throat. "Is she inside? Let me see her!"

"I can't do that, ma'am. We'll be bringing her out in a minute."

"Let me in! This is my home! I want to see the Leiti!" Tahiti tried to push her way past the detective, who put her in a bear hug to restrain her.

That was too much for Kraken. He brushed the nearest cop out of his way and lifted Sims into the air before anyone could react. The detective's cellphone flew through the air. Tahiti ran toward the hut.

Modoc shouted, "Don't shoot! You'll hit Sims!"

I reached up and grabbed Kraken by the arm. "Put him down, Kraken. You're only making things worse."

A scream sounded from inside the hut.

Kraken dropped Sims to the muddy street and bounded toward the hut. Shots rang out, but I couldn't tell if any of them hit the adaro, who never slowed. I ran in after him.

Inside the hut, Tahiti was kneeling next to the body of Leiti La'aka, which was sprawled face up on the floor. One of the Leiti's legs was tucked under the rest of her body in an unnatural position. I stepped toward the Leiti and looked into her eyes, which were still wide open. They were dull, unseeing. From where I stood, I could see no marks on her body, no indication she had been harmed in any way. Nevertheless, it was obvious that the Leiti was dead.

Kraken gently pulled Tahiti away from the Leiti. A trail of blood ran down the back of his leg from a hole in his upper thigh, but he didn't seem to notice. The other cops filled the hut, but no one was shooting now.

Something about the Leiti seemed... wrong. Something beyond the fact that she was dead. I couldn't quite put my finger on it at first, but suddenly it was obvious. Sims was standing next to me, and I was about to ask him for an explanation, but Modoc pushed me away from him. "Get back outside, asshole. This is a crime scene."

Tahiti turned away from Kraken and shouted at Modoc. "Leave him alone! He's my guest." It didn't make a lot of sense under the circumstances, but people say odd things under stress.

Modoc grabbed Tahiti by the arm. "You need to go outside, too, ma'am."

"Let her go, little human." Kraken's voice dripped with menace.

Modoc released Tahiti and slammed a fist into Kraken's abdomen. The full weight of his body was behind the blow, and it would have shattered a concrete slab. It was the second solid body blow Kraken had received that night, and this one was delivered with far more force than the first. Kraken's only response was to lift the detective off his feet by both shoulders. On his way up, Modoc wrapped both of his hands around the adaro's throat and began to squeeze with everything he had. His chest and shoulders swelled as he pushed his thumbs into the big adaro's neck. Kraken's lips parted, revealing a mouthful of shark's teeth. He began to growl.

Four uniformed officers lifted their guns.

"Put him down, Kraken!" I shouted.

Kraken either didn't hear me or didn't care. He stopped growling and began to pull Modoc's neck toward his wide-open mouth. The cops positioned themselves to pump lead into the adaro without hitting the detective. I had less than a second to act.

The wooden kava bowl was on the coffee table. I snatched it up with one hand, and, in the same motion, shattered it against the side of Kraken's head. Kava flew through the room. The blow didn't hurt the adaro, of course. I didn't think it would—his skull was harder than his belly—but it took his attention away from Modoc. Kraken spun toward me, thrusting the detective away from him in the process. Modoc slammed into one of the cops, and the cop's gun went off with a crack that sounded like a bomb blast in the small crowded room. Kraken, eyes wild and teeth bared, reached for me with both hands. I stepped back out of his reach and bumped into one of the other cops. He must have tripped over something, because his arm shot around my waist, and, next thing I knew, both of us were sprawled on the floor.

Kraken roared and was preparing to come after me, when Tahiti stepped between us and slapped Kraken, hard, right in the chops. To my surprise, that stopped the big man cold.

"What's the matter with you!" Tahiti shouted.

Kraken opened his mouth to answer, but Tahiti cut him off. "Leiti La'aka is dead, you... you... you dumb *gruurl-braaplorp!*" Whatever Kraken was going to say died on his lips, and he hung his head like a dog caught gorging on the Sunday roast.

Sims, unruffled by the commotion, looked about the room. "Would everyone please settle down and start acting like professionals? Stop waving those gats around before one of you gets hurt. Speaking of which, did that shot hit anybody?"

We all looked at each other and confirmed that no one was bleeding, except Kraken, and it was from the bullet he'd taken earlier. I noticed rain leaking through a hole in the ceiling and pointed. "Looks like the only thing hit was the house."

I climbed to my feet. "What happened here, Sims?"

Sims took off his glasses and began rubbing at them with a dry handkerchief. "Police business, Mr. Southerland."

I pointed at Tahiti with my thumb. "She has a right to know."

Sims put on his glasses and turned toward Tahiti. He studied her for a moment before nodding. "Very well. Our operator at the precinct received a call informing us that Leiti La'aka was dead. The Leiti is an important person in the settlement. I was called at home. I was dreaming about sunshine and beautiful young dames with a thing for middle-aged authority figures with graying beards and receding hairlines. I dragged myself out of bed and here we are."

"How did she die?" I asked. "Murdered?"

Sims adjusted his glasses. "Can't say. We haven't found any indication of it. No blood. No wounds. No signs of a struggle. Maybe she had a heart attack."

Tahiti shook her head. "The Leiti didn't have a heart attack. Someone killed her."

Sims lifted his eyebrows and smiled slightly. "Oh? And how would you know that, my dear?"

I knew it, too. "The Leiti's tattoos."

Sims turned to me. "What tattoos?"

"Exactly," I said. "They're gone."

***

Sims wanted to take the body to the precinct for an autopsy. Tahiti wasn't having it.

"I must prepare her body and take it to the shore, where she will be taken by Havea Hikule'o to Pulotu, the land of the dead. There, she will dwell throughout time with the other honored Leitis."

"She may have been murdered," Sims objected. "We have to find out how she died."

Tahiti continued to stare down at the body of the Leiti. "I know how she died."

The detective's eyes widened. "Oh? Care to enlighten me?"

"She was killed. That's all that matters."

Sims put a comforting hand on the adaro's shoulder. "If someone killed her, don't you want to know who did it?"

Tahiti turned to the detective. "When she reaches Pulotu, she will tell Hikule'o what happened. Hikule'o will decide whether further action is necessary to restore order to the *manu* of this place."

Sims gave Tahiti's shoulder a squeeze. "Sure, miss. I don't know about moomoo or Havvy Hikayayhoo, but I'm the one with jurisdiction here. This is a police matter. You can have the body once we're done with it, and then you can send it off to Poloville or wherever you want it to go."

"No!" Tahiti pushed Sims's hand away. "I forbid you to cut her up. The Leiti must go intact to Pulotu."

Sims scowled. "You forbid? Miss, you forget who's in charge here." He turned to the other cops. "Go ahead, guys. Take the body to the station."

"No!" Tahiti shouted at the cops. "You can't!" She turned to Kraken, who had been standing with me near the doorway watching the argument unfold. "Kraken! Stop them!"

"Here we go again," I muttered to no one in particular. I lunged after Kraken, but I wasn't fast enough. The towering adaro reached the Leiti's body in one long stride, shoving aside everyone in his path. Four cops and two medics found themselves thrown against the walls of the shack, which shook as if it were in the grip of an earthquake. Modoc flung himself onto Kraken's back and locked his arms around the adaro's neck in a chokehold. Two cops drew guns and pointed them at the combatants.

I reached into my coat pocket for the gun I had taken from the cop and fired it into the ceiling. Everyone turned in my direction. I wrapped an arm around Sims and pointed the rod at his temple. "Get the picture, fellas?"

Everyone froze. "Modoc!" I shouted. "Climb down off the adaro. The rest of you, put down your weapons. Now." When no one moved, I touched the side of Sims's head with the muzzle of the pistol, which was hot enough to leave a mark. "You tell them, detective."

Sims winced. "Ow! Alkwat's balls, somebody shoot this motherfucker!"

That wasn't the response I had hoped for.

Things might have gone sour then, but I had a fierce adaro giant on my side. Kraken tore Modoc from his back and flung him into the cop pointing the heater. Modoc and the cop went down in a heap. He grabbed two other cops who were waving their gats and pounded them into the corrugated metal ceiling before releasing them and letting them fall to the floor. Water began pouring down into the room. I spotted another cop with iron in his hand and swung in his direction, putting Sims between us. "Don't do it!" I shouted. The cop raised both arms into the air in surrender, but hung on to the piece.

Sims wrapped both arms around my extended arm, planted his mouth on my bicep, and bit down hard. He caught me by surprise, and I let the pistol slip from my fingers. Suddenly, three cops, Modoc and two bulls in blue, were flashing gats and drawing a bead on me. I held them off by planting Sims in their line of fire.

Modoc's lips parted, and he showed me the toothy smile that undoubtedly dazzled every teenybopper he'd ever met. He turned and shot Kraken in the stomach. Tahiti put her hands to her mouth and screamed. Kraken doubled over, roaring like a beast, but kept his feet. The two other cops shifted their aim to the tottering adaro.

That's when the ceiling collapsed.

***

Fifteen minutes later, medics were tending to the injured cops outside the ruins of the Leiti's shack, shielding them from the rain to the best of their ability. Tahiti was nearby trying to examine the bullet hole in Kraken's midsection.

"Leave me alone, I'm fine," Kraken protested through gritted teeth. But blood was leaking from a hole in his midsection and from his silvery scaled leg.

Tahiti looked up at me with alarm. "We've got to get him to the ocean."

Kraken nudged her away from him with a gentle shove. "I'll get the Leiti." He breezed past the cops and entered the fallen shack, streams of scarlet trailing after him in the muddy ground.

Before anyone could stop him, Kraken had reemerged from the rubble with the plump body of Leiti La'aka slung over his shoulder like a wet sack of flour. No one was in the mood to get in his way. I heard sirens in the distance, the kind used by the MAs.

"We're leaving," I told Sims, who glanced at me and nodded once before turning his attention back to the wounded cops.

Modoc, a bandage wrapped around his head, called after me. "This isn't over, asshole. I'll be seeing you soon."

"I won't be hard to find," I told him.

## Chapter Nineteen

As we sped away from Leiti La'aka's ruined shack, the rain began to let up. It died altogether by the time we reached Fremont Street, although the sky remained threatening. Tahiti guided me to a quiet stretch of deserted beach a little to the west of the settlement. As soon as we were parked, Kraken, resisting any offers of assistance, marched resolutely into the surf and disappeared into the crashing waves.

"He'll be fine now," Tahiti told me. "The ocean will heal him."

"Are you sure? It couldn't give him back the finger he lost."

"The wound may leave a scar. He'll probably be proud of it." Tahiti's lips pursed, and she made a gurgling sound.

"Wanna run that by me again?" I asked.

She grinned at me. "Loose translation? I said, 'Foolish boy.' A more literal translation might shock you."

"I doubt it. Not even coming from a nice young girl like you." I nodded toward the ocean. "You like him, don't you."

Tahiti made a sour face. "Maybe. But I'm a *kwuurlplup*, a priestess, so…. Anyway, I have no desire to compete with other women for his attention." She looked up at me, her eyes moist. "Will you help me with the Leiti?"

I carried the heavy body of Leiti La'aka from the beastmobile to the shore and stretched it out on the sand. "What happens next?" I rasped, out of breath from the exertion.

"She will be taken to the Island of Pulotu, the realm of the dead. The Leiti was an acolyte of Havea Hikule'o, the ruler of Pulotu, and she will be welcome there. Hikule'o will be unhappy if the Leiti isn't on the beach when her oarsmen come to get her. That's why I couldn't let the police keep the body. You really don't want to get Hikule'o upset. Especially now."

"What do you mean?"

Tahiti frowned. "I'm not exactly in her good graces right now." She sucked in a breath and shook her head, as if shaking off a bad dream. "I'll stay until they come for her. Thanks for your help tonight. If we don't see each other again, I want you to know that I'm glad I met you. You seem like a decent person. For a man."

I raised my eyebrows at her and showed her a smile. "You don't like men?"

She smiled back and pushed her hair off one shoulder. "I'm sorry, that didn't come out right. It's nothing personal. It's just that I don't associate with men all that often. It's that way for most adaro women, especially those still in the water. It's different with us than it is for humans."

"Because there's so many more adaro women than men?"

"Mostly, yes. Throughout our history, the highest aspiration for most women has been to become a wife, but, as you say, we outnumber the men, so there's a lot of competition for the few men who are available. Only a small percentage of adaro women become wives."

"And the rest are out of luck?"

Tahiti crossed her arms and stared down at the sand. "Many of our women feel that way." She scratched a figure-eight into the wet sand with her toe. "But being married to a man isn't easy. Our men are strong, and when it comes to their wives they are extremely protective."

She looked up at me. "You have to understand something about adaros. There are many dangers in the ocean. Throughout our existence, we have been protected by two things: strong nature spirits and the strength of our men. Strength and ferocity are highly valued in our men. It can't be any other way if we are going to survive as a species. Our society has always been run by physically powerful men, and our customs encourage men to be strong and protective."

She ran her foot across the figure-eight and obliterated it. "Our society has given strong men a great many privileges. It is customary that a man—even a married man—may have intimate relations with as many women as he can manage, as long as the women are unmarried. But wives are expected to be faithful to their husbands, to honor their place, not only as the leaders and protectors of our communities, but as the leaders and protectors of their families. It is a great shame for a wife to have relations with a man she is not married to. It's disrespectful."

"Must be swell for the men," I said. "But it doesn't seem fair to the women."

Tahiti's lips curled into a wry smile. "You think humans are any different? I've been around enough of you to know that human and adaro men have very similar ideas about marital relationships."

I couldn't argue with that, and I didn't try. Sometimes I'm smart enough to keep my trap shut.

"Also," Tahiti continued. "In our society, a man may set aside his wife at his pleasure and choose another for his wife, even if he has already fathered children. A woman does not have this right. A woman who has been released from the marriage bonds is not permitted to remarry."

"That's rough. Can a divorced wife fool around with single men?"

"Of course not! In our society, it is forbidden for a woman who has been married to be intimate with any man other than her husband, no matter what, even if he has divorced her, or died."

"So divorced and widowed women are out of luck?"

"That's our way."

"What about single men, like Kraken?"

She pursed her lips again. "Although married men have many privileges, unmarried men are supposed to wait until they are married before having sexual relations with women, and they are forbidden from having relations with the wives of other men. At least, that's how it's supposed to be. In practice, our boys and men have license to do whatever they can get away with."

I hashed this over. "To be honest, that sounds a lot like life among humans, too. Although, in practice, enforcement of the rules is probably a lot looser among humans than what you're describing. And, of course, divorced and widowed women are free to remarry."

Tahiti's face hardened. "Humans are shameless! How do you even know which children are legitimate and which aren't? So many of your children are born outside the bonds of marriage. How you ever maintain such a population of bastard children is unfathomable to me. Adaro bastards have a low standing in our society. Men born outside legitimate unions are not respectable. Women of illegitimate birth are not permitted to marry men of legitimate birth. It happens sometimes, but it's not supposed to. And it shouldn't. It's not our way."

I thought back to Leena Waterfowl and her sister, Mila. "The adaro women I've met lived different lives than what you've been telling me about."

Tahiti scowled. "I know what you humans think of us. You call us 'nymphs' and see us as vessels for relieving your sexual tensions."

"Hey, not all men are like that," I protested.

"Is that your defense? Human males aren't guilty because a few of them are innocent? And how innocent *are* you, Mr. Southerland? What's the first thing that comes to your mind when you see an adaro woman? You think I can't see what you're thinking when you look at me?

Even now, standing above the corpse of a friend I knew well and admired? Tell me you have never referred to any of us adaro women as 'nymphs'!"

I threw my hands up in surrender. "All right, already. But don't look at me! I've been a perfect gentleman around you. And, to be fair, it isn't easy for us men. You know what kind of effect you girls have on us."

"Girls? Do you think of me as a child?"

"No!" I protested. "I mean, sure, you're young, but you're all woman. I'm just saying that adaro women..., I mean, it's a well-known fact that..., but I don't have to tell *you*, right?" I didn't want to continue. I wanted to climb into the hole I was digging and bury myself alive.

Naturally, Tahiti wasn't going to let me. "A strong man controls himself." She curled her upper lip. "Unfortunately, human men are not strong."

"Look, Tahiti. I'm not going to argue with you. All I'm saying is that I think some of the adaro women I've met would be uncomfortable living within the rigid social conventions you've described. I knew of a couple in particular who were quite free-spirited."

Tahiti sighed. "Living on the land has not been good for us. Too many of us have adopted the licentious values of humans. Removing them from our traditional society has been a terrible crime. It has destroyed our way of life!"

"Is having more liberties such a terrible thing?"

"It's not our way." Tahiti's face reddened as she glared at me. "It would be much better if the women of the settlement returned to the sea, the way Kanoa wanted them to."

I indicated the body at our feet. "She didn't think the adaros were all that hot on leaving."

Tahiti's eyes flashed. "The Leiti was a great woman. But she was *not* an adaro. She didn't know us as well as she thought."

I shrugged. "We are all products of our own culture, I guess. I don't know a lot of human women who would willingly trade lives with the women in your society, at least not the way you've described it. No sex outside of marriage? No remarrying after a divorce? Not even a Dragon Lord could enforce your society's rules among most of the women I know."

Tahiti glanced at the roaring surf and let some of the tension out of her shoulders. "If I'm being honest, Mr. Southerland, I have to admit that there are fewer virtuous women in our society than I've let on. Scandalous behavior among us is... not infrequent."

I shot her a grin. "Scandalous behavior, eh? I suppose since there are so many more adaro women than men, a lot of women must find themselves in relations with other women."

Tahiti nodded. "Yes. But that's not scandalous. Same sex relationships among unmarried women are common and perfectly acceptable. Many of these develop into an official lifelong coupling with the same benefits as marriage, although with less status. It's the same with our men, too. They spend a lot of time training and fighting together. It's only natural that they would build close relationships with each other, too."

I thought about that. "Doesn't that leave even fewer men as husband material for the women?"

"Not at all. Almost every man takes a wife, even if just for the purposes of having children."

"But doesn't that leave most of your women unmarried for life? What sorts of lives do they lead without husbands?"

Tahiti shrugged. "Productive ones. They don't have the same status as married women, of course, but they fill many vital roles in our communities. Most of our food is gathered and processed by unmarried women, or women in female couplings. They do most of the service and domestic work. They conduct a great deal of business. And a woman can always apply for the… for the priesthood, as you would call it. Like I have."

"Are there a lot of you?"

She grinned a bit at that. "I don't know how many you would call a lot, but, yes, I suppose there are. It's a good way to avoid living with a man." She giggled, and for a moment she seemed more like a young human girl than a serious adaro priestess. "They aren't usually as docile as Kraken, you know."

I grunted at that. "You think of Kraken as docile? He seems like a swell kid, but I watched him crack the skulls of two gangsters and slam two cops into a metal ceiling tonight."

Her smile broadened a bit. "Not many of our men would have let any of those policemen live. Or you, either, for that matter. When our men get into a fighting mood, they are difficult to control."

"You stopped him," I pointed out. "And you're half his size."

Tahiti's face became serious, and her blue eyes met mine. I felt myself falling into them. "In the middle of it all," she said, "when Kraken was coming at you? He would have killed you if I hadn't been there."

"And you sobered him up with one slap?"

"Yes. I'm a *kwuurlplup*."

"At least you didn't send him crawling into a corner."

She looked away from me.

"Sorry," I said. "I guess that was an insensitive thing to say."

Tahiti sighed. "It's okay. It's who I am. Some of the powers I possess are... terrifying, even to me. But my skills are nothing compared to what the Leiti could do. That young man I had to deal with will recover. If the Leiti had been there, she could have called up a *qaitu*, what you might call a ghost. These *qaitus* are fearsome, even to look upon. The *qaitu*'s touch freezes the blood, and its scream brings madness. There is a reason the Leitis are feared. Leiti La'aka may have seemed like a kindly old woman, but she had power beyond belief."

"And yet, someone killed her."

"Yes." Tahiti gazed down on the Leiti's body.

Leiti La'aka had power beyond belief. What did that say about whoever killed her? I didn't want to think about that.

"What did you mean when you said you knew how the Leiti was killed?"

Tahiti didn't answer right away. After a few moments, she shook her head. "I don't want to talk about that yet."

"Okay."

Tahiti turned toward me and smiled. "After what you saw tonight, you must think I'm a monster."

I met her eyes and matched her smile with one of my own. "Not at all. And if I did, I wouldn't say so."

Her smile faded, and she grew thoughtful. "I'm glad to hear that. In a way, I *am* a monster. I didn't use to be. I was a normal child before I went into my training. But knowledge, the kind of knowledge I've received, changes you. *Kwuurlplups* can do monstrous things. We command ancient spirits, spirits older than adaros, and not all of them are friendly. We intercede with these spirits in order to protect our people, and we are given a great deal of responsibility. And sometimes that means doing things that others might consider evil. Like what I did to that young man tonight. It seemed like an evil thing, but is an action really evil if I do it to protect others? He might have done something terrible to you and Kraken if I hadn't stopped him."

"He might have," I agreed. "And I'm still in one piece, thanks to you. That makes you an all right gee in my book."

"I'll be as powerful as a Leiti one day. Maybe more. Sometimes I wonder what kind of person I'll be when I can summon up *qaitus* and command them to possess the bodies of the living. Or deprive a person of his *manu* and leave him to live an empty life without luck or hope. Will I have the will to live a simple life, like Leiti La'aka did, or will I be seduced by my powers and live a selfish life, forgetting that I am a servant of my people and choosing to serve only myself? Especially now that she is no longer here to teach and restrain me."

I shook my head. "These are questions you have to answer for yourself over time. But you're young. You'll solve them."

The faraway look left her eyes, and she smiled at me. "How old do you think I am?"

"I couldn't say. I don't know how adaros age."

"Much like humans do until we reach forty or so years. Then we remain physically unchanged for many years."

"In that case, I'd say you were about ninety."

She gave me a playful tap on my shoulder with her fist. "Don't be silly. I'm twenty years old."

"Really? You look fourteen."

"I do not!"

"Yes you do. I feel like your babysitter."

"So I'm a baby now?"

I looked her up and down, aware of the rain spilling down her bare shoulder. "Well, okay, you're not a baby. A baby couldn't have kept Kraken from tearing me apart."

Tahiti's lips parted, exposing the tips of her pointed teeth. "Kraken is a little boy, but he's smart enough to know how to behave around a *kwuurlplup*. Even one who is still in training."

Tahiti's eyes held a strange gleam, and, with reluctance, I tore my gaze away from hers. The ocean seemed gray and cold after looking into those eyes. "I guess I owe you my life. Thank you."

"You're welcome. But I had an ulterior motive."

"Oh? And what's that?" I was suddenly apprehensive.

She smiled, and her nose crinkled in a way that made my heart skip a beat. "I needed you to help me bring the Leiti here. Why? What were you thinking I meant?"

I listened to the waves crashing in the darkness. "That was important?"

Tahiti smiled at me for another second before turning her own gaze to the incoming waves. "More than you can possibly imagine."

I was going to question her further, but I was distracted by movement on the water. I pointed. "Is that what I think it is?"

Tahiti peered out into the ocean. "Where? I don't see anything."

"It's a ship of some kind. A small one." I honed in on the object. "Not a ship—a canoe! With two men paddling it. They're too small to be adaros. They must be human."

"They're coming for the Leiti." I was aware of the beating of Tahiti's heart, and she struggled to calm her breathing. "They're from Pulotu."

"What's Pulotu?" I asked. "You've mentioned it, but I've never heard of it before."

"It's an island, but it's not in this world. It's the land of the dead. That is where they will take the Leiti."

I stood next to Tahiti, transfixed, as the two oarsmen steered their canoe through the treacherous waves far more quickly and easily than I would have thought possible. When they drew near the shore, the rowers slipped out of the canoe and dragged it up the beach until they reached the body of the Leiti. The men were human, broad-shouldered and thickly built, each clothed only in a kind of grass skirt that resembled the *ta'ovala* Tahiti was still wearing. Before I realized it had happened, Tahiti's hand was in mine. I shot her a quick glance, but her attention was on the two oarsmen, who, without a word, effortlessly lifted the Leiti and placed her with care into the canoe. When the body was in place, the two men stood on either side of the canoe with their heads lowered. Tahiti's head was lowered, too, and it seemed right that I should lower mine, so I did. A warmth spread through the cold, moist air, and for a moment it was as if we'd all been transported to the tropics. I heard unfamiliar sounds—calling birds, grunting beasts, and the rushing of a river—and I knew these sounds did not come from a Caychan beach.

After a minute or so, the two men raised their heads in unison. The tropical sounds were replaced by the crashing of waves, and the tropical warmth by the Yerba City cold. Without so much as a glance at Tahiti or me, the oarsmen dragged the canoe into the surf. Tahiti's hand was still in mine as we watched the canoe holding the body of Leiti La'aka vanish into the darkness, and for several minutes afterwards we continued to gaze out over the roiling black water and listen to the arrhythmic pounding of the incoming surf.

After a time, my breathing grew heavy, and my head became light. Tahiti must have noticed something, because she slid her hand away with an apology. The breeze had blown her hair over her eyes, and she reached up to brush it clear. "I'm going to miss the Leiti," she said.

"Do you have somewhere to go?"

"I have some friends who live near the marketplace. I can stay with them for a while."

"Need a lift?" I asked.

She smiled at me, but shook her head. "Thanks for your help tonight. You didn't have to get involved, and I appreciate everything you did for me. I'm going to check in on Kraken and make sure he's okay. After that I'll find my own way back into the settlement."

"At least give me your number. I'll call you."

She took a cellphone from her *ta'ovala*, and we entered each other's numbers into our contact lists. She hugged me then, and kissed me on the cheek, causing my head to grow light again. We said our goodbyes, and I watched her walk away and disappear into the waves.

On the way home, the winds calmed, and the clouds parted in the early morning sky. After parking the beastmobile at Gio's, I looked up and gazed at the bright quarter moon, like the one I had seen in my dream the night after researching Taufa'tahi a few months before. It was surrounded by a panoply of twinkling stars. No deluge today, I thought to myself. So much for prophecies.

I was a hundred yards from my house when I became aware of the chrome moon hubcap propped up against my front door. I picked up my pace, scanning the street as I approached the building, trying to pick up any surveillance. If anyone was watching me, I didn't catch them at it. When I reached my porch, I scooped up the hubcap and carried it inside before examining it. Once in my office, I wiped it dry and studied the surface. I stared at it for several seconds, blinked, and stared at it some more. Etched into the surface, as if with the tip of a needle, was a single word: SUNNY.

## Chapter Twenty

I awoke to the sound of Detective Kalama's laughter.

"Uhhmmrawha...," I managed. I tried again. "Wha'? Uhh..."

"Wake up, gumshoe! You're talking in your sleep."

I rolled over in my bed to escape the drool that had pooled up on my pillow and was sliding down my chin. My phone fell to the sheets, and I returned it to the side of my face. "Issat you, detective? Was I saying something?"

"You sure were. Unfortunately for you, I'm a married woman, and you're not my type. We've really got to fix you up with a date."

"Lord's balls."

"That's not what you were asking for a second ago."

"Shuddup, Kalama. Whaddoyouwan'?"

"What are you offering, ya big lug? And are you sure you're in good enough shape to deliver?"

"Does Kai know you talk like this to strange men?"

"You should hear how I talk to him!"

"Yeah, well, skip it." I forced a yawn until it took over and became real. "Excuse me, detective, but you woke me out of a sound sleep, and I've got to go take care of some urgent business."

"Don't you dare take me into the bathroom! Call me back when you're done. But be quick about it. This is important."

Five minutes later, properly armed with a cup of coffee seasoned with a splash of rye, I speed-dialed the detective's mobile from my office. "Okay, detective, I'm back and almost awake. What's up? And don't say what I know you want to say."

Kalama's voice turned innocent. "I have no idea what you mean by that, gumshoe."

"Right. What time is it, anyway?" I silently sipped some of the coffee and winced. I might have slipped a little when I was adding the rye.

"Eightish. I wanted to catch you first thing. Got something interesting on the wire this morning from the Placid Point Precinct. A notable woman named Leiti La'aka was murdered last night or early this morning, and among the persons of interest in the case is a private snoop called Alexander Southerland. We've been asked to find him and pick him up."

"The Placid Point cops aren't coming for me themselves?"

"They're shorthanded, and you live in our jurisdiction. Also, an adaro buck was spotted on the scene, and they're helping the MAs look for him. Wanna tell me what's going on now, or should I send someone to bring you here?"

I sighed and sat up in my chair, gathering my thoughts. "I had a chat with the Leiti last night regarding my investigation."

"Looking for Ten-Inch."

"Right."

"Find him yet?"

"Not yet."

"Continue."

A sip of coffee got me to coughing, and it took me a few moments to regain control. "Sorry," I said. "Where was I?"

"You had a chat with Leiti La'aka last night."

"Right. So I took the Leiti's apprentice, a young adaro called Tahiti Whiteshell, with me to The Dripping Bucket."

"Lord's balls, gumshoe!" Kalama interjected. "That's the last place you want to take a date if you're trying to impress her."

I rubbed my eyes. "It wasn't a date, and I wasn't trying to impress her. She was there as a representative of the Leiti in some kind of negotiations with the acting head of the Northsiders."

"Man named Doman?"

"Right."

"And what do these negotiations have to do with you?"

I sighed. "Nothing. I went there to ask around about Ten-Inch. Anyway, we go back to the Leiti's place afterwards. When we get there, we find the shack filled with cops, and the Leiti is lying on the floor, dead. Murdered."

Kalama waited for more, and when I didn't offer her any she asked, "How was she killed?"

I shrugged, even though she couldn't see it. "Beats me."

"Then how do you know she was murdered?"

I opened my mouth, closed it, opened it again and asked, "What do you know about the late Leiti La'aka?"

"I know about Leities. They're witches, essentially. Maybe not on the level of Madame Cuapa, but not the frauds that grift the tourists on the wharfs, either. Definitely the real thing. Leiti La'aka was supposed to be a strong one. She was a respected person in the adaro settlement. She arbitrated disputes among the inhabitants and acted as a liaison between the settlement officials and the members of the community. In a lot of ways she was the unofficial mayor of the adaro settlement. Her death is going to cause a lot of trouble, especially if it's established that her death was a homicide. So talk, Southerland. What makes you think she was murdered?"

"The Leiti was heavily tattooed, and a lot of magic flowed through that ink. You're right when you say that she probably wasn't in Madame Cuapa's weight class. Cuapa's in a league by herself. But I don't think Leiti La'aka was all that far off. Anyway, when I saw her on the floor, her tattoos were gone."

"Gone? Are you saying they'd been removed?"

"They were just gone. And so was the magic."

"Hunh! And you're sure about this?"

"I am. I'm working on a theory that someone killed her in order to strip her of her magic."

Kalama was probably the smartest detective I'd ever met, and I could almost hear her considering the implications. "Maybe she wasn't murdered. Maybe the magic just left her when she died. A collateral effect."

"That's possible," I admitted. "But Tahiti, the Leiti's apprentice, concluded she'd been murdered, and it seems to me that she would know. She also says she knows how it was done, but she's not talking about it. Still, I guess we shouldn't rule out a natural death based on her word alone. I'll talk to an expert about it."

"You'll do no such thing, gumshoe," Kalama told me. "You're a person of interest in the case. That means you can't investigate it. You'll gum it up."

I paused to take a healthy swallow of the coffee, which was going down more smoothly now. "The only reason I'm a person of interest is because I took the body away from the crime scene."

"You *what*?" Kalama was incredulous. "Explain yourself, Southerland!"

"Tahiti insisted that the Leiti needed to be taken to the ocean so that she could be carried off to someplace called Pulotu. Tahiti says that's the land of the dead. So after the shack's roof collapsed, Kraken—that's the name of the adaro buck—grabbed the body, and I drove us all to the beach."

"Hold on! Wait a second!" Kalama made a few attempts to come to grips with everything I'd just dumped on her. "Pulotu? Land of.... Wait! Did you say Kraken? What was he doing there?"

"Kraken was helping me look for Ten-Inch. He went with me to the Leiti's and to The Dripping Bucket."

"And he was with you when you went back to Leiti La'aka's house?"

"More of a shack, really, but, yeah, that's right."

"What's this about the roof collapsing?"

"Well...."

"*Southerland*? Don't clam up on me now!"

"Kraken and me had a little altercation with Placid Point's so-called finest. A couple of swell detectives, Sims and Modoc, were on the scene. Modoc put his hands on Tahiti, and Kraken didn't take it well. Things got out of control."

"And the roof collapsed," Kalama said, finishing my edited summary of the events.

"Well, it was raining pretty hard, and the Leiti's shack wasn't exactly up to code."

"Hmm." Kalama sounded less than satisfied. "Let's get back to that later. Sims, yeah. According to the wire, Detective Sims arrested you on Wednesday morning."

"For jaywalking. They have a big jaywalking problem in Placid Point."

"So I hear. The report also says you were drunk and disorderly."

"Allegedly. I was never tested."

"Little early in the morning to be soused, wasn't it?"

"I wasn't soused," I insisted. "It was raining. I had a couple of belts to chase away the chill."

"Uh-huh."

I set my coffee cup on my desk, a little off to the side. "I'm cutting back."

"Sure you are, gumshoe," Kalama said, sounding skeptical. "About time, too."

"What's *that* supposed to mean?"

Kalama got the conversation—interrogation, actually—back on track. "So you and Kraken, and this nymph, Tahiti, took the stiff to the ocean. What'd you do, dump it?"

"No, I didn't dump it, detective. Two emissaries from Pulotu rowed in on the tide and took the body away with them."

"I see. So you dumped it."

"I'm serious, detective. I watched the oarsmen row the Leiti off into the night. You'd have liked them. Dark, handsome, no shirts, rippling muscles...."

When Kalama didn't respond, I said, "Come on, detective. It was no stranger than the shadow-dog who possessed that witch. Or the hag from the abyss. The whole thing was actually rather dignified."

Kalama sighed. "Whatever you say, gumshoe. Bottom line, the body's gone. For good, I assume?"

"That's a safe bet."

"Do the Placid Point dicks know what happened to it?"

"No. That's probably why I'm a person of interest."

"What are you going to tell them?"

"The truth. I'm sure they'll understand." I reached for my coffee and took a swallow. I didn't want it to get cold.

Kalama snorted. "Sure they will. Look, gumshoe. Watch out for Sims and Modoc. Rumor is they're on the pad. Either with the LIA or the Hatfields or both. Sims is smart, but he's got his own rackets going. Modoc is a real piece of work. Suspects check into that station house, and they don't check out again. How'd *you* get out?"

"I had some help."

"Let me guess—Lubank?"

"Maybe."

"Watch out for him, too. I'll bet you already owe him your life savings."

"He and I have an arrangement."

"Right. You do the work, and he gets the dough."

"Usually," I admitted. I reached for my coffee, but the cup was dry.

"All right, gumshoe. My advice is to keep your head down for a while. Don't let Sims get you back into one of their sweatboxes. Steer clear of Modoc. Stay out of the adaro settlement. And never, ever, set foot in The Dripping Bucket again, especially with a date."

"Sure, Mom. And I promise to eat my vegetables, too."

"Fuck you, Southerland. You get in trouble, don't expect any help from me. Kai and I have tickets for the opera tonight."

"Opera?"

"Entertainment for respectable people, gumshoe. You'd hate it."

"No doubt."

"One more thing before I go. This Tahiti Whiteshell? She's listed as a person of interest, too."

"So?"

"She may be mixed up in some kind of resistance movement in the settlement. The NCIS has its eye on her."

"Who could blame her?" I wondered if Tahiti knew she'd come under the attention of the Naval Criminal Investigative Service.

"Take care of yourself, gumshoe."

The detective disconnected.

\*\*\*

For breakfast, I washed down a slice of day-old pizza with a glass of orange juice instead of a bottle of beer, because oranges are chock full of vitamin C, and because I was cutting down on alcohol. I felt pretty good about that. Fueled and hydrated, I decided to go for a run, something I hadn't done in weeks. Throwing on a sleeveless sweatshirt and some sneakers, I prepared to hit the pavement.

Ominous clouds hung low in the sky, and the air was thick with droplets, but the rain had stopped during the night. I listened to the passing cars splashing through the still-wet streets, water rooster-tailing off the back tires, as I glided over the sidewalk, dodging the occasional puddle. I picked up my pace, generating heat to combat the cold breeze that wanted to drive me back indoors. I marveled at the ease of my stride, wondering why I'd been denying myself the pleasure of the run, and thinking I hadn't lost a bit of my form or stamina since the last time I'd worked out. I kicked the pace up another notch, cruising past the storefronts, bars, and working-class homes of the Porter District, tossing out a quick "good morning" to oncoming pedestrians, and an "on your left" to the pedestrians I caught and passed from behind. I was invincible, but, knowing it was my first run after a long layoff, I resolved to keep it short, maybe four miles, five at the most.

A mile out, I was hunched over, hands on knees, sucking in gulps of chilled air and trying not to puke. My stomach was clenched like a fist, trying to fight off the acid burn from the orange juice, and the leftover pizza was pushing its way through my intestines like viscous lava. After taking a few minutes to catch my breath, I began to walk slowly back the way I'd come, lamenting the fact that I'd left my phone at home and couldn't call a cab.

Halfway home, I'd recovered enough to wonder if I might be able to jog the rest of the way, as long as I didn't push it. Just as I'd finished convincing myself to give it a try, I heard a familiar voice calling to me from an expensive beige SUV parked along the street.

"Excuse me, sir! You look like a man who could use a ride."

I stopped alongside the vehicle and peered into the open window at the driver, a large heavily muscled man in his twenties. "Are you offering me one?"

"Of course not, sir. The way you're perspiring? The Madame would be furious if I let you into her car in your present condition."

Cody, personal assistant to Madame Cuapa, the most powerful witch in western Tolanica, was grinning at me from ear to ear. One look at his motorist attire, and I couldn't help grinning back. He gazed at me through a pair of vintage black-framed aviator goggles, and the cashmere scarf double-wrapped around his neck was dyed a neon pink so bright it almost glowed. He wore no shirt under a buttoned black-leather vest that exposed a hairless chest almost as broad as a troll's. His long black hair was tied back in a ponytail, and a black leather bowler was perched at the top of his head.

"What are you doing here in the Porter, Cody?" I asked. "Slumming?"

"Waiting for you, actually. The Madame told me you'd be here about now." He looked me up and down. "She didn't tell me you'd be looking like something the cat dragged in."

I laughed. Cody's "cat"—Mr. Whiskers—was a four-hundred pound manticore, a lion-like creature with eagle's wings, a scorpion tail, and claws that could tear through steel. "It can't be that bad. I've still got all my limbs."

"What happened? Did that pimpmobile of yours finally break down?"

"The *beast*mobile is fine. I went for a run."

"What'd you do, twenty miles?"

"Fuck you, Cody."

Cody's grin widened. "Not until you clean yourself up. I've got standards."

I shook my head in surrender. "I might have let myself get a little out of shape in the last couple of months. I'm trying to fix that."

"Good for you! But don't try to do too much too soon. A man your age has to ease into it."

"Smartass! I'm only a few years older than you."

Cody nodded. "Sure you are. But don't forget, we are very definitely on opposite sides of thirty."

I sighed. "What does Madame Cuapa want with me?"

Cody's grin disappeared, and he paused before speaking. "She says you're in trouble. Or will be soon. I've got something she wants me to give you."

Cody opened his glove compartment and pulled out a pint flask made of polished silver. "Here. Take this. The Madame says you should drink this at the end of the day as you are retiring for the night." He held up a finger in warning. "But not until you are ready to sleep. It packs a punch."

I took the flask and eyed it with suspicion. "Is she serious? Drinking her potions hasn't worked out all that well for me."

Cody rolled his eyes. "So she tried to kill you a couple of times. Don't be such a baby."

I took the stopper off the flask and sniffed the contents. "Is this kava?" I asked.

Cody's face lit up. "Excellent, sir! It is, in fact, kava. And a few other ingredients you probably don't want to know about. The Madame says it will fortify you for what's to come."

I narrowed my eyes at Cody. "For what's to come? You got any details, or does Madame Cuapa want to save it for a surprise?"

"She said to tell you there's a storm coming. And when the storm is at its height, someone will try to kill you." He indicated the silver flask. "We're hoping the kava will help keep you alive." His eyes widened. "Oh, I almost forgot. When you drink the kava tonight, be sure to leave a swallow for later."

"For later? What do you mean?"

Cody bit at his lip. "I'm not exactly sure. The Madame says you will need the last swallow to activate the kava's protection when you find yourself needing it." He smiled. "I guess you'll know when that is when the time comes."

"Terrific. Let's hope it's not a sneak attack. I don't suppose she told you who it is that's going to try to kill me."

Cody shook his head. "She didn't say. You know how it works. If she tells you too much, your reaction to her warnings will cause you to behave in a way that will *increase* your danger, rather than reduce it. You have to do what the Madame advises and let it play out."

"Well, isn't that just swell."

Cody laughed. "I'm sure everything will be fine, sir. The Madame is of the opinion that you have a good chance of surviving."

"A 'good' chance? How good?"

Cody shook his head, suddenly serious. "That's all she would tell me, sir." He lifted his eyes to meet mine. "To be honest, she seems a bit upset by it all. But I choose to be optimistic. She said a *good* chance. That's better than a *bad* chance, right?"

"Wonderful."

Cody's grin returned. "Cheer up, sir. You've proven yourself to be a resourceful man in the past, and you aren't *entirely* past your prime." He gave me a critical look. "I hope."

"Gee, thanks."

"You're welcome, sir. I will tell the Madame I found you hale and hearty."

Cody started up the SUV, and, as it veered into traffic, it started to rain. Hard. Great, I thought. Could this morning get any worse? I threw my head back and opened my mouth to catch the drops of rain on my tongue.

And then I spit it to the pavement. The rainwater was salty. Not the kind of salty you taste in the fog that rolls in regularly over the peninsula, the mild kind of salty that lets you know you live on the coast. No, this was the robust briny tang of seawater. It was as if the Nihhonese Ocean itself had risen into the air and was raining down on the city.

I jogged back to my house, thinking about prophecies and vengeful spirits.

# Chapter Twenty-One

Leiti La'aka had told me that I'd be returning to the settlement the next day to pursue my investigation, and who was I to argue with a Leiti? Anyway, I wanted to try to find Doman, and I needed to start at the adaro marketplace. I had a plan, and it required me to put on my cleanest shirt and best tie. Once I was suitably dressed, I grabbed my coat and hat and prepared to head out. Before I did, I strapped on a shoulder holster and retrieved my loaded thirty-eight from my desk drawer. Even in the daytime, the adaro settlement was a dangerous neighborhood, especially when a couple of Placid Point cops wanted me in an interrogation room. Besides, a killer was on the loose. Maybe more than one. Unearthly spirits were in the wind, too, and bullets wouldn't help me against them. Still, I found some comfort in the weight of the iron against my chest.

I was going to leave my whiskey flask at home, but at the last second I topped it off and stuffed it in my outside coat pocket. Like the gat, it gave me comfort. I didn't have to drink from it. I could always use it to hit someone over the head.

*** 

"Shit! The bottle's empty, and I forgot to pick up a refill." Holly's smile was resigned. "Sorry, baby. But don't worry, I won't leave you hanging." Her smile grew mischievous as she reached under the sheets and circled me with her fingers.

"Do you need to take it every time?" I asked her, my voice husky.

"That's the way it works, darling. A teaspoon after play keeps the baby away."

In the shower afterwards, I asked her, "Where do you get that stuff, anyway?"

"The potion? Ella's cousin is a witch. She keeps all the girls at the club supplied, and we give her a little off the top from our tips. Turn around and I'll wash your hair."

"Is it safe?"

"You're afraid I'll get soap in your eyes?"

"I mean the potion, smartass."

Her body pressed against my backside as she massaged shampoo into my hair. "Of course it's safe. Effective, too. You haven't got me pregnant yet, have you? And Lord knows we've been putting it to the test." She giggled.

"I don't doubt that it works," I said. "But what about the side effects?"

She continued rubbing the soap into my scalp. "It's fine. It gives me a little dry-mouth, but a drink or two takes care of that."

"You should be careful," I told her. "Those potions can be bad for your womb. The magic doesn't go away completely, and it builds up over time. If you use those potions for too long, they can make it impossible for you to have a baby when you want one later on. That's why you can skip using them from time to time. You know, if you've been using them for a while."

I felt Holly's fingers stop moving, and she pulled them off my head. "Where'd you hear all that?"

I turned to face her. "I don't know. It's just something I picked up."

"Really." She slid a half step back from me, about as far as she could go without bumping into the wall of the shower stall. "Did you hear it from a doctor?"

"Uh, no, I don't think so."

"From a woman?"

"No."

"I see." All of the amusement was gone from Holly's face. "So based on what you probably heard from a bunch of your ignorant army buddies when you were a teenager, you think you can give me medical advice about my reproductive system?"

"No, of course not. It's just that I don't think these potions are as safe as they're cracked up to be. I've run into some of these witches. A lot of them are fakes. How do you know Ella's sister, or cousin, or whatever... how do you know she isn't running some kind of racket?"

"You think you know more about my uterus than I do?"

"What? No, I didn't say that. I'm just saying—"

"I know what you're saying." She turned and stepped out of the shower.

"Hey, what about my shampoo?"

"A smart man like you can figure out how to wash his own hair." She grabbed a towel off the rack and began drying herself off.

"Hey, what's the big deal, babe? I was just concerned about you, that's all. If you say the potion is safe, it's safe. And if you say you've got to take it every time, well, I guess you would know." Holly had already left the bathroom, and the shower was suddenly the last place I wanted to be. I rinsed my hair as if I were trying to set a speed record.

Once out of the shower, I wrapped myself in a towel and hurried into the bedroom, where Holly was getting herself dressed. "Where're you going?" I asked. "You don't have to be at work for another hour, do you?"

"I thought I'd get there early and grab a drink." She grabbed a blouse from her closet. "Unless you want to talk to me about my drinking habits."

"There's nothing wrong with your drinking habits."

"Thank you. I'm certainly relieved to hear that."

"Holly," I started.

"Because if I ever start drinking too much, or drinking the wrong kind of drinks, I want you to let me know."

"Holly, what's going on here? Am I missing something?"

Holly buttoned up her blouse. "Missing something? How could you be missing something? You know everything, don't you? You know more about my lady parts than I do."

"I never said that. I never meant to imply anything like that."

Holly stopped mid-button. "No. Of course you didn't. But you're a man, and I'm just a woman. A woman with sex organs that you know more about than I do, even though I've lived with them all my life, and you've only known them intermittently for a few months."

"Where's all this coming from? I'm just trying to take care of you."

Holly's eyes told me what she thought of my self-appointed role as her caregiver.

I held out a palm. "Okay, forget I said that. I know you don't need me to take care of you, and that's not what I meant. I was curious about the potion, that's all. I just wanted to make sure...." I stopped, because I wasn't sure exactly what I had wanted to make sure of anymore.

Holly was there to tell me. "You wanted to make sure I knew what I was doing. Because feminine care isn't something you actually know anything about, but, because you're a man, you think you know more about everything than any woman could possibly know." She *pushed past me to the closet to dig out some shoes, and I felt as if I'd been slapped by a cold breeze.*

"Don't go running off. Let's talk about this."

"How 'bout we don't." She picked up a pair of shoes, studied them, and set them back down again.

"I don't want you to go away mad."

"*How* would you like me to go away?" She settled on another pair of shoes and carried them with her to her vanity table.

"I don't want you to go away at all. Do you have to work tonight? Why don't I take you out to dinner, instead?"

She shot me a glance that froze my bones. "You think that will fix things? That might work for you, but if I skip work, the club will be short a cigarette girl tonight, and I'll probably lose my job."

"So what? It's a crap job. You work all night and come home exhausted. If you worked for me, you'd make just as much money and you wouldn't have to work so damned hard. I could use you, you know. You could be my right hand."

Holly threw the shoes in her hand to the floor. "I am not a fucking appendage! In case you haven't noticed, I'm a whole person! You want me to give up *my* job so I can be a part of yours? Well, I've got my own life, buster, and my 'crap' job is part of it." She slammed her feet into her shoes and stood to leave.

"Look, Holly," I said. "If you would just calm down—"

Holly whipped her body around, and the look in her face caused me to back away a step.

"Did you just tell me to *calm* down? Let me tell *you* something, mister. I will calm down when I feel like calming down, and you don't get to tell me how I should feel. First, you don't have that kind of authority over me just because we *might* have something good going on between us. Second, you're not qualified to know what I should be feeling, just like you're not qualified to tell me about things a man knows nothing about." She took a step toward me and raised a finger. "Now, I'm going to go to work, where I will smile sweetly at spoiled rich men and their even more spoiled wives, who will look down their noses at me with something evil in their eyes, or their young dates, who will warn me away with their greedy smirks like I'm trying to steal money out of their pockets. I will charm those self-important old goats out of their ill-gotten gains, and I will walk away from them with a big smile on my face knowing that I gave them nothing I couldn't afford to lose and left with enough of their dough to pay my rent and buy me some good times. And I will enjoy every fucking minute of it. It's my job, and I like it just fine, but it's just a job. I'll put up with things on my job that I won't put up with when it comes to you! I'm nothing to those rich old men but a friendly smile, a nice pair of gams, and a little glimpse of cleavage, just enough to get their juices flowing and keep them coming back. They can think about me any way they want to. They think they're treating me right because they give me a big tip when I sell them an overpriced cigar. But you gotta respect me, mister, if you want me to be with you. The way you treat me right is to listen to me when I talk to you, and to let me feel what I want to feel for as long as I want to feel it. My feelings are not yours to control. And don't you ever try to tell me how to take care of my body. It's my body, not yours." She pointed her finger at my lips. "Don't say nothing to me right now. Not a fucking word, if you know what's good for you. I know you want to fix this mess, but, believe me, anything you say right now will only make it worse. Now, at the start of all this, if you had offered to participate in our birth control, and volunteered to wear a rubber from time to time, this whole conversation might have gone in a different direction. But you didn't. Instead, you put all the burden on me, and then you questioned my choices, like this isn't something I've had to deal with for a long time. You came on like you were the expert, and like I didn't know any better. You're probably sorry now, and I might be willing to accept your apology later. But not now." She lowered her finger and picked up the traveling case that contained her work clothes. "You can stay here tonight, if you want. If you're not here when I get back, I'll understand."

    She never raised her voice when she spoke her piece that night, but every word had been a punch to the gut. I'd been there when she got back, of course, and we made up. Afterwards, I tried to pretend the argument had never happened, which, of course, was exactly the wrong way to handle it. Holly stayed with me for four and a half months, and that was the longest intimate relationship with a woman I'd ever had. Eventually, I think I learned some valuable lessons from Holly, about women and about myself. But it was much too little and far too late, and, by the end of it, Holly was exhausted. And maybe I didn't really learn anything at all.

***

    On the way to Placid Point I turned on the car radio, hoping to hear something about the peculiar saltwater rainstorm. I wasn't surprised when the newscasts made no mention of it. I assumed that some kind of noteworthy supernatural force must be at play, which would certainly be newsworthy, but news stories couldn't be aired to the public until they had cleared the government censors, and the appropriate agencies were probably still deciding what kind of spin to put on this troubling development. No doubt they were waiting for word from Lord Ketz himself, and the immortal dragon was not known for making hasty decisions. I didn't doubt that the internet would be filled with theories about the salty rain by now, but any useful information would be buried beneath a mountain of uninformed opinions, misinformation, and ignorant speculation. I wouldn't get much help there.

Apart from the government-controlled media and the unreliable internet, I had other, less accessible sources of information. A young witch-in-training divining my future had shown me a storm card. The most powerful witch I'd ever met had warned me about the coming storm. A different kind of witch had told me of an adaro priestess emerging from the sea with a prophetic warning about storms, a vengeful spirit, and a deadly deluge. I'd begun searching for Ten-Inch on a whim, and my search was leading me into the center of the storm. As I entered the settlement I hoped the answers I needed would be waiting for me there.

I parked the beastmobile near an open marketplace just outside the settlement's center and opened my umbrella. Adaros don't carry umbrellas in the rain, but benevolent uptown gentlemen do. I had a plan. Not a well thought-out plan, maybe, but a plan, nonetheless. I straightened my tie and made my way to the market.

Open markets were a novelty in Yerba City. Huaxiatown had one, but it was only open in the summertime at the height of tourist season. Other markets were open here and there throughout the city for a few hours at a time during certain days of the week. The adaro settlement's market was open from sunup to sunset, seven days a week, every day of the year, rain or shine, and it had never failed to open its booths to the public since the day it started. No grocery chains operated in the settlement, so the open marketplace was the primary source of food for the community.

Like much of the settlement, the marketplace had sprung up spontaneously, a few independent booths at a time with no central plan. As the marketplace began to grow, the adaro residents established a local committee to oversee the operation of the markets. The marketplace committee established rents for booth space and taxes on the sale of goods, and under the committee's supervision the marketplace began swallowing up block after block of settlement property until it had become one of the settlement's most essential institutions. Nearly all of the adaro residents frequented the marketplace. In addition, humans, trolls, gnomes, and dwarfs—most of them from outside the settlement—could be found running the booths or shopping for supplies at the market during daylight hours. In short order, the open marketplace became the beating heart of the landed adaro community.

No vehicle traffic was allowed on the market grounds, and on most days bustling and diverse crowds of shoppers surged shoulder to shoulder from booth to booth during peak hours. Because of the rain, however, the crowds were sparse when I entered the grounds, and almost all of the shoppers were adaros. I spotted a cluster of adaros examining the fish laid out in troughs at one of the largest booths in the market and made my way in that direction.

Drawing near, I spotted an adaro child standing near the booth watching the booth's proprietor like a hawk. She was wearing a colorless torn dress that hung on her bony shoulders like rags on a clothesline. When the proprietor was busy with a customer, the child darted forward and plucked a whole unscaled tilapia from the trough. As the girl scooted away from the booth, she plunged her pointed teeth into the side of the raw fish and made a loud slurping sound. My stomach lurched, and I willed it to be still. Different customs for different sentient species, I reminded myself. I reasoned that the girl would have a similar reaction to watching me eat a microwaved waffle with peanut butter and chocolate syrup. And we'd both have the same response when watching trolls eat yonak. In fact, given the choice, I'd bite into that raw tilapia before I'd try yonak.

I took several deep breaths to acclimate myself to the odor of decaying fish, and began asking the adaros lined up at the booth if any of them knew a man called Ten-Inch. If any of them did, they weren't willing to admit it to me, even after I flashed a roll of bills and waved it around. I moved on to the other booths, along with anyplace else the marketplace patrons were clustered. I asked dozens of adaro women about Ten-Inch, making sure everyone got a gander at my bankroll, and in response, I received polite apologies, rude insults, unhelpful advice, cold shoulders, and a few business propositions I regretfully declined. After more than two hours of non-stop wandering and fruitless questioning in the unrelenting rain, I found myself back at the fish booth where I'd started, soaked to the bone, footsore, and frustrated.

My excursion through the marketplace had been enlightening. I'd seen other children like the tilapia thief, some clutching the hems of their mothers' dresses, some wandering alone or in small groups, like raccoon packs. Their skin seemed unnaturally pale, and some of them had the kind of bloated bellies you find on people who have had too little to eat, rather than too much. Outside a booth that sold fresh kelp I spotted a young woman grasping a child by her stick-like arm, both of them regarding the bags of kelp with hungry eyes. I approached the woman and asked her if I could buy a bag of kelp for her little girl. The woman stared at me with alarm before scooping up the child and scurrying off as if I had threatened to take the girl away from her. I took a closer look at the adaros passing through the marketplace and realized fewer than half of them were actually buying anything. The rest were either looking for scraps in trash cans or on the ground, stealing food when no one was looking, or gazing longingly at the goods on display. I'd wandered through the slums on the south side of the settlement, and I'd driven through streets crowded with thin, ill-dressed adaros. On a previous trip through the settlement, I'd seen skinny young adaro hookers with track marks on their arms soliciting men from outside the settlement as they cruised by in their slick cars. I'd known that poverty was a problem in the crowded settlement. I'd read about it in the paper and seen news reports about it on TV. But, somehow, on that rainy morning strolling through the marketplace, watching so many of the residents gazing at booths filled with food they didn't have the means to acquire except by theft, it struck me for the first time how desperately poor many of the adaros in the settlement really were. If this was what it meant to be a "protected species" I wondered what our government was protecting them from. The perils of overeating? The curse of prosperity? Decadence?

While inquiring after Ten-Inch, my attention had been drawn by an adaro who looked to be in her mid to late twenties haranguing passers-by from a corner of the street. My attention was first drawn by her hair, or rather her lack of it. Every adaro woman I'd ever seen had thick luxurious waves of dark blue hair, and I'd seen scores of adaros that morning with long wet hair matted to their shoulders and backs by the rain. A few of the women I'd run across that morning, however, had cut their hair close to their heads and were sporting blue buzz cuts. I noted that most of these women were young, probably in their teens or early twenties, though I had to admit I was a poor judge when it came to determining the age of adaros. The woman on the corner had shaved her head so recently that her scalp appeared to be a blue-tinged billiard ball. She was shouting at the other adaros in their own burbling language, which I, of course, didn't understand. Whatever her message was, it seemed to be lost on most of the women in the marketplace. One older adaro stopped to argue with her for a few minutes before shaking her head and walking away. Most walked past her as if she weren't there.

Curious, I approached the woman. "Excuse me. I don't mean to be rude, but can I ask you what you are trying to tell these people?"

She gave me a quick look, and her eyes darted this way and that to see if I was alone. "You a cop?" She asked me.

I put up my free hand, palm out. "No, and I'm not from the Navy, either. I'm just curious."

She looked me up and down from the top of my umbrella to the toes of my shoes before settling on my chest, like she knew I was packing heat.

"My name's Alex," I said, trying to come across as friendly.

She looked up to peer into my eyes. "They call me Piper. If I'd wanted you to know what I was saying to my adaro friends, I'd have said it in human."

I nodded. "All right, I get it. Like I said, I was just curious."

She frowned. "You sure you're not a cop? You look like one, and you're carrying a gun under that coat."

"I'm a private detective," I admitted. "I'm looking for a guy. You might know him. Goes by Ten-Inch. The real cops are after him, and I'm trying to find him before they do."

Piper tilted her head. "Is there a reward for him?"

"Not that I know of. He's an old friend of mine. I'm trying to keep him out of trouble."

She made a kind of coughing sound at that. "Too late for that. He's the boss of the Northsiders. Those guys are nothing *but* trouble."

"You know where he is?" I asked.

She shook her head. "I don't know him. I only know *of* him. But from what I hear, I hope he's gone for good."

"Why? What did you hear?"

She stared at me for a moment before answering, weighing her words. "He was supposed to be protecting someone, but he didn't do a very good job of it. She got killed."

"You're talking about Kanoa?"

Piper's eyes widened. "I don't know anyone by that name, and I don't know where Ten-Inch is. I've gotta go." And, just like that, Piper was gone.

Another dead end, I thought, and went on to try my luck with the next person I saw.

Back at the tilapia booth where I'd started, I found three adaro adolescents laughing and conversing in their own burbling language. They seemed to have no interest in the booth's wares. Like all adaro women, these three were gorgeous, and I had to steel myself against an impulse to stare at the results of the rain flattening the thin fabric of their dresses against their skin. The rotting fish smell from the booth helped.

But something else drew my attention to these three young ladies. Like Piper, these girls had all cut their hair down to the nubs. A fashion trend? Or some sort of protest? Maybe both.

Approaching the girls and interjecting myself into their conversation, I launched into a variant of the same huckster's patter I'd repeated dozens and dozens of times over the past hour. "Excuse me, ladies. My name is Alex, and I'm a private investigator. Would you mind if I asked you a few questions?" I held up my roll of bills. "I can make it worth your while."

Up close, I realized that their shaved heads had made the girls seem a little younger than they probably were. My original guess had been about twelve, but now I was thinking more like fifteen or sixteen. The scowls on their faces let me know what they thought of strange men flashing money at them. The one who seemed to be their leader squared up to me and put her fists on her hips. "We look like hookers to you, mister?"

"No, ma'am. You seem like fine upstanding young citizens."

The three girls gave each other knowing smirks, and the one who had spoken spat near my feet. "I think he's a cop."

"No, ma'am," I said. "I'm a private investigator. I work independently of the cops."

She rubbed her hand over the blue stubble on her head. "I don't like coppers."

I smiled. "I'm not fond of them either. A cop knocked out one of my teeth."

She eyed me with skepticism. "Oh yeah?" she challenged me. "Which one?"

I pulled at my bottom lip and indicated a gap in the back of my mouth. "'Aa' uhhn," I said.

"A cop did that?"

"Yep. A troll."

Her lips twisted as she considered my story. She looked to her friends, who nodded at her, then turned back to me. "Hmm. Okay, ask a question."

"Have you heard of a human man who calls himself Ten-Inch?"

The woman leered at me. "Yeah, we know Ten-Inch." She smirked at her two friends. "More like Four-Inch, though."

All three women giggled.

"Oh, come on," one of the women protested. "It's at least six."

"Maybe five," said the third, holding the palms of her hands in front of her to indicate the appropriate length. I noted that she was the only one of the three wearing gloves, which extended well beyond her wrists.

"Well I don't know what you two did to him," said the first adaro, "but you only left four inches for me!"

I waited for the laughter to settle before asking, "Do you know where I might find him?"

The first adaro studied me, her blue eyes bright and aware. "Who did you say you were again?"

"Alex. Alex Southerland."

"You're a dick?"

"A private dick."

She continued to study me. "Where'd you get all that money?"

I shrugged. "I've got a little stashed away."

The adaro stared into my forehead, and I felt like she was looking into my brain. I sensed intelligence in her eyes, and I knew I'd have to be careful with her. I'd been trying to attract the attention of the adaro crew hustling for Doman, and I was beginning to think I'd found them. My plan had been to let them solicit me and take me to Doman to be rolled, but now I didn't think it was going to go that way.

The adaro turned to her companions, and the three seemed to come to a silent consensus.

Turning back to me, the adaro asked, "Are you a fighter?"

"I was in the Army many years ago."

She nodded. "Can you use that gun under your coat, or is it just for show?"

I sighed mentally to myself. Could everyone in the marketplace see I was armed? "I can use it if I have to."

"Are you going to use it on Ten-Inch?"

"I don't plan to. I want to find out what happened to him. See if he needs any help."

"You're a friend of his?"

"Not really."

"They why do you want to help him?"

"Because I think he needs me to."

The adaro held my eyes as she licked rainwater off her lips with the tip of her tongue. "If you kill someone for us, we'll tell you how to find Ten-Inch."

## Chapter Twenty-Two

I stared at the adaro, trying to figure out whether she was serious. "You want me to kill someone," I said.

She returned my stare without flinching. "That's right."

"Why?"

"Because he's a fuckin' bully. He tried to rape Coral."

"Who's Coral?"

The adaro pointed at one of her friends, the one without gloves. "That's Coral. She's my little sister. And that's Sandy, and you can call me Sunny."

Sunny. My heart skipped a beat, and I took a second to steady myself. "Because of your disposition?" I asked.

Sunny put her fists on her hips. "What the fuck is that supposed to mean?"

"Nothing." I turned to Coral. "Is Sunny telling the truth? This mug tried to rape you?"

Sunny cut her sister off before she could speak. "Coral doesn't want to talk about it. If you kick this motherfucker's ass, we'll tell you how to find Ten-Inch. If you don't want to do it, then fuck off."

"Is this guy's name Doman?"

Sunny's lips spread slowly into a knowing grin. "I knew you were trying to use us to get to Doman. How'd you find out about our racket?"

I shrugged. "I'm a private dick, remember?"

She smirked at me. "Well, I hope you're tougher than you are smart. You really think you were fooling anyone by struttin' around like a fuckin' peacock and flashing that dough? This is the settlement. If you ever *really* want to find little girls here, quit being clever and just ask around."

"I'll keep that in mind. So what's the plan?"

Predatory smiles appeared on the faces of all three adaros. "Simple," Sunny said. "We take you to Doman, and you shoot him. We take everything he's got, and then we tell you how to find Ten-Inch."

"Sounds a little too simple. Is Doman alone?"

Sunny shrugged. "He usually has a couple of his guys with him. But you'll be taking them by surprise. Just go in and start shooting at anything that moves. Piece of cake for an ex-soldier." Coral and Sandy each nodded vigorously, expressing their approval.

It sounded like a good way to get myself killed, but I shrugged and went along. After all, "SUNNY" had been the name scratched on the hubcap left in my doorway. Was that reason enough? Leiti La'aka believed that Kisikisi, a powerful, but mischievous spirit was the one dropping messages in my path. Was he helping me or fucking with me? Only one way to find out. "All right. Where are we going?"

"We'll show you," said Sunny. "Follow us."

Sunny and her crew led me out of the marketplace in the direction of the ocean. They talked amongst themselves in their own language, Sunny in the lead with Coral and Sandy on either side of me. I felt exactly like a prisoner being led to a firing squad, and I kept all my senses on high alert. The most likely scenario, I thought, was that the women intended to give me up to Doman. Either that, or Sunny really *did* have it in for Doman. Maybe he really had tried to rape her sister. It was possible she was hoping Doman and I would gun each other down, and she and her chums would be there to loot the bodies. It was obvious that none of the adaros were hiding firearms in the wet fabric glued to their bodies by the rain, but I wasn't going to underestimate them. Contrary to what they might think, however, I had no intention of killing Doman unless he forced me to. Once Sunny realized I wasn't going to go along with her plans, I was going to have to watch my back. Truth be told, I was winging it. Why not? I had a trickster spirit on my side, right? I pulled my collar up against the rain, kept my hands free, and trudged through the length of the marketplace with Sunny and her little band of hustlers.

As we were walking, we came across another adaro with a buzz cut coming at us from the other end of the street. She didn't look up as she approached, but when she drew near she raised her hand in a kind of salute, her fingers and thumb curved into a circle. My three companions raised their hands and returned the salute with ones of their own.

I half-turned to Sandy, the adaro with the gloves. "What was that?"

It was Sunny who answered. "None of your fuckin' business, human."

We continued walking. At the end of the street, we turned right and approached a booth selling a kava-flavored drink. My companions drew near, and I thought they were going to stop to buy a drink. Instead, they walked behind the booth and lightly slapped a silver oval that had been spray-painted on the booth's back wall. It was the same image that Jaguar had ordered to be painted over on the way to the Leiti's hut the night before. I caught Sunny glancing my way as we continued onward, but I didn't say anything.

After a half hour of walking, Sunny stopped near the entrance to an alley and pointed down the street to a small military-issue prefabricated hut made of corrugated steel with a wooden door. The adaros all turned to face me.

"That's where Doman lives," she told me. "He's probably drunk. He usually is at this time of the day."

"How should we play this?"

"I'll go first with my arm in yours. He'll think I've convinced you that I've brought you here for fun and games. That's how we usually play it. Coral and Sandy will come up behind us. I'll knock on the door and get out of the way. Doman won't suspect a thing. He'll have a gun, but he won't have it out. When he opens the door, start throwing lead."

We were all smiles as we approached the hut, Sunny's arm locked in mine, my other hand holding my umbrella. When we got to the door, Sunny released my arm and knocked three times. "Hey!" she shouted. "It's me. Open up!" She ducked out of the way and moved in to join her friends behind me. I reached into my coat for my gat. Even if I wasn't going to rush in with guns blazing, I wanted to be ready for anything.

The door opened. Without turning, I was aware that Sunny, Coral, and Sandy were hightailing it back the way we'd come. I stared at the figure in the doorway, and my gun hand fell to my side.

"Hello, Ten-Inch," I said. "I've been looking for you."

***

Ten-Inch stared through me like I wasn't there, his expression vacant, as if he were asleep. Or dead. The supernatural energy pouring out of his body was causing my skin to tingle and making my hairs stand on end. The air around me grew cold. Gradually, his eyes focused, and his lips widened into a tight smile as he seemed to see me for the first time. "Sarge," he said. "You'll be wanting to come in out of the rain." He moved away from the doorway to give me room to enter. Once I'd stepped inside the hut, the door slammed shut behind me of its own accord.

The hut, constructed of recycled plastic waste, was the same standard military unit I'd seen a thousand times during my years in the service. Its efficient design enabled a living room, dining area, kitchen, bedroom, and shower room to fit into a cozy two thousand cubic feet of space. The beefy bruno I'd seen standing next to Doman at The Dripping Bucket the night before was lying on the floor of the living room area, his body slack, his legs twisted into uncomfortable angles. A nine-millimeter rod lay on the floor next to his hand, and the hot odor of gunpowder filled the room. The bruno's mouth was wide open, silently screaming, his eyes locked in an endless stare into nothing.

I looked from the body to Ten-Inch, who was hovering next to it and watching me without speaking. "Did you kill him?" I asked.

"In a manner of speaking." Ten-Inch seemed distracted, almost bored. He pointed toward the door to the shower room, which opened a crack. "Doman is in there."

I crossed the room and pushed on the door, but something was blocking it. I put my weight into it and felt something heavy slide across the floor. I leaned into the door one more time and was able to push my head around it to see inside. Doman's body was curled into a heap on the tiny shower room's floor, which was flooded with blood. I counted six kitchen knives buried to the hilt into Doman's back.

Ten-Inch stood impassively where I'd left him.

"Did you do that, too?"

"Yeah," he drawled. "It was necessary."

"I see. And now what. Is it going to be necessary to kill me?"

Ten-Inch's eyebrows shot up in surprise, the first hint of animation I'd seen from him. "What? Of course not." He shook his head like he'd just been clocked and was trying to regain his senses. "Sorry. This must all seem weird to you." Life seemed to come into his face, which lit up in a welcoming expression. "It's good to see you, Sarge. I wish the circumstances were different."

I stared at him. "What happened here, Ten-Inch?"

The old gang boss glanced down at the bruno and sighed. "This one was scared to death. Literally, I mean. He might've had a bad heart. I always told the mug that steroids and meth don't mix." He turned from the body to me. "Look, Sarge. You better sit down. I got some shit to tell you, and some of it's gonna be hard to understand. Fuck, I don't understand all of it myself."

Once we were seated, he drew in a breath and let it out. "Let me start by saying that I'm not really here."

"You want to run that by me again?"

In response, he leaned toward me and extended his hand for a shake. After a brief hesitation, I reached to grip his hand—and encountered nothing but air. My blood chilled, and I began to shiver. A cloud of mist streamed from my mouth as I let out a breath. I fell back into my chair and stared at Ten-Inch with eyes that must have been wide as saucers.

"Take a breath, Sarge." He indicated the body of the bruno. "Moose dished some lead, but the pills passed right through me. Then he tried to put me in a bear hug." He looked at me hard. "I wouldn't recommend it. That chill you felt when you tried to shake my hand? That was just a taste. He got it full force. Anyway, you're a lot tougher than he was. You'll be okay in a few minutes. I think. Truthfully, I'm kind of new at this."

I took a moment to calm the beating of my heart, using exercises I'd picked up in the Army. When I was able to, I asked, "What are you?"

"We call it a *hau*, the disembodied spirit of myself."

"Who calls it a... a how?"

"A *hau*. My family comes from the South Nihhonese Islands. All us kids were taught that everyone has two spirits, a spirit that stays with the body, and a spirit called the *hau* that can exist apart from the body. I always thought it was bullshit. Guess I was wrong."

"Are you a ghost?" I asked. "Are you dead?"

"I'm alive, but my body is somewhere else. Don't ask me where, 'cause I don't fuckin' know. A lot of things are unclear to me. Some of my short-term memories are foggy, like I'm dreaming or something. I think I might have a bad concussion."

"What's the last thing you remember?"

"Getting my ass kicked. Someone fucked me up real bad."

"You don't know who? Sounds like you could use a private investigator."

Ten-Inch—or whatever he was—slouched back into the sofa, looking more like the cocky old street thug I remembered. It only bothered me a little that the couch cushions didn't give under the illusion of his body. "I saw you walking in the rain the other night," he said, his lips tightened into a grimace. "You were fuckin' shitfaced. I knew you were looking for me, but after seeing the state you were in I didn't know if I wanted you to find me. You didn't look like the champ that beat me like a bitch in front of my family. That cost me a lot of cred, you know.

You look a little better now, but I think I could take you if we had another go."

I smiled. "I was lucky. You'll always be the champ, babe."

Ten-Inch shook his head. "Nah, man. You might've pulled it out of your ass and caught me by surprise, but a win is a win. Anyway, I'm getting old. It gets harder every day to keep my family in line. And now the fuckin' Hatfields are trying to take us over. I don't know, man. If I live, I might have to retire. Makes me wonder how much longer I want to live."

The deadening chill I'd felt when my hand had passed through his was lessening, but it was being replaced by the discomfort I was experiencing at the direction our conversation was taking. "Hey, man," I said. "You want to find out who got the jump on you, right?"

Ten-Inch's expression grew cold. "That's what's keeping me going."

"Was it Doman? Is that why you're here?"

Ten-Inch turned his head toward the shower room. "I thought it could've been. I guess I was wrong about that."

"But you killed him anyway."

The old gangster's eyes flashed. "That motherfucker thought he was gonna steal my tribe and sell it to the fuckin' Hatfield Syndicate while I was temporarily indisposed. I couldn't let that happen."

"Maybe he thought you were dead."

"He should've waited to see a body."

"How do you know he was taking over? Last night he introduced himself as your chief of staff."

In response, Ten-Inch extended his arm to his side and held up his hand. Something flew into it from the direction of the dining area. I flinched and my eyes blinked involuntarily. After I recovered, I stared at the object in Ten-Inch's outstretched hand for a few seconds before recognizing it as the conch shell that Tahiti had brought to The Dripping Bucket.

"Leiti La'aka had this delivered to our headquarters as a gift for the leader of the Northsiders," said Ten-Inch. "That's me until somebody convinces me otherwise. Doman took it and brought it here to his home. By stealing the Leiti's gift to me, he was stealing my position as leader of the tribe. I was sent here to retrieve it."

"What do you mean you were 'sent'? Who sent you?"

"My spirit guide. Maui-Kisikisi."

"Kisikisi? Is he the one who's been sending hubcaps my way?" When Ten-Inch gave me a quizzical look, I said, "Never mind that for now. Maybe you should start from the beginning."

Ten-Inch nodded. "It begins with a special nymph called Kanoa, a shitload of rain, and something called the Eye of Taufa'tahi."

He told me how Kanoa had come out of the sea during a rainstorm and started telling all the adaros in the settlement that the sea spirit, Taufa'tahi, was going to drown Yerba City in the ocean. "He's pissed at the Dragon Lords for declaring war on the adaros, and for forcing the adaro women into settlements."

But an even more powerful spirit, Havea Hikule'o, wasn't happy with Taufa'tahi's operation, and she sent Maui-Kisikisi to stop him. Kisikisi stole the Eye of Taufa'tahi from its guardian, the priestess Kanoa, and took it to Yerba City. Kanoa was forced to leave the ocean, find it, and return it to its rightful place. "She knew it was in Yerba City," Ten-Inch said. "But she didn't know where. She thought it might be somewhere in the settlement. When she met me, she recognized that I had been chosen by Kisikisi, and she accused me of stashing the fuckin' thing somewhere. I told her that was bullshit, and I thought she believed me."

Ten-Inch paused, remembering. "When I first met Kanao, I knew she was a special lady. She got to me, Sarge. You know how it is with adaros. I'd hung around enough of them so's I thought I was fuckin' immune, but Kanoa was something else. She was beautiful, sure, like most of them, but that wasn't it. She had a quality about her, like she'd been touched by a spirit. I never messed with her, though. It wasn't that way between us. And, anyway, she was a priestess, and all of us Islanders know about that. It would be like messin' with your sister."

"I never knew you were an Islander," I said.

"Feleti Latu."

"Excuse me?"

"That was the name I was given at birth. Feleti Latu. I moved to the mainland when I was a kid. They started calling me Ten-Inch in the Army the first time they saw me in my glory in a public shower."

"Right. You were telling me about Kanoa?"

Ten-Inch smiled. "That's right, I was. My mind seems to want to wander. Maybe I'm less alive than I thought. Anyway, like I say, she's a priestess. What the adaro call a *kwuurlplup*." Ten-Inch surprised me by pronouncing it just the way I'd heard it from Tahiti, Kraken, and Leiti La'aka.

"And she isn't just any priestess, either," Ten-Inch went on. "She was an important lady among the adaros in her homeworld, chosen by Taufa'tahi himself to watch over his Eye, which has a lot of the sea spirit's *mana* in it. Kanoa was respected in her community. But she didn't get the same respect here on land, not even from the adaros. People here didn't listen to her like they would've if they'd all still been in their old homes in the ocean. When she told them that Taufa'tahi was whipping up a storm that would destroy the settlement, they didn't believe her. When she tried to get them to return to the ocean, they resisted her. She started getting threats, so she asked me to protect her. Maybe she just wanted to keep me close to her because she thought I could lead her to the Eye. Anyway, I protected her from the threats. Kept her safe. And, in return, she played me for a sap."

Kanoa had come to Ten-Inch's apartment, something she'd done before on numerous occasions. But this time she'd done something to Ten-Inch, something he couldn't describe. "It was like being drugged, but worse. After that, I don't remember much. Someone else came in and started asking me about the Eye. I didn't have nothing to say about that. After that, I remember pain. Someone pounded the crap out of me. Trying to make me talk, I guess. And then...."

And then he'd found himself near death in some place he didn't recognize. Kisikisi was with him. "He looks like an ordinary Islander dressed in one of those old-fashioned lavalava kilts you see them wear for the tourists. But he talks to me through my mind. And he talks about you. He told me you were looking for me, and that when I was ready, you'd find me. And then we'd fight Taufa'tahi."

"We're supposed to fight against a sea spirit trying to drown Yerba City?"

A grim smile split Ten-Inch's face, and his eyes hardened. "It's a war, Sarge. A war between spirits honored by my people. Fuck yes I'm going to fight. And Kisikisi says you are going to fight right alongside me."

That was the Ten-Inch I remembered. A warrior out of place in a world of peace-loving civilians. People like him had to be in a fight in order to feel alive. Talking about a war brought life into the eyes of his *hau*, his disembodied shade. The ghost was coming alive in front of me.

"I'm not a soldier anymore, Ten-Inch. I don't know these spirits you're talking about, and I'm not a part of their battle. Tell your spirit guide that I'm gonna take a pass."

"We're not always in command of our own lives, Sarge. Taufa'tahi has brought the war to you. Your only choice is to fight back or die."

"I've found that when someone tells me I've got two choices, there's a third choice they're not telling me about."

Ten-Inch smiled. "Yerba City is about to find itself buried under the ocean, Sarge. Kisikisi says you can help me do something about it. I don't see a third choice here."

"What does he say I can do?"

The smile disappeared from Ten-Inch's face. "That's the problem with spirits. They tend to talk in hints and riddles."

"I hear you loud and clear, champ. I've got a spirit guide of my own. Cougar."

"No shit? When did this happen?"

"About a year ago. I went on a spirit quest. It wasn't an entirely voluntary act on my part."

Ten-Inch lifted his hand in my direction. "You see what I'm saying about not being in command of your own life?"

I couldn't argue with him. "Look. I'll try to find out who roughed you up. But I'm not committing myself to anything beyond that."

Ten-Inch nodded. "That shouldn't be hard. Just find Kanoa and get her to talk."

I caught my breath. "You don't know?"

Ten-Inch stared at me.

"Kanoa is dead. Murdered. Probably raped, too. The same night you disappeared."

It occurred to me then that I hadn't seen Ten-Inch breathe. He didn't breathe now, either. Neither of us said anything while I waited for him to process that information. I'd been wondering if Ten-Inch himself had killed Kanoa, but I didn't think so now. He was too obviously shocked by the news. When he spoke, his voice was filled with the desire for violence. "Find out who did this, Sarge. She betrayed me, and maybe I would have iced her myself for that. I would have given her a chance to explain herself, but I wouldn't have hesitated to put an end to her if I didn't like her justification. But she was a priestess. Whoever raped her took that away from her. There is no justification for that. None. You're right, Sarge. I need your professional services. Find out who did it, and tell me. I'll take care of the rest."

I nodded. "Deal."

A darkness my senses couldn't penetrate grew in the air around Ten-Inch, swallowing up colors and shapes until all I could see was Ten-

Inch himself, still holding the conch shell in his hand. He began to shrink, as if he were speeding away from me into the distance. The darkness disappeared, and I was alone in the hut with two dead bodies.

I got to my feet and walked out the front door into the rain.

## Chapter Twenty-Three

As I was leaving the hut, I spotted Sunny and her crew hanging out in a narrow alley just up the avenue trying and failing to be inconspicuous. When they saw me, they ran down the alley and disappeared. I didn't give them a second thought.

I checked my phone and found a text from Ralph's burner. The text consisted of a single question mark, Ralph's way of telling me he wanted a progress report. I texted, "Got something. Stay tuned." Terse, but at least I spelled out all the words and used punctuation.

I also had a voicemail from Walks in Cloud: "Call me when you can, Jack. I think we may have a problem."

I clicked on call, and Walks answered after four rings. "Where are you, Jack?"

"Walking in the rain through the adaro settlement."

"That doesn't sound like my idea of a good time."

"You have no idea. But I gotta go where my work takes me."

"Glad I work indoors. Anyway, when can you tear yourself away from whatever it is you're doing and come over here?"

I hesitated. I wanted to find out more about Kanoa, and it struck me that Tahiti might be able to help me out. I didn't know where she was staying now that the Leiti was dead, and I wanted to find out. But Walks had never asked for my help before. "Does this have something to do with the you-know-what?"

Walks responded with a brief chuckle. "The you-know-what? Is that some kind of fancy professional code you private eyes use?"

"Only the good ones."

"Right. It might be nothing, but I need to talk to you about it. Not on the phone. Phones aren't secure."

"Everyone keeps telling me that."

"That's because it's true. When can you be here?"

"I'm heading out right now. Give me forty-five minutes or so."

"That'll work. But don't hurry. Like I said, it might be nothing."

"Have some coffee ready. I'll be there as soon as I can."

We disconnected, and I tipped rainwater off the brim of my hat as I set out for the marketplace. A steaming hot cup of Walks in Cloud's Ghanaian coffee sounded like it was going to be the best part of my day.

This part of the settlement wasn't as hard to navigate as the maze in which the late Leiti La'aka had lived and died, and I found my way to the marketplace without any problem. It was mid-afternoon, and the market's main thoroughfare was a bit more crowded than it had been when I'd left it. I even saw a few humans holding canvas bags, braving the rain to shop for fish, fruit, and vegetables at the settlement's bargain prices. I turned past a booth selling chic leather gloves suitable for hiding registration tattoos and headed off in the direction of the beastmobile.

Sims and Modoc were waiting for me just outside the marketplace grounds. Sunny, Coral, and Sandy were with them.

"That's him!" Sunny was pointing at me, her face twisted in anger. "He's the one who tried to rape my sister!"

Modoc glared at me, a cold smile on his face.

Sims took off his glasses and attempted to dry them with a handkerchief. "Well, well, well, Mr. Southerland. This is a bit more serious than jaywalking. Even more serious than a drunk and disorderly. I'm placing you under arrest. I advise you to come in quietly, although my partner would like for you to try to make a run for it. Your choice. What's it going to be?"

I came in quietly, even though something inside me was itching for the opportunity to put some bruises on Modoc's pretty face. Wrong time, wrong place, I told myself. I had little doubt a better time would present itself in the near future.

The detectives left Sunny, Sandy, and the allegedly violated Coral behind and, after depriving me of my gun and cuffing my wrists behind my back, loaded me into the back of an unmarked car. "Don't you want to bring the precious little angels in to make a statement?" I asked Sims.

"No need," the detective answered. "We got what we need from them."

Modoc, who was driving, snarled at me via the rear-view mirror. "What's the matter, Southerland? You can't find no pussy downtown? You gotta go slumming in the settlement to get your rocks off?"

I met his eyes in the mirror. "I heard your mother had a place around here. They said she'd blow me for a sip of whiskey."

Tires screeched as Modoc slammed his foot on the brake. The expression on his flushed face was twisted with rage as he whipped his head around to glare at me through the prisoner partition separating the back of the vehicle from the front. Sims put a hand on Modoc's shoulder. "Not here, Modoc. Plenty of time for you to have fun with him later."

\*\*\*

They didn't take me back to the station. Instead, we pulled into an empty parking lot in front of a small one-story office building that looked brand new and appeared to be empty. Next to the building was an unmarked structure about the size of a one-car garage with no windows and thick metal walls. It looked like an oversized vault. Heavy iron pylons raised the building about two feet off the ground, and a wide plastic hose ran from underneath the vault into an opening in the side of the office building. A similar hose ran from the ceiling of the vault and back through the same opening in the building.

With Modoc following at my heels, Sims led me up a metal step to the front door of the vault, which he unlocked by punching a number into a keypad and staring into a retinal scanner. When the door opened, Modoc pushed me through and followed me inside. Sims came in last and closed the door behind him. I heard the ka-chunk of a substantial bolt sliding into place.

The inside of the vault had the look of a typical interrogation sweatbox, minus the one-way mirror and the camera. Two uncomfortable metal chairs sat on either side of a steel table, which was bolted to the floor. Sims removed my cuffs and my coat, and Modoc indicated that I should take one of the chairs. Once I was seated, Sims cuffed me to a short length of chain hanging from the underside of the table. The chain had enough slack to allow me to lean back in my chair, but I wouldn't be able to stand without crouching. Sims took the seat on the opposite side of the table and smoothed rainwater out of his beard, while Modoc leaned against a wall facing me, arms folded, his lips stretched into a leer.

Lord's flaming balls, I thought. Here we go again. You'd think I'd be accustomed to police interrogations by now. I'd suffered through plenty of them. But the fact was I was starting to become a little tired of them. Sick and tired.

Sims removed his glasses and wiped them dry with his handkerchief. He fitted them back on his nose and regarded me with a pleasant expression. "This is our precinct's special interrogation unit. It's brand new, Mr. Southerland. You have the honor of being our first guest."

He waited for me to respond, but I had nothing to say. I tilted my head and took note of the vent in the floor under the table.

Sims saw where I was looking and nodded. "This room is sealed, Mr. Southerland. Air is pumped in through that vent. Up there on the ceiling...." He pointed. "That's the exhaust vent. The air comes from a compressor and humidifier in the building next to us, and the exhaust is cooled, re-oxygenated, and recycled. I'm told it's a one-hundred percent closed system. The plastic piping itself is reinforced with flexible steel webbing. You couldn't damage it with a hurricane."

Sims leaned forward. "I bet you can guess why I'm telling you this." When I didn't answer, he continued. "We've learned a little more about you since you were last in our custody, Mr. Southerland. For instance, we learned that you are an air elementalist. I'm told that you can summon and command air elementals that produce tornado-force winds. Impressive!"

"That might be a bit of an exaggeration," I said. "Mostly I just summon little fellows."

"Oh?" Sims adjusted his glasses. "Well, be that as it may. Once that door is closed, this room is proofed against elementals of any kind, no matter how big or small. These walls are made of titanium steel, and they're a foot thick. The only air that gets in or out goes through those hoses, and the hoses themselves are airtight. Waterproof, too, by the way. You can summon all you want, but no elemental can get inside this room." He chuckled. "And no lawyers, either, or their drivers."

I made a show of looking the room over. "This place must have cost some dough. I didn't know you Placid Point cops were so well-funded." I looked over the table at Sims. "I guess this is where your LIA connection comes in handy."

Sims flashed a tight smile, but otherwise went on as if I hadn't spoken. "That was a neat stunt your attorney pulled on us, but he doesn't know you're here. Neither does anyone else. The only way you leave here in one piece, Mr. Southerland, is to answer our questions truthfully, holding nothing back. Only when I am satisfied that I have heard everything you can tell us will you be allowed to leave. Hopefully on your own two feet, although...." He chuckled softly. "My partner may have something to say about that, especially after that crack about his mother." He shook his head. "Not that Modoc is particularly close to his mother, but that was an extremely rude thing to say to an officer of the law. It was disrespectful. And Modoc and I both demand that you show us the respect due to people in our position."

Modoc pulled a roll of tape out of his pocket and pulled off a large strip, using his teeth to tear it from the roll. He began wrapping the tape around his knuckles.

I sent out a summons for Badass. Sims believed his brand new interrogation room was airtight and proof against elementals, but that wasn't going to stop me from putting his theory to the test.

Sims readjusted his glasses, which, judging by the creases that had formed on the bridge of his nose, undoubtedly pinched the detective's skin enough to cause him some mild discomfort. I nodded toward the detective with my chin. "How long has it been since you bought new ones?"

Sims stopped fiddling with his glasses. "What did you say?"

I lifted a finger, causing my chain to scrape noisily across the end of the table, and pointed at his face. "Your spectacles. Those frames of yours were all the rage about twenty-five years ago. I'm guessing you were a lot thinner back then. Your increased weight has broadened your nose, which is why the pads squeeze more than they should. They're bifocals, aren't they? I've noticed you wear them every waking hour of the day, even when you're reading. You're probably so used to the sensation of the pads digging into the sides of your nostrils that you're unaware of how often you toy with those things in order to alleviate the irritation. You really should get them refitted."

Sims took his glasses off and examined them. He turned to look at me, his pupils dilated and slightly unfocused. "There's nothing wrong with my glasses, Mr. Southerland."

I shrugged. "Just trying to help."

Sims frowned and sat up in his chair. "The only person you should think about helping is yourself."

I leaned back in my chair as far as I could, surreptitiously testing my wrist restraints and the chain holding me to the table. They seemed all too secure, unfortunately.

Sims replaced the glasses on his nose, his face wincing microscopically.

I decided to change the subject. "So have you figured out who killed Leiti La'aka?"

Sims flashed a bored smile. "I haven't decided whether to write it up as an accident or finger you as the killer."

"Me!" I exclaimed, as if horrified. "You and I both know that I wasn't there when she bought it."

Sims raised his eyebrows. "You say that as if it makes a difference."

"Don't you want to solve the crime?" I asked, all innocence.

A chuckle forced its way through the detective's lips. "Lord's balls! Who's got the time for solving crimes?"

"Isn't that your job?"

"Lord no! My job is to make sure the paperwork is properly filled out and filed. Calling it an accident would end the matter quite satisfactorily. No fuss, no muss. But pinning the murder on you would kill two birds with one stone. It would end the investigation into her death, and it would give me the excuse I need to make you disappear from my life once and for all." He indicated his partner with a quick nod. "I already know which option Modoc would prefer."

"I didn't realize I had become such a problem for you. I mean, we just met, right? Maybe we didn't get off to the best start. To be fair, that's mostly on you, but I'll admit that maybe I share in some of the responsibility. I'll try to do better in the future." I gave the detective my most disarming smile, the one I use when I tell a distraught client that her husband could easily have been telling the truth when he claimed that he'd had too much to drink that night at the digital information tech's convention and had gone straight to bed and fallen right to sleep instead of calling home to check in first like he'd promised he would.

"You'll be a lot less of a problem if you answer my questions honestly and truthfully with no bullshit."

"Sure, detective," I said. "That's why I'm here, isn't it?"

Narrowing his eyes at me, Sims pulled a pen and notepad from his jacket pocket and began his interrogation. "You were poking around the marketplace asking about Ten-Inch. Did you find out anything?"

"What about Sunny and her sister?" I asked.

Sims frowned. "What?"

"Didn't you bring me here because I'd been accused of rape?"

The detective's frown disappeared as he brushed my question aside. "Oh, don't worry about that. If Coral got raped as often as Sunny claims she does, she wouldn't be able to walk. It's just a gag they pull when they get bored. We don't take her seriously."

"What if she ever really *did* get raped?"

Sims shrugged. "I suppose that's always a possibility. But those teeth and nails of hers aren't just for show."

I turned to see how Modoc was doing. The leer on his face had deepened, and his nose twitched ever so slightly, reminding me of a cat stalking a mouse. Something caught my attention. The scars I'd seen on his face the last time he'd had me in a sweatbox were gone. I examined his face for signs of makeup, but his skin was clear. The scars that had been there before were gone without a trace. Curious, to say the least.

"You haven't answered my question, Mr. Southerland. If you don't, I'll conclude that my interrogation methods have failed. It will then be Modoc's turn to ask the questions." Sims's smile was as sincere as a politician's promise. "His methods are a bit extreme, but generally effective."

Modoc's nostrils flared as he drew in a breath. In my mind, I could sense Badass outside the interrogation room trying to batter his way in, but the vault-like chamber was too well-built for the big air spirit to overcome with force. I'd summoned a dozen smaller elementals, too, and I mentally commanded them to enter the building next to the vault and search for a way into the air hoses. According to Sims, the air filtration system was airtight, but in my years working with air elementals I'd found few places they couldn't find their way into eventually. Government bureaucracies almost always contracted out to the lowest bidder, and I figured there'd be a crack or two somewhere. I only hoped I wouldn't run out of time before one of the elementals found one.

I turned to look Modoc square in the face. "Ten-Inch? That's gotta be, what would you say, Modoc—about four of you?"

Modoc, an evil smile on his face, pushed himself off the wall. "This is going to be fun," he informed me.

"Wait," I said. "I'm just pulling your leg. You want to know where Ten-Inch is right now? I can tell you. As a matter of fact, I spoke to him recently. He's real pissed off, by the way."

Modoc's eyes flared, but Sims put a restraining hand on the bigger man's forearm. "Hang on a sec, Modoc." Sims turned to me. "You know where he is? Tell me." He put his pen to his notepad.

"Sure I will," I said. "Just as soon as you let me call my lawyer. You do that, and I have some assurance that I'll walk out of here alive. That's when I start talking."

Sims looked up from his notepad and glared at me. "Stop playing games, Southerland."

"It's no game, Sims. I know the score. If I tell you where Ten-Inch is, you'll turn your pet ape on me. Not that I wouldn't mind if my hands were free, but I guess Modoc prefers it when the odds are stacked in his favor. I get my lawyer on the phone, I'll tell you where to find Ten-Inch. Cross my heart. As you say, no fuss, no muss."

"I've got you for rape and murder, Southerland." I noticed that Sims had dropped the 'Mr.' "You either tell me what I want to know, or Modoc beats it out of you. You give it to me now, and you go free. Modoc gets it from you, and you get hit with both charges. And," he smiled. "Modoc feeds you to the sharks. You go down in my reports as 'disappeared at sea while trying to escape.' Two ways, Southerland: my way or Modoc's way. Your choice. But whichever way you choose, I get Ten-Inch."

"I don't know, Sims. Modoc here is likely to kill me before I talk. He doesn't strike me as a guy with a lot of self-control. You turn him loose on me, and you lose Ten-Inch. I'm guessing someone wants you to find him, bad. Someone named Leea. I'm your best hope, but you lose that opportunity the minute Modoc lays a finger on me. You say I've got two ways. I say *you've* got two ways. You let me call my lawyer, you get your information. You turn Modoc on me, you have to tell your LIA overseer that you fucked up."

I sat back in my chair with my hands in my lap, knowing that Badass was hurling itself against the interrogation chamber with the force of a tornado. Not that it was having any success moving the heavy vault. All I could feel were the faintest of vibrations. I mentally commanded the powerful elemental to direct itself at the air hoses leading into and out of the vault. Sims claimed the hoses could withstand hurricane-force winds, but it was worth a shot.

They say that in a negotiation, once you've given it your best pitch, the best thing you can do is keep your mouth shut and wait for the prospective buyer to give in. I clammed up and waited.

It didn't go the way I would have preferred.

Sims put his pad and pen on the table. "Modoc," he said, keeping his eyes on mine. "Get this man to tell me where to find Ten-Inch. But I don't want him checking out on us until he gives it up, you understand me? Keep him alive until he gives you an address. Once we check it out, he's all yours."

Modoc's baby face lit up like a kid's when he gets the new bike he's been bugging his parents about for weeks. His hands balled themselves into fists, his knuckles bulging under the tape. He took a quick step in my direction.

I waited for the precise moment and shot my leg out from under the table, catching Modoc square in the side of his knee with my heel. I put everything I had into it, and my aim was perfect. Unfortunately, the chair I was sitting in slid back a couple of inches on the slick metal floor, lessening the impact. I got a satisfying yelp out of Modoc. He staggered and nearly collapsed. But, although I had halted his momentum, the big man kept his feet.

"Mother*fuck*!" Modoc's screech echoed throughout the steel-enclosed room.

Wild-eyed, face the color of blood, the detective rushed me. I slid down the front of my chair, intending to drop below the table, but my restraints made me clumsy, and I didn't get as low as I needed to. Modoc nailed me with a roundhouse to the temple that spun my head around. Sparks of light dotted my vision, and a gutful of coffee rose to my throat. My muscles suddenly refused to work, and I found myself sprawled on the floor, arms held up by the restraints on my wrists.

Hands gripping my hair pulled me back into the chair. Modoc aimed a straight jab at my kisser, and I blocked it with my cuffed wrist. The detective howled and shoved my chair away from the table until the slack was gone from the chain. My restraints kept my arms extended out in front of me, leaving me helpless to use them to defend myself. I aimed kicks at Modoc with both feet, but he was ready for them, and I couldn't put anything behind them. A solid rabbit punch connected behind my ear, and I thought my head would roll off my neck.

I conjured up an image of a waterfall in the jungle. "Cougar? Little help?" A faint feline odor filtered into my senses, and my vision cleared.

Which meant I had a clear view of the taped fists that clobbered my face, each punch following the next in rapid succession, pounding against the bones in my head like sledgehammers. Modoc kept me pinned to the chair, with the restraints keeping me attached to the immovable steel table stretched taut. Try as I might, I couldn't get the leverage I needed to pull myself forward and give my arms room to operate. Cougar must have been blocking the transmission of pain from my nerve endings to my brain, because all I could feel was a dull throbbing, like the mother of all hangovers. I was all too aware, however, of the damage those punches were inflicting. My teeth felt loose, and I was pretty sure my nose was shattered. I hoped my jaw wasn't broken, as well. I figured it would only be a matter of time. I was getting my ass kicked.

After what seemed like hours, but was probably only a couple of minutes, Sims put a stop to it. "Don't kill him! We need Ten-Inch's location."

The ass-kicking stopped, and I peered up at Modoc through eyes that were swollen nearly shut. The tape on his hands was stained with blood—mine, of course—and he was rubbing his knuckles with the palms of his hands to soothe them. Good, I thought. I hoped he'd broken a few of them on my skull.

"Are you ready to tell me where Ten-Inch is, Mr. Southerland?"

How nice. The 'Mr.' was back.

I turned my head toward Sims and nodded. "Okay." I groaned. It hurt to draw enough breath to breathe, much less talk. "I'll tell you. You ready?"

"Just a sec." Sims picked his pen and pad from the table. "Go ahead."

"Right. Okay. Write this down." I drew in a deep rasping breath before speaking. "He's staying at the Fuck You House. That's eff you see kay why oh you. Corner of Kiss Street and My Ass Avenue."

Sims threw the pad to the tabletop. "Alkwat's flaming pecker, Southerland! Do you *want* to die? Do you have some kind of suicide complex?"

Modoc scowled. "He doesn't know where Ten-Inch is. He's fuckin' with us." He slammed a bloody fist into my jaw. Even if the taut chain hadn't been preventing me from lifting my arms, I don't think I could have stopped it. I didn't have the energy.

My head dangled to one side, my neck unable to support it. Through half-closed eyes, I saw a tiny smudge in front of my face. I blinked, thinking my eyes might have been damaged. I shivered at the thought that I might be going blind. I looked away from the smudge, but it didn't move when my peepers moved. I shut my eyes and opened them. The smudge was still there. I felt the tiniest glimmer of hope.

"Is he right, Southerland?" Sims asked. "Were you lying about talking to Ten-Inch?"

"I was telling the truth. I talked to him, and I know where he is right now." My voice slurred as I forced words through clenched teeth. "But you'll have to get someone tougher than this pretty boy to pry it out of me. Sunny hits harder than he does."

That got me three more crunching jolts from Modoc's jackhammer fists. Red drool spilled from the corner of my mouth to the floor. I was done. If it weren't for Cougar, I'd have been unconscious. Or worse. I wondered how much longer my spirit guide would be able to keep me alive, much less awake. But I needed to hang on just a bit longer. I just needed a little more time.

Desperate, I searched for the smudge I'd seen. It was still there, floating in front of my face, a shimmer in the air no more than half an inch tall. It was whirling and shooting off tiny droplets of water that stung when they spattered against my lips.

I ran my tongue over my lips and tasted salt. Hope brushed at my mind like the edge of a feather. One of the tiny air elementals I had summoned had found its way into the supposedly airtight filtration system and made its way into the vault to hurl droplets of salty rainwater into my face. I tried to send a mental command to the elemental, but my brains had been too scrambled by Modoc's fists for me to make a connection. I'd have to try to speak to the drop of sentient air out loud.

Sims was shouting at me, but I ignored him, focusing instead on the whirling drop of air. "Go back the way you came in," I muttered, trying to enunciate the words with a tongue that felt like a balloon. "Find the big spirit. Show it how to get inside this room."

"What's he saying?" Sims demanded. "Is he giving us an address?"

"Nah." Modoc gave me a knuckle sandwich that turned my mouth to ground chuck. "He's gone loony." Another blow landed on my temple, and a silent explosion went off in the back of my head. Cougar or no Cougar, I wasn't going to be able to take too many more of those.

"Stop that!" Sims's voice sounded like it was bubbling up from the bottom of a deep well. A bass drum was beating a slow, irregular rhythm in my head, and I couldn't see the walls of the room anymore.

"No more, Modoc," came the voice. Whose voice was it again? Some mug's. Some fucking mug.

"Can't you see he's had it?" Who was the mug talking about? Was he talking about me? Was I dead?

"Tell me where Ten-Inch is, Southerland. Don't you even think about dying until you give up Ten-Inch!"

As the room around me grew darker, I became aware of a distant piercing noise coming from deep within the intake vent beneath the table, a high-pitched squeal, faint, but more urgent than the steady hum produced by the air shooting up through the vent to circulate inside the chamber. It was the sound of a thin jet of pressurized air streaming out of a pinhole in a balloon. I let my body go limp until I slid off the chair and under the table. I leaned toward the intake vent, guided by the sound of the distant squeal. After a few moments, the air rising from the vent began to change, becoming more substantial, until it shaped itself into a gray whirlwind flinging large drops of seawater in all directions. Ice-cold water hit me in the face and chased away some of the fog that was threatening to overwhelm my senses. Focusing on staying conscious, I drew in a breath, and, with a croak in my voice, I shouted at the swirling funnel with as much strength as I could muster: "Badass!" I pointed at Modoc, who was trying to drag me out from under the table. "Attack!"

My breath rattled in my chest. Sounds of pain were coming from somewhere. The growing darkness rushed into my head, and I saw and heard nothing.

## Chapter Twenty-Four

I woke in darkness to the sound of roaring winds. I was lying on a cold metal floor, or maybe on the roof of the bus that had run me over. My head was spinning, and I was too dizzy to move. Or open my eyes. Or breathe. I wanted to go back to wherever I'd been, but I couldn't remember where that was, and something was telling me it wasn't anywhere I wanted to go back to anyway. Eyes still closed, my senses, enhanced by elf magic, told me I couldn't stand without banging my head against the underside of a table, so I pushed myself along the floor until I was clear.

When the spinning in my head let up to the point where I thought I might be able to stand without falling, I opened my eyes and pushed myself to my feet. I became aware of a number of things. First, a fiercely spinning gray twister that filled a corner of the room was hovering over the prone body of a man who wasn't moving. Second, the room was filled with other, much smaller whirlwinds, maybe a couple of dozen or so, each one hovering in place in the air as if waiting for something. Third, my hands were free, and something told me they shouldn't be. Fourth, a hubcap was lying on the top of the table in the center of the room.

Memories came flooding back to me. The body on the floor was Modoc. The door to the chamber was wide open, and Detective Sims was nowhere in sight. The handcuffs that had been around my wrists were lying on the floor. They were still closed and locked, and the chain that had attached them to the table had been ripped in two, the center links stretched and broken. After a quick assessment of the situation, I dismissed all of the elementals in the room except Badass. I still couldn't send mental commands, and it took me three tries to get the words out without gagging on them. My head felt like one giant exposed nerve ending, and the act of speaking sent bolts of lightning through my jaws and into my inner ears. I shuddered to think what my face must look like. Well, it wasn't that pretty to begin with, I reminded myself. Maybe a new one wouldn't be so bad.

After commanding Badass to stand down and wait in a different corner of the chamber, I bent down to examine Modoc. The first thing I noticed was Sims's pen poked deep into Modoc's left eye. Not deep enough to pierce his brain, I concluded. Pity. Modoc's face had been mauled as badly as mine had, and I noted with perverse satisfaction that he didn't look so pretty anymore. That would have brought a smile to my face if the pain of stretching my lips hadn't stopped one from forming.

He wasn't dead, but he was on the doorstep. His body was still as death, but I could hear a slow shallow heartbeat and the barest hint of a gurgle deep in his lungs. When I listened more closely, I could hear the grinding of his clenched teeth, as if he were in great pain and unable to do anything about it. I considered several options. Even though he was obviously suffering and probably dying, I felt no sympathy toward him at all. Instead, the sight of him lying there helpless and hurting stirred an intense hatred from someplace deep inside me. I still had no idea why he affected me the way he did, but my reaction to seeing him at the edge of the great abyss left me torn between two hopes. First, that he was suffering tremendously, and that he would continue to suffer until he died the death of a thousand slices. Second, that he would somehow survive, and that we would meet again, and that I would kill him slowly and painfully.

With an effort, I shook my irrational feelings away and stood. Turning to Badass, I asked, "What happened to the other man who was in this room?"

A moan rose from the whirlwind. "Human open door and go through."

Okay, I had deduced that for myself. "Was he hurt?"

"This one doesn't know."

Getting information from elementals was a tricky business. "Was blood coming out of his body?"

"Yessss."

Good, I thought. The pudgy weasel hadn't escaped unscathed.

Forgetting about Sims for the moment, I turned my attention to the most out-of-place object in the room, the familiar-looking hubcab on the table. Now that I was concentrating on it, I could sense the vibration and lightness of air that signaled something otherworldly at work.

"Badass, who brought this thing into this room?"

"This one doesn't know."

"How did it get here?"

"It fell from the air."

Of course it did. Kisikisi wasn't willing to stop Modoc from beating me to death, but he had no problem delivering me another cryptic message. "And no one else was in this room?"

"Noooo."

I indicated the broken chain. "How did this break?"

"This one doesn't know."

"Did I break it?"

"Noooo."

Had Kisikisi freed me? Maybe I owed him a little gratitude after all.

Interrogating the big elemental wasn't doing anything for the pain in my head, and, anyway, I was about out of questions. "Okay, Badass. You can go. And thank you, bud. You saved my bacon."

The whirling funnel bowed slightly in my direction. "Badass is happy to serve Alex." The elemental disappeared through the open door.

Alone in the room with the nearly dead Modoc, I picked the hubcap off the table and studied it. It matched the other three I'd already recovered, and, like them, it had a message scratched onto the outer surface. I read the message, and the hairs on the back of my neck rose to attention. Scratched on the surface of the hubcap were three capital letters and a punctuation mark: RUN!

At that moment, the inside of the chamber lit up with a white light that seemed to have no source. Something dropped from the ceiling of the room and fell like a wrinkled lump on Modoc's body, partially covering it. More help from Kisikisi? My first thought was that the covering was a rug, or maybe a heavy blanket. A second look revealed the covering to be the pelt of an animal, although I couldn't immediately tell what kind. I sniffed, and the scent of decaying flesh assaulted my nostrils. I took a step toward the animal pelt and came to an abrupt halt when it moved of its own accord and began to spread over Modoc's body. Modoc rose to a sitting position, and the pelt melted through his clothes and into his skin. Modoc's face began to alter its shape. His jawline lengthened, and his nose stretched into a snout. His mouth opened, revealing sharpened teeth, and his single functioning eyeball locked onto me like a laser. As I watched, horrified, the thing that had been Modoc reached up and wrapped his hand around the pen poking out of his eye. He yanked it free and flung it to one side. Thick dark matter poured from his eye socket and slid down his face like molten rock. An otherworldly energy emanated from the detective, buzzing and crackling like the electric current between the test prongs of a stun gun.

Maybe this wasn't Kisikisi's work after all.

I cast my eyes down at the message on the hubcap I was still holding. RUN! Good advice, I thought, as Modoc, or whatever he'd become, rose slowly to his feet. Best advice I've received in years. I turned and stumbled out the door.

***

A steady rain soaked the asphalt as I broke into a painful jog across the parking lot away from the interrogation chamber. I saw no sign of Sims, and the car he'd used to bring me to the empty office complex was gone. Given the scene inside the vault when I'd come to, I couldn't blame the detective for not sticking around. When I reached the street, I looked back over my shoulder and spotted the creature that had been Modoc emerging from the vault a hundred yards behind me. A growl emerged from somewhere deep inside my chest. An impulse, the product of a burning animalistic hatred, bubbled to the surface of my thoughts: stand and fight! I considered the idea for maybe half an eye blink before deciding to wait until I was in better shape before plunging headlong into a confrontation with something I didn't understand.

I was running, but I hoped I wouldn't have to run far. I was already gasping for air, and my head was spinning so badly I could barely keep my feet. I risked another glance back the way I'd come and saw Modoc standing at the edge of the parking lot, watching me. He didn't seem to be in any condition for a footrace, either. Whatever magic was present in that animal pelt apparently needed some time to revive him. I hoped the combination of my spirit animal and the elf magic in me would be faster, but I wasn't going to take any chances. A taxicab was sitting outside a bar a block ahead of me, and I made my way toward it at a fast jog.

When I reached the hack, the back door was locked. The cabbie rolled down his window and, without looking directly at me, shouted, "I'm booked."

"I don't see anyone," I said.

"He's in the bar. He'll be out in a sec."

I walked up to the driver's window and leaned down far enough for him to get a good gander at my face. His eyes widened at the sight of it.

"I'm injured. I need to get to a hospital," I told him.

"Not in this hack, buddy. I'll get dispatch to send another one out here."

"The mug who did this to me is looking to finish the job."

"That's your problem."

I checked my pockets and found that the detectives hadn't relieved me of anything but my gun, and that my phone and wallet were still with me. I took a credit card out of my wallet and showed it to the cabbie. "Double fare. Triple if you run the lights."

His eyes moved from my card to my face, and back to the card again. "All right, get in. Try not to bleed on the seat."

When I was in the cab, the cabbie asked, "Which hospital?"

"Never mind the hospital," I told him. "Get me to the adaro settlement. My car is parked there."

The cabbie turned to look at me over his shoulder. "You sure about that, buddy?"

"I'm sure. Just get me there fast."

He shrugged and jammed the accelerator.

I looked back and saw Modoc, about thirty yards behind me, glide to a stop and glare at me through the back window. Allowing myself a brief smile, I lay back in the seat, closed my eyes, and listened to the sound of my blood pulsing through my temples. Questions crowded through my brain, bumping shoulders and elbowing at each other as they competed for my attention.

Who, or what, was Modoc? He was definitely more than he seemed. Was he human? What was the deal with our mutual antagonism? It seemed instinctual and beyond all reason. What was behind that?

My eyes popped open. Walks in Cloud! I'd told her that I'd be seeing her in forty-five minutes. How long ago had that been? I checked the time and was surprised to discover that it was still mid-afternoon, and so far I was only about a half hour overdue. I found my phone and tapped on her name in my contacts list.

"You're late, Jack"

"I know. A lot has happened. You okay?"

"Sure. Are you on your way?"

I had to think about that. I was exhausted, but my body would heal. It would take a while, probably several days, or even weeks, to get back to normal, but as long as I didn't try to lift anything heavy, or let myself get beat nearly to death again for another month or so, I'd probably manage. "I can be there in an hour. I hope."

"You okay, Jack? You sound a little tired."

"I'll be fine. Uh.... You wouldn't happen to have a first-aid kit in your shop, would you? Or just some disinfectant and a few bandages?"

"Shit, Jack. What'd you do this time?"

"My face got in the way of someone's fists a few times. I think my nose got the worst of it. Or maybe my jaw. Or my mouth. Hard to tell."

"Lord's balls! You sure you don't need a doctor?"

"What for? My own healing magic will help me more than a doctor could. I just want to make sure the worst of the cuts get cleaned up."

She let out a breath. "Okay, Jack. Get here as soon as you can. But be careful."

We disconnected. It had been a long day. My head was throbbing and I was tired. I settled into my seat and once again let my eyes fall shut. Suddenly, I was no longer sitting in a cab cruising the rainy streets of Yerba City. I didn't remember opening my eyes, but I found my attention drawn to a bright full moon in a clear night sky above a line of trees, branches swaying in the breeze. Rather than cold and dank, the air was heavy with warm tropical moisture. From nearby, I heard the low roar of a waterfall. I breathed in and picked up a faint feline odor.

The voice of Cougar filled my throbbing head. "Be aware, Speaks with Wind," warned my spirit animal, referring to me by the name he'd given me when we'd bonded. "The one you call Modoc plots your death."

I concentrated, ignored the pain, and found that I was able to form words in my head. "No shit. What is he?"

"Your enemy."

"Thanks. I kinda got that. Can you be more specific?"

"He is a skinwalker."

"A skinwalker? Isn't that some kind of shapeshifting witch?"

I heard a growl in my head.

"What animal does he change into?" I asked.

More growling. A pause. Finally: "A cougar."

"Modoc shapeshifts into a cougar?"

"Partially. He is possessed by the spirit of one."

"Wait. Aren't you the cougar spirit?"

I waited through a pause before hearing, "It's complicated. He is possessed by a memory of me."

"Seriously?"

I "heard" a sound with a lot of syllables, many vowels, and several guttural stops.

"Um, excuse me?"

"That is his name."

"Whose—Modoc's?"

"It is what he calls himself."

The pounding in my head had not disappeared, and, in fact, was stronger than ever. "How 'bout we just stick to Modoc." I felt faint. Faced with an unexpected trip to the tropics in the aftermath of a savage beating, I was having some trouble keeping my bearings. I couldn't tell if I was having a vision, or if I was severely concussed. Maybe both.

The air in front of me shimmered, and Cougar appeared, head lowered and tail swishing from side to side in an irregular pattern. His eyes lifted to meet mine.

I took a deep breath and spoke out loud. "Why does he want to kill me? And why did he make me want to wrap my fingers around his neck and squeeze until his head pops even before he started using my head as a punching bag?"

Cougar spoke out loud. "Once, long ago, I chose him to be one of mine. I gave him much strength and taught him many things. He took my gifts and wandered down paths I did not choose for him. I expressed my displeasure with his choices, and he spurned me. The power in him had grown. He showed me no respect. I rejected him, and I walked away, but I left a part of me behind."

"The memory of you?"

"Yes. But... more."

I decided to let it go.

Cougar paused, and I waited. I'd learned not to rush my spirit guide when he was in the mood to speak to me.

Cougar lowered himself to the ground and gave his paw a lick with his thick tongue. Again his voice filled my head. "The one you call Modoc studied many forbidden arts. He stalked and hunted an old cougar who was dear to me. He killed him and took his skin. He learned to draw upon the spirit of the cougar, to take on the essence of his material form and natural properties, and he became a creature of fear."

"Wait," I interrupted. "When did all this happen? How old is he? He doesn't look like he's more than twenty-five."

"He is many times that, Speaks with Wind. Many summers have passed since I last saw him. He has traveled far. Now he is here."

I thought about that. "Okay. But what's he got against me?"

"He sees me in you. It is me he hates. He hates you because I am your guide. Your fur rises when you are in his presence because you sense the hate he feels for you, and for me. And because you are rivals for the same territory. He is dangerous. You have wounded him, but skinwalkers heal fast. Faster than you do. Healing is one of their gifts. Killing is another."

My head continued to pound. "Are you saying that this town isn't big enough for the two of us? You aren't actually saying that, are you? Because that's just stupid."

"You are his rival, Speaks with Wind. He is your rival."

"Everyone wants me to fight in their war. Well fuck that. I'll tell him the territory is all his. I don't fight turf wars."

Cougar stared at me and I sensed, rather than saw, something my brain interpreted as a smile. Cougar's voice sounded, "But *I* do, little one. And so you must, as well."

"Hold on there," I protested. "This isn't part of our deal."

Cougar stood, and his tail rose like a banner of war. "You will oppose the one you call Modoc."

"Don't I get a say in this? What if I refuse?"

Cougar turned, showing me his backside. I heard his voice in my mind. "You won't, Speaks with Wind. You want this. He has hurt you. He has angered you. You desire revenge."

I couldn't argue with that. As the big cat began to stride away, the scent of tropical breezes was replaced by the stale fumes of gasoline and burning oil, the roar of the waterfall by the sounds of tires on wet asphalt, and the clear night sky by the interior of a taxicab, whose driver was eyeing me curiously in the rearview mirror.

"You okay back there, bud? I think you were talking in your sleep."

"I'm okay. How much farther?"

"Just another couple of blocks, but traffic is getting heavy."

I gazed out the window at the falling rain. Ten-Inch had told me that I wasn't always in command of my own life. Whether I liked it or not, I was in the middle of a war between two South Sea spirits, and the fate of Yerba City depended on the outcome. At the same time, I was apparently caught up in a power struggle between a shapeshifting witch and his former mentor, and there was nothing I could do about that, either. I knew I should have been upset by this turn of events, but something deep inside me was... well... pleased. I *wanted* to go up against Modoc again, preferably with my hands free. Modoc was a killer. According to Cougar, he'd been at it for a very long time. And now he was in my territory. I had no doubt that he had tried to kill me in the interrogation vault and wanted to finish the job. He hadn't cared whether I'd known where Ten-Inch was or not. If I was being honest with myself, the prospect of stopping that son of a bitch for keeps felt pretty good. It went beyond revenge, although that was part of it now. But I'd hated him the moment I'd first encountered him outside Ten-Inch's apartment. Where had this anger come from? Was Cougar manipulating me? It didn't feel that way. It felt like something deeper, and it felt familiar, like an old friend. It felt like my own natural instincts, the same love of fighting I'd felt as a kid growing up in the neighborhood. The same instincts I'd brought with me into the military. The same bellicose spirit that my army trainers had recognized and molded when they sent me to a special training school before unleashing me against the Qusco insurgents in the Borderland. I was glad Modoc hated me. I was glad he'd tried to kill me. It was something I needed. His hatred made me feel alive in a way I hadn't felt since... since Holly. I wasn't sure what that said about me, but I was more than willing to put off thinking about it until later. Or never.

## Chapter Twenty-Five

"Don't take off your coat, Jack. You're taking me out."

Walks was already dressed for the rain when I arrived at her workshop, and she kept me in her entryway only long enough to grab an umbrella before waiting for me to wheel her out the door.

"Let's go. Down the block to the right. Ever been to Sharky's Bar?"

I opened the umbrella and held it over both our heads. "I must have missed that one."

"It's nothing special, but it's nearby and there's no stairs."

"I was thinking I might fix my face before we went anywhere."

She gave me a quick glance. "All right. Get a wet towel and wash off the blood. I don't have any bandages, but I don't think you need any. You're not leaking blood, and bruises suit you." She studied my face more carefully. "Hmm. Someone really did a number on you. Anything broken in there?"

"Yeah, but I'll be all right. Good thing I'm filled with elf magic. Give me a week and I'll be my old handsome self again."

"Lucky you. Just keep your hat brim pulled low so you don't scare anyone on our way to Sharky's."

After I'd guided Walks's chair down the block a ways, I asked, "Why are we going to a bar?"

"We're meeting someone there."

"Who?"

Walks looked back at me over her shoulder, a sunny smile on her face. "Captain Flinthook of the Placid Point Police Department. He says you've met, and he's very anxious to see you again."

I stopped. "Excuse me?"

Walks chuckled as she lit up a cigarette. "Lord's balls, Southerland. You got a problem with the cops? If I didn't know better, I'd say you were acting like a wanted criminal."

"Did I mention that the lug who rearranged my face today was one of Flinthook's detectives?"

"You didn't." She sighed. "But I'm not surprised. The captain told me that a couple of his coppers were looking for you, and I gather they didn't have your best interests at heart. Come on, Jack. We're almost there. The captain says he'll explain everything."

We got to Sharky's in time to beat the dinner rush, if the place ever had one. The inside of the joint was dark, but the captain of the Placid Point Precinct was easy to find. Over seven feet tall with a belly the size of a small whale, Flinthook sat at the back of the bar on a reinforced bench specially made for trolls. His cane lay beside him on the bench, and a quart-sized goblet of red wine sat on the table in front of him, still full. Either Flinthook had just received a refill, or he'd been waiting for us to arrive before starting in on it. The troll turned his gleaming red eyes on me and waved us over to join him. I pushed Walks in his direction, pausing near the bar to tell the barkeep that the lady and I would be needing black coffee.

"Pardon me for not rising," Flinthook told us when we reached his table. "This rainstorm has got my knees acting up."

"You won't get any grief from me," said Walks, patting the side of her wheelchair.

I remained standing. "If you're here to put the elbow on me, let me remind you that this is Nihhonese Heights, not Placid Point. You're out of your precinct."

Flinthook waved away my protest. "As if that mattered. But relax, Mr. Southerland. Take a load off. I'm not here to take you in. I'm here to help you, although I'm not sure how much I can do." He shook his head, looking sad. The skin on his gray face was all drooping bags and hanging jowls, giving his hairless head the appearance of a lump of wet clay. Trolls typically live more than twice as long as humans, and this one appeared to be old even for one of his people. I wondered that he was still an active member of the police force.

Walks pulled at the sleeve of my coat. "Sit down, Alex. The captain has some information for us."

I sat in a chair opposite Flinthook and placed my soaked fedora at the end of the table just as the barkeep brought over our coffees. I wrapped my hands around the coffee mug to warm them. "Someone want to tell me what's going on?" I asked.

In response, Flinthook turned his glowing red eyes on my face. "Modoc do that to you?"

"You should see *him*," I retorted.

Flinthook let his laser-like gaze linger on me for a few moments. "Will I be able to?" he asked.

"He's still alive, if that's what you're asking."

"Hmm. Pity. I was hoping you'd killed him."

That wasn't the response I'd been expecting, though maybe I shouldn't have been surprised. "You haven't seen him?" I asked.

"No, but I just left Sims. He was... upset. Whatever you did really rattled him, not that he told me much." Flinthook's thick red lips twisted into a scowl. "I must admit that it was good to see that pompous rat bastard knocked off his high horse. He thinks you killed his partner."

I studied the captain before speaking. "You don't seem to care much for the detectives who work for you."

Flinthook's face looked as if a bug had flown into his mouth. "Work for me. Right." He closed his eyes and sighed. "I may be the captain, Mr. Southerland, but I'm afraid I don't have much authority at the Placid Point Precinct. Not anymore."

"Are you saying Sims runs the place?" I'd suspected as much from my time there.

But Flinthook shook his head. "No, Mr. Southerland. Although he probably has more pull around the station house than I do. But he just follows orders, same as me."

I nodded. "He's LIA, right?"

Flinthook looked down at the table. "Through and through."

"Thought so. I know they have a presence everywhere, but..."

"The LIA runs our department, Mr. Southerland. We all get our marching orders from someone calling himself Mr. White. A human, I think. I've talked to him on the phone, but I've never seen him. The members of the force just do what he tells us, like good little monkeys."

"That's rough, captain. But why are you telling us all this?"

Flinthook turned his gaze on Walks. "Because the LIA believes *you've* got something they want very badly."

The troll turned back to me. "As for *you*, Mr. Southerland.... They want to make you disappear. For keeps. But first, they want you to tell them where to find Ten-Inch."

I let out a breath and lied. "Everyone thinks I know where Ten-Inch is. I haven't seen him in almost three years."

Flinthook sighed. "That's unfortunate. They know you've been looking for him, and they suspect you've either found him, or that you know where he's hiding. If they don't think you've got information concerning his whereabouts, or any way of getting it, they'll remove you from the picture."

Walks put a hand on my elbow. "The captain called me earlier. He said the LIA has been watching my office. They've got people staked out in the building across the street." The look in her eyes told me she hadn't told Flinthook why the LIA might be interested in her.

I looked Flinthook up and down, from the warts on his close-set pointed ears and sagging face to the bulbous roll of fat hanging over his belt. "How do you know all this?"

Flinthook was silent for a few moments, thinking. Finally, he reached for his wine goblet with a huge four-fingered hand and took a sip. He set it back down on the table and let out a resigned breath. "I've been a Placid Point cop for a long time, longer than either of you have been alive. I like being a cop, or I used to. Being a cop made me feel useful. I was serving the public, and it felt good. Placid Point used to be a quiet district, once upon a time. When I was on the beat, I used to hang out with the shopkeepers, eat free meals at the restaurants, get drinks on the house.... A big day for me was breaking up a back-alley craps game, or keeping the dips out of the pockets of the tourists at the Old Placid Point Pier. But I broke up some robberies, too. I arrested some bad people and took them off the street. I helped keep Placid Point quiet. Helped make it a nice place to live. And, eventually, I rose through the ranks, from street cop to detective, to lieutenant, and right about when the old pier was closed down, to captain. It was a proud day for me."

The troll shook his head and took another swallow of his wine. "But the neighborhood changed when they closed down the pier. The tourists stopped coming, and businesses closed. People started buying cheap illegal shit from the black market. Gangs formed and started selling drugs and running numbers and women. Crime increased and got more violent. The adaro settlement opened, and things got worse, fast. Then the LIA showed up. Started sending us after targets, or telling us to look the other way when certain people turned up dead, or disappeared. Mr. White became my main Leea contact. Eventually I came to realize I was working for him, and only him. Crime in Placid Point escalated. It changed from being a nice place to raise a family to becoming a crime-ridden cesspit. And all under my watch. But that wasn't our main area of concern anymore. We stopped being a local police department and became a branch office for the Lord's Investigation Agency."

The captain was building to a point, and I let him get there at his own pace. He tossed back the remainder of his wine, about a pint in two big gulps, before continuing. "Sims showed up last summer. I don't know if Sims is a card-carrying LIA agent, or if he's just under their control, but from the moment he set foot in the precinct he started running the department like he owned it. He reports directly to Mr. White, which makes me nothing more than a figurehead."

Flinthook turned his glowing eyes directly on me. "I'm not stupid, Mr. Southerland, although a lot of people seem to think I am. I know better than to fuck with the LIA, but I've got eyes, and I've got ears. Sims has a strong interest in Walks in Cloud's shop. I think he was sent here to keep an eye on it. I know he has it under surveillance, even though it's not technically in our jurisdiction. Whenever I ask him about it he tells me to take it up with Mr. White. Bastard. He doesn't even pretend that I'm supposed to be his superior in the department."

I'd suspected Sims was Leea since I'd researched his job history. All those transfers, and so little time in any one place... it wasn't a typical résumé for a cop without any black marks on his record. It made more sense, however, if he was troubleshooting for the LIA. I studied the troll. "What's your angle in all this, captain? Why are you telling us all this?"

Flinthook leveled his glowing eyes at me. "I'm sick of it, Mr. Southerland. I want to be a captain again. A real one. Not a stooge for the LIA. This rainstorm is flooding my town. The people in my precinct need help from its police department. We're supposed to serve our public. But the LIA has my whole department wasting its time with LIA business. Searching for the leader of a street gang who may or may not have been involved in the murder of some nymph? Why? It's not even our case. The LIA took it off our hands. But we're supposed to drop everything and do all their work for them. And does the round-the-clock surveillance of a computer tech outside our jurisdiction stop while we've got all other available hands on deck looking for some petty gangster? Not on your life! That's an LIA job, too, so it continues, day and night, using our officers. It's not right. Being captain of the Placid Point Precinct used to make me proud, but it's been a long time since I felt that way. I'm ashamed of what I've become, Mr. Southerland. And I want to do something about it."

A police captain with a sense of public duty. Huh! Well, why not? A cop had the same need for self-esteem as anyone else.

I nodded at Flinthook, inviting him to continue.

"So. Anyway. Tuesday morning, I get a call from Mr. White. We're to drop everything and look for Ten-Inch in connection with the killing of an adaro nymph. He makes certain threats about what will happen to me if we don't find him fast."

Flinthook nodded in my direction. "The next day, Sims and Modoc pick you up and lose you. They don't tell me anything about you, except that you got picked up by the LIA, which I find curious, since Sims seemed to be surprised by it." He chuckled. "I hear you and your lawyer pulled a fast one on him. Very smooth! Anyway, yesterday morning, Sims gets a call."

Flinthook leaned back in his seat and smiled like a cat who's just polished off a canary. "A couple of months ago, I hired a tech witch to rewire Sim's phone so that I could listen in on his calls without him knowing about it." He turned his smile on Walks. "No one in *your* league, of course. I can't afford anyone like you. But he was competent enough. Since then, I've been listening in on Sim's calls whenever I get the chance. Anyway, this call's from Mr. White. Their surveillance has spotted *you*..." Flinthook nodded at me, "in *her* shop..." Flinthook indicated Walks in Cloud, "and someone needs to beat feet over there right that second and pick you up for questioning, chop chop! Sims hangs up and calls Modoc."

Flinthook turned his gaze on me to make sure I was getting the picture. I was, and I nodded.

But Flinthook wasn't done. "One more thing, Southerland." He leaned toward me over the table. "Modoc is dirty. The Hatfield Syndicate has had him in their pocket since he first showed up. They might have even arranged to put him here. To tell you the truth, I can't think of any other reason why a brute like him would ever be a cop. Everyone at the station knows there's something unnatural about him. He's a freak, but he usually does whatever Sims tells him to. Most of the time, anyway. Good thing, because that savage don't respect *me*, that's for sure."

My brain leaped into overdrive, making connections, putting pieces together. Modoc was working for the Hatfields? Of course. A few things were starting to make sense.

The barkeep finally made his way to our table, and we waited until he'd taken away the glasses. He walked away when he was done without asking any of us if we wanted refills.

When the barkeep was out of earshot, Flinthook resumed speaking. "Earlier today, Sims and Modoc started out the door. I ask them where they are going, and for once I get an answer. You've been spotted at the settlement, and they're going to pick you up. After they leave, I decide to call Walks in Cloud. I don't know if she's connected to this Ten-Inch case, but I know that you were at her office the other day when Modoc went after you, and that the LIA is looking at both of you. I wanted to warn you to watch yourselves. I don't know what's going on, and I don't know what I could do about it if I did. I'm just the captain of the local precinct, that's all. I'm not in the loop for the big picture. But the LIA wants you, Southerland, and they're spying on Walks in Cloud here. And I'm getting fuckin' sick and tired of being pushed around like I don't matter. If talking to the two of you throws a monkey wrench into the LIA's plans for you, then I believe I will have done something... something... I don't know. Good, maybe? I don't know. Maybe just disruptive. I'll settle for that."

Captain Flinthook slumped on his bench, looking exhausted.

\*\*\*

Once back in Walks in Cloud's workshop, I insisted on scanning it for elementals.

"Knock yourself out, Jack. But the Cloud Spirit has it covered. They snuck one by us once, but it won't happen again." She wheeled herself to her coffeemaker and began preparing a fresh batch of nature's nectar. "You know," she called. "I don't get it. An air elemental? What could Leea get from it? What's it gonna see? It's not like I go anywhere, and it's not gonna be able to figure out what I'm doing on the computer, right?"

"I don't see how. It could listen to your side of any phone calls, or let someone know if you have any visitors."

Walks thought for a moment. "I can't think of any phone conversations I've had recently that would interest the LIA. And the only visitor they've reacted to is you."

"It doesn't make much sense," I admitted. "But they've got Placid Point cops watching your shop round the clock. They must want something. I'd feel better if we both took a good look around."

While the coffee was brewing, I searched for elementals, and Walks checked her security scanners.

As we were conducting our inspection, Walks in Cloud stopped, a thoughtful expression on her face. "Hey, Jack. Can you see through an elemental's eyes?"

"Elementals don't actually have eyes."

"Stop being technical. Can you see what an elemental sees? Or hear what it hears?"

"No, I can't. If I want to know what information they've picked up I have to call them back and get a report from them."

"Is that true with all elementalists?"

"Yes, as far as I know. I mean, I'm one of the most powerful elementalists I know, thanks to the elf. After he shoved that crystal into my forehead I could contact elementals directly without having to draw glyphs. I don't know of anybody else who can work without visible glyphs. Lately I've learned how to communicate with elementals telepathically. I think Cougar might have something to do with that. But I can't see or hear what elementals are experiencing directly." I paused. "It would sure be handy if I could."

Walks in Cloud frowned. "What if someone else could do that? You've told me that other elementalists are more powerful than you are."

I thought about it for several moments. "It's conceivable, I suppose. But I've never heard of such a case. It seems unlikely."

"Hmmm.... If you say so."

I shrugged and concentrated on searching for security risks.

Once I was satisfied we weren't being watched or overheard, I relaxed and filled two mugs with hot coffee. Handing a mug to Walks, I asked, "Do you think the LIA knows we saved a copy of the RAA formula, or do you think they're just guessing?"

The computer wizard took a sip from her mug before answering. "I've been thinking about that. I don't think they know. I don't see how they could. But they've probably guessed I made a copy. I mean, that's what *I'd* be thinking if I were in their shoes. It's the logical thing for me to do."

"So they probably bugged your shop to find out for sure."

She shrugged. "Or they might be interested in one of my other projects. I've got a lot of important clients, you know, and I handle a lot of sensitive shit. The LIA could be looking at me for any number of things. And even if they think I've got the RAA formula, there's no way they could have found it by watching me work. Once I stored it away, I forgot about it. I never accessed it again, so I never gave them anything to see."

"How do you know it's still there?"

"Why wouldn't it be?"

"Is there some way you could check without anyone knowing about it?"

"Sure I could. But I'm not going to. Let it go, Alex. It's safe. Trust me." She wheeled herself around her worktable until she was sitting next to me. "And anyway, what if the LIA somehow managed to steal the file. Is there any reason why we should care?"

I thought about that. "Lord Ketz would use it to hatch an egg and make himself a junior Lord Ketz."

Walks shrugged. "So what?"

When I didn't answer, Walks put a hand on my knee. "The only reason you prevented the LIA from getting that formula in the first place is because they wanted it, and you don't like them. You were planning on destroying it. We still could, you know. Then you'd never have to worry about it again. You want me to? Just say the word."

I sipped at my coffee without tasting it, relishing its warmth on my bruised lips and in my throat. "To be honest, I'm not sure what I want. But I have to admit that I like having something the LIA doesn't want me to have. You're right. I hate those bastards. If holding on to that formula pisses them off, then I'm all for it. But not if it puts you in any danger. Do you think we should erase it?"

Walks chuckled, a deep husky rasp from a heavy smoker's lungs. "You know me. I'm a techie. I *hate* destroying data. It's like destroying art. And this RAA formula is fucking brilliant!"

I smiled at her. "Let's keep it then. Who knows, it might come in handy someday. I don't know how, but it might."

Walks nodded, but the expression on her face was thoughtful. "We have another option, you know. We could release the formula to the public."

"Huh? Why would we do that?"

She shrugged. "Why not? It's a process for reinvigorating dead cells. Think of the potential for something like that." She took her hand off my knee and slapped at her motionless thigh perched on the seat of her wheelchair. "That formula could do a lot of good."

"I thought your condition was more the result of a deal you made with the Cloud Spirit than with any physical cause."

"It is, but I'm not thinking of myself. A lot of disabled people out there would like to have an opportunity to walk. Reifying Agent Alpha might give them some hope."

"It would more likely be weaponized by the Dragon Lords. Lord Ketz wants it so he can make a little dragon assistant. Ketz-Alkwat and Son. If all seven of the Dragon Lords get hold of it, we might wind up with a whole new generation of dragons. And don't forget, the guy who came up with the formula thought it would be impossible to use because of the huge amount of power it required in order to make it work. Lord Ketz was going to drain the power from a spirit who is practically a god.

I hate to think what the other Dragon Lords would do in order to activate the formula. Or what they'd use it for."

A sly smile appeared on Walks's face. "All that might happen, and maybe it won't. Or maybe it will cure paralysis. Who knows? You had something no one else had. The LIA tortured you, and Night Owl tried to kill you in order to take it from you. Now you're hanging on to it out of spite. Admit it. You're stubborn."

"I'm not stubborn."

Walks's smile broadened. "Whatever you say, Jack."

I shifted in my seat, trying to get comfortable. "You could always release the formula yourself if you wanted to."

The computer wizard shook her head. "That would be highly unprofessional on my part. I would never do anything like that without your say-so. You entrusted that data to me. As far as I'm concerned, it belongs to you. I can advise you what to do, but, in the end, it's your decision."

"Mm. Well, I'll think about it. Let's talk about it another time. I've had a long day."

Walks put her hand back on my knee and examined my face. "You took a beating today. How are you feeling?"

"I'm fine."

"You're not fine, Jack. You got your face bashed in. Tell me about it."

"Not much to tell. A very bad man chained my wrists to a table and bruised his knuckles on my head while Cougar dulled the pain and kept me conscious."

"And the man who did this to you is the cop I ran out of here with my shotgun?"

"Yep. Detective Modoc of the Placid Point Police Department. Also on the payroll of the Hatfield Syndicate. Running errands for the LIA, too, and threatening innocent computer technicians. Cougar tells me he's one of his chosen people who turned on him and became a skinwalker."

Walks's eyes widened. "Shit! That's bad, Alex. That's real bad. I wish I'd pulled the trigger."

"He and I seem to have some kind of instinctual hatred for each other." I smiled over clenched teeth. "I'm looking forward to seeing him again."

"Captain Flinthook heard you'd killed him."

I grunted. "Nah. The only thing I was able to do was to sic Badass on him. Badass kicked his butt pretty good, but it didn't kill him. I passed out and missed most of it. While I was out, someone cut me loose from the chains cuffing me to the table, but I'm not sure who. It might have been a spirit called Maui-Kisikisi."

Walks smiled at that. "Kissy kissy?"

I couldn't help chuckling. "It's a long story. Wanna hear it?"

"I do, Jack. But there's something I want to do first."

Walks's hand moved from my knee to my belt buckle.

My whole body stiffened. "What are you doing?"

She lifted her eyes to meet mine as she undid my belt. "What does it look like I'm doing, Jack?" She popped the button loose from my trousers and unzipped the fly.

"I thought you said you were dead from the waist down."

Her face grew serious. "True. But I'm alive from the waist up. Things have been rough for you lately, and you're so tense you're about to jump out of your skin. You need this, Speaks with Wind." She reached up and touched my battered face with gentle fingers. "You need this. And you know what? I need it, too."

***

Later, after the cab I'd called had pulled up and double-parked in front of the shop, I turned to Walks, who had wheeled herself up to the door to see me out. I cleared my throat, not quite knowing what I wanted to say. "Look, Walks.... I... I mean—"

She lifted a finger to cut me off. "It's okay, Jack. You don't have to say anything." Her smile was pleasant and genuine. "You don't have to say a word." Without warning, she clapped me on my backside with the flat of her hand. "I'll see you when I see you, gorgeous. Now get out of here! I've got work to do."

## Chapter Twenty-Six

Back in the beastmobile, I considered returning to the settlement to look for Tahiti, but decided to return home for the evening, instead. It had been a long day, and I needed a night to recuperate.

Friday night traffic in Yerba City is a mess at the best of times, and the unremitting storm had slowed it to near immobility. As a longtime resident, I knew how to skirt the most congested sections of the city, but on this night even my tried-and-true alternate routes were stop-and-go. To make things worse, I hadn't eaten in hours, and I was hungry enough to devour a manticore. Fortunately, no matter where you might find yourself in Yerba City, you're never far from a decent place to eat. I spotted a sterile-looking bar and grill in a residential shopping complex and steered the beastmobile out of the traffic and into the parking lot.

The B&G wasn't half bad for a neighborhood joint. Construction workers, schoolteachers, and landscapers crowded the dining area, and the pleasant fragrance of spicy barbecue sauce, hot coffee, and cold beer filled the air. I found a seat at the bar between a brown-faced middle-aged lug dipping deep-fried shrimp into a cup of cocktail sauce, and a pert dame nursing a beer and wearing the glum expression of someone who had just walked out on her drunken husband. Both of my neighbors snuck a peek at the bruises on my face and tried their best to pretend I wasn't there. That made them my favorite kind of dinner companions, and I knew we'd get along just fine.

Even with healing powers granted to me by the magic in the crystal shard the elf had planted in my forebrain, I figured I needed plenty of fuel if I was going to have a speedy recovery. I ordered a barbecued beef sandwich with all the trimmings on a sourdough roll, a side of potato salad, and a twenty-ounce beer. With all that nutrition, I reckoned I could recover from malaria. I told the barkeep I was on a diet and to make sure the beef had at least marginally more meat on it than fat.

TV screens lined the wall above the bar, each one tuned to a different station. The sound was muted on all of the screens except one, which was tuned to a basketball game. The screen in front of me was showing a newscast with no audio, but between the video clips and the graphics I could pretty much tell what was going on. The news report was covering the unusual weather, of course, and I saw scenes of flooding that probably hadn't been staged. Yerba City sits on forty-eight named hills, and clips showed muddy water pouring down asphalt slopes. Rushing streams swamped parked cars, and traffic was at a standstill. Another shot showed waves crashing over piers, flooding beaches, and even washing up into the yards of expensive shoreline mansions. I wondered how the working-class neighborhoods along the coast were faring, but as far as our television stations are concerned it's only news when it affects the rich.

The newscast cut to an anchorman, and, after he jawed a bit in silence, I watched a clip of heavy rains and rising waters along the coastline of what I thought was the adaro settlement in Placid Point. When a graphic appeared on the screen identifying the location as the adaro settlement in Amaterasu Harbor in Nihhon, I sat up and paid attention.

As the newscast continued, I realized that, in addition to Nihhon, the freak storm we were experiencing in Yerba City was also hitting the Southern Caychan province near Angel City, the port of Callao in Qusco, the city of Gadi in southeastern Nyungara, and the seaport city of Shen Hu in the Huaxian Empire at the mouth of the Dajiang River, each region the location of an adaro settlement. It wasn't that I didn't believe in coincidences, and any storm activity on the coasts of the Nihhonese Ocean was bound to affect the adaro communities in the realms of Tolanica, Qusco, Nihhon, Nyungara, and Huaxia, but I couldn't help thinking about Kanoa's warnings about the wrath of Taufa'tahi.

I drove home from the B&G wondering how serious this storm was going to get. I never spent much time worrying about weather, because what's the point. It's going to do what it's going to do. But if this storm was really the product of a powerful and wrathful nature spirit, maybe someone could intervene to calm that spirit. Maybe someone like an adaro priestess. Finding Tahiti was taking on a new sense of urgency. Maybe if she knew that I had swallowed the Eye of Taufa'tahi, which, according to Ralph, was believed to have some kind of power over storms, she'd know what to do with it, provided, of course, I could cough it up.

But that was a problem for another day, and I reckoned the city would just have to survive another night without my help. I was beat.

I arrived at my place without incident, and, after making sure to leave some yonak in Chivo's dish—nearly rancid, the way he liked it—I went upstairs to hit the sack. As I was throwing back the covers, I spotted the silver flask next to my bed and remembered Cody's warning. I removed the cap, took a deep breath, and threw back the contents. At the last second, I remembered to leave a swallow in the flask for later. I waited a few moments to see if I was going to be visited by talking snakes, or if my head was going to explode. With Madame Cuapa's potions, you never knew. When nothing happened right away, I climbed into bed. Sleep took me before I saw it coming.

My dreams that night were vivid, but, as is the way with dreams, I remembered only fragments upon waking. Mostly I remembered taped fists pummeling my face, over and over again. In my dream, my arms were free, but the fists flew right through them as if they weren't there. More than pain, I was overwhelmed by the frustration of being powerless to stop the blows. At one point, I looked up, and it wasn't Modoc striking at me, but my father. I saw his eyes, dead as a shark's, and I smelled the whiskey on his breath. The scent of the tropics came to me, and I put my senses on high alert, listening for the sounds of enemy soldiers. I found a depression near the base of a tree and crawled in, hoping no one would see me until the fighting was over. I peered around the tree and found Ten-Inch staring into my eyes, mouth twisted in an expression of disapproval. He shook his head and vanished in darkness. The moon made its appearance over the treetops. I was sitting by a waterfall with Cougar at my side. I heard his voice saying, "Revenge." "Revenge is stupid," I answered, but he was gone. Rain was pouring down from a dark sky, and everything around me was dark, too. I sensed nothing but rain and the taste of salt water on my lips, no people, no traffic, no city lights. From nearby I heard the crash of a huge wave, and a wall of water rushed in my direction. I scrambled up rocks that appeared suddenly, climbing above the oncoming surf, but the water continued to rise until I was swept away. I heard the voice of the old elf telling me I was both the drop of water in the ocean and the ocean itself, but the idea brought me no relief, and all I wanted to do was find dry land. Walks in Cloud was looking up at me and into my eyes. We were in her shop. I kissed her forehead, and her head slid down my chest to my abdomen. Holly watched me from across the room, her bedroom now. "I just want you to hear me," she said. "I *do* hear you," I protested. "Then what did I just tell you?" she asked. I wanted to answer, but I couldn't remember what we'd been talking about. The rain fell, and Ten-Inch looked at me through the torrential downpour. He was holding something in his hand, a leaf folded into the shape of a shark. I wanted to ask him what it was, but I was too weak to open my mouth. I tried to move, but my limbs wouldn't respond.

My life was draining from my body. I felt my consciousness fading, fading.... "No," I mumbled to myself. Blood pounded through my temples, and everything around me grew dark. The elf stood at the end of the Old North Point Pier, his fishing pole hanging over the railing. My heart continued to pound. The elf's hooded head turned suddenly in my direction. "Awake," he commanded.

I awoke. My pillowcase and sheets were soaked, presumably from perspiration, though I remembered the salty taste of the rain in my dream. My heart was thudding in my chest like I was sprinting home at the end of a Ten-K. I couldn't move a muscle, and I was afraid to close my eyes. It took me a good five minutes before I could roll out of bed. The effort exhausted me, and I barely made it to the bathroom before I started spilling the contents of my stomach into the toilet with great massive heaves.

The potion, I thought to myself. Had I just lost Madame Cuapa's protection? I hung my head over the toilet. Potions. At least she hadn't been trying to kill me. I hoped.

\*\*\*

I felt better once my stomach was empty, but now, in the wake of the departed potion, I had a void longing to be filled. I took care of that with a hearty breakfast consisting of two toasted waffles smeared with peanut butter, sprinkled with sliced bananas, and drowned in maple syrup, all washed down with two cups of black coffee as hot as molten steel. When I was done, I made my way downstairs to my office feeling alive and ready to challenge skinwalkers, stormlords, underworld syndicates, and the LIA. Maybe some of Madame Cuapa's potion had entered my system after all. I hoped so. I needed all the help I could get.

I knew that Ralph was waiting to hear from me, so I sent him a text message asking for a meeting. I got an immediate response asking me to come out to the pier that evening. That suited me fine.

My plan for the day was to drive to the adaro settlement and find Tahiti. Before leaving, I turned on the television to see what was happening with the storm. The news wasn't good. The rains had continued non-stop during the night and were causing serious flooding throughout the city. Several streets were closed, including one of the main downtown arteries. Mudslides had destroyed some homes near the coast, and a mansion belonging to a famous retired sports star was in danger of being washed out to sea. A grim-faced city councilman speaking as a guest on a local news show declared that further flooding would plunge Yerba City into an economic disaster from which it might take years—if not decades—to recover.

I was about to turn off the television when the news anchor announced that a story was developing in the adaro settlement in Placid Point. The broadcast cut to a pert young woman in a fashionable clear plastic raincoat reporting live from the adaro settlement marketplace, which hadn't yet opened. With her was Piper, the adaro I'd seen shouting at shoppers the previous morning, standing stiffly before the camera as the rain rolled down her shaved head.

The reporter introduced Piper, identifying her as a member of the Daughters of Taufa'tahi, an adaro resistance movement whose aim was to free the "prisoners" of the settlement and return them to their homes in the Nihhonese Ocean. The reporter turned to her guest, and I expected her to ask Piper for details about the movement and its goals. Instead, her first question was, "Why did you cut off all your beautiful blue hair?"

I groaned at the insipidity of the question, but it turned out to be pertinent. Piper faced the camera, and the camera operator zoomed in for a close up of her face as she answered: "We have shaved our heads in memory of the prophet Kanoa, who rose from the waters to declare that the sea spirit Taufa'tahi is angry with the people of the Dragon Lords for their unprovoked war against the adaro nations, and for the forced migration of adaro women into unfree settlements. Taufa'tahi is going to destroy Yerba City and all of the other cities illegally holding adaro women against their will."

The reporter tried to withdraw the mike, but the adaro yanked it away from her. "Taufa'tahi is going to flood these cities and pull them into the ocean. Before Kanoa was viciously murdered, she told all adaro women to loose themselves from the chains of their oppressors and return to the ocean before the destruction of the cities was complete. Be warned! The destruction of Yerba City is underway. Every rain drop falling on the city is a bullet fired from above by the sea spirit Taufa'tahi. People of Yerba City, your time is through! I have a message for all adaros watching this broadcast: prepare yourselves for a return to our homes in the Nihhonese. The time is at hand! And I have a message for our adaro men, too. Get ready for change."

As the reporter reclaimed her microphone and kicked the broadcast back to the anchor, Piper held up her hand in the curled finger salute I'd seen Sunny and her crew use to greet other young adaros with shaved heads.

The news anchor apologized for the content of the report, laughing it off as the consequence of live reporting, and took the time to assure all his listeners that they were in no real danger, and that Dragon Lord Ketz-Alkwat had everything, by which I assumed he meant the weather, under control. I shook my head and switched off the television.

According to Ten-Inch, I was a player in the war against Taufa'tahi. Kanoa had believed that Ten-Inch had the Eye of Taufa'tahi, a magical object reputed to have the power to create floods and call up sea monsters. Kanoa had been wrong. Ten-Inch didn't have the Eye: I did. Kisikisi had stolen it, and it had wound up in my possession. Somewhere. Possibly in my stomach, although it seemed to me that an object that size would affect me physically in some adverse way if it were lodged in my innards. I dismissed the thought. It was a magical object, and my possession of it was magical, too. It wasn't anything I was going to be able to understand.

But maybe Tahiti did, and maybe she would know how to use it to stop Taufa'tahi's storm. Kisikisi had been pushing me in her direction, hadn't he? He'd steered me toward Leiti La'aka by dropping a hubcap with her name on it in my path, and he'd sent Ten-Inch, or his *hau*, to tell me his war against the storm spirit was coming to me, and whether I liked it or not I had some kind of part to play in it. Logically, the Eye of Taufa'tahi had to be the key. Otherwise, why me?

I called Tahiti's number, but it went to voicemail. I left a message telling her that I was headed for the adaro marketplace and asked her to call me or meet me there.

As I drove the beastmobile through the flooded city streets, I was less and less convinced that the news reporter's faith in Lord Ketz had any merit. Several streets were blocked, and traffic was jammed as vehicles inched their way through a meandering series of detours by teams of cops in heavy raincoats with bright flashlights. I wondered if anyone was on the streets fighting crime. Robberies were going to be a cinch for any heist jockeys willing to brave the weather. I gave the downtown area a wide berth, going miles out of my way to avoid the most heavily clogged avenues of the city. I saw a line of cars stalled in a deep pool of water filling an intersection at the base of a hill. I passed the sites of several fender-benders. At one of them, the two drivers had left their vehicles and were throwing roundhouse haymakers at each other in the pouring rain. I'd left home soon after eating breakfast, and it was almost lunchtime by the time I found a parking spot on the fringes of the adaro settlement.

Once I was out of the car, I took a moment to watch the sheets of rain sweeping over the city in the near gale-force winds. A gust threatened to tear my umbrella from my grasp, and I had to crush my hat to my head in order to keep it from flying off into the rainy darkness. Deciding that neither the umbrella nor my hat were doing anything to keep me dry, I threw them both into the car and locked them inside. Turning up my collar and huddling inside my trench coat, I hoofed it toward the heart of the settlement.

Tahiti hadn't called me back. She'd told me she was going to be staying with friends near the marketplace, and I was heading in that direction. The settlement wasn't that large, and everyone in the adaro community had known the Leiti, so I'd assumed that one of the adaro vendors or shoppers in the marketplace would be able to tell me where her former apprentice was holing up in the wake of the Leiti's death. Maybe I'd even find Tahiti herself at one of the booths picking up some supplies to replace what she'd lost when the Leiti's shack collapsed.

It wasn't until I reached the marketplace that I truly recognized how serious the effects of the storm had become. The market hadn't opened and didn't look like it was going to. The booths were unmanned, and no one was in sight. Large sections of the street were underwater, and a few of the puddles were more than a foot deep. I kicked myself (figuratively) for not wearing rain boots, even while knowing I didn't own a pair.

Disappointed and frustrated, I took out my phone and called Tahiti's number again, but again my call went to voicemail. I put my phone away and stared at the driving rain, wondering what to do next.

I sensed rapid movement behind me and turned in time to stiff-arm a charging Sunny.

"Th'fuck you doing?" I shouted, and then I pulled my head back to avoid having my face slashed by her ungloved nails.

She hissed at me like a cat. I spotted Coral and Sandy flanking me on either side, closing with slow, deliberate strides.

"All of you, stop. I don't want to have to hurt you."

All three were hissing now, mouths open to expose pointed teeth capable of ripping chunks of meaty flesh from my throat. Sunny tensed to spring, but I'd had enough. I backhanded her across the face hard enough to stop her in her tracks. She backed off a step and rubbed her jaw, glaring at me.

"You killed Doman," she screeched.

"No, I didn't."

"Yes, you did. We saw him. You stabbed him in the back and left him there."

"It wasn't me. Well, okay, I left him there. But I didn't kill him."

Sunny continued to glare at me, her eyes narrowed, her face twisted in hate. "If you didn't kill him, who did?" Coral and Sandy had each closed within a few feet of me.

"What's it to you?" I asked.

"Doman was our partner," hissed Sandy from my right.

"Doman took care of us," hissed Coral from my left.

I kept my eyes on Sunny. "And now you're wondering how you're going to run your little racket without him?"

"We don't need him for that now. We're getting the fuck out of the settlement before Taufa'tahi pulls it into the ocean. Doman was going to get us past the Navy cops."

I relaxed a notch and showed Sunny a smile. "What if I do it?"

Sunny's shoulders unclenched. "Get us out of the settlement? You can do that?"

"Sure I can." I put plenty of confident assurance in my voice. "Let's talk about it, okay? How 'bout we go under that awning over there so I can get out of the rain."

Sunny glanced at her companions, uncertain.

"Come on," I said. "Maybe you can help me. You help me, and I'll help you. That's a lot more reasonable than brawling in the street like animals, don't you think?"

Sunny shrugged. "All right. But if you're lying to me, we'll rip out your stomach and eat your liver."

"Better make it my heart. I've been pickling my liver a little too much lately."

Sunny smiled her toothy smile. "Okay, your heart. If you're lying, we eat your heart."

"Deal," I said.

## Chapter Twenty-Seven

We gathered under the awning of a streetside café that was closed for business because of the storm. The building provided a windbreak, and the awning kept the rain from pounding onto my head, but water from the street was lapping over the sidewalk and soaking my leather shoes. The shoes had cost me some good dough, but I was going to have to replace them once the weather dried up. If it did. From what people had been telling me, I was going to have to help make that happen.

I caught Sunny staring at me. "What happened to your face?" she asked, showing what I thought was a definite lack of tact.

I returned her stare. "I cut myself shaving."

"Did Modoc do that to you?"

"What do *you* think?"

She had the grace to lower her eyes. "It wasn't my fault. I had to rat you out, even though you didn't do nothing. He made me."

"What did he do—offer you a lollipop?"

Sunny ignored my jab. "He wanted to know where we'd taken you. We had to tell him. He's a cop."

"You always cooperate with the cops?"

Sunny wrapped her arms around her chest and squeezed, as if her heart were threatening to escape her body. "We had to tell him. He... he..."

"He raped me," Coral interjected.

I refrained from rolling my eyes. "Sure he did. Has anyone told you that gag is getting old?"

Sunny's eyes shot up to meet mine, her face tight. "He really did rape my sister, asshole! A couple of years ago. Coral was just a kid, and he hurt her bad. We couldn't stop him. Sandy hadn't come out of the ocean yet, and it was just Coral and me. That freak turned into some kind of animal and raped my sister and I couldn't stop him. I'm not lying!"

I looked into her face, all defiance and suppressed rage, and nodded. "I believe you. And I'm sorry."

Sunny wiped her eyes and shook her head vigorously, trying to drive away her grief. She narrowed her eyes at me, daring me to show pity for her or her sister, letting me know that any attempt to do so would be unwelcome. "If I had known that Doman was dead," she said through clenched teeth, "I would have told Modoc that you killed him. We didn't find out until after they took you away. When you were all gone, we went back and found him and Moose. Were you lying when you said you didn't do it? We saw you go in, and nobody else went in until you came out."

"That wasn't Doman or Moose who opened the door. You didn't see him?"

Sunny and her friends looked at each other with blank expressions.

"It was Ten-Inch who let me in."

Sunny's eyes widened. "No fuckin' way. He's dead!"

"I don't think so," I said. "Do you know what a *hau* is?"

"Oh, shit!" Sunny let out a breath. She turned to her friends, who looked back at her with their own widened eyes in silent communication. Sunny turned back to me. "Did you talk to him?"

"Yes. He told me Kanoa went to his place last Monday night and drugged him or put some kind of whammy on him. Then she let someone in to give him a beatdown."

Sunny's face hardened. "Kanoa wouldn't do that!"

"That's what Ten-Inch told me. You want to argue with him, be my guest."

Sunny shook her head. "No. She... she..."

"Look. I know what your buzzcuts and your little salute mean." I made an 'o' with my curled fingers and thumb. "I know about the Daughters of Taufa'tahi, and how you've been inspired by Kanoa to escape into the Nihhonese. You need to think hard about that, by the way. The Navy executes registered adaro nymphs they find loose in the ocean. And if you're wearing gloves, they'll assume you're covering up a registration tattoo. Also, I've heard they put tracking devices under your skin when they gave you those tattoos. When they find you, they'll shoot first and ask questions later. Anyway, I know how you feel about Kanoa. But she thought Ten-Inch had something she was looking for. Something important to her. And she thought he was keeping it from her. So she got someone to try to beat it out of him. But she was wrong. He didn't have it."

Coral and Sandy stared at each other with glum expressions. But Sunny refused to accept my story. "You're lying! Kanoa was a prophet. She was going to take care of us. She..."

Coral put a hand on Sunny's shoulder, stopping her. "I think he's telling the truth, *bruurbruur*. We know Kanoa was looking for something. Remember? She wanted us to tell her if we heard anything about the Eye of Taufa'tahi." Coral held up her fist in the 'o' salute, and it occurred to me that the 'o' was supposed to represent the Eye.

Sunny whirled on her. "I fuckin' know that, but she... Ten-Inch was helping her! She wouldn't've... She wasn't like that." But the fight had drained out of her, and she ground to a halt. Coral wrapped her arms around her sister, and Sunny lay her head on her shoulder, eyes shut.

Sandy turned to me. "Did you really see Ten-Inch's *hau*?"

"I did."

Sandy put a hand on Sunny's shoulder. "We need to take him to see *her*."

With her head still on Coral's shoulder, Sunny nodded. She opened her eyes and lifted them to meet mine. "We're going to take you to see somebody."

"Who?" I asked.

Sunny gently disengaged from her sister and straightened. "Do you know Leiti La'aka?"

"I met her," I said. "But she's dead."

Sunny nodded. "She had an apprentice. More like an assistant, actually."

"Tahiti."

"Right. We're going to take you to see her. She and the Leiti knew Kanoa. Tahiti is a *kwuurlplup*. A... um...."

"A priestess," I filled in.

Sunny nodded. "Yeah. Close enough, I guess. Anyway, she knows about *haus* and *qaitus* and shit like that. If you really saw Ten-Inch's *hau*, then you need to talk to her."

I smiled. "She's who I came to the settlement to see. I've been trying to call her, but I can't get through. Do you know where she is now?"

"I think so," Sunny said. "Come on. We'll show you. But then you have to get us past the Navy assholes and out of the settlement. Whoever it was who told you about those tracking devices, they were right. We aren't supposed to, but all of us adaros know about them."

I nodded. "I know some people who can get you out. One of them is an adaro man named Kraken. Heard of him?"

Sunny and Coral both looked at Sandy, who blushed and looked away.

Sunny smiled. "We know who he is. Sandy's in love with him."

"I am not!" Sandy protested.

"Yes, you are. And now he's going to carry you off to the depths of the sea."

"Shut up!"

I rolled my eyes. Kraken was going to love this. I hoped. Taking care of the tracking devices—if they really existed—was going to be tricky, but I had some ideas about that. And, the more I thought about it, the more likely it seemed that the government would have a way of finding adaros who entered the ocean from outside the settlement. Tahiti was right: the adaros were prisoners. I felt something cold in my chest when I thought about that. I found myself sympathizing with the devious Sunny and her little band of delinquents. In spite of the fact they'd dropped the cops on me, I owed them. Because of them, I knew that Modoc had been the one to work over Ten-Inch, and that he'd raped and killed Kanoa.

***

The Sunny Trio, as I'd come to think of the three street urchins, led me westward out of the marketplace into the teeth of the wind. The adaros leaned into the watery gusts and moved with little trouble. I, on the other hand, being a big clumsy air-breathing human, fought the storm every step of the way. The last thing I wanted to do was carry on a conversation, but I needed to know something.

I caught up to Sunny and leaned toward her so she could hear me over the howling wind. "How do the three of you know Kraken?"

Sunny smiled. "We don't actually *know* him. But we've seen him a couple of times when he sneaks in here at night. Sandy wants to have his baby."

"Shut up!" Sandy shouted. "I do not!"

"So you've never met him?" I asked.

Sunny shook her head. "Do you know him?"

"We've hung out."

The Trio regarded me with something that looked like longing. Sandy was practically melting. "Really?" She hesitated. "What's he like?"

"I bet he's a fuckin' jerk," Sunny cut in.

Sandy was aghast. "No, he's not!"

"How would *you* know?" Sunny taunted.

Sandy looked at me, hope in her eyes. "He's not, is he?"

"He's an okay kid," I offered.

Sandy turned to Sunny in triumph. "See? I told you!"

Sunny gave her friend a severe eye roll. "Like he's going to look at a skinny punk like you. A dreamy dude like him could have any girl he wanted."

"His last girlfriend was a street punk," I said for Sandy's benefit. "She was a member of the Northsiders. She died a couple of years ago."

Sandy's chin dropped. "Ohhhhhh. How sad. And he hasn't had a girl since?"

"Not as far as I know."

Sunny's face screwed up in disgust. "You're a fuckin' idiot, Sandy."

"If everything goes well, I'll introduce you," I said. Sandy smiled as she lost herself in a dream involving a hunky ocean prince. Sunny fired a vicious glare in my direction. It was the reaction I was going for.

We walked in silence after that for another block before stopping at a long box-like cement structure extending back from the street. Save for a large silver spray-painted egg-shaped oval on the double doors, the building was unmarked. With its unpainted outer walls and small shaded windows, the building was innocuous and anonymous.

Sunny gestured toward the building "This is where she's staying now. She came here yesterday morning."

"What is this place?" I asked.

Sunny smiled, showing me her teeth. "I don't know what it used to be. The Navy put it there and abandoned it. But now it's the meeting hall for the Daughters of Taufa'tahi. Tahiti got the building for us. She's the leader of our movement now that Kanoa is dead. She's going to get us out of the settlement and return us to the ocean where we belong."

I nodded, thinking about my conversation with Tahiti on the beach the night before, the young adaro priestess standing in the darkness, rain rolling off her bare shoulder, wind in her hair, telling me: "It would be much better if the women of the settlement returned to the sea, the way Kanoa wanted them to." Leiti La'aka had felt differently. Had she known her apprentice was leading a movement to try to make that happen? I couldn't say, but I thought it would interesting to know.

I was aware of the Sunny Trio, staring at me with feral eyes and bared teeth, when the door to the building opened and three figures emerged. I recognized them as the hoods Jaguar had left outside the Leiti's shack after escorting Kraken and me to her door. All three were holding gats at their sides, the business ends pointed at the ground. The one in front wore a copper medallion on a leather thong hanging around his neck. They stood outside the door trying to look casual and waited for me to make a move.

I turned toward Sunny. "Tahiti's in there?"

She nodded.

"Then let's go see her."

Without waiting for the adaros, I walked toward the entrance to the building. I stopped when I reached the three gangsters and held my arms away from my sides. "You want to frisk me?"

They did. The one with the medallion gave me a good going over, but I hadn't thought to pack any iron when I'd left my house that morning. When they were satisfied I was clean, the gangsters ushered me into the building. The Sunny Trio followed me through the door.

The meeting hall was large enough to host a modest wedding reception or a funeral service. A couple of dozen mattress pads that looked like they came from a Navy warehouse were lined up in a row stretching back from the entrance on the left. Young adaros with shaved heads and glum expressions sat on half of the pads, some sharing bits of raw fish and carrying on whispered conversations. One of them was lying back and staring at the ceiling, and when I got closer I recognized her as Piper. Her bright eyes were listless now, like the rest of them. Piper and the others looked as if their engines had been running non-stop for days and had finally run out of gas. I was struck by how young they all were. Piper appeared to be the only one amongst them more than a year or two older than Sunny and her crew.

I peered past the adaros to the head of the hall, where Tahiti lay prone, face down, on a bare mattress. Her nude body was covered from head to toe in black ink formed into bars and symbols that reminded me of what I'd seen on Leiti La'aka's skin when she was alive. Some looked identical, and I knew the tattoos hadn't been on Tahiti's skin two nights before. The unearthly energy flowing through those inked bars vibrated my back teeth in the same way the magic in the Leiti's markings had. I looked around for tattooing equipment, but didn't see any. Jaguar, also nude, lay on a second mattress a few feet away from Tahiti. His body was gleaming with sweat and blistered all over, as if he'd spent too many hours under a strong heat lamp. He appeared to be unconscious, or maybe just sleeping.

Tahiti turned to her side and propped herself up on her elbow. The front of her body was as covered with ink as her back. She met my gaze with a dreamy smile. Her voice drifted down the hall, "Come in, Alex. You're just in time."

A dozen pairs of eyes followed me as I walked past the adaros, my wet shoes sloshing and squeaking on the slick surface of the cement floor. "What am I just in time for?" I asked when I reached the end of the hall.

Tahiti closed her eyes and drew in a long breath. "You might say it's my coming of age. Or my fulfillment." She opened her eyes and gazed into mine. "The spirits have seen fit to transfer the agreements they'd made with Leiti La'aka to me. I now have all of the powers of the Leiti, and more besides." She pushed herself up and sat cross-legged on the pad. "I feel... amazing!"

I indicated Jaguar with my chin. "What about him?"

"Hmm? Oh. Poor Jaguar. He suffered some pain, but he'll recover in a few days."

"Was he part of your... how did you put it? Fulfillment?"

Tahiti lifted her arms into the air, and stretched. I wanted to look away, but, well, maybe I didn't really. She lowered her arms and touched a bare patch of skin over her left breast with her fingernail. As I watched, fascinated, she pierced the skin and dragged her nail over the top of her breast to a tattooed symbol over her upper sternum. Black ink flowed from the abstract symbol and filled the line that she'd etched into her skin. She looked up with glazed eyes at nothing, smiling, chest rising as she filled her lungs with a satisfied breath.

The atmosphere in the hall was charged with tension. I turned and met the dull silent stares of the dozen adaros seated along the wall. Otherworldly energy crackled over their heads like balls of lightning I could neither see nor hear, but they didn't seem to notice. My skin tightened as chill bumps formed on my arms, legs, and neck. Steam rose off my coat and from inside my collar, as rainwater and sweat boiled away into the air. The adaros stared past me and did nothing.

I turned away from the adaros to see what was happening to the Sunny Trio and Jaguar's hoods. They were all gazing at Tahiti, awestruck in the presence of something beyond their experience. I turned my attention to Jaguar, whose unconscious body was vibrating like the engine of a badly tuned racecar. His eyes were closed, but his face was twisted in agony.

"Tahiti!" I shouted. "Are you sure he's okay?"

Tahiti let out a sigh. "He's fine. He's just exhausted. We've been at this for a day and a half without rest or sleep. But this is the last of it. It's done. Look." She extended her left arm, palm up, giving me a good look at the numbers tattooed on her wrist. As I watched, the numbers faded and disappeared, leaving unmarked flesh behind. She smiled up at me. "Do you see? I'm now a free nymph, which means I'm officially an enemy combatant."

She looked up at the gangsters and gestured toward Jaguar. "Find something to cover him. Give him water when he wakes up. He'll be hungry, too, but don't let him eat too much." She looked around herself until her eyes fell on a gown lying on the floor nearby. She slipped it over her head, stood, took a step toward me, and staggered. Everyone in the room drew in a quick breath.

I caught her in my arms and held her before she could fall. The energies in the room were causing the hairs to rise from my scalp. Tahiti looked at me, eyes beaming. "You can feel them, can't you. The spirits of air, earth, and sea. Isn't it wonderful?"

"Yes. I can feel them. I feel too much of them."

"Please excuse me," she said. "I've been up for two nights. I should sleep and refresh myself." I lowered her to the mattress, and she rolled onto it.

As I was about to stand, she grabbed my arm. "Wait. I need to talk to you. But... later. Will you come back tonight after I've had a chance to rest?"

"Sure," I said, because I needed to talk to her, too. I had questions that needed asking, and the sooner the better. But now was clearly not the time.

Tahiti closed her eyes and was asleep within seconds.

I turned to the Cartel gangsters. "Jaguar needs a doctor. Right now."

One of them shrugged. "Tahiti says he's fine."

"He's not fine. He'll die unless you can get him to a doctor. Better yet, a witch."

"Fuck you." The hood folded his arms and turned away from me.

"How long has he been like this?" I demanded.

The hood stared up at the ceiling. "Couple of days."

I looked at all three of the hoods. "What's she been doing to him?"

No one met my eyes. No one answered.

I stepped toward Jaguar and examined his skin. "Did he have tattoos when he got here?"

The hood with the medallion shuffled his feet and lowered his eyes.

I grabbed him by the arm. "Did he?"

The hood shook me off. "Yeah. So?"

"And someone removed them, right? That's why his skin looks like that?"

"She took them away from him," he said. "With her magic."

I looked at Jaguar and understood. "Get him to a doctor! He'll die if you don't. Look at him!"

The gangster with the medallion did, and his eyes widened at what he saw. But he shook his head. "This ain't your business, man."

Giving up, I turned to Sunny. "Can you three look after Tahiti? She'll be fine once she wakes up, but she needs someone to stay with her." I looked out over the other adaros, most of whom had followed Tahiti's example and were curled up on their mattress pads.

Sunny frowned at me. "Where are *you* going?"

"I've got things to do. I'll be back later. Probably in a few hours. I'm trusting you and your friends to keep an eye on things until I get back." I gestured toward the gangsters. "Try to convince these idiots to get their boss to a hospital. Maybe they'll listen to you."

Sunny seemed surprised. "You trust *me*?"

I nodded. "Yes. I probably shouldn't, but I do. At least you have some life in you." I indicated the other adaros. "I take it they are all part of this movement to escape the settlement?"

Sunny's face grew intense. "We are the Daughters of Taufa'tahi."

"See if your crew can find them some food. They look hungry."

Sunny looked like she wanted to argue, but couldn't find the words. I walked away before she could.

When I reached Piper, I stopped. "Remember me?" I asked.

She met my eyes and sat up. "You're the man from the market."

"Are you okay?"

"Sure. Just a little tired. And anxious. The storm is here. We're all going home."

I nodded. "Best of luck to you. Can I ask you a question?"

Piper looked me up and down. "You can ask. I can't promise that I'll answer."

I gestured toward the other adaros. "I saw you on television today. What did you mean when you told the adaro men to get ready for change?"

She sighed. "I'm sure it hasn't escaped your attention that I'm the oldest adaro in this room. The reason most of these young ladies want to return to the ocean is so they can meet young adaro men. They have a much romanticized idea about what adaro men are like."

"And you?"

She set her jaw, and a glint came into her eyes. "I was processed into the settlement nearly three years ago, right after my husband was killed and my home destroyed. When I arrived here, I hated humans. All humans. But I didn't stay in the settlement long. I wanted to see how humans lived. As it happens, I spent most of my time in the city among human women. Professional women."

I nodded. "Sex workers?"

She shook her head. "Attorneys, doctors, teachers, business owners, a career Army officer, a CPA...."

"Oh."

"I've had many enlightening talks with them about the unrealized potential of women in both human and adaro society. I've thought about ways the role of adaro women must change in order for our nations to become stronger." She looked up at me. "Kanoa wanted us to return to our homes because she believed we had been changed by life on the land. She's right. We've had to change in order to adapt to our new situation. But she wanted us to return to our old ways of living, to a life under the rule and mastery of men. Tahiti agrees with her." A tight smile formed itself on Piper's face. "But some of us—including some of these younger ones here today—have something different in mind. Our old ways have led our civilization to the brink of destruction. Our men haven't been exposed to a new idea for thousands of years, but some of us women have learned a few things while living on the land. It's time for us women to stand up, take charge, and bring some new ideas into our culture, ideas we need if we're going to survive. That's all I meant."

She looked away, a signal she was done talking to me. I thanked her and left the hall.

Back out in the rain, I took out my phone and punched in Captain Flinthook's personal cellphone number, which he had given me at Sharky's the day before. After telling him what I needed, I placed a call to Walks in Cloud and told her I would be coming by. I let her know what I wanted her to do. We argued a bit, but she came around in the end. I placed a third call while I was driving home, this one to Detective Kalama. It was her day off, but she was more than happy to put in a little overtime once I told her what I was up to.

After the detective and I disconnected, I placed a final call. Just when I thought the call would go to voicemail, Rob Lubank picked up.

"Th'fuck you want, Southerland! It's Saturday! Gracie wouldn't let me go to the office because the streets are flooded. She's making me take the whole fuckin' day off so we can watch this shitty chick-flick rom-com she's been wanting to see. I don't know anything about it, and I already know the fuckin' plot. This pretty young dame is in love with some handsome rich asshole who's a no-good bastard. And this other poor loser she's known all her life, the son of a local druggist or hardware store clerk or some shit, is in love with her, but he's too much of a fuckin' pussy to tell her. They're friends, and she's jake with that, but he's an ordinary jerk, not rich or handsome like the other asshole. And in the end, the rich asshole is mean to the innocent young lady, and she discovers that the fuckin' pussy boy is the right man for her after all, and they're both happy as clams, looking forward to raising a dozen brats with no money. Stupid dame. She shouldn't sell herself short! She's a real looker, at least once she takes off her glasses and brushes her hair and puts on a dress that boosts her ya-yas and shows off a little more of her gams. She should go for the fuckin' gold! But, no, she fuckin' settles for mediocrity, and we're supposed to be happy for the dumb cluck. And I've got to watch this shit? It's killing me! I'm telling ya, I can feel my balls shrinking! Tell me you've been arrested. I need an excuse to get out of here before my dick shrivels up and falls off!"

  I told Lubank what I wanted. He objected. I insisted. When he gave in, I knew that he had figured out how to turn what I wanted into money. It was a long drive through the flooded streets back to the Porter, but we'd worked out the details by the time I reached Gio's lot.

## Chapter Twenty-Eight

I hadn't known Holly was going to be waiting for me in my office when I staggered through my front door with a bullet in my chest. I'd been hired by a prominent businessman to find out who was selling designer brain candy to his fifteen-year-old daughter, and my investigation had led me to a sleazy racket involving the illegal resale of legal hallucinogens to underage users in one of Yerba City's most upscale residential neighborhoods. When I discovered that the Hatfield Syndicate was behind the whole operation, I hadn't been surprised. Unfortunately, the Hatfields caught onto me somehow and sent one of their torpedoes to take me out.

The slug missed my heart, but the damage it did to my lung would have punched the ticket of anyone whose body hadn't been fortified with elf magic. As it was, I was going to need a solid week of bedrest before getting in the ring with a heavyweight contender. Or trying to walk around the block. But I figured I'd be okay as long as I didn't run out of peanut butter sandwiches, frozen pizzas, and whiskey.

Holly had a different perspective. She took one look at my blood-spattered chest and wanted to haul me off to an emergency room. I didn't want to tell her how an elf had used his magic to enhance my body's awareness of its own inner workings, enabling it to heal injuries and wounds in practically no time flat. I was afraid she would think I was crazy, man, crazy. I thought it was better for her to go on believing that elves existed only in monster movies and horror stories. And I certainly didn't want to tell her I was involved in the elf's insane plot to end the rule of the Dragon Lords. To my credit, I was trying to protect her. I thought she would be safer if she didn't know about elves and their secret plots. So I lied. I told her the Army had used experimental magically enhanced drugs to increase my body's ability to heal wounds. Somehow that story seemed less complicated and more plausible.

I may have been wrong. "You expect me to believe that bullshit?" she'd asked. "Even if that were true, you can still die, right?"

I had to admit that I could. I probably wouldn't have survived a bullet tearing up my heart, for example. But, I reminded her, the bullet had missed my heart.

"But you have a hole in your lung!" she'd pointed out.

I had to admit that she was right about that, too, but I explained reasonably that I had another lung, and it would do the job until the first one healed, as long as I didn't put too much stress on it.

"Are you a doctor?" she'd asked me.

I didn't know why she'd asked me that, because, as I calmly pointed out, she already knew I wasn't. But, as I explained, I knew more about how my body worked than any doctor did.

"I'm calling an ambulance," she told me.

I explained how that would be a bad idea, because I was going to tell Chivo to eat anyone who tried to come through our front door. And then I dragged myself up the stairs, falling only once, and made it almost all the way to the bedroom before collapsing.

At least, that's the way I remember it. I heard Holly's version of the story after I woke up in a hospital room and found her sitting at my bedside. The way she remembers it, my responses to her suggestions had been neither reasonable nor delivered in a calm, mature fashion. According to her, I had raised my voice as loud as my one working lung would allow and assailed her with rough language and verbal abuse. I had insulted her intelligence, brushed her away when she'd tried to examine my wound, and, at some point in our discussion, hurled a full pot of coffee at the wall. And, by the by, the doctor had told her I'd nearly died trying to get to my bedroom without help.

"I was trying to help you," she told me, "and you responded by getting pissed off at me."

I was genuinely sorry, and I told her so. "But," I went on, "to be fair, I was in a lot of pain. I knew that bullet wasn't going to kill me, but that didn't mean it didn't hurt."

"That bullet probably would have killed you if I hadn't called for the ambulance," she said.

"I know. You're right. I should have let you call the ambulance."

"Good thing for you I called it anyway. But that's not the real problem, Alex."

"I said 'I'm sorry.' What more do you want?"

"See?" Holly's jaw tightened, and her eyes misted over. "There it is. You don't get it. When I saw you come through the door with blood all over your shirt, I was scared. I was really scared, Alex. I thought you were going to die. I love you, and I thought you were going to die right then and there! I was scared, and I wanted to help you. Try to imagine how I was feeling. Can you? Is that something you are capable of doing? Getting inside my head, seeing the situation through my eyes?

*I was a woman in love, and blood was pouring out of your chest. You could barely stand. Can you picture that from my point of view?"*

I didn't say anything, and she wiped a tear from the corner of her eye. "I don't think you can. Your response to me, the girl who loves you and cares about you, was to get mad. I get it. You were in pain. But your response to any emotional situation is anger. It's like anger is the only emotion you know." She narrowed her eyes. "Admit it. You're getting angry now, aren't you."

"I'm not angry," I snapped through clenched teeth.

She continued to stare into my eyes. I let out a breath. "Okay, I see your point. I have a temper. But I keep it under control most of the time. I've never hit you, right?"

Her face fell. "That's your bar? As long as you don't hit me, you think it's okay?" She took my hand in both of hers, leaned in and kissed my forehead. "It's all right, Alex. I know who you are, and it's all right. I love you, and I'm not one of those dizzy dames who thinks she can change a man into something he doesn't want to be."

"It's not that I don't want to be a better man," I started.

She cut me off with a smile. "You're already a good man, Alex. By the way, the doctor says you'll be fine. He's amazed at how fast you're recovering from what he says was a real bad wound. He said you need rest, a lot of leafy green vegetables, and plenty of non-alcoholic liquid." She laughed softly. "I told him you'll be up in a day or two, feasting on deep-fried calamari, and drinking spiked coffee."

*Turns out her estimate wasn't far off.*

*Five nights later, Holly and I were sitting in a booth at the Black Minotaur, washing down breaded calamari with shots of rye. She had a lot of things to tell me that night. She told me I was who I was, and that's who I should be. She told me I was a good man, a giving man. That I bought her nice dresses and shoes. That I took her places she wanted to go and showed me the kind of time she wanted to have. That I always said I was sorry when I thought she wanted an apology. She said it wasn't my fault that I couldn't give her what she really wanted from me, that I couldn't let her inside and give her what was in my heart. Vital parts of me, my rawest emotions, were locked away in a box and buried so deep, she said, that I couldn't reach them. The only emotion that ever escaped that locked box was anger, and I was always quick to force it back where it came from whenever it rose to the surface. She told me that the suppressed anger in my heart was a vital part of me, part of what made me good at my job. It was what motivated me to strike out against injustice, to stand up against immorality, and to stubbornly keep going when the going got tough. She didn't want to take that away from me. That was who I was, and it was who I wanted to be, and that was okay. But, she told me, what a man like me needed in his life was a stalwart, supportive woman who would patch her man up when he came home bloody, and not ask too many questions while she was tending to him. She wasn't that kind of person and never could be. She was the type of lady who would sit up all night worrying about me when I stayed out till dawn, and who would come apart at the seams when I came home with a bullet wound. She told me she was a goodtime gal who liked dolling herself up, going out on the town, and having a ball, and that the only thing she wanted to worry about was whether she had the right shoes for the occasion. She didn't want to change me, she told me, but she didn't want to be changed by me, either. She loved me, she said, but she told me it was over, and that it wasn't me, it was her. I was who I was, and she couldn't be the woman I needed in my life.*

*When she'd said her piece, she stood and left the restaurant. But before she did, she paid the check. She insisted on it, and, even though it pissed me off a little, I gave in to prove to her I wasn't stubborn. She was a sweet gal, a picnic in the park. I gave her everything I thought she should want, but I couldn't give her what she actually needed. She told me it wasn't my fault, but she was being generous. The truth was I'd made it impossible for her to be with me without becoming somebody she didn't want to be. She left me out of self-preservation. It was the only sensible play she had.*

***

I found Gio in his office with Gemma. The mechanic launched right into me when I entered. "What the fuck happened to your hubcaps?"

I shook water off my umbrella and set it down near the door. "Someone stole them."

"Th'fuck! Where were you parked?"

"Placid Point."

Gio shook his head. "Not a good place to leave a car unattended. Especially yours. That flashy motherfucker is a beacon for thieves."

"I count on its size to scare the punks away."

"Lord's freakin' balls, Alex. Your typical junkie is gonna be drawn to that beast like a moth to a flame. Those hubcaps will buy a lot of nose candy."

"I think the guy who stole them has something else in mind. He's pulling some kind of gag on me."

The mechanic raised his eyebrows, sending a ripple of wrinkles well up into his bald scalp. "Ah! Not an ordinary thief?"

"Not this guy, no."

Gio wiped sweat off the side of his face with a greasy red rag. "Nothing you can't handle, though, right?"

"So far, so good."

"Huh! Well I hope you get those caps back. The beastmobile ain't the same without them. Replacing them will be a bitch."

Gemma had been sitting at her father's desk, staring at me. "That's some shiner, Mr. Southerland. Were you in a fight?"

I smiled and touched the side of my face. "What, this? Nah, I fell down the stairs."

"Were you drunk?"

"Gemma!" Gio shouted. "That was rude. Apologize to Mr. Southerland right now."

"I'm sorry, Mr. Southerland."

"That's okay, Gemma. I deserved that for lying to you. I didn't really fall down the stairs."

Gemma's eyes widened. "So you really did get into a fight?"

The memory of Modoc pulling a pen out of his eye came to me unbidden. "You should see the other guy."

Gemma's face grew serious. "Was it a werewolf? Because I did a reading on you yesterday. Don't worry, Mrs. Keli'i was with me. The cards said that you would be obstructed by a shapeshifter."

"He wasn't a werewolf," I said. "But he was a kind of shapeshifter."

Gemma nodded. "Actually, Mrs. Keli'i said the card could mean a lot of things. But she said you need to be on the lookout for a shapeshifter. A real bad one. I said werewolf, because it was the werewolf card, but Mrs. Keli'i says you aren't supposed to take the cards literally. But sometimes you *are* supposed to take the cards literally. So that's why I thought you got in a fight with a werewolf."

I rubbed my jaw. "He was tougher than a werewolf. Too bad her warning came a little late."

"I'm sorry. I should have called you." The expression on her twelve-year-old face was heartbreaking.

"That's okay," I assured her. "It turned out all right."

Gemma's chin lifted, and her jaw set. "Let me do a reading for you right now."

"Ix-nay," said Gio. "Not without your teacher."

"But Daddy!" Gemma protested. "The cards said Mr. Southerland was close to finishing something important, but it could go either way. Mrs. Keli'i said that the storm could be a literal storm, like the bad one we're having, or some kind of other bad disaster." She turned to me. "I didn't warn you in time about the shapeshifter. Let me make sure there's nothing else out there I should warn you about."

Gio shook his head. "Mrs. Keli'i says—"

"I can do this, Daddy. And... and the cards are telling me I should."

"Gemma..."

His daughter put her hands on her hips and frowned. "You'd let me do it if I was a boy! You let Antonio do anything he wants."

Gio opened his mouth to speak, but thought better about what he was going to say.

Gemma looked up at her father with the expression little girls have been using on their fathers since the beginning of time. "Please, Daddy? Please?"

Gio's eyes narrowed. "The minute you sense any kind of trouble...."

"Thanks, Daddy!" Gemma began shuffling the cards.

*\*\**

It was well past sunset when I finally reached the Placid Point Pier. I'd stopped at my place long enough to chow down a couple of peanut butter and banana sandwiches and wash them down with half a pot of coffee. After that, I had a couple of things to arrange before my meeting with Ralph. The storm made the trip to the pier difficult. Fewer drivers were willing to risk the heavy weather, but the ones who did were cautious, meaning slow. A growing number of streets were now blocked off because of the flooding. To top it off, power was out in parts of the city, which meant signal lights had ceased operating at several busy intersections. I listened for traffic reports on the radio and tried to avoid the worst of the problems, but all too often avoiding one meant running into others. I tried to relax and go with the flow, whenever I found a flow, that is.

Ralph was waiting for me in the pier's parking lot, his stumpy frame perched on the padded seat in the beat up van that had carried him to Yerba City from Lakota Province the previous summer. The van was pointed toward the entrance to the lot. I pulled up next to him, facing the opposite direction toward the ocean, our driver's side windows a few feet apart.

We each rolled down our windows. "You don't want to walk to the end of the pier?" I asked him.

Ralph glared at me through our windows from inside his hooded overcoat. "You shittin' me? Those waves are going to wash it out to sea!"

I looked out over the pier and watched a rolling wave crash against it, sending spray high into the air and ocean water spilling over the walkway. "Fine," I said. "We can talk here."

"What do you got on Ten-Inch?" Ralph asked.

"I saw him yesterday morning. Or rather I saw his ghost."

Ralph's eyes widened. "What are you talking about? Is he dead?"

"I'm not sure. Probably not. I saw his *hau*. His spirit form, or something like that. My hand passed right through him, but he could make objects in the room move."

"What, like making doors open and close?"

"And plunging kitchen knives into someone's back."

"He did that?"

I nodded. "He was looking for whoever got the jump on him and tortured him. Kanoa was convinced he had the Eye of Taufa'tahi and was keeping it from her, so she set him up. Went with him to his apartment and drugged him or whammied him. Maybe both. Then someone came in and tried to get him to give up the Eye. Hurt him pretty bad, I guess, but he was rescued by Maui-Kisikisi before he could be killed. He didn't know what happened to Kanoa until I told him, but it looks like whoever tortured Ten-Inch also raped and murdered Kanoa. Ten-Inch thought it might have been his chief-of-staff, a fellow named Doman. That's who got the knives in the back. Doman was taking advantage of Ten-Inch's absence to muscle his way to the top of the Northsiders. Then he was going to sell the gang off to the Hatfields. Ten-Inch didn't like that, but he says Doman isn't the one who jumped him."

Ralph took it all in and lit up one of his stogies. "But you think Ten-Inch is still alive? Physically, I mean?"

"I think so. Kisikisi has him holed up somewhere, probably not on this earth. And the only thing Ten-Inch knows about the Eye of Taufa'tahi is that Kanoa thought he had it and was willing to fuck him over in order to find it."

Ralph sighed. "So what you're telling me is I ain't got no reason to kill him."

"That's what I'm telling you."

"You wouldn't lie to me, would you?"

I stared at him and didn't bother to answer.

Ralph sunk further back into his hood and thought about it while I listened to the rain beating down on the roof of the beastmobile. Finally, he flicked his stogie into the night and watched sparks trail it down to the asphalt. "Okay, good job. Even if Ten-Inch is alive, the LIA no longer has an interest in him. Let me know how much I owe you and I'll send a courier to your office with the dough."

"Hang on," I said. "I got something else I need to talk to you about."

"Yeah? Well make it quick. I got a warm fire and a big bowl of yonak waiting for me at home."

"I need to talk to the elf."

"So talk to him."

"I don't have any way to contact him. You know that."

"That's your problem."

"Come on, Ralph. I need you to give him something. He'll want it."

Ralph shot me a look. "Have you tried sending him a message through Thunderbird?"

"Uh-uh. Too hit and miss. I never know if it's going to work or not, and this is important."

Ralph sighed. "What makes you think I have a direct line to the elf?"

"I know you do. I don't know why he'd rather talk to you than me, but I know that's how it works."

A short laugh, like the barking of a sea lion, emerged from Ralph's hood. "All right, all right. I'll get a message to the elf. I can't guarantee he'll talk to you, though. That's up to him."

I leaned back in my seat and watched the waves rolling past the pier. If the tide rose any higher, the waves would wash into the parking lot. I turned back to Ralph, who was waiting for me. "Why is the elf more willing to talk to you than me? It can't be because of your sunny disposition. Have I given him any reason not to trust me?"

Ralph pulled the hood off his head and scratched at his jaw. "Maybe he's known me longer. Maybe it's because I'm less reluctant to help him than you are. Maybe it's because you're a human and I'm a nirumbee."

"What's he got against humans?"

Ralph picked a bit of unsmoked laurel leaf out of his teeth with his fingernail. "Elves are natural forces, Southerland. We nirumbees are a natural part of this world, too." He gave me a sidelong glance. "You humans aren't as close to nature as we are."

I was skeptical. "Are you saying humans are unnatural?"

Ralph stared at the rain running down his windshield. "Not exactly. I mean, humans were created by the natural energies of this planet, same as us. But you humans have separated yourselves from nature. I think old Ketz and the other Hell-born Dragon Lords had a lot to do with that. Under their rule, their human subjects have turned their backs on nature." He leaned out his window toward me and pointed at the lights of the city. "Look at the places you've built for yourselves. Have you ever thought about how fuckin' unnatural cities are?" He paused in thought for another few seconds before continuing. "According to the stories my people tell, the nirumbees were a kind of anchor to the tribes of humans living in the Baahpuuo Mountains before Lord Ketz came along and grabbed up everything for himself. We reminded humans where they came from. But the ties between nirumbees and the human tribes dissolved after Ketz came along, and you humans lost your natural connection to this world. That's why the elf and you have so much trouble communicating. He's an earthbound natural force, and you're a city boy." He grinned at me. "That's why he'd rather talk to me. Because, like him, I'm a motherfuckin' force of nature."

I shook my head. "If you say so."

Ralph chuckled. "Besides...." His grin grew broader. "I don't think he thinks you're all that smart."

I gave Ralph a sidelong glance. "Hmph. Well, he may be right about that. If I had any real brains I'd be in a bar right now knocking back some shooters instead of sitting in my car on a freezing rainy night listening to you yap about nature."

Ralph laughed and pulled his hood back over his head. "Yeah, well, you've got a point there. Give me your message and I'll see that the elf gets it."

I pulled a thumb drive from my pocket and held it out to Ralph. "This is for him."

Ralph looked at the drive without taking it. "What's on it?"

"It's the formula for Reifying Agent Alpha. Give it to him with my compliments."

## Chapter Twenty-Nine

Ralph snatched the thumb drive from my hand. "You son of a bitch. You told me you didn't make a copy."

"I didn't. Someone else did."

Ralph chuckled. "Don't tell me. Walks in Cloud, right?"

When I didn't say anything, he continued. "I figured as much. I tried to put some bugs in her place to find out for sure, but her security is air tight."

"An LIA team has her under surveillance. Is that one of yours?"

Ralph shook his head. "No, but I know about it. They're wasting their time. The Cloud Spirit is keeping a close watch over your gal. The agency couldn't get in there without bringing down a shitload of attention on itself. It's not worth the effort."

"I spotted an air elemental they were using to keep tabs on Walks."

Ralph tilted his head, and I saw his pug nose wrinkle. "An air elemental? Nah, those joes ain't using nothing like that. One of them reports to me on the sly. He'd've told me if they were using an elemental."

"I saw it. A tiny one, no bigger than a raindrop."

Ralph shrugged. "Well it wasn't one of ours. Maybe it just wandered into the shop on its own."

"It flew out the door when I spotted it."

"Maybe you scared it off with that ugly mug of yours."

"I commanded it to stop, but it didn't."

"Maybe you're not as good as you think you are."

I started to argue, but stopped. Was Ralph right? Had the elemental simply drifted into the shop? The Cloud Spirit hadn't stopped it. Was that because it was too small and insignificant for the spirit to detect, or was it because the little elemental posed no threat? I remembered how startled it had been when I'd discovered the tiny air spirit hovering above Walks in Cloud's worktable. I'd been looking for a security threat. Maybe all I'd seen was an innocent semi-sentient drop of air.

I didn't buy it. "Do you know anyone capable of experiencing sensory input directly through an elemental? Seeing and hearing what it's seeing and hearing?"

"Sure," Ralph said. "The elf can do it."

"Really?"

"All elves can do it. It's something they're born with."

"I didn't know that."

Ralph grunted. "Not surprising. You're not that bright."

"Can you think of any reason why the elf might be spying on Walks in Cloud?"

"Who knows? The elf doesn't tell me everything. Just more than he tells you. But there are other elves out there."

I nodded. "Do you know if anyone else can do it?"

"No humans," Ralph said.

"What about non-humans?"

"Well...." Ralph frowned. "There's the Dragon Lords."

That stopped me cold. Lord's flaming balls. The idea that old Ketz himself might have a direct interest in Walks in Cloud.... I couldn't get my mind around it. Despite his irrefutable existence in the world I woke up to every morning, I had trouble conceiving of Lord Ketz-Alkwat as more than a distant, even transcendent reality. The idea that he might directly intervene in my life, or in the life of someone I was close to, was unsettling.

I glanced at Ralph, who was studying the thumb drive I'd given him as if it were a chess piece that had magically returned to the board in the middle of a game. I interrupted his scheming and brought his attention back to the mysterious elemental. "Why would the elf—or the Dragon Lord—plant an elemental in Walks in Cloud's shop? What were they hoping to find?"

"Hmm?" Ralph looked up. "I don't know. But what makes you think the elemental was spying on Walks in Cloud?"

"Huh?"

"I doubt that an air elemental could have stayed hidden from the Cloud Spirit for any length of time, no matter how small it was. It seems more likely that it was following you and came into the shop when you did."

"Wait. You think someone was using the elemental to keep tabs on *me*?"

Ralph shrugged. "Why not? You're a pretty shady character, you know. You've been poking your nose into places it doesn't belong for quite some time now, and you know a lot of things you shouldn't."

I opened my mouth to respond, but found I had nothing to say. I felt a prickling in the back of my neck, as if large shadowy figures were creeping up on me from behind. Wild thoughts crashed into my brain, and I nearly turned my head to look, but managed to restrain myself when I realized how unlikely it was that a Placid Point cop, or an LIA agent, or the elf, or Lord Ketz himself, would be sitting in the back seat of the beastmobile waiting for the right moment to pounce. I shivered for an instant and slowly shook my head. Crazy, man, crazy.

I heard Ralph saying something. "Sorry, what was that again?"

"I said, why are you giving me this thumb drive?"

I forced myself back to my present circumstances. "I'm not giving it to you. I'm giving it to the elf."

"Don't be a wise guy. Why are you giving this to the elf?"

I let out a breath. "Walks thinks I've only been hiding it out of stubbornness. No one was asking for it in a way that suited me. Maybe she's right. When she asked me why I was hanging on to it, I couldn't give her a good answer, except that I thought I was sticking it to the LIA."

Ralph barked out a laugh. "Not the worst reason."

"Walks wanted to release it to the world. She thinks maybe it can cure paralysis."

Ralph's eyes widened. "Tell her not to do that. Something like this could stir the Dragon Lords into a worldwide war over power sources big enough to activate it."

"Well, I don't know about that. But I don't want the Dragon Lords to have it."

Ralph leaned away from me in surprise. "What's this? Is this the apolitical Alexander Southerland I'm hearing? When did you become such a wild-eyed radical?"

"It's not like that," I insisted. "I just don't know that the Dragon Lords would make the best use of something like RAA. I don't want to see them turn it into a weapon."

A smile crept onto Ralph's face. "Fine. Have it your way. "

The subject was making me uncomfortable, and I decided to change it. "Hey, I want to ask you something, Ralph. Does the Navy inject tracking devices into the adaros when they're giving them their tattoos?"

Ralph tilted his head. "Officially? No. The Navy does not inject the adaro nymphs with tracking devices keyed to their registration numbers. Those devices do not send out alerts to Navy trackers whenever they enter the water, which allows the Navy to send search-and-destroy vessels to intercept the adaros and execute them on the spot if they refuse to cooperate by returning with them to the land. The governments of the Seven Realms do not believe that these devices are a better alternative than putting walls around the settlements to keep the nymphs from escaping into the ocean. That answer your question? Good. Never ask it again, especially in the presence of an LIA agent who isn't, in fact, a double agent working for an elf who is trying to overthrow the government."

I nodded and sat up as I became aware of a shape coming out of the rising waves.

Ralph noticed my reaction. "What is it?" He leaned out the window and looked over his shoulder. "Is that...?"

"Yep. It's Kraken."

The big adaro waved at us and began loping through the rain in our direction.

"Hey guys," Kraken called when he drew near. "What's shakin'?"

"Kraken," I acknowledged. "I'm glad to see you. Want to come with me into the settlement?"

Ralph shot me a questioning glance.

"Maybe," Kraken said. "Why?"

"I want to introduce you to the guy who raped and killed Kanoa."

Kraken scowled, and Ralph's jaw dropped.

"You know who killed the nymph?" Ralph asked after his jaw had reset. "Who did it?"

"A cop named Modoc. He raped and killed her after he beat the shit out of Ten-Inch. And we're going to nail his ass to the wall tonight."

\*\*\*

Kraken had a hard time believing that Kanoa could have set up Ten-Inch, insisting that a *kwuurlplup* would never behave in any way that wasn't honorable. I forgave him because he was young, but the kid had a lot to learn. His objections were buried by his rage after I reached the part of the story where Modoc assaulted the adaro priestess.

"Why do you think it was Modoc?" Ralph asked me.

"It was the scars on his face that first got me thinking about him," I said. "When I first saw them, I thought they were from some older encounter. They were almost healed, and it had only been a couple of days since Kanoa was attacked and murdered. But when I saw Modoc again two days later, the scars were gone. Like they'd never been there. I realized he had healing abilities like mine, but better. That means the scars I'd seen weren't from an old fight, but a recent one. I wondered if he'd got them from Kanoa."

Ralph popped another stogie between his lips, and I waited for him to light it up before continuing. After he'd let out a stream of smoke and nodded at me, I went on. "Then I heard from his captain, Captain Flinthook, that Modoc was a Hatfield plant. The Hatfields have been trying to merge the Placid Point gangs into their service, but Ten-Inch wasn't playing ball. At the same time, Kanoa was getting frustrated with Ten-Inch because he wouldn't give up the Eye of Taufa'tahi."

"Which he didn't have," Ralph pointed out.

"Right. But Kanoa was convinced that he did because she knew he'd been chosen by Kisikisi. And Kanoa knew that Kisikisi had stolen the Eye in the first place and sent it to someone in Yerba City. Kanoa put two and two together. Unfortunately, she got the wrong answer."

Kraken looked confused. "It's four, isn't it?"

Ralph and I both stared at him for a few moments before I continued. "So Kanoa decided to get someone to help her get the Eye from Ten-Inch. I don't know how she and Modoc got together, but he was more than happy to help Kanoa get the Eye while getting rid of a big obstacle to the Hatfield Syndicate's plan to gain control of the street gangs."

Kraken's face brightened. "Ten-Inch. The Hatfields had to get rid of Ten-Inch because he wasn't letting them take over the Northsiders."

Ralph looked at me and nodded, his eyes twinkling. "The kid's getting it."

I went on. "But Ten-Inch wasn't talking, and before Modoc could finish him off, Kisikisi took him away somewhere."

Kraken nodded knowingly. "Probably to Koloa."

I looked at him, surprised. "Koloa?"

"It's an island that's only partly in this world. That's where he lives."

Sounded good to me. When it came to powerful South Sea spirits, the kid was a lot more in his depth than I was.

"Modoc was frustrated," I continued. "Kanoa probably was, too. Maybe they argued, I don't know. Maybe Modoc had just been in close proximity to an adaro woman for too long. It was an emotional situation. Anyway, Modoc is a violent asshole with little control over his impulses even in the best of times. He attacks and rapes Kanoa. We all know that an adaro woman can defend herself. And she did. She scarred Modoc's face. But I've learned that Modoc has raped an adaro before."

Ralph cut in. "When was this?"

"A couple of years ago. She was young, a child. Not as strong as Kanoa. But it tells us what kind of man he is, and what he's capable of."

Kraken, furious, was spitting out sharp throaty barking sounds that rang into the night. A flock of pelicans, startled from their sleep, rose into the air and wheeled away from us.

"One other thing," I said, peering into Ralph's hooded face. "Modoc is a skinwalker."

Ralph let out a stream of smoke. "Shit." He stared back at me. "What kind?"

"A cougar."

"A cougar? You mean like...." Ralph knew about my spirit guide, just as I knew that his spirit guide was Badger. "Fuck," he concluded.

Kraken agreed to come with me into the settlement. He'd never heard of skinwalkers, but he'd once fought a troll, so he didn't care.

Ralph wished us luck. "I've got to deal with this other matter," he told me as he tucked the thumb drive I'd given him inside his overcoat. "Don't underestimate that skinwalker. Those things are tougher than old boots and almost impossible to kill. The two of you together won't have a chance unless you can pull his skin off."

I blinked. "Say what?"

"He's not a true shapeshifter," Ralph explained. "His strength comes from wearing a skin he's taken from a cougar he's hunted down and killed as a sacrifice to a dark nature spirit. In this case, it's a cougar hide. The hide becomes a part of him, so you can't just grab it and yank. First you have to separate the hide from him somehow. A shaman or medicine man can do it, if you happen to know one. Can you get in touch with Madame Cuapa?"

I sighed. "I could try, I guess. But she's not exactly at my beck and call. Besides, she's already given me something, and I'm not keen on pressing her for more. To be honest, I'm a lot more scared of her than I am the skinwalker. But I'll give Cody a call. How about you? You have any medicine men at your disposal?"

"Not in these parts."

"That's too bad."

Ralph gave me a worried expression. "Do you have a plan?"

I nodded toward Kraken, who was burbling to himself under his breath. "I thought I'd turn the kid on him."

Ralph's expression didn't change.

"I had a gun, but a couple of Placid Point detectives took it away from me."

Ralph shook his head slowly. "It was nice knowing you. At least I won't have to pay you for finding Ten-Inch."

***

After Ralph drove away, I told Kraken I'd pick him up in an hour. Before pulling out of the parking lot I placed a call to Madame Cuapa's residence. Cody answered, of course. Madame Cuapa was notorious for avoiding telephones, something that had nothing to do with her practice of witchcraft and everything to do with her unwillingness to communicate with people unless it was on her own strict terms, which usually meant face to face.

"Cody. It's Alex." I had to shout to be heard over the pounding of the rain on the roof of the beastmobile.

"Sir! I trust everything is going well? You drank the potion?"

"Last night. It gave me some odd dreams. I'm afraid I may have puked most of it up this morning, though."

"Not to worry, sir. That was expected. One of the herbs in the potion was a strong emetic. Your system needed to be purged of certain impurities in order to maximize the effectiveness of the potion. That diet of yours. You should really think about eating healthier."

I raised my hand to my forehead and pinched the bridge of my nose. "I see. You think you might have wanted to warn me about that?"

"Oh, there was no need of that, sir. I didn't want to worry you."

"Great."

"No problem. Just thinking of you, sir."

At least he had the grace not to laugh out loud, but I still detected a bit of a smirk in his voice. For all his dedication to his role as the right-hand man to the most powerful witch in western Tolanica, if not the entire realm, Cody had a free and sometimes annoyingly lighthearted spirit that often belied the gravity of his responsibilities.

"Cody? We won't be seeing a repeat of that experience, will we? The emetic has finished its job?"

"Yes, sir. Any upchucking you experience from here on in will be entirely your own doing."

"Good to know. Is the Madame available to come to the phone?"

"I'm afraid not, sir. She is indisposed."

"I see. When will she be free?"

"With luck, in another two days' time. She's involved in a rather intense negotiation with a nasty spirit I wouldn't care to name out loud due to the... umm... consequences of such a slip of the tongue. May I be of assistance, sir?"

"I hope so. What do you know about skinwalkers?"

"Enough to avoid them at all costs, sir."

"That ship has sailed." I sighed. "I'm very likely going toe-to-toe with one tonight."

"I'm sorry to hear that, sir. I hate to be the bearer of bad tidings, but you are most likely fucked."

"Thanks for the vote of confidence."

"Sorry, sir. It's just that they are quite deadly, most aggressive, and nearly impossible to kill."

"*Nearly* impossible?"

"Well, yes. Anything can be killed. But it's extremely difficult to kill a skinwalker. Especially in this day and age."

I groaned. "I was able to wound it, but he's a fast healer."

"Yes. That's how it all started. With healing. In older times, certain tribal people desired to be healers. A laudable aim. But these people were prideful and ambitious. They wanted to use methods of healing that were forbidden by the traditions of their tribe."

"What sorts of methods?"

"Dark ones. Methods that involved blood sacrifices to dangerous spirits. In their arrogance, these would-be healers made secret deals with these spirits and gained healing powers greater than those of the more traditional tribal healers. They were cast out of their tribes. In the wilderness, they merged with the spirits of animals they had hunted down and killed in order to become stronger. As they grew in power, many of them forgot about their original benevolent intentions and began to serve themselves instead of their tribe. They became deadly creatures of the night."

"Secret deals with dangerous spirits in return for great power? That sounds familiar."

Cody paused a beat before answering. "Point taken. The Madame is quite aware of the balancing act she has to engage in with much of her work. It takes a unique personality and an overwhelming strength of will to command and contain the spirits she must deal with, and to command and contain herself in order to avoid the temptations of the power she wields. She would be a very evil creature if she ever succumbed to those temptations. In part, that's why she employs me."

"Both of you scare me to death, you know."

"Sir! When have I ever given you reason to be wary of me?"

"Sure. We'll just forget all about your overgrown housecat attacking me from behind and then forcing me on his back so he could give me a joy-ride through the downtown cityscape."

"Exhilarating, wasn't it? Mr. Whiskers is always available if you'd like another go."

"Never mind. Look, Cody. I need to know how to stop one of these skinwalkers. You say it's possible?"

"I believe what I said, sir, is that it is nearly *im*possible. It used to be easier. A knife or bullet coated with powder from the bark of the white ash tree could weaken them enough to remove their skin. But over time, skinwalkers have improved their witchcraft. It takes a little more than that now. What animal spirit has merged with the skinwalker in question?"

"A cougar."

Cody was silent for a moment. "Did you say, a cougar?"

"Yes."

"Aren't you...?"

"Yes. Cougar is my spirit animal. He was once this skinwalker's spirit animal, too, but they had a falling-out."

"Well, sir, this could be your lucky day. Remember when I said that it takes more than white ash powder to weaken a skinwalker? The second ingredient is the dried urine of the type of animal associated with the skinwalker. In this case, a cougar."

"So all I need is powder made from the bark of an ash tree and some cougar piss?"

"A *white* ash tree," Cody corrected me. "You can find some in any decent herbalist's shop."

"And the cat piss?"

"Cougar urine, sir. *Dried* cougar urine."

"So all I have to do is run down a stray cougar?"

"No, sir. The Cougar is your spirit animal. That's had an effect on much of your own body chemistry."

"Wait! Are you saying?"

"Yes, sir. A good quantity of your own pee-pee should do the trick. A couple of beers should help generate a sufficient amount."

I was halfway home, but Cody raised some other problems, especially concerning methods of injection. It seemed that skinwalker technology had improved with the times, and neither knives nor bullets could penetrate a skinwalker properly protected by the pelt of his spirit animal. The only reason Badass had been able to jam a pen in Modoc's eye was because he hadn't been wearing his cougar skin at the time. But Cody assured me that if I could secure some readily available white ash powder and boil enough of my urine to leave a nice mineral-rich deposit, I'd be well on my way to making a potion that might cause Modoc some serious inconvenience if I could find a way to convince him to swallow it. It sounded shaky to me, but it was a start.

    I found the white ash powder at a shop in the Placid Point business district not far from where Crawford used to peddle his jewelry and novelties. I wondered how the quirky little mug was getting along, wherever he was, and whether I'd see him again. I hoped so. I missed sharing cheeseballs and whiskey with him. I even missed his ridiculous fedoras.

    The woman who ran the herbalist shop let me pee into a cup in her restroom. She even boiled it down for me and mixed the residue with the ash powder and a bit of saline solution. She seemed like a smart lady, smart enough to know what I needed the mixture for. She told me I had enough to stop a charging bull, or whatever I was after, provided I could find a way to inject it into the critter's bloodstream. I told her I had a plan for that. She shook her head, made me pay cash, and wished me luck.

## Chapter Thirty

On my way back to the pier, an SUV in front of me suddenly swerved to the left and spun to a stop across two lanes of traffic in the middle of an intersection. I hit the brakes in time to watch a wall of mud slide down the cross street and on through the intersection, sweeping up the SUV and pushing it down the road. A jagged flash of blinding light lit up the night sky over the ocean. A roar of thunder sounded four seconds later, which meant the lightning blast had split the sky less than a mile away. Rain continued to drench the streets, and the wind blowing in from the direction of the South Nihhonese had turned into a steady gale. I'd seen storms before, but nothing like this one had hit Yerba City since I'd been living there. The night sky glowed with distant lightning. Nothing about this storm seemed natural.

Nearly two hours after I'd left Kraken, I was back in the parking lot, waiting to pick him up. I'd parked the car as close to the beach as possible, and I'd only had to wait a couple of minutes until he emerged from the waves. I wondered how he'd known I was there. I knew that he had the ability to communicate with sea creatures. Maybe he'd stationed a sand crab to alert him the minute I arrived.

"You're late, Dickhead" Kraken informed me after he'd slid his wet naked body into the passenger seat.

"Storm's got the streets tied up," I explained.

He shook his head. "I don't know what that means. Your car is cool, but the way you use it is stupid. You have too many dumb rules, like the one that says you have to get behind other cars in a line. You should be able to go around them, instead of behind them. Also, your car is big. You should be allowed to push smaller cars out of your way."

"I'll take it up with the mayor. Listen to me, Kraken. This storm is becoming a disaster, and one thing you can count on during a disaster is a big increase in street crime, especially after dark. The animals are going to come out and start looting, and the cops won't be far behind. There's going to be a shitload of MAs—Navy cops—swarming over the settlement, and they'd be happy to try to capture or gun down any adaro bucks they happen to run across. That means you have to stay out of sight. Keep the windows closed. They're tinted, and no one will see you.

When we get to where we're going, get inside and stay inside until we leave. Got it?"

Kraken nodded. "Got it. Are we going to The Dripping Bucket?"

"No. We're going to see some adaros who call themselves the Daughters of Taufa'tahi. Tahiti will be there. Also maybe some members of the Claymore Cartel."

Kraken's eyes lit up. "Are we going to fight them?"

"I don't think so. I hope not. But after we get there, if everything goes according to plan, we're going to meet Detective Modoc. You remember him?"

Kraken's eyes narrowed, and his hand fell over the scar on his stomach. "He shot me! And he hurt Kanoa!"

"That's right."

The adaro's eyes bored into my head. "Are we going to fight him?"

I turned to meet his gaze. "We sure are."

Kraken smiled. "Good! Let's go."

*\*\**

Surprisingly, we drove into the settlement without incident. The storm had convinced people to spend this particular Saturday night off the roads, and traffic was light. The settlement was only a mile or so from the pier, and fortunately I didn't run into any mudslides on the way.

Inside the settlement we passed by a few MAs, but I kept my speed well under the limit, and Kraken stayed behind the tinted windows. I made it to the meeting hall, where about two dozen adaros—twice as many as I'd seen earlier—were standing outside in the storm in small groups, chatting together in the wind and the rain like humans at a summer barbecue. I saw Piper talking to three of the adaros, who were nodding along to whatever she was telling them. The feathery gills on either side of the adaros' necks, exposed when they'd shaved their heads, served as a reminder that these young women were not human. That didn't lessen their appeal, however. I tried to ignore the fact that they were wearing next to nothing, and that the falling rain was doing wonderful things to what little covering they had. After making sure the coast was clear of cops and other authorities, I took out my phone and called Flinthook.

"We're here and in place," I told him when he answered.

"Affirmative," he responded. "Modoc is here, like you wanted. I put out an 'all hands on deck' notice because of the storm. I gotta tell you, he's in an ugly mood."

"Good. So am I. Tell him the MAs have spotted Ten-Inch at the Daughter of Taufa'tahi meeting hall I told you about before. Tell him I'm there, too. That should motivate him."

"Yeah.... You sure about this?"

"I'm sure. How about you? Are you willing to go through with your end? It's not too late to back out."

"Are you kidding? I'm looking forward to it. It's about time we shook things up around here."

"Glad to hear it. What about Sims? Is he there, too?"

"Yep. I'll have to send him with Modoc. They're partners, and it wouldn't look right if I tried to dispatch one without the other."

"Understood. Thanks, captain."

"I sure hope you know what you're doing."

"You and me both." We said our goodbyes and good lucks, and I disconnected the call.

Kraken and I made a beeline for the entrance, and the adaro nymphs, blue eyes and slick bronze skin practically glowing in the darkness, all followed us inside. We trailed puddles of water into the entryway as we came through the door. Tahiti spotted us from across the hall and threw us a beaming smile. The Sunny Trio was with her, watching Kraken and me as we approached. Sandy's eyes widened and her face blanched at the sight of Kraken, and she appeared to be close to fainting. Two Claymore Cartel hoods stood a little apart from Tahiti with surly expressions and arms folded over their chests. On the floor behind them, the third Cartel hood sat cross-legged next to the prone body of Jaguar, who was lying with closed eyes on a mattress pad and wrapped tight in a thin blanket. My mind eased a bit as I watched his chest rise and fall. Jaguar was hanging in there. I still thought he belonged in a hospital, but I didn't owe him anything, and it wasn't my call to make.

I turned to Sunny. "You girls okay?"

Sunny shrugged. "Sure." She pointed at the hoods. "Those idiots tried to hit on us, and we told them to fuck off. Now they're pissed off."

I looked at Sandy, whose eyes hadn't left Kraken since we'd entered the hall. Her lips were parted in a wistful smile. "How about you, Sandy? You all right?"

Sandy continued to gaze at Kraken. "Uhhh...."

Sunny slapped her shoulder. "Stop it, Sandy! You're gross."

Kraken ignored them both as he scanned the hall, scowling. I knew that given the choice he'd rather be out in the storm than enclosed in this cement box, but he'd agreed to do things my way, and that meant waiting for Modoc inside the hall.

Tahiti was regarding me with an expression of satisfied serenity. "I'm glad you came back. Both of you. Isn't it a lovely night?"

I wanted to slap her across the mouth. "This storm is out of hand," I told her. "The whole fuckin' city is flooding."

Tahiti was unfazed. "Yes. Taufa'tahi has come. We adaros will soon be free."

"And.... You're okay with this?" I made an effort to stifle my growing anger. Flying off the handle wasn't going to solve anything.

Her eyes seemed to lose focus as she stared over my head at nothing. "Kanoa told us what was going to happen. This city will be destroyed."

"So will the settlement and everyone in it if we don't get you all out of here. Everyone thinks this is just a heavy storm, and you'll all be okay once it stops raining. But if what you've been telling me is true, and I'm beginning to believe it is, then even you adaros are at risk while you're on the land. Will you be safe in the water?"

Tahiti's eyes focused on me. "Once we get deep enough, yes."

"How much time do you think you have?" I pressed.

"A few hours, I think. The storm will reach its peak at dawn. By then, we need to be deep in the ocean."

"How do you plan to get everybody past the Navy patrols?"

Tahiti shrugged. "Taufa'tahi will take care of the ships. The storm will destroy them. We need only to wait a little longer."

"The city will be destroyed, the Navy ships will be destroyed.... You seem awfully casual about all this destruction."

She continued to smile, but said nothing.

I was getting frustrated by her offhanded attitude. "You're a priestess. Isn't there anything you can do to stop this Taufa'tahi character?"

She tilted her head. "Like what?"

"I don't know." I pointed at her new tattoos. "Didn't you say you've received all the Leiti's powers? Can't you cast some kind of whammy and slow him down? Or talk him out of it?"

"Why would I do that?"

"A million people live in this city," I reminded her, raising my voice a little so she'd get the point.

Her smile disappeared, and her eyes became frosty. "And every one of them is an enemy to the adaros. They stood by and did nothing when we were swept out of our homes and herded into settlements like sardines. They won't all die. But I won't cry for the ones who do."

I studied her face and saw things in it I hadn't seen when she was holding my hand and watching the oarsmen take Leiti La'aka out to sea. A new tightness in her jawline. An intensity in her stare, aimed somewhere beyond me. A hint of a smirk in her smile. Her lips were parted just enough to expose the points of her teeth. She seemed taller than she had before, and she held her shoulders back in a way that caused her chest to expand. My eyes fell on her tattoos, which no longer appeared to be black ink, but colorless fissures that fed on the light in the room. I had the sudden impression that if I reached out with a finger to touch one of those tattoos, my finger wouldn't encounter skin, but would sink into emptiness.

"Tahiti?" I raised a hand to catch her attention. "Are you okay?"

She blinked and the tension seemed to leave her body. "Sorry to be so blunt, Mr. Southerland. It's not that I want to see more death and destruction. I've seen enough to last a lifetime. I just want my people to be free, and the only place we can truly be free is in the ocean."

I indicated the adaros in the hall, clustered together in an enclosed space that could have comfortably held five times their number. "It doesn't seem like many of your people are all that anxious to leave."

Tahiti stiffened for a moment, but made an effort to relax. "You sound like Leiti La'aka. She thought it would be best for adaros to accept the fact that we are a conquered people and to assimilate with the people of the land. But she never really understood us. She lived among adaros, and she had our respect, but she wasn't an adaro. She deluded many adaros into believing that the Dragon Lord would eventually lift our so-called 'protected species' designation and allow us to pass back and forth from sea to land as free people. These women were quick to dismiss Kanoa's warnings of a coming storm, and they still believe that the storm will come and go and leave the settlement intact. And some of the weaker-willed women in the settlement have simply given up and become resigned to their lives. They've become complacent and have no desire to change anything, even for the better. The Leiti is partly to blame for this, too. She had great status, and the weaker ones among us might have listened to her if she had encouraged them to resist their oppression." She sighed, and a self-deprecating smile came to her lips. "Maybe I could reach them if I had more time. Or maybe Kanoa could have changed their minds if she hadn't been violated and lost her connection to the spirits. Or if she had been stronger and chosen to go on without her connections." Her eyes dropped, and she slowly shook her head before stiffening once again and lifting her eyes to meet mine. "But the strong young women here with us tonight are ready to defy the people of the land and return to the ocean with me. We may not be many, but our numbers don't matter. The storm is here, and as their *kwuurlplup*, it is my responsibility to lead them to safety."

My heart skipped a beat at her words, and a sudden chill ran through my veins. I kept my breathing shallow and my features composed, as if I'd just filled an inside straight flush and didn't want to tip my hand to the other players.

"Okay. What's your plan, then? Are you just going to charge past the Tolanican Navy into the ocean?"

"We're going to be a little sneakier than that. We'll wait for the storm to get a bit stronger so that the MAs are less inclined to stop us. If any of them get too enthusiastic, well, I've got ways of distracting them." She tapped at her temple with an extended finger.

I shuddered a little, remembering what she had done to the hood in The Dripping Bucket, how she'd left him whimpering for his mother. "And you're counting on the storm to keep the Navy from intercepting you once you're in the water?"

"Mm-hmm."

"What about the tracking devices? Eventually things will settle, and they'll hunt you down."

Tahiti frowned. "That's a problem. Once I reunite us with our men, we can work together to find a solution." She brightened. "Maybe Kraken will help us find more of our people in the deep waters. He seems like he might be willing."

I followed her gaze and saw Kraken mingling with the adaro girls, the Sunny Trio amongst them. He kept reaching out and rubbing the soft blue fuzz on their shaven scalps, receiving slaps and giggles in return. Judging by the wide-eyed stares and goofy expressions, Sandy was going to have some competition. I figured she'd better get used to it. Competition among the adaro women was built into their social system, and maybe into their DNA.

"Look, Tahiti. I might have a better idea. But it depends on us doing something about this storm before it drowns the city. Are you sure you can't put in a call to this Taufa'tahi and tell him to back off?"

She shook her head. "It's too late for that. You seem like a decent man, Alex. I like you, I really do. But your Dragon Lords brought this storm down on you when they decided to wage war on the adaros, and there's no turning back. You want my advice? Leave the city before dawn."

I wanted to tell her that Taufa'tahi, not the Dragon Lords, was bringing the storm down on us, but I knew it was a stupid argument. The Dragon Lords had launched a war against the adaros in order to seize control of the Nihhonese Ocean from them. They had herded the adaro women into "protective custody," not, as they claimed, to assimilate them, but, as Tahiti had explained the first time I'd seen her, to prevent the adaro men from going on the offensive. I had no reason to doubt that she was right about that. It made too much sense. But it was an act of cruelty and injustice, an evil act against an innocent people. Taufa'tahi's storm was nothing more than a retaliatory strike.

Unfortunately, the storm the spirit had unleashed threatened the lives of people whose only crime was not defying their ruler. Maybe that was crime enough in the eyes of Taufa'tahi. Maybe it was enough for Tahiti and the other adaros. But what choice did we ordinary people living under Dragon Lord rule have? Who were we to stand up to the Dragon Lords? Why should we throw away our lives in a suicidal attempt to right a wrong when we had no chance of succeeding?

But I knew the answer to that question. The strength of the Dragon Lords and our own weakness was no excuse. We should stand up to the Dragon Lords because to do otherwise meant capitulation to an unjust ruler and an acceptance of that ruler's unjust acts. Refusing to say no to that ruler was the same as saying yes. Yes, go ahead and destroy a complex society more ancient than the human race. Yes, treat an entire sentient and intelligent species as if they were animals. Yes, round up their women and hold them hostage for the good behavior of their men. Yes, register them and designate the ocean nymphs as inferior to humans, trolls, gnomes, dwarfs, and the other sentient species—even fresh-water nymphs—because our rulers have decided to take their homes away from them for their own gain. Yes, do whatever you want to do—no matter how unjust—because might makes right, and the rest of us are too weak and apathetic to stop you. Yes, we will love you unconditionally. Yes, our love for you is greater than our own self-respect. And may the LIA remove anyone from our midst who feels otherwise.

Stand up and fight? Right. Easy to say. Lofty sentiments, to be sure, but not very practical for the average joe and jane. Most people have enough problems just trying to get by. To make enough dough to put a roof over their heads, to put food on the table, and maybe raise a family. Take a stand when you know in your heart of hearts you have no chance of succeeding? Where's the percentage in that? It's a sucker's play, a game for idealists and dreamers. It's a game I'd avoided all my life. But standing in that hall that night arguing with Tahiti, I knew it was the only game in town, and anyone who didn't play it to the best of their ability, despite the impossible odds, had already lost.

For a few moments, I watched the adaros in the meeting hall gathered around Kraken. He was obviously relishing the attention the group of bright-eyed girls were giving him, girls who had gathered in the hall for a desperate chance at reclaiming their freedom, even if some or all of them would be killed in the attempt. I examined their faces and saw no tears, no fear as they dished out the patter with Kraken and yakked it up with each other. I wondered if they knew how unlikely they were to succeed. I wondered how many of them would still be alive when the sun rose.

I thought about what I might be able to do to increase their chances. Through no intention of my own, or any effort on my part, I'd been placed in a position where I might be able to affect the game. Maybe not in any way anyone would notice, but I'd been given a tiny bit of influence over some of the shit going on around me. I'd seen an injustice, and I had the means to do something about it. I might fail. Trying might cost me my life. But I had a chance to save the lives of those two dozen insignificant adaros. Even if I succeeded, it wouldn't be enough to end the injustice, not by a long shot. But doing nothing would make me as unjust as the Dragon Lords. I didn't think I could live with that.

And after tonight? If all went well and I lived to see the morning? What then? Like it or not, I was part of a broad long-range scheme to bring down the Dragon Lords. It wasn't my scheme, and I wasn't even sure it was the right thing to do. I wasn't at all convinced that people would be better off under the rule of elves than dragons. All I knew was that a regime willing to do what it was doing to the adaros was an unjust one. Without asking for my approval, an elf had given me a modicum of power and a role to play in a plan to overthrow the Dragon Lords, to remove an unjust regime. Just a tiny role in a larger movement, nothing more. But if I could do anything at all to strike a blow—even a slap—

against a giant injustice, then it was my responsibility to put the weight of my whole body into that slap and make it sting.

"Look, Tahiti," I said after a time. "Maybe you can get these kids out of here, and maybe you can't. I've seen what you can do, and now I guess you can do even more. But if we can stop this storm, I can get them all out of the settlement safely. No one gets hurt. And after they're safe I can do something about their tattoos and their tracking devices. Once we've taken care of that, it's just a matter of getting them into the ocean undetected. Kraken goes back and forth from sea to land all the time. He can lead them all to a safe place. But before we can do any of that we have to stop this storm."

It was an eloquent speech, I thought, but I could see that Tahiti wasn't buying any of it. Her mind was made up. "You don't understand, Alex," she said. "I'm no longer the little girl you saw waving goodbye to the Leiti. I'm more than that now. I know you mean well, but you're a human. We adaros can get along without you. I don't need your help. I don't want it. I'll return these young women to their homes. And our oppressors will suffer."

"I can't let you do it, Tahiti. You're not the right person for the job."

She raised her eyebrows in surprise. "Of course I am. I have all the Leiti's powers now, and more. You have no I idea what I'm capable of doing."

"I think I do, Tahiti. I think I know exactly what you're capable of."

She frowned, and I saw a bit of doubt cloud her blue eyes. "What are you saying?"

"I know what you've done, Tahiti. I know that it was you who killed Kanoa."

Tahiti's eyes widened, and she opened her mouth to respond. Before she could say anything, the front door opened, and a monster stalked into the hall.

## Chapter Thirty-One

The monster wore a parody of Modoc's baby face. The jawline was longer, and his open mouth revealed a set of carnivore's teeth capable of ripping through boiled leather. He was taller, thicker, and the arms hanging from the sleeves of his hooded raincoat reached to his shins. The claws extending from his fingers looked strong and sharp enough to slice a man's head from his neck with one swipe. Below his raincoat, his bare legs were covered with thick fur, and lethal-looking talons curled from the toes of his bare feet. He glared at me through a single yellow eye, its pupil dilated. An ugly yellow and green scab covered the socket where his other eye should have been.

Detective Sims stepped into the room behind him and stopped just inside the doorway.

When the monster reached the center of the hall, the adaros closest to him bunched against the wall and gave him plenty of room. Kraken eyed the monster with a puzzled expression, trying to make sense out of what he was seeing. I figured it would come to him soon enough.

The voice emerging from the monster was Modoc's, but with a bestial growl. "Police." He pointed in my direction. "Everyone step away from that man."

Tahiti never flinched. "Whatever for, officer?"

The monster lifted a long arm and displayed a police buzzer. "It's detective, ma'am. Detective Modoc, remember? That man is under arrest."

"For what?" I asked. "Jaywalking?"

"For assaulting an officer of the law and fleeing custody. And for anything else we can think up on the way to the station."

"You're planning to take me in?"

The monster's jowls split into a smile, exposing more of his teeth. "Oh, I'm taking you in, asshole. One way or the other." He began to stride past the adaros in my direction. I noticed that Sims was hanging back by the door and wondered why he was leaving his partner to act on his own.

I stayed where I was. "While you're here, skinwalker, why don't you explain to these young ladies why you attacked and raped Kanoa."

Gasps arose from the adaros. Modoc slowed and looked around the room, seeming to notice the adaros for the first time. He stopped when his eyes fell on Kraken, whose menacing expression suggested that he'd figured out who the skinwalker really was.

Modoc whirled on the adaros clustered near the wall, and they jumped back a few paces. He turned back to me and shouted, "I didn't rape her. She was coming on to me. I gave her what she wanted."

"That's not what she wanted. She wanted you to make Ten-Inch give up the Eye of Taufa'tahi. It should have been easy. She had Ten-Inch all laid out for you so he couldn't fight back. That's the way you like your victims, isn't it. Restrained, drugged, or bewitched. But you still couldn't make him talk. Big bad Modoc couldn't get the job done. And then he got away. I bet Kanoa wasn't happy about that. I bet she said some things to you that you didn't like. What'd she call you? Incompetent? Loser? Weak?"

Modoc licked his lips and leered. "She was nothing but a slut, just like all these little nymphs. She did something to my mind to get me hot, so I nailed that bitch just the way she wanted it and left her moaning."

"If she wanted it, why did she scar up your pretty face? Seems to me she put up a fight."

"Yeah, she fought me. That was jake with me. I love it when they got some fight in them." He reached up and rubbed at his scabbed eye. "No one can hurt me for long. Even this will heal."

"No, skinwalker. No one can hurt you. But you can hurt them, can't you. You can hurt them bad."

He shook his head. "I didn't hurt that bitch. I gave her what she wanted and left her wanting more."

"You didn't kill her?"

"What? Of course not. Why would I?" He leered again. "I think she was in love with me."

That was too much for Tahiti. "She was a *kwuurlplup*—a priestess! And she was a prophet! You took all that away from her when you violated her, you bastard!"

Kraken's shout, like the bursting of giant bubbles, echoed through the hall. "*Borrgloop-borrbl*! I'll kill you!" He flung himself at Modoc.

The skinwalker met his attack, grabbing Kraken's wrists and holding them off in a surprising show of strength. Strong as he was, though, the adaro was stronger, and he began driving Modoc to his knees. The skinwalker suddenly fell to his back, caught Kraken in the stomach with his feet, and rocked backwards, flipping the adaro head over heels. The girls in the hall screamed as Kraken plopped to the cement floor.

Kraken rolled to his feet, unhurt. He lunged for the skinwalker, but Modoc was too fast for him. The skinwalker's hood fell back, and his long arms shot out, one after the other, in a blur of speed too fast for my eyes to follow. He stepped back just in time to avoid Kraken's grasp. After a moment, blood began to drip from the deep scratches crisscrossing Kraken's chest.

Kraken lunged again, and this time the skinwalker ducked underneath the adaro's grasping arms. He spun on his heel and thrust out a leg, catching Kraken at the side of his knee and sweeping the adaro off his feet. The young women all fled to the end of the hall to cluster near Tahiti.

Modoc threw himself on the fallen Kraken, but Kraken caught him and thrust him to one side. The nimble skinwalker landed on his feet and kicked Kraken twice, hard, in the ribs. Kraken grunted, but managed to struggle to his feet. He tried to go on the offensive, throwing punch after lightning punch, but the skinwalker slipped them with ease. Modoc began to showboat, feinting one way and the other, drawing fists that sailed harmlessly over his shoulders and past his ears. The skinwalker's jaws stretched in a monstrous smile, as he mocked the futility of his opponent's attack. He stepped in with an attack of his own, drawing blood from Kraken's cheek with a sweeping slash before retreating away from the adaro's counterpunch.

"You're too slow, fish boy!" Modoc taunted. "You can't touch me." He ducked a punch and drew blood from the base of Kraken's neck with a jab from his long right arm that left Kraken rocking back on unsteady feet. Modoc was sticking and moving, and the larger, stronger Kraken couldn't close on him. If the big adaro didn't get his hands on Modoc soon, the catlike skinwalker would slice him to ribbons.

A patch of utter darkness appeared near the hall's ceiling over the center of the room, and a figure fell from it to the floor. Ten-Inch—in the flesh—holding the conch shell in one hand, landed on his feet, his knees bending to absorb the blow. He carefully placed the shell on one of the mattress pads lined up against the wall and turned to face Modoc.

"Hey! Assbite! Remember me?" Ten-Inch charged, ducked, and hit Modoc with a perfect flying tackle that sent the skinwalker's head crashing to the cement floor.

A smack to the noggin like that would have hurt me. A lot. It probably would have knocked me out for the count and given me a weeklong headache. Modoc, unfazed, kicked Ten-Inch away and spun to his feet with a snarl.

It was time for me to act.

"Smokey!" I called. "Just like we talked about. Do it now!"

A tiny dark splotch hovering unnoticed in a darker corner near the ceiling of the hall streaked toward the skinwalker. Modoc never saw it coming, but when the elemental shot under his raincoat and plunged itself up the skinwalker's ass, he felt it.

"What the fuck!" Modoc leaped off the ground and grabbed his butt cheeks with both hands. He glared at me and let out a growling hiss.

Kraken and Ten-Inch gaped at me, open-mouthed. I held up my hand. "Wait for it," I said.

Modoc's hiss turned into a surprised yelp, and he fell to one knee. His eyes narrowed, and his glare was replaced with a questioning frown. The white ash and piss mixture I'd had Smokey apply like a suppository was working its way rapidly through the skinwalker's intestinal lining and into his bloodstream. Modoc's arms shortened and his jaw receded as he began to shrink in on himself. Folds of skin appeared on his face and on the back of his neck.

"Kraken!" I shouted. "Now!" I hoped he remembered what I had told him to do as we were driving to the meeting hall.

He did. He might have been a little slow on the uptake in most matters, but when it came to a fight he was sharp as a tack. As Modoc started to rise off his knee, Kraken was upon him, throwing back his hood, and grabbing the loose skin on the back of the skinwalker's neck. The powerful adaro yanked with all his strength and pulled an animal pelt—the skin of a cougar—off Modoc's body and out the back of his raincoat. Kraken examined the pelt for a moment, wrinkled his nose at it, and tossed it up the hall in my direction. I plucked it out of the air and tucked it under my arm.

Fear flooded Modoc's face as he found himself staring at a grinning Ten-Inch.

"Payback time, motherfucker," Ten-Inch said. The gangster's fist was a blur as it slammed into Modoc's jaw and sent his head spinning. Modoc's eyes rolled up into his head, and his body went slack as it dropped to the floor.

Ten-Inch rubbed his knuckles. "Hmm. Too easy." He started to drive a kick into Modoc's ribs, but stopped himself at the last minute. "Ain't worth it," he concluded. He turned to Kraken and gave him the once over. "Kraken," he said. "Long time no see. Keeping fit?"

Kraken nodded at the old gangster. "Hello, Ten-Inch. Me and Dickhead have been looking for you."

As the two of them were getting reacquainted, I summoned Smokey, thanked the elemental for doing a dirty job well, and freed it from its service. It zipped away, and I whirled on Tahiti. "We don't have much time. Talk. After Kanoa was raped, she came to see the Leiti. Isn't that right?"

Tahiti stared at me. "What? I...."

"Don't play dumb with me. She'd been raped—violated—and it was the absolute worst thing that could have happened to her. She'd been a priestess, and more. She was the guardian of the Eye of Taufa'tahi. But all of that required her to be a virgin, and now that had been taken from her. She had nothing left. So she came to Leiti La'aka. What did she want, Tahiti? What did she want the Leiti to do?"

Tahiti's eyes softened. "She wanted the Leiti to take her life. You're right. She came to see Leiti La'aka. She told us what had happened, but she wouldn't tell us who did it. I think she was ashamed. We thought it must have been Ten-Inch, especially after he disappeared the same night." She turned and narrowed her eyes at the unconscious Modoc. "But it was him? He's the one?"

"He's the one." I glanced at Sunny's sister, Coral. "Kanoa wasn't the first adaro he's raped."

Tahiti continued to stare at Modoc, studying him. "After he did what he did to Kanoa, she lost everything. She wanted to die."

"But the Leiti wouldn't do it, would she."

Tahiti redirected her narrow-eyed stare to me. "No. She wasn't an adaro. She didn't understand."

"So you did it."

Tahiti looked away, but didn't respond.

"How?" I asked.

She looked back at me. "Does it matter? She went peacefully. I did what she wanted. You'd have to be a *kwuurlplup* to understand. Believe me, it was an act of mercy."

I hesitated, but nodded and told her to go on.

"When it was done, the Leiti performed a ritual to capture Kanoa's *hau* and send it to Pulotu, but Havea Hikule'o rejected her *hau* because she had served Taufa'tahi. It wasn't fair."

"What happened to Kanoa's *hau*?"

Tahiti lowered her eyes. "There are things we aren't meant to know."

I nodded, accepting this. "What did you do with Kanoa's body?"

Tahiti shot a glance at Jaguar, still out, but breathing easily on the mat under the watchful eyes of the Cartel gangsters. "*He* was supposed to dispose of it in the ocean."

"Seems a little callous."

Tahiti tilted her head at me. "Why? Her *hau* had been released, and her body was defiled. Letting the ocean reclaim the body was the best thing we could do for it. But, *he!*" She tossed a hateful sidelong scowl at Jaguar. "He took her into the city, instead. He claims he was compelled by Kisikisi."

"And was he?"

Tahiti's scowl disappeared. "Perhaps," she conceded. "It's something Kisikisi would do. He's not trustworthy." She frowned. "I think Kisikisi wanted the body to come to the attention of the city's authorities." A sly grin appeared on her face. "That's how *you* got involved in all this, right?"

I thought about it. "I guess so."

"I might never have known who did that to Kanoa if you hadn't found out. The real reason Leiti La'aka sent me to see the Northsiders was to find out if they knew where Ten-Inch was. But it was obvious from the start they didn't know."

I heard a groan and turned to see what was happening down the hall. Modoc was starting to come around. Kraken and Ten-Inch were standing over him, prepared to step in if he decided to be belligerent, but Modoc looked beaten to me.

Realizing I'd forgotten about Modoc's senior partner, I looked toward the front door to where Sims had been standing. Curiously, he was no longer there. I guessed he'd decided to pull off a strategic withdrawal. Smart move on his part.

As I was watching, the doors flew open and a team of YCPD officers charged out of the storm and into the hall, splashing through the puddles in the entryway. Detective Kalama, barely recognizable in her heavy rain gear, came in last, and pulled the doors shut. She paused in the entryway and scanned the room, assessing the scene. She saw me and headed in my direction, pausing to take in the sight of a dead-eyed middle-aged thug and a naked seven-foot adaro buck standing over the body of a miserable-looking one-eyed young man on the floor rubbing the purple bruise forming on his swollen jaw. Kalama looked from Modoc to Ten-Inch, and let her gaze linger on Kraken, who shrugged. She looked in my direction, and I waved her over.

Kalama signaled two of her officers. "Keep an eye on these three," she told them. "Don't let any of them leave." She yanked a thumb at Kraken. "If this lug tries to go anywhere, shoot him. Use all your bullets."

When she'd crossed to the end of the hall, Kalama flashed her buzzer to Tahiti, the adaros, and the Cartel hoods. "I'm Detective Kalama, YCPD." She turned to me. "This better be good, gumshoe. This storm is tearing the city apart. It took me forever to get here."

"I could have used you earlier, but actually you're just in time."

She nodded back toward Modoc. "Why is a Placid Point detective laying on the floor with a gang boss and an enemy of the Realm standing over him like they've given him a beatdown?"

I shot a quick glance at Tahiti before turning back to Kalama. "Modoc raped and murdered Kanoa, the adaro dame the LIA picked up in South Market a few days ago."

Kalama grimaced. "Modoc did that? You're sure?"

"He's a bad cop. He's also a skinwalker." I held up the cougar pelt. "Here's his skin."

"Is that cougar skin?"

"Yes. Modoc can't shapeshift without it. He's trying to summon it right now, but he's been weakened by a potion, and Cougar, my spirit guide, is keeping it from him. Problem is, the potion is going to wear off soon. When it does, he'll be able to get his skin back, at which point he's probably going to start killing a lot of people, starting with me."

Kalama pursed her lips and nodded. "Any way to stop him?"

"Yes. Cougar is going to destroy the skin. I wanted to let you know what was going on first, though."

I laid the skin on the floor at my feet. "You all might want to step back a little," I warned.

The presence of Cougar filled my senses, and I gave the spirit free rein over my body. Obeying Cougar's will, I knelt and placed the palms of my hands on the pelt. A surge of hot energy passed through my arms to my hands, and the pelt burst into flames.

Modoc screamed, a scream of loss rather than pain. Of my own volition, I stood and took a step back from the flames, which only lasted for a few seconds. When the flames were gone, nothing was left of the pelt but ash. I turned to look at Modoc, who was lying flat on the floor, his face buried in his arms, sobbing.

"I think he'll go quietly now," I told Kalama.

Kalama frowned. "You say he raped and killed the adaro nymph? Do you have any evidence?"

"You'll have to ask the LIA. But he confessed earlier tonight to Captain Flinthook. The captain has already written up a statement and is willing to testify. I know Modoc told his partner, Detective Sims, about it, too, although I don't know if Sims will be willing to cooperate. He was here earlier, but he snuck out just before you arrived. He's LIA, by the way. Maybe you can use that somehow."

"You've been busy, gumshoe. I'm going to need a full statement from you. Tomorrow okay?" Her expression told me I had no other option but to agree, so I did.

"I'll tell you the whole story in the morning," I promised.

Kalama nodded, and her eyes narrowed. "Which brings us to the matter of your two friends."

"Ten-Inch and Kraken? Why are you interested in them?"

"Don't be a fuckin' wise guy, Southerland. You know as well as I do that Ten-Inch is wanted by the LIA as a person of interest in the Kanoa murder."

"You don't need him anymore. You know he didn't do it, and you've got the testimony of a police captain that it was Modoc who did. Isn't that enough? Why not let the LIA worry about Ten-Inch?"

Kalama thought about that for all of one second before giving a sharp nod. "Okay. But I can't just ignore the adaro buck in the room."

"He'll be tough for your officers to take. Some of them could get hurt trying. And, besides, he's really not a bad guy."

"Damn it, Southerland—he's an enemy combatant! I'm obligated to turn him over to the Navy. Failure to do so could cost me my job."

I took in a breath and let it out. "I know. I was hoping to keep him out of your sight until you'd taken Modoc away. It's going to get a little complicated now, but you should be able to keep your job. You might get chewed out a little. Sorry about that. But you've got a good service record. Lord's balls, you're the best homicide detective they've got. I think you'll be okay."

Kalama frowned. "What are you talking about, gumshoe? If you're planning some kind of gag...."

I turned to look down the hall. "Kraken?" I called. "Time for Plan B."

Kraken's mouth formed into a circle, and he frowned as he tried to recall Plan B. He brightened after a few moments. "Oh—the *gruurbluurbl!*" He held up a thumb and flashed me a broad smile. "Got it!"

One of the puddles of water that had formed just inside the front door rose like a wave and streaked across the floor toward Kraken. When it was still a few feet away, Kraken leaped toward the rushing water. Kalama's officers opened fire on the adaro, but they'd been caught with their pants down, and their bullets went wild. In the next second, Kraken disappeared head first into the wave, which reversed direction and crashed through the doorway into the stormy night. The doors hung open, letting in the wind and the rain.

Kalama narrowed her eyes at me. "That was Plan B?"

I shrugged. "He got away in a water elemental. A big one. There was nothing you or your officers could do. I'm sure your bosses will understand."

Kalama shook her head. "Lord's flaming pecker, gumshoe. Eight o'clock. In the fucking morning. I'm going to want a full statement. If you're not there—on time—I'm going to put an APB out on you with orders to shoot to kill. You understand me?"

"Loud and clear, detective." I gave her a military salute. A sloppy one, but I think she was suppressing a grin as she turned and ordered her officers to put the cuffs on Modoc. Of course, that might have been wishful thinking on my part.

## Chapter Thirty-Two

When Kalama and her officers were gone, the adaros scattered into small groups and began to prepare for their great escape into the sea. Rather than join them, Sunny and her crew stayed at the end of the hall and exchanged some banter with the Cartel hoods. They seemed to be getting downright chummy. I ignored them. Ten-Inch had retrieved the conch shell from where he had set it down, and brought it to the end of the hall. He looked for a place to put it before finally giving it to Sunny and telling her to look after it. Sunny studied the shell, awed by its beauty, and assured Ten-Inch she'd keep it safe.

Tahiti asked me why I hadn't turned her in. "You told that detective that Modoc killed Kanoa. You knew that wasn't true."

"Modoc all but killed her when he violated her. It was his fault she died. And, anyway, I still need you to help stop this storm," I told her.

She crossed her arms. "I've already told you. There's nothing I can do. And, if there was, I wouldn't do it." She gestured toward the front door. "This settlement is a crime against adaros. Taufa'tahi is going to put an end to it."

"This storm is going to bury the whole city. Innocent people are going to die." I caught her eyes in my own. "You can't want that."

She tore her gaze away. "No one is innocent, Alex."

"No? How about you? You're a kworb... a kwuub... a fuckin' priestess, right? Aren't you supposed to be pure and innocent?"

She turned to me, a severe expression on her face. "You're upset because of what I did to Kanoa. I explained that to you. I did what she wanted. It was necessary."

I held her eyes. "And Leiti La'aka? Was it necessary to kill her, too?"

Her eyes widened in surprise. "What? You're saying I killed the Leiti? That's ridiculous!"

"Stop it, Tahiti. It couldn't have been anyone else. You were the only one who wanted her dead."

She laughed, and it was a laugh as phony as a grifter's gold tooth. "I couldn't have killed the Leiti. I was with you at that awful bar when she died."

"You killed her all right. She might not have died by your hand, but you're the one who had it done. This wasn't like helping Kanoa commit suicide. This was coldblooded murder, and you made it happen."

Ten-Inch and Sunny were watching me, Ten-Inch with a face of stone, Sunny with a mixture of uncertainty and curiosity.

Tahiti shook her head. "You're being silly, Mr. Southerland. Why would I have done such a thing?"

"Oh, I've figured out the why. That's easy. Leiti La'aka was respected by everyone in the settlement, including the Northsiders, even though she had the Claymore Cartel working for her. All of the adaros listened to her. But when Kanoa came along and warned them that a great spirit was unleashing a storm and encouraged them to return to the ocean, the Leiti wouldn't go along. She didn't approve of the way the adaro men dominate your communities and use their strength to force the women into a subordinate role, even though the women outnumber the men. She thought the adaros would be better off learning to live with the people of the land. But you disagreed with the Leiti. You don't believe your society should change its age-old ways of doing things. You thought Kanoa had the right idea. And you thought the adaros in the settlement would be more willing to follow Kanoa's advice if the Leiti wasn't around to tell them different."

Tahiti shook her head. "No. You're wrong. Adaro women can make up their own minds."

"Maybe. But you don't really believe that, do you. You thought they were giving too much weight to what the Leiti was telling them. And she wasn't even an adaro."

"You're crazy! The Leiti was my mentor. I loved her like my own mother!"

"Maybe you did," I said. "But you didn't think she understood the adaros. You've told me that more than once. But there's another thing. She was a powerful witch. A priestess in her own way, able to communicate with great spirits. She was an acolyte of Havea Hikule'o, the ruler of Pulotu, and a powerful spirit. You told me that. But Havea Hikule'o doesn't approve of what Taufa'tahi is doing with his storm. You told me that you weren't in Hikule'o's good graces. Leiti La'aka didn't know it, but you're an acolyte of Taufa'tahi, aren't you. You don't have to answer. I can see it in your face. You approve of what he's doing to this city, isn't that right? And in a struggle between two great spirits, Leiti La'aka was on one side, and you are on the other."

I saw pride in Tahiti's face then. In the upward tilt of her chin. In the way she pushed her shoulders back and stood tall. In her satisfied smile. "I have offered my life and service to Taufa'tahi. We formalized our agreement in secret after I met Kanoa. Taufa'tahi is striking a blow for the freedom of the adaros, and I will help him any way I can. He's on the side of justice."

"That may be. I'm not going to argue with you there. I can't justify what the Dragon Lords have done to your people. But your murder of Leiti La'aka was not an act of war or retribution. In the end, you killed her for her power. The tattoos are the giveaway. I felt the magic in the Leiti's tattoos, and the magic was gone along with the tattoos when she was killed. I'll admit I'm no expert in magic, but I've been learning a lot about it lately. Magic has a signature. I can feel the magic in your tattoos right now, in my temples, at the base of my jaw, and in my back teeth. And a lot of the magic I sense in you feels just like the magic I sensed in the Leiti. Even some of your tattoos are identical. She doesn't have the magic anymore, and you do. You took it from her."

Tahiti sighed. "Alex. I was with you when she died. I didn't take anything from her. I didn't start getting these tattoos until yesterday."

"That's right," I agreed. "Taufa'tahi helped you lift the tattoos from the man you convinced to kill the Leiti." I gestured toward Jaguar. "The Leiti's magic fell on him when he killed her. I'm sure he'll tell us all about it once he's conscious."

Tahiti's smile was cold.

"But you're not planning to let him regain consciousness, are you," I said. The Cartel hoods were listening now. "When he killed Leiti La'aka, the tattoos left her body and covered Jaguar's." I half turned towards the Cartel hoods. I wanted to make sure they were listening. "A lot of mysteries are solved by following the money. This one is a case of following the magic. Jaguar carried the Leiti's magic for you until you could take it from him. Those burns on his body. That's what was left behind when Taufa'tahi transferred the Leiti's magic to you. It was a painful process for him. You told me yourself that he suffered. You didn't think he'd live through it. But you underestimated how tough he is. He may survive yet if we can get him to a hospital with a witch on staff."

One of the hoods spoke up. "Is that right, Tahiti? Did you try to kill Jaguar?"

Tahiti looked over her shoulder at the hoods. "Don't listen to him. He doesn't know what he's talking about. You know that Jaguar and I are friends."

I scratched my chin. "The only thing I can't figure out is how Jaguar was able to kill the Leiti, especially without leaving a mark on her."

"She gave this to Jaguar." It was Ten-Inch who had spoken. He was standing a few feet from Tahiti and holding something in his hand. It appeared to be a dried leaf, but it was folded into the semblance of something I couldn't make out right away. Ten-Inch turned his hand, giving me a better view of the leaf, and I saw that it resembled a shark. It seemed familiar to me somehow, but I couldn't imagine why.

A look of shock came over Tahiti's face. "Give me that!" she demanded. She reached for the leaf, but Ten-Inch pulled it back out of her reach.

"What is it?" I asked.

"Kisikisi called it a taufa'anga. He said that followers of Taufa used it for protection. But it can also be used to kill. You hold it up to someone, and they die. Kisikisi took it from Jaguar after he'd used it on the Leiti. I'll bet Tahiti had a fit when she found out Jaguar didn't have it anymore. But she didn't know that Jaguar was chosen by Kisikisi, just like I was. It is one of the reasons we fought each other so much. Kisikisi loves a good rivalry. I wouldn't advise looking at this thing. Kisikisi says it can drain the life out of just about anyone."

"You idiot!" Tahiti shouted. "You don't know what you're doing with that. Give it to me!"

Ten-Inch held the leaf over his head with one hand and fended Tahiti off with the other. "She gave one of these to Jaguar and told him to go see the Leiti. They probably shared some kava. Then he whipped one of these out on her. Anyone can use it if they know how. Tahiti must have taught Jaguar what to do."

"Wait a minute," I said. "Jaguar killed the Leiti with a leaf?"

"A magic leaf," Ten-Inch confirmed. "A motherfuckingly kickass magic leaf."

It struck me then why the leaf seemed familiar to me. I had dreamed of the shark-shaped leaf under the influence of Madame Cuapa's kava potion. I remembered the leaf in Ten-Inch's hand, siphoning away my life's energy. I looked straight at the leaf, and the rest of the room began to fade, as it had in my dream. A great weariness began to settle over me, and I found myself growing faint.

Ten-Inch thrust the leaf inside his coat, and I felt my head clear as a surge of blood pumped through my temples.

"Give me the taufa'anga!" Tahiti clawed at Ten-Inch's leather coat, trying to reach inside.

Ten-Inch held her back. "Back off, lady. I don't want to have to hurt you, but I'm not above it."

Tahiti stepped away from Ten-Inch a pace and began to peer into his eyes, which widened suddenly.

I knew what was coming. "Don't do it, Tahiti!" I shouted.

Ten-Inch drew in a sharp breath and lifted his forearm in front of his face, as if he were fending off an unseen attack.

"You *bitch*!"

Tahiti's head spun at the sudden shout from one of the Cartel hoods, who was pointing a heavy pistol at her.

"You tried to kill Jaguar!"

"Shut up, you id—"

The boom of the pistol was unexpectedly loud as it echoed through the hall. The adaros screamed, and I flinched backwards reflexively. Tahiti faced the hood as if nothing had happened. She showed no signs of having been drilled with lead, even though the shot had come from only a few feet away and couldn't possibly have missed her.

A second shot rang out, and Tahiti didn't so much as flinch. Tahiti narrowed her eyes at the hood, who let out a yelp and dropped the gun. He held up both arms to protect himself from something only he could see and sank to his knees.

I reached out and grabbed Tahiti by the shoulders. "Stop all this crap!" I shouted. "All of you!" I whirled Tahiti around until she was facing me. "You don't have time for this, Tahiti. Have you forgotten why you're here? The storm is out of hand. You need to think about these young women."

She blinked her eyes and nodded. "Yes. Yes, you're right. None of the rest of this matters."

I kept my grip on the priestess's shoulders. "I'm asking you one more time, Tahiti. Can you do anything to stop this storm? Anything at all?"

She wrapped her hands around my wrists, and I let her pull them off her shoulders. "No. The storm is here. Even if I wanted to, I can't do anything about it."

Ten-Inch, recovered from Tahiti's light touch of mind-messing, let out an attention-getting whistle, and both Tahiti and I turned to look at him.

"Kanoa told me that the thing she was looking for could stop the storm," he said. "The thing she thought I was hiding from her. The Eye of Taufa'tahi."

Tahiti's jaw dropped. "The Eye would make the storm stronger. With the Eye, Taufa'tahi could bury the whole Tolanican coast!"

Ten-Inch met her stare, which, given the glimpse he'd had of what the priestess could do, was an incredibly brave act on his part, I thought. "Kanoa told me that the Eye could *control* the storm," he told her. "It could make the storm bigger, or it could calm it down."

Tahiti considered that bit of information and sighed. "Well it hardly matters. We don't have it."

Ten-Inch nodded at me with his chin. "Is that true, Sarge? Kisikisi told me what he'd done with the Eye. He says he gave it to someone who sent it to someone else. You got any ideas about that you want to share?"

"Alex?" Tahiti's eyes were bright as she locked them on mine. "Do you know where the Eye is?"

I gave her my most innocent look. "Not at the moment," I said. Technically, I wasn't lying.

She continued to stare, and my head began to ache under the pressure. Her eyes lit up. "*You* have it! You have the Eye!"

I tried to deny it. "I don't...." My throat tightened. I had a powerful urge to cough, but I couldn't breathe in or out. I fell to one knee and opened my mouth as wide as I could, trying to force open a passage. Ten-Inch, seeing what was happening, darted behind me and wrapped his arms around my waist. He buried his fist into my stomach, covered it with his other hand, and forced it inward and upward. I felt an obstruction slide up from my throat and out of my mouth. I took a gasping breath and looked down at the egg-shaped ruby-red jewel resting on the floor in front of me.

Before anyone could stop her, Tahiti reached down and scooped the Eye of Taufa'tahi off the floor and held it up to the light. "This is it— the Eye!"

I tried to call her name, but managed only a raw croak. I cleared my throat and tried again. "Tahiti. You can use it to calm the storm."

Tahiti's eyes were wild as she turned them on me.

"I've got a way to get your people out of here. But you have to calm the storm."

She looked from me to the Eye, but said nothing.

"You have to trust me." I gestured out over the hall. "Look at your people, Tahiti. They want to go home. I can arrange it. I've got a driver coming with a bus. I can get everyone out of the settlement. I can arrange for professionals to remove their tattoos and their tracking devices. And then I can get them all safely out into the ocean. I just need you to use the Eye to stop this storm before it floods the city. Trust me, Tahiti. We can do this together."

Tahiti turned to the other adaros, who were all watching her, wondering what she would do. She turned back to me. "Trust you? A human? I don't need your help to free my people. They don't need a human to lead them to freedom. I can do that without your help. Stand back!"

Tahiti held up the eye, grasping it by the narrower end and holding the wider end upwards. Outside the meeting hall, thunder cracked. A powerful gust of wind caused the doors of the building to slam shut and the walls to groan. Gasps and screams filled the room.

I scrambled to my feet. "Tahiti! What are you doing? This is crazy!"

Ten-Inch was faster. He lunged toward the adaro priestess, but stopped as if running into a wall. He whirled and dove to the floor, as if a bomb had detonated nearby. I saw the Sunny Trio cringe and crawl toward the wall. The Cartel gangsters were on their hands and knees.

Tahiti held the Eye higher into the air. A thunderclap sounded so nearby that I thought it must have hit the roof of the meeting hall. The hairs on my neck stood on end. I tried to shout, but it came out as a choked plea: "Tahiti?"

I took a step toward the priestess and found myself in a jungle, moonlight casting a dim light through the blade-like leaves of the tagua trees hanging overhead. I saw a shape in the corner of my eye, but when I snapped my head around to get a better view, the shape disappeared. Cold dread settled in my stomach. I sensed movement just out of my vision, but when I spun to see what it was, nothing was there. I felt an otherworldly presence pressing down on me, and I knew there was no escaping it. An oppressive quiet filled the air, heralding the coming of death. The silence was shattered by the clatter of machinegun fire, and I was about to hit the deck when I saw that I was not, in fact, standing in a jungle clearing, but on a cement floor inside a hall. Tahiti was standing in front of me, still holding the red jewel. "Tahiti," I breathed. "Stop this."

Tahiti stared at me, a confused look on her face. She disappeared, and I was in an alley I recognized from my childhood neighborhood. I was eight years old. Bigger kids surrounded me. They'd been taking turns kicking me, and I was on my knees. A teenaged brute with dead eyes and a cold grin took a step toward me, leg cocked. I braced myself. A vague taste of kava filled the back of my mouth.

I was in the meeting hall. Ten-Inch was lying prone at my side, screaming epithets at men who weren't there. The Cartel hoods were whimpering. Sunny and her crew were crying out, and I heard screams and cries from nearby. I took a step toward Tahiti.

She saw me coming. Darkness surrounded me, a darkness without walls. A whisper came to me, and I turned my head, trying to find the source of the voice.

The whisper became a wail: "You said you would help me." I whirled, but saw only darkness.

A ghostly silhouette appeared in the darkness in front of me.

"Look what you did to me." The silhouette resolved itself into the figure of a man, a young man with the face of a child. But that face was battered almost beyond recognition. One eye was shut and swollen. The nose had been smashed into a shapeless ruin, and blood streamed from both nostrils. An ear had been ripped off the side of his head, and thick blood oozed from the fissure it left behind. A purple and black bruise covered one side of the young man's swollen face, and his drooping mouth revealed chipped and broken teeth.

It was the Northsiders headband holding back long, thick, curly black hair that told me who this young man had been. "I didn't do that to you, Quapo. You did that to yourself. I gave you the chance to run after you ratted out your gang to the cops. But you tried to talk Ten-Inch into giving you another chance. That was on you, kid. Not me."

Quapo slowly raised a hand and pointed an accusing finger at me. "You shouldn't have tried to help me. You only made things worse."

I told myself that whatever I was speaking to, it wasn't really Quapo, whose dead and broken body I'd last seen hanging from the rafters in Medusa's Tavern. In the back of my mind, I knew that Tahiti had summoned a *qaitu*, a ghost. A chill spread from my chest and froze my lungs. When I spoke, it was if my throat were lined with razor blades. "You'd've been okay if you'd've just taken that bus," I rasped, my voice shaking. "You should have listened to me."

"Why did you think you could save me? You can't save anyone. You can't even save yourself." Quapo's ghost faded, became smoke, his accusing finger the last of him to disappear.

The smoke reshaped itself, and I found myself staring at the floating figure of a woman with strawberry-blond hair, brown eyes, and a smattering of freckles across her cheeks and nose. She was there, clear as day in the surrounding blackness, and I could see right through her into the void at her back.

She stared past me, as if she were blind. Her face was waxy and bloodless, the face of a corpse. My blood turned to ice, and a wave of panic seized my mind. I was freezing to death. I suppressed the scream rising from my chest. "Cindy?" Her name turned to steam as it passed over my numb lips.

The woman stared straight into my eyes and recoiled as if she'd seen something evil. She raised her arms to defend herself against blows. Her lips curled, and she let out a piercing screech that made me want to cover my ears.

"Cindy! What is it? What do you see?" Did I want to know? Cindy Shipper had been alive the last time I'd seen her. Was this a *qaitu*? Did this mean Cindy was dead?

"Cindy! Where are you? You can't be dead! You can't!"

Her scream turned to maniacal laughter, and the laughter turned my stomach to ice. "Can't I?" she asked, her voice mocking. "What did you do to stop it from happening? Where were you when I needed you? You told yourself that you cared for me, that you would help me if I needed it, but you never even tried. You forgot about me."

"I... I didn't know... I..." The skin on Cindy's face reddened and blistered. Flames rose from her hair. She shrieked in pain, and my heart wrenched at the sound. Her blistered skin blackened and peeled from her face, and a sudden stench of charred flesh unleashed a violent wave of nausea that caused my insides to clench like a fist. I closed my eyes, and my head began to spin. My consciousness started to slip out the back door, and I wanted to let it go. All at once, the sickening odor of scorched meat was replaced by the sharp tang of kava. My stomach uncoiled, and my head cleared. When I opened my eyes, Cindy was gone.

Everything was gone. I was surrounded by a darkness without color, not even black. My entire body had gone numb, and my tongue had swollen to fill my mouth. I felt myself falling, endlessly falling, picking up speed with every second. I had a distinct sense of up and, especially, down, but I saw nothing in the darkness to provide any orientation. I was accelerating at an impossible speed, plummeting through emptiness toward an inevitable sudden death. Once again, I became aware of the bitter taste of kava in the back of my mouth. I reached out....

I touched Tahiti's arm. "Tahiti!" I shouted. "Stop this!"

Startled, Tahiti pulled back from my touch. "I don't know how you are resisting me," she said. "I'm sorry to have to do this to you. But you're leaving me no choice."

She pushed me away from her and held up something for me to see. It was the leaf folded into the shape of a shark that Ten-Inch had shown me. The motherfuckingly kick-ass magic leaf. The taufa'anga. I tried to look away, but my head wouldn't move. I tried to close my eyes, but they were locked open. I tried to step away, but I found myself on one knee. The room around me grew hazy and began to fade. I heard the rhythm of my heart grow slow... slower... slower with each passing beat. My eyes were focused on the leaf, and my thoughts faded along with the surrounding room. I felt myself grow numb.

I became aware of something hard and cold touching my hand. Desperate for any sensation at all, I grasped the object. A faint taste of kava came to me, like a memory. I remembered Cody telling me something... something about saving a swallow....

Barely able to think, I sensed, rather than felt, my hand pulling something out of my coat pocket. I felt my heart beating again, and found I could move my eyes. Looking down, I saw a silver flask in my hand. I took a deep breath, ripped the stopper off the flask, drew it up to my mouth, and threw the last swallow of Madame Cuapa's potion down my throat.

Immediately, I began to cough, and, as I coughed, my mind cleared until I was fully awake, awake as only a person whose awareness has been magically enhanced by elf magic and witchcraft can be. I heard Tahiti's breath catch in her throat. Her hand holding the leaf spasmed, and she took a quick step backwards. I slapped the leaf out of her hand and watched it flutter to the floor.

Beside me, Ten-Inch groaned. Tahiti turned to look at him, and I grabbed at her hand holding the Eye with both of mine. She raised her other hand to the Eye, and we fought over it. I was bigger than the adaro, but whatever Tahiti had done to me had left me weak as a kitten. Her two-handed grip on the Eye was firm, and she was determined. She kicked out and caught me just below the knee. Pain shot up my leg, and my grip on the Eye slackened, allowing Tahiti to pull the jewel into her torso.

Outside the hall, thunder boomed, one crash after another in rapid succession. The double door at the front of the hall crashed inwards and splintered. A powerful gust of wind tore through the room. Tahiti was doubled over the Eye with both arms wrapped around it, burying the jewel into her midsection. I grabbed for her wrists, intending to rip the jewel from her grip, but I couldn't get my hands on it.

"Let go!" Tahiti shouted. "Let—"

Ten-Inch had risen to his feet behind the priestess. He wrapped his arms around her neck, grabbed her chin, and yanked. Tahiti's neck snapped with a crack that sounded louder to me than the thunder.

## Chapter Thirty-Three

Tahiti's body lay sprawled at my feet. I wanted to scream at Ten-Inch. I wanted to punch him in the face. I wanted to rip his head off his shoulders and smash it against the wall. But before I could do anything, I saw the haunted look in his eyes and the twitch in the corner of his mouth. It was the face of a strong man who had awakened from a nightmare that had left him shaken to his core. I heard whimpering sounds around me and turned to see Sunny, Coral, and Sandy holding each other, tears streaming down their cheeks. The Cartel thug who had fired shots at Tahiti scrambled to his feet and ran into a corner of the room, where he stumbled to his hands and knees and began vomiting. The other two hoods were curled into fetal positions on the floor, gasping for breath. I looked out over the hall and saw the two dozen adaros with blue-tinged scalps wiping tears from their eyes or sobbing out loud and letting the tears run free. Piper was stretched out on the wet floor, staring up at the ceiling with hollow eyes.

Outside the meeting hall, the storm continued to rage. Lightning cracked non-stop, the wind howled like a chorus of demons, and rainwater poured through the open doorway into the hall.

I knelt next to the unmoving form of Tahiti and picked the Eye off the floor where it had fallen.

Ten-Inch peered down at me. "Can you do anything with that?"

Heat from the jewel scalded my hand, forcing me to drop it to the floor. The strong buzz of magic vibrating the bones in my head threatened to loosen my teeth.

"We need a practitioner," I said. "A strong one. There's a shitload of energy in this thing, but I have no idea how to control it. I can't even fuckin' touch it."

As the otherworldly energy from the jewel shook my skull, the sound of running water, like a fountain, reached me from nearby. I turned toward the sound and saw Sunny standing at the wall, her blue eyes wide and her mouth open in a circle. Next to her, water flowed from the conch shell Ten-Inch had brought with him and gathered into a pool at Sunny's feet. Coral and Sandy scrambled away from her. After a few moments, Sunny's lips formed into a smile.

She stepped from the pool of water and slid her hands down her sides to her hips. Her eyes closed as she sighed. "So slim," she breathed. "So young. I could get used to this."

Her eyes opened and she stepped in my direction. As she drew near, her eyes narrowed as she spotted something on the floor. "Could one of you do something about that thing? I had to leave my body in order to keep it from pulling me into the abyss, and I can still feel it trying to finish the job."

I followed her eyes to the taufa'anga lying on the floor. I snapped my head up. "Leiti? Is that you?"

"Yep. Well, my *hau*, at least. That's all that's left. But that was always the most real part of me. Would one of you gentlemen be a dear and step on that thing? It's an abomination."

Ten-Inch did the honors, stomping on the leaf and crushing it under his heel. For good measure, he picked it up and ripped it to shreds.

"Thank you, Ten-Inch." The voice sounded like Sunny's, but the rhythm and intonation of her words were Leiti La'aka's. "It's amazing what one can do with a coconut leaf, isn't it? I didn't think Tahiti had it in her to make a taufa'anga that could be used by someone without the talent." She glanced at Jaguar, who was still unconscious. "I can only think she must have got it from Taufa'tahi himself. It's my own fault. I never knew the extent to which he had his hooks in her."

"Leiti?" I tried to look through Sunny's eyes to find some visible evidence of the Leiti's *hau* inside her, but it wasn't in my skillset. "Can you stop this storm?"

She turned her attention to the Eye of Taufa'tahi and studied it for a few seconds before bending to pick it up. She straightened and examined the ruby-red jewel with a discerning eye. At least it wasn't burning her hands. I figure that was an encouraging sign.

After murmuring a few phrases I couldn't hear over the crashing thunder and the wailing wind, she looked up from the jewel. "This little son-of-a-bitch is energized. Its strength is increasing, too. I'm afraid it may be too late for any of these girls to escape into the ocean. They'll get tossed around and crushed by the floodwaters and storm tides before they can reach water deep enough and calm enough to swim through."

"But can you connect with the Eye?" I asked. "If you can, then I think I know how you can use it to stop the storm. A young witch did a reading for me earlier today. The last card she turned up showed a jewel. It didn't look like the same jewel as this one, but she said that wasn't important. She told me that the jewel on the card represented strong natural energies spilling out into the world. But the card was upside down—reversed—and, according to her, that meant that the jewel was taking those energies *away* from our world."

I pointed at the jewel. "Tahiti was holding the Eye with the fat end up. I think if you hold it with the narrow end up and do your mojo..."

The Leiti focused on the jewel through Sunny's eyes. "Yes... yes, that might work. But it couldn't be that simple, could it?" She held the jewel away from her body, narrow side up.

We waited. The thunder continued to crack. The storm continued to rage. Leiti La'aka's frown appeared on Sunny's face. We waited some more. Finally, the Leiti pulled the stone down and stared at it, biting her lip.

She gazed at the jewel for several long moments.

"Leiti?" I asked.

"Shut up!" She never took her eyes off the stone.

Seconds passed. The seconds became a minute. The storm continued to rage. Water poured in through the doorway and swamped the mattress pads on the floor. I heard a window shatter. No one dared move. At any moment, I thought, floodwaters would tear the meeting hall from its foundations and send us all tumbling through the city, like a ship caught in a tidal wave. My plan had been to put the adaros on a bus and get them out of the settlement while the authorities were busy with the storm. I had a driver, and I had assurances that professionals would be on hand to remove the tattoos and the tracking devices from the adaros. Kraken would then be able to smuggle the adaros out of the city and into the ocean undetected. But I'd misjudged Tahiti, hadn't realized the depths of her ambitions. Until I'd returned to the meeting hall, I hadn't known she'd had Leiti La'aka killed and had acquired all her spells and connections to spirits, or that she'd become a creature of Taufa'tahi. Once she seized the Eye of Taufa'tahi, she'd used it to intensify the storm until it was completely out of control. I don't think it occurred to her that her actions were making it impossible for her adaro followers to escape into the ocean. Her judgment had been overwhelmed by the acquisition of too much new power in too short a time. Tahiti had handled it like a fresh squad of boots on their first night in a Borderland hooch house. Many of *them* had drunk themselves blind, too.

My thoughts slammed to a stop when I became aware of the smile slowly spreading across Sunny's face. "Oh, Taufa'tahi," she muttered. "You cunning little shark."

She turned slowly, scanning the room. "Stand back," she said. She held the Eye in front of her face, narrow side up, and muttered a few words. She turned and met my eyes, opened her mouth as wide as she could, and swallowed the jewel.

\*\*\*

Clouds still filled the sky as I helped the adaros load their belongings into the minibus. It was a tight fit, but we managed to squeeze all twenty-four of them inside.

"You good, Luano?" I asked.

"I think so. The roads are messed up, but I shouldn't have any trouble once we get these girls out of the settlement. Lubank had me drop a few mugs off after we drove in. They're some pretty hard numbers, and I figure they'll keep the MAs too busy to care about traffic leaving the area." Luano snapped his fingers. "Oh, that reminds me. Lubank said to tell you that he's putting the dough he had to pay those goons to create the distraction you need on your account. He said you wouldn't mind because, and these are his exact words, 'Southerland knows that all good deeds have a fuckin' price tag.'"

I shook my head. I should have known that chiseler would figure out a way to score a handsome profit for helping me smuggle innocent adaros out of the settlement and return them to their homes in the ocean. I doubted that he was paying a dime to the muscle he'd sent to trash the settlement and keep the MAs busy. If I knew Lubank, those thugs were working off debts they owed him for keeping them out of prison. His expense report would show that he'd given them a wage, and he'd bill me for their time. He'd also charge me plenty for finding people to remove the tattoos and tracking devices from the adaros. As far as Lubank was concerned, a good cause was nothing but an opportunity to make money. Not that I minded. I was going to pass Lubank's bill on to Ralph, and Ralph would find a way to get reimbursed by the LIA. I can't lie: knowing that Leea would wind up funding my whole operation made me feel pretty good, even if Lubank was the only one who was actually going to make any dough in the end. And at least the people he lined up for me would be reliable. "Okay," I said. "Better get going. And thanks, Luano. For this, and for getting me out of the Placid Point stationhouse."

Luano winked. "Sure thing, boss. If you ever need a driver again, look me up."

When the bus was out of sight, I turned to Sunny, who, along with Coral and Sandy, had elected to stay behind. Sunny held the conch shell at her side.

"You okay, Sunny?" I asked.

She nodded. The rain had all but disappeared, and she wiped freshwater drizzle from her eyes.

"You're sure you didn't want to go with them?"

She shrugged. "Leiti La'aka is going to help me become a *kwuurlplup*."

"We're going to help her," Coral said, and Sandy nodded.

I looked into Sunny's eyes, trying to see what might be lurking inside. "Is the Leiti still in there?"

Sunny tilted her head. "Not at the moment. She says she'll come whenever I need her to. And we can talk to each other. It's crazy, but she kind of rocks!"

"Yeah," I agreed. "She kind of does. Do you know what she did to fix the storm?"

Sunny frowned. "Not exactly. She said it had something to do with reversing pol... polo... polar-somethings."

"Polarities?"

Sunny shrugged. "Maybe. Also something about saying some spells backwards, or inside-out. Something like that. Also, Havea Hikule'o has the Eye now. I don't get it all—yet! But I will." Her eyes narrowed, and her face lit up with a devious smile. "And when I do—look out!" She turned to Coral and Sandy. "The cops are going to be busy all night chasing down looters and cleaning up the flood damage. Let's go have some fun!"

The Sunny Trio sprinted away into the night, whooping as they ran. Lord's balls, I thought. I hoped the Leiti knew what she was getting herself into.

I went back inside the meeting hall to find Ten-Inch, who was kneeling beside Tahiti's body. The Cartel hoods had already taken Jaguar away, hopefully to a hospital, and no one else was in the hall, filled now with mud, abandoned mattress pads, and the half-eaten remains of raw fish. Ten-Inch looked up at me as I drew near.

"I don't regret killing her, Sarge. She was a soldier of Taufa'tahi, and she had to be stopped. It was an act of war."

"Battles have a way of finding you, Ten-Inch. But it looks like this one is over."

Ten-Inch continued staring at the body of Tahiti. "There will be others. There's always a war going on." He rose to his feet. "But for now, we need to clear the fallen from the battlefield. I'm going to take her body to the beach and wait for the emissaries from Pulotu to claim it. Will you come with me?"

I nodded. "Yes. I know just the place. My car's outside. We can use it."

A small grin appeared on Ten-Inch's face. "You still driving that pimpmobile?"

"I call it the beastmobile."

Ten-Inch chuckled. "I'm sure you do."

We wrapped Tahiti in a wet blanket that had been left behind, and she was surprisingly heavy as we carried her out of the hall. We were halfway to my car, when the temperature plummeted, and an icy wind chilled me to the bone.

We stopped walking. Ten-Inch and I stared at each other, and I'm sure we were both thinking the same thing. Had the storm returned? The wind gusted, and marble-sized balls of ice fell from the sky. Without a word, we hunched our shoulders against the impossible cold piercing our hearts like razor-sharp knives and began to speed walk toward my waiting car.

We had only walked a few steps when a shadow darker than the night rose from the wet ground. The shadow loomed over us, and from within the darkness I heard cracking and clanging noises that brought visions of snapping tree branches and rattling chains. Those sounds were drowned out by a long moan that caused both Ten-Inch and me to let Tahiti's body slip from our nerveless fingers and drop to the ground. I felt my bowels loosen and fought to keep myself under control.

The shadow drew in on itself until we were staring at a human-shaped figure. Glimpses of facial features, an eye, a nose, a mouth, a head of hair, flickered into view and disappeared, bits at a time, until they settled into place, and I could discern the translucent image of a fully formed human—no, not a human—but an adaro woman. She never quite solidified, and I could look through her and make out the blurred sight of the beastmobile parked behind her. As she became more visible to us, the wind gusts died and the ice stopped falling, although the unearthly chill in the air remained.

My chattering teeth made it difficult for me to speak, which was fine because I didn't have anything I wanted to say. But Ten-Inch managed to fight through the freeze to force out a one-word query: "Kanoa?"

The mouth of the *qaitu* didn't move, but the sound of the adaro's voice came from the freezing air itself, and the words drove me to my knees: "Help me."

How Ten-Inch managed to keep his feet and speak to the apparition, I'll never know. He was a tougher man than I.

"I can't," Ten-Inch hissed through gritted teeth.

"Help me," Kanoa repeated.

Ten-Inch sucked in a breath of frozen air. "Tell me how."

In response, the *qaitu* let out a moan, a forlorn sound filled with such loneliness and anguish that I was forced to cover my ears with my hands.

"Send me to Taufa'tahi," the *qaitu* wailed.

Ten-Inch forced himself to take another breath. "I don't know how."

This was followed by another moan, and I thought I was going to be sick.

"Then send me to Pulotu," demanded the *qaitu*.

Ten-Inch turned to me, a question in his eyes. I could only shake my head.

Ten-Inch seemed to gain some strength, and his voice was clearer when he spoke. "Hikule'o has rejected you, Kanoa."

Another moan filled the air, but the power was gone from it. I sucked in a breath, shook my head to clear it, and managed to climb to my feet.

The *qaitu*'s words filled the air. "Then kill me."

Ten-Inch stared at the ghostly form of Kanoa. "You're already dead."

The apparition's mouth opened, and a quiet groan escaped from it. It was the groan of someone wounded to the point of death, but still alive. Kanoa spoke, and the words chilled me in a different way than the freezing air. "There is no death for me."

Kanoa lifted her face to Ten-Inch and extended a hand to him. Her plaintive voice sounded almost normal. "I'm alone, Ten-Inch. So alone. I don't have anywhere to go. Please, Ten-Inch. Please help me. Come with me, Ten-Inch. Please come and be with me. I have no one. Nothing. I don't want to be alone. Please come be with me."

I was aghast. Even though the words hadn't been directed toward me, I could feel their pull, their compulsion. My voice was locked in my throat. I watched, helpless, as Ten-Inch lowered his eyes to gaze at Kanoa's ghostly hand.

Ten-Inch snapped his head up so that he was staring straight into the apparition's eyes. "Fuck you, bitch. You betrayed me. Get the fuck out of my face."

The sudden gust of wind that hit us blew us off our feet and threatened to freeze us solid. I thought I would crack when I hit the ground. A deafening screech filled the air, rising in pitch until it faded into the night. When I opened my eyes, the *qaitu* was gone, leaving behind such a deep feeling of loss and hopeless abandonment that I thought I would die from it. An image of Kanoa, the adaro priestess who had once been the esteemed guardian of a sea spirit's artifact, who had risked everything to retrieve it when it had been stolen away, who had been violated and deprived of everything that gave her life meaning, and who, as a result, had been rejected by everyone and left to wander alone, lost, with no destination, burned itself into my brain. Tears poured from my eyes and froze on my cheeks. I buried my face into the collar of my coat so that Ten-Inch wouldn't see them.

# Epilogue

Modoc never made it to the downtown YCPD stationhouse. No one noticed when he lost consciousness in the back of the squad car. The storm had flooded most of the major streets and knocked out power in large sections of the city, and with most of the stoplights out, traffic was more of a mess than usual even with fewer cars on the road. It took the cops more than an hour to get from the settlement to the police station. By the time they turned their attention from navigating the storm-tossed streets to checking on the condition of their prisoner, Modoc was dead.

I couldn't be certain, but I had what I thought was a pretty good idea about what might have killed him. After Cougar destroyed his pelt, Modoc lost much of his magical power to heal. He'd still been in the process of patching up his last major wound, the one caused by a pen piercing his eye, when he lost his healing mojo. Maybe it had pierced his brain after all. I felt a sense of profound, if somewhat guilty, satisfaction at the thought that I might have been the one to do him in.

I'd taken Kalama's threats seriously and arrived at the station fifteen minutes early. Kalama had hardly slept and was in a grumpy mood when she joined me in the interrogation room to take my statement. I gave her a full and accurate accounting of my search for Ten-Inch and the deaths of Kanoa and Leiti La'aka. Well, perhaps not entirely full, and maybe not quite accurate. I stuck with the story that Modoc had both raped and murdered Kanoa. I figured no one was going to tell it any different, and, besides, as far as I was concerned Kanoa died because Modoc raped her. Why complicate matters? I told Kalama how Tahiti had used Jaguar to kill Leiti La'aka. As far as I knew, Jaguar was still alive and would corroborate my account. I left out the part about Ten-Inch snapping Tahiti's neck. Ten-Inch didn't need the aggravation. He'd helped save the city. We all owed him for that.

Kalama knew I'd left some vital information out of my story—she was much too sharp not to—but she didn't press the issue, and I knew she was reasonably satisfied with my version of things. She told me she'd have to verify my story with Tahiti before she could close the case.

"If she tells me a different story, I'll have to bring you back in," Kalama told me. I told her that was fine with me. I didn't tell her that she'd never see Tahiti again.

Ten-Inch and I had taken Tahiti's body to the same beach where she and I had sent Leiti La'aka on her way to Pulotu. We lay her body on the sand and awaited the oarsmen. A few minutes after we arrived, Kraken joined us, rising from the ocean waves. The three of us waited for several hours. No one came for her.

As dawn was breaking, Ten-Inch threw a pebble into the outgoing tide. "Havea Hikule'o knows how to hold a grudge."

"What happens to Tahiti now?" I asked. Ten-Inch had no answer.

"I'll take her body to my elders," Kraken declared. "She was a *kwuurlplup*. We'll take her to the deep waters and conduct funeral rituals."

And that's how I knew the cops would never find Tahiti. Wherever she'd gone, she was out of their reach.

\*\*\*

Sims never returned to the Placid Point station. Walks in Cloud and I joined Captain Flinthook at Sharky's, and he told us how the precinct had been turned inside out.

"They gave me a golden parachute." Flinthook gulped red wine from his goblet. "Early retirement, a gold watch—well, gold plated, anyway—and a nice fat pension. All I had to do in return is sign a few agreements not to talk about LIA involvement at the station, which means we're not having this conversation."

"What do you think happened to Sims?" I asked.

The newly retired Captain Flinthook swirled the wine in his goblet. "Oh, I'm sure he'll turn up somewhere. The LIA will plant him in another precinct, and he'll introduce his moneymaking rackets. You'd be surprised at how much dough Leea rakes in from jaywalking citations."

"Are they still watching my office from across the street?" Walks in Cloud asked.

Flinthook shrugged. "I have no idea. But Mr. White seems to have disappeared, so maybe not. I never found out what they were looking for."

I glanced at Walks, who blew smoke toward the ceiling and crushed her cigarette out in an ashtray. "It bothers me that they were watching," she said. "Until I hear otherwise, I'm going to assume they still are. But I might have to do something about it."

Flinthook held up a hand. "Whatever you're planning, don't tell me about it. I'm done with the LIA and their schemes. I'm done with

Placid Point, too. It's turned into a real shithole, especially with all that nonsense going on in the adaro settlement. Now that the weather's cleared up, I'm gonna buy me a little boat and spend the rest of my life pulling fish out of the Bay."

I wished him luck.

*\*\**

According to news reports, more than forty adaros had disappeared from the settlement on the night of the freak storm, but, thanks to the Navy's heretofore secret tracking program, all had either been returned or, in some rare cases, executed.

So much for the veracity of the official news outlets.

Over the next few months, the Navy made massive renovations to the settlement. The entire settlement was fenced off with chain link steel and barbed wire. Heavy equipment arrived unannounced and cleared away the slums. All adaros living in the slum were relocated into the settlement proper. All non-adaros were left to make their way, homeless, into the city. Fremont Street was re-routed through the newly cleared area, and three new roads were built leading from Fremont through newly installed naval checkpoints into the settlement. The walls and nets separating the settlement's cove from the open sea were strengthened and reinforced, and naval patrols off the coast were increased. With no announcement of their intentions, the Navy effectively turned the settlement into a prison.

The booths in the marketplace remained open throughout the transition, but they took on a new look. The Navy contracted the whole enterprise to the Hatfield Syndicate, who organized the loose collection of merchants into a unified operation. Members of the Hatfield family contested the charge that they'd taken on this legitimate business venture in order to secure a foothold for the expansion of the illicit rackets they ran in the shadows of the settlement, but no one took their denials seriously. The Claymore Cartel remained a visible presence in the settlement, but word on the street was the gang now operated there as subcontractors for the Hatfields.

The Northsiders disappeared from the settlement after The Dripping Bucket mysteriously burned down. First Medusa's, then the Bucket. I sensed a pattern, one that might be worth investigating if I could make any money from it.

\*\*\*

It had taken Lubank's hired specialists a full week to successfully remove the ink and the tracking devices from the two dozen adaros wanting to free themselves from their status as "protected species." I didn't ask where Lubank had found the tattooists, or where he'd found the thugs who'd occupied the Navy's Master-at-Arms while Luano was driving the adaros out of the settlement. I was sure that none of them could be found in a legitimate business, or by using an unsecured internet search engine. I'd been afraid that the MAs would swoop in on our operation before all of the adaros had been treated, but the Navy had found themselves occupied with other more pressing problems. The settlement had seen the worst of the storm and had been almost destroyed by the high winds and tides, not to mention the excessive vandalism and looting. The resulting chaos kept the Navy far too occupied to worry about tracking down a busload of adaros who had fled the scene.

I wondered how Kraken was getting along with the adaro nymphs he led into the deeps. He might be on the verge of building himself a nice little harem, I thought. Of course, he might also be bringing big trouble into the secret adaro strongholds. Piper and her like-minded reformers were determined to shake things up in a big way with stories of their experiences among human women. Those poor adaro bucks. After thousands of years of maintaining a social structure in which a male minority dominated a vast female majority, preserving that unjust structure in the face of new ideas from the land was going to be a bitch.

\*\*\*

I was a block from Lefty's, wearing a fresh splash of aftershave and my best suit, a half-dozen long stem roses gripped in one hand. It was a Saturday evening, and the other revelers waiting at the crosswalk for a green light were throwing side-eyed glances and amused grins my way. A yellow cab taking the right turn too fast hit a puddle by the curb, but it was a small puddle, the rains having finally stopped a few days earlier, and the splash didn't reach my new leather shoes. I was nervous and hoping it didn't show, but, just in case, I kept my eyes focused straight ahead and forced myself to steady my breathing.

I reminded myself that I wasn't going to ask Holly to take me back. I was going to give her the roses and tell her that even though we'd both moved on I still thought about her from time to time and there were no hard feelings and I hoped she was doing well. I'd sit in a quiet booth and enjoy the show. What was it again? Oh, yeah. Some band that was supposed to be good. I'd have a couple of drinks, maybe buy a cigar from Holly or one of the other cigarette girls, and slip away at about midnight when things were getting hot.

The light turned green, but I decided to wait and get the next one. I was in no hurry. It was a nice night. Maybe a little humid after the recent storm that almost drowned the city. The palm of my hand holding the roses was soaked with sweat. I transferred the flowers to my other hand and dragged the sweaty one down the side of my coat. I should have worn gloves, but I didn't own any nice ones, and I'd spent too much on the shoes.

The light turned red, and a new crowd of revelers pulled up around me to give me their side-eyes and their grins. I wondered how Holly would react when she saw me. Would she come to my table right away, a big smile on her face, and ask me what took me so long? Would she sit down with me, let me buy her a drink?

Would she be upset at me for invading her turf? Would she tell me to please go away and leave her alone? Would she send a bouncer to my table to facilitate my departure?

Would she pretend not to see me at all and send one of the other girls my way?

When the light once again turned green, I didn't move. Lord's flaming balls, what the fuck was I doing? I lifted my eyes across the street to the neon Lefty's sign above the entrance of the swanky joint. The door opened and orchestral music streamed out into the night. I listened closely and heard the Saturday night sounds of cheery voices and joyful laughter. Crazy, man, crazy.

The reverberating echoes hit me like a wall. I turned on my heel and walked away. When I reached a trash can, I dropped the roses inside. I pulled the brim of my fedora down over my forehead, slid my hands into my pockets, and walked past the shops, restaurants, office buildings, bars, and apartments of downtown Yerba City in no particular direction except away from Lefty's. And Holly.

I'd been kidding myself. Relationships with women like Holly weren't in the cards for a mug like me. Aftershave and long stem roses? They had no place in my world, the world of a private dick in a dirty city. A world of alleys and cheap motels, of greasy calamari, bitter coffee, and too much cheap booze. A world of witches, deadly shapeshifters, sleazy lawyers with shadowy connections, and otherworldly spirits with a taste for blood. A world of hunting down small-time dealers selling drugs to prep-school kids from well-to-do neighborhoods, of cheap hoodlums and button-men, of greedy men and greedier women, of death at the hands of cops and friends. Who brings a decent lady into a world like that, leaves her to wait up into the early morning hours wondering if this is the night the man she loves finally runs into that piece of lead with his name on it, or that shadow creature from another world with his one-way ticket to the land of the dead? Only a selfish heel would put a dame through that kind of sorrow and grief.

I thought about Walks in Cloud, what we had between us. Two lonely professionals, good at our jobs, tied together by nothing in particular. No illusions of love or foolish dreams of happily ever after. Not even any lust, really. Just a mutual respect for each other's privacy, a shared appreciation for a good cup of coffee, and a convenient friendship that might drift into something else on occasion when we needed it. That was the relationship for a man like me.

I walked a little more, listening to tires kick up the mud and the last of the moisture from the rain still clinging to the asphalt. I passed by the other pedestrians without making eye contact, looking instead at the glow of the lights spilling into and out of the streets. I turned a corner and breathed in the aroma of roast beef, fried chicken, and coffee drifting out the door of an upscale diner. I kept walking and heard the urgent squeal of burning rubber and blaring horns, followed by shouts and curses. I heard a distant shout, the sound of running feet, a woman screaming: "Somebody stop that man!" I passed by a group of young men on the corner singing a perfect song in perfect harmony without instruments and dropped a bill into an upturned hat at their feet.

I walked a little farther and stopped. It was still a couple of hours before midnight. I took out my phone and called Walks, but got her voicemail. I didn't leave a message. I resumed walking, searching for a bar. When I found one, I stepped inside.

The End

# Thank You!

Thank you for reading *A Nymph Returns to the Sea: A Noir Urban Fantasy Novel*. If you enjoyed it, I hope that you will consider writing a review—even a short one—on Amazon, Goodreads, or your favorite book site. Publishing is still driven by word of mouth, and every single voice helps. I'm working hard to bring Alex Southerland back, and knowing that readers might be interested in hearing more about his adventures in Yerba City will certainly speed up the process!

# Acknowledgements

What a ride this has been! When I slapped down that first long sentence describing a troll standing in the entryway of a bar, I had no idea I'd be finishing up a fifth book in a series (plus a standalone novella set in the same world). I'm immensely grateful for everyone who has picked up one of my books and given it a shot. I could never have made it this far without a lot of help along the way. First and foremost, as always, I want to thank my wife, Rita, my full partner in everything I do, not to mention the best pal any mug could ever hope for.

I want to thank my parents, Bill and Carolyn, for their unending support and encouragement. Thanks, also, to my sisters, Teri and Karen, who once again read this book in advance and not only cleaned up a lot of typos, but gave me great suggestions that I incorporated into my story. I also want to thank my cousin Juliana for her continued support and encouragement.

I want to thank Elaine, who read an advance copy of this book *three times* (are you kidding me?) and helped make it a much better book.

My thanks once again to Assaph Mehr, author of the fantastic *Stories of Togas, Daggers, and Magic* series, not only for reading an advance copy of this book, but for being there from the beginning and offering me his continual support.

My thanks also to Lucy McLaren, who's "counselling session" with Alexander Southerland inspired much of the interaction between Southerland and Holly.

A special thank you goes out to veteran voice actor Duffy Weber, who somehow squeezes thirty hours into every working day and still manages to pedal his bicycle into exotic locales. Thanks for the cookies, buddy!

I thank anyone who ever gave me the slightest bit of encouragement or support. I've received a lot of great advice, and, if I didn't take it, that's my fault, not yours.

Finally, a big thank you to anyone and everyone who has read my books and taken the time to rate or review them. Every review—good or bad—helps me in the end. Readers have an abundance of choices, and I appreciate every one of you who chose to read something I wrote. Southerland has at least one more story to tell, and after that? Well, let's just say I'm far from done, and I hope you'll stick with me.

## About the Author

My parents raised me right. Any mistakes I made were my own. Hopefully, I learned from them.

I earned a doctorate in medieval European history at the University of California Santa Barbara. Go Gauchos! I taught world history at a couple of colleges before settling into a private college prep high school in Monterey. After I retired, I began to write an urban fantasy series featuring hardboiled private eye Alexander Southerland as he cruises through the mean streets of Yerba City and interacts with trolls, femme fatales, shape-shifters, witches, and corrupt city officials.

I am happily married to my wife, Rita. The two of us can be found most days pounding the pavement in our running shoes. We both love living in Monterey, California, with its foggy mornings, ocean breezes, and year-round mild temperatures. Rita listens to all of my ideas and reads all of my work. Her advice is beyond value. In return, I make her tea twice a day. It's a pretty sweet deal. We have two cats now, Cinderella and her new pal Prince. Both of them are happy to stay indoors. Cinderella continues to demand that we tell her how pretty she is, especially since we brought an interloper into the fold. Prince is excitable and loves to play for hours at a time until he drops from exhaustion.